Chronicles of the Imagination

Lizard Face

David Scott Fields II

Thrive
Christian Press

Jupiter, Florida
www.thrivechristianpress.com

Thrive Christian Press
1095 Military Trail #8584
Jupiter, FL 33468

First published by Thrive Christian Press on March 1, 2008.
Republished by Thrive Christian Press on October 24, 2022.

Paperback ISBN: 978-1-945995-06-4
Hardcover ISBN: 978-1-945995-07-1
Also available for Amazon Kindle.

Printed in the United States of America.

Dedication

*T*his book is dedicated to both my grandfathers –
John Walter Fields (1928-2000) and Loy
Douglas Graham (1927-2008) with whom I
will share eternity. Remember, once we get to Heaven, our
true lives have only just begun.

Before

"Hold her steady, Ensign!"

"I'm doing my best, sir."

Captain Micah Turrock, of the Stararockan vessel *Dragon's Blood,* rubbed the fur on his face. Something was out there, but what and where he had no idea. For the last two hours, the *Dragon's Blood* had been tracing what appeared to be a ghost ship. It emitted no energy signature, had no fuel trail, and no life signs were detectable. However, nearly a dozen times in the past few hours a tiny metallic object and shimmer in the distance had sent a pulse of laser light in the direction of the *Dragon's Blood.* What could it be?

Ensign Toby Nakan, a recent transfer from Staranana, reported from the helm, "The…whatever it is, is moving too far into the asteroid field for us to safely maneuver, sir. I recommend backing off."

"Thank you, Ensign, but I think it's a little too early to be giving up," Turrock replied. He turned to his first officer, a plump bear in his mid-forties named Elijah Honeytub, and asked, "What do you think, Commander?"

"I'm afraid I agree with Mr. Nakan, sir. Is it worth risking damage to the ship just to chase down something that may not even exist?"

"How do you explain those flashes of laser light?" Turrock asked. "Something is out there. And I intend to find out what that something is."

"Sir, maybe I…" Toby began, but a beep from his control board turned his attention back to the helm.

"What is it?" Turrock asked.

"I don't know, Captain. Some sort of signal is being routed through the helm. I think I can put it through for you."

"Proceed."

Toby tapped a few controls, and the bridge erupted. The hands of all the officers present shot to their ears as a sound of unparalleled volume and terrible pitch ripped through the room. Agonizing pain slashed at their eardrums, and everyone began to scream. What was this madness, and where was it coming from?

Toby felt a trickle of blood drip from his ears as his eyes fell on his console. He tried to make himself heard over the noise, "It's a virus! Our course is being diverted, Captain; we're going to crash into the large asteroid just ahead! There's nothing I can do."

Turrock, his cheeks now covered with blood, forsook his destroyed ears, and returned his hands to his controls. "All hands, this is the Captain. Prepare to abandon ship. Our systems have been compromised by a virus. The ship is on a collision course for one of the asteroids and…"

The sound died.

Honeytub asked, "Can anyone still hear me?"

Toby nodded, "I can, sir!" And a few others acknowledged that their ears were working too.

Captain Turrock, though now deaf, asked, "How much damage?"

Honeytub attempted to transfer the data to his Captain's console, but before he could, the lights on the bridge snapped off.

"What's going on?" Toby cursed.

In the blackness, a single point of light began to form. At first, it was just a pinprick, but then it started to grow exponentially, and it brought with it another sound. Only, this one was not painful. It was more like a chime, and an instant later, that chime deposited twenty hooded figures onto the bridge.

"Who is the captain of this vessel?" The hissing voice came from a short, hooded figure in the center of the bridge. Toby shuddered, recognizing the voice.

Turrock hadn't heard the question, but being the captain, he stood and responded. "My name is Turrock. I am captain of this vessel. Who are you?"

The figure removed his hood to reveal a scaly head and a stubby, reptilian snout. "Pleased to meet you, Captain," he said. Then he pulled a pistol from his side and shot Turrock.

"NO!" Honeytub screamed.

"Hear this," the figure screeched. "This vessel is now under the command of the Evilandian Empire. Goons, hoods and masks off!"

Toby fell to the floor, wrapped his arms around the bottom of the helm, and squeezed his eyes tightly shut. He could hear the screams of his comrades as the goons began to kill them, and he felt like a coward, but he couldn't move. Fortunately, he didn't have much time to wallow in self-pity. Something hard hit him in the back of the head, and everything went black.

Chapter 1

Christmas Tree Emergency

"Are you sure it goes that way?"

"Would you stop bugging me, Berry? Scotty wants this done, and he put me in charge of doing it!"

"I know, General, but whoever heard of putting a tree inside a building; much less one five stories high?"

"Scotty tells me they do it on Earth all the time."

"People on Earth don't typically have five-story homes."

"No, but they put smaller ones in their houses at the end of every year."

"What for…I mean, I know it honors Christ's birth, but what in the world does an evergreen tree have to do with the birth of the Messiah?"

"I don't know, but this is only the beginning. Once we get it standing, we have to cover it with those things over there." General Shortstop was standing on the balcony of the second story of the Palace, directing the large Christmas tree into place. Berry was on the first level, and Shortstop pointed to a box near him. It was filled with red and green glass bulbs, strings of tiny lights, little candies that looked like fishing hooks, and many more objects of various shapes and sizes.

"Humans certainly have weird holidays and traditions. What is this one called again?" Berry asked.

"Christmas, but I wouldn't go calling it weird around the Emperor. He loves this holiday. As I understand it, many humans have robbed it of its true meaning. Scotty wants to celebrate his first Christmas on Staranana with all its true meaning attached. He wants it to be totally honoring to God."

"How have humans robbed it of its true meaning?"

"Scotty said they give gifts to each other, which isn't bad. In fact, it is very good, but many people are more concerned about getting than giving. Plus, this holiday was supposed to be all about Christ, but even people who don't believe in Christ celebrate it, making it more about themselves than the Savior."

"I can see why it's so important to Scotty then."

"Yeah, and wait till you find out what Scotty has planned for you."

"What?"

"Are you sure you want to know?"

"Yes, come on now!"

"A feast of astronomical proportions! He has invited every bear on the planet to a huge party here in the Palace."

"What! I'd better get on the menu right now! How long until this party?"

"It happens on the night before Christmas, or Christmas Eve as the humans call it. That is about a week away."

"Ugh! Who does this kid think he is?"

"Um, the Emperor!"

"Oh, yeah, well…"

"General!" Chef Berry was cut off by a frantic voice coming from several stories above. Shortstop looked up to see Spikey Moonbeam leaning over the fifth story balcony.

"What is it, Captain?" Shortstop asked.

Spikey cringed a bit. Scotty had given him the rank of captain in the newly created Starananian Space Force. He held the position of chief engineer of the fleet. He loved his job and all the opportunities that came with it. Unfortunately, the formality that also came with it was often annoying.

Spikey replied, "I was just up on the Command Deck. We received an emergency transmission from the *Dragon's Blood.* The signal was interrupted, but before it was, they said they were being attacked."

"Attacked? The *Fire Cruiser* blew the *Space Shark* to ashes three months ago without so much as getting her own paint scratched. As I understand it, other than its name, the *Dragon's Blood* is identical to the *Fire Cruiser*."

"Yes, I know, General. You need to come see the data we've collected."

"I'll be right up."

Shortstop secured the tree and headed up to join Spikey. Berry called out after him, "What am I supposed to do?"

"Best get cooking," Shortstop called back, and then he and Spikey disappeared into the upper halls of the Palace.

"Great, just great!" Berry sighed.

~

"Report!" demanded Shortstop as he stepped onto the Command Deck of the Palace. The Command Deck, or CD as Scotty liked to call it, was located on the 100th story of the Palace, just down the hall from Scotty's chambers. It had two levels. The upper level circled the lower and was ringed by workstations, flashing with colored lights and switches. A theater-size screen was mounted on the front wall and was currently displaying a view of the Ice Sea. A single console had been set up on the lower level, though it was easily fifteen feet long and had half a dozen bears working at its controls. Twenty other bears manned the upper stations. The entire room was about 100 feet in diameter.

In the center of the CD was a command chair, normally reserved for Scotty, but Shortstop slid into it for the moment. Spikey took a station at the lower control board. He sat next to Cak Nakan. The teen clearly looked agitated.

Spikey tapped a few buttons, and the icy tides of the sea dissolved to be replaced seconds later by a tiny, silver disk floating in the center of a backdrop of stars and asteroids. Spikey flicked a few more switches, and the silver disk swelled into a *Fire Cruiser*-class vessel.

"General, our satellite network has detected this vessel moving deeper into the asteroid belt of our solar system. We have confirmed that it is the *Dragon's Blood*."

"So, she wasn't destroyed! That's good news."

"Yeah, for the ship, not the crew."

"What do you mean, Spikey?"

"This image was taken about ten minutes after we got the distress call. We have tried to make contact, but no one onboard is responding."

"Could the crew have been incapacitated?"

"Possibly, but I think it is a little more involved than that. Our Stararockan cousins have technology much more sophisticated than ours, and they detected this." Spikey tapped a few more controls and said, "Oh, you all might want to cover your ears."

Shortstop was confused, but he and the rest of the bears complied. Spikey tapped one last button, and the screen was flooded with what at first appeared to be random streaks of color. Shortstop looked closer and thought he could make out numbers, well, two numbers anyway, zeroes and ones. The colors were pulsing and succeeded in making the General dizzy. In addition to that, he thought he heard a shrill whine beyond the protection of his ear-covering hands. He released his ears momentarily, but the sound was so horrible, he instantly covered them again. Spikey tapped another control, and the image and sound were gone.

"What was that?" Shortstop roared.

"The Stararockans have analyzed it and believe it to be a computer virus. It can be sent over regular communication channels, but once it infects a system, it renders the computer useless. The sound it produces has the added effect of incapacitating a crew."

"So, what are we saying here?"

"It is the belief of the Stararockans, and mine as well, that the *Dragon's Blood* has been commandeered by some hostile force."

"That's definitely not a good thing. When I was on the *New Life,* the *Fire Cruiser* didn't even break a sweat, so to speak, when it took down the *Space Shark.* If some enemy has one of those ships, there is no telling what kind of damage it could do. What do the Stararockans plan to do about it?"

"That's just it. They can't do anything about it. All their vessels are vulnerable. This virus is so insidious it can infiltrate any system. They so much as use their onboard intercom system to contact each other, and they're dead."

"So, we have a rogue ship with enough firepower to wipe out a planet, and we can't do anything about it?"

"Not exactly. We do have three distinct advantages over these hijackers."

"And these advantages would be?"

"In order of importance: God, Scotty, and TB."

"What?"

"Well, we always know we can come to God in prayer, and no one can overcome Him. We all learned that the hard way three months ago."

"So, how do Scotty, and who did you say, fit in?"

"Oh, TB. You remember him. He is the artificial intelligence that operates the *Door*. I have been working on a way to make him portable."

"You've completely lost me, Spikey."

"Sorry, okay, look. Scotty has a jeweled necklace that I created for him. It creates a duplicate of him to send to Earth anytime he is here. That device scans Scotty's brain so the duplicate will act exactly like him."

"Yeah, so?"

"So, TB must stay patched into that necklace in order to keep it connected to the duplicate. However, TB's micro-circuitry is small enough that it could fit inside of the necklace and control it directly."

"Still not getting it, Captain."

"Hang on. Hang on. If we are going to rescue the crew of the *Dragon's Blood,* we will have to send in another ship. Now, you can bet that if the Stararockans were vulnerable, we will be even more vulnerable. But if we send in a ship with all its computer systems in black mode, we might stand a chance. I can modify TB's brain scanner so that he can communicate with any crewmembers we send telepathically. He can also control the ship independently of the primary computer."

"What makes you think that TB won't be vulnerable as well?" Shortstop asked.

"TB isn't what you would call a typical computer. Aside from being self-aware, his technology is far more sophisticated than anything on Staranana, Stararocka, or even Earth for that matter."

"How did you manage that?"

"It's a long story. But in brief, about ten years ago, an alien probe crashed in the Northern Mountains. I found it, analyzed it, and in time, incorporated it into what later became the *Door*. It wasn't until sometime later that I discovered that TB was sentient. In any case, his alien circuitry has already been tested on a sample of this virus. He eliminated it within 2/1,000,000ths of a second."

"Wait a minute," Shortstop halted him. "Ten years ago? Isn't that about the time you disappeared, right before your…"

"Yes, General!" Spikey huffed, not wishing to recall the incident Shortstop had in mind. He then redirected the conversation back where it needed to go, "TB's systems are still a bit of a mystery, even to me. So, we will have to replace the ship's computer system with him, and let him take control, but after that, we should have a distinct tactical advantage against this threat."

Cak interjected, "The question remains, what ship do we send?"

Shortstop scratched his head, "That's a good question. Staranana only has a fleet of fifteen ships. Ten of those are pod shuttles with a maximum crew capacity of two, a fixed-position laser cannon, and a maximum speed capability of ten thousand kleps per hour. It would take weeks to reach the asteroid belt at that rate, and assuming that the *Dragon's Blood* was still there, the shuttles wouldn't stand a chance against it. Four of the remaining vessels are cargo transports. Their speed capabilities are impressive at one-quarter light speed, but they lack maneuverability, and their weapons are no better than the pods. The last vessel is the rebuilt *New Life*. We have improved its hull and added reinforced titanium armor and seven multi-positioning laser cannons. The engines have also been enhanced to one-quarter light speed, but that is still no match for the *Dragon's Blood*."

Spikey smiled, "Not to worry. I've got that covered too."

He tapped a few more buttons, and the rotating exoskeleton of a small vessel appeared on the screen. From what Shortstop could make out, the vessel had three compartments: a rear living cabin, a central multipurpose deck, and a forward flight deck. Nacelles were attached to the sides of the ship with sophisticated thruster arrays below them. The fuselage was rectangular, but with aerodynamic contours. The upper hull was also littered with a series of jutting metal projections which Shortstop could only guess housed any number of weapons and sensor arrays. It was a small ship, but it looked like it packed a punch.

Spikey said, "Allow me to introduce the *Zerubbabel.*"

"The what?" Cak asked.

"The *Zerubbabel.* In the *Bible*, after the Babylonian captivity, Zerubbabel was the man primarily responsible for rebuilding the Jewish Temple. Since we are rebuilding our world, the name seemed appropriate."

"Great, so how does it help us?" Shortstop asked.

"I have constructed the *Zerubbabel* using a combination of human, Starananian, Stararockan, and even Takillian technologies and supplies. The hull is triple reinforced with titanium. It is also protected by a magnetic bubble shield that will repulse even the highest levels of laser energy. The weapons systems are decidedly human with a few Stararockan adaptations."

"Such as?" Cak asked.

"Over the past century, humans have been experimenting with nuclear-based weapons. These weapons are highly dangerous, and many human nations have seen fit to ban them. However, thanks to a little Stararockan technology, I have created a cold fusion nuclear weapons array. Nuclear energy beams have replaced the standard lasers. The beams can inflict considerable damage, even to a Stararockan vessel's hull. In addition, the vessel has a compliment of twenty micro-sized, plutonium torpedoes. Based on our best data, the *Zerubbabel* should be more than a match for a *Fire Cruiser*-class vessel."

"Excellent! How fast is it?" Shortstop asked.

"One-half light speed."

Shortstop balked, "That's impossible!"

"I will admit, I haven't tested the vessel yet, but its fuel economy and engine thrust have been designed to be twice as effective as the best engines currently in service."

"What does it run on?" Shortstop asked.

"Standard hydrogen for launch and short-range maneuvering, but the interplanetary drive is nuclear-based."

"Well, Spikey, once again you've impressed me. We had best get on this mission immediately. There are lives at stake. Where is your ship?"

"On the roof. It can accommodate a crew of five."

"Good, you and Gloria will come, along with Speedway and myself."

"Sir, that leaves one space left. I would like to volunteer," Cak piped up.

Shortstop shook his head, "Sorry, Ensign. I know you're close to this because of your brother, but the only other possible choice is Scotty."

Cak didn't like that, but he felt a little better knowing the Emperor would be on the crew. After what Scotty had done to Seth, everyone had a great deal of confidence in his abilities. He hoped the young ruler would prove up to the task again.

"Where is Scotty?" Shortstop asked.

"On Earth," Spikey replied. "I'll go contact him, and I'll get TB ready."

"Very well; get on it," Shortstop ordered. Then he sighed, "So much for the Christmas party!"

Chapter 2
Alarm Clock Message

Nine-year-old Scotty Fields rubbed his gloved hands together and watched as his breath turned into a vaporous cloud in the air of the late December night. Above him, a voice called, "How does that look?"

"A little to the left, Dad." Scotty looked on as his father carefully stepped across the icy roof of their home, trying to get their last plastic reindeer into the perfect spot.

Finally, Mr. Fields said, "There, I think that should do it! Plug it in."

Scotty smiled. This was his favorite part. He picked up both ends of the extension cord and thrust them together. Simultaneously, the entire yard exploded in a rainbow of color. Scotty looked around to admire their handiwork as Mr. Fields climbed down the ladder. Soon the man was beside his son with an arm around the boy's shoulders. This was one of Scotty's favorite times of the year. He knew his dad shared that sentiment.

The fence around their yard and the rim of the roof had been strung with dazzling, multi-colored lights. At Mrs. Fields' request, they were not twinkling lights, which she said always made her sick. In the yard, there were glowing elves, snowmen, and tin soldiers, and on the roof was the most magnificent Santa Claus, sleigh, and nine tiny reindeer. Rudolph, at the head of Santa's team, boasted a huge, glowing red nose.

However, the most impressive sight of all was the Nativity

scene in the side yard facing the road. Mr. Fields had built a tiny wooden stable to house the plastic Messiah and His family. Mary and Joseph, with a few chips of paint flaking away from their plastic bodies after years of use, sat under the roof of the stable. They shone in an almost holy way over baby Jesus in His manger. Scotty's dad, as a career fireman, had refused to put a light bulb in the baby Jesus who lay in a manger of hay. The next best thing was a light attached to the roof of the stable that shimmered down on the holy infant. The artificial baby had lost all its paint. Mr. Fields often talked about replacing it, but the Nativity scene was a family heirloom, and somehow, it didn't seem right.

In addition, there were a few shepherds and plastic animals in the scene. And in keeping with biblical accuracy, the three Magi were standing in a line at the far end of the yard facing the Nativity. Their distance from the rest of the scene represented their holy pilgrimage, a journey they would not complete until well after the birth of the Messiah. Finally, a ring of ten caroling angels circled the entire display.

Scotty walked over to the Nativity and knelt to adjust the baby Jesus. He asked, "Dad, do you think this will be a good Christmas?"

"I hope so," Mr. Fields said. "We can only…"

"*Scotty!*"

Scotty recognized the deep voice screaming his name and yelled back, "What do you want, Noah?"

"That stupid alarm clock of yours is going off!"

Scotty felt a pounding in his chest, and he got up immediately. His *alarm clock* going off at this hour could only mean one thing. He left his dad without so much as another word. When he reached the front door, he saw Noah. The tall and athletic sixteen-year-old, in his trademark baggy clothes, looked annoyed. Scotty couldn't blame him, but to be honest, he didn't care.

He pushed past Noah and stepped into the house. Mrs. Fields and his sister Samantha were putting the finishing touches on the Christmas tree in the living room, and Scotty could smell hot apple cider and baked party mix coming from the kitchen. Yes, Christmas was getting very close in the Fields' home, but Scotty feared it wouldn't be a very happy one for a few of his friends.

He got to his room seconds later and heard the wailing of his alarm clock. He locked the door and sat on his bed next to the clock. For all outward appearances, the alarm was a normal digital clock with a built-in radio. Scotty knew it was much more than that, though. The time flashing 11:34 was a dead giveaway, especially since it was only a few minutes past 8:00 p.m. The clock was, in fact, a two-way communicator between Earth and Staranana. Scotty could use it to contact Spikey anytime he wanted to go back to Staranana. However, because of the enormous amounts of electricity it required to bridge the gap between their respective worlds, the bears rarely used it to contact him.

When Spikey had first given him the clock, Scotty had used it so much that he had nearly tripled his parents' electricity bill. After that, Spikey had formulated a code system using the time display, and he suggested that they only use the clock in the event of an emergency (beyond Scotty's typical requests to open a *Door*). The time 11:34, which upside down spelled the word *hell*, indicated a major disaster.

He tapped the snooze button three times and then set the clock back to its proper time. That would tell Spikey to open a *Door*. Scotty tensed as the shimmering gateway began to form in his room. Whatever the problem was, he hoped he would prove up to it. But with God to help him, he had no doubt he would. When the *Door* had fully formed, he stepped through.

Chapter 3
The Mission

"What is it, Spikey?" Scotty felt the last tickle of the energy field as his bedroom in Prineville dissolved, only to be replaced with Spikey Moonbeam's large and cluttered workshop. On the closest table to the *Door,* Scotty saw his particle duplicator, the device that would send a double of himself back to Earth to take his place until he returned. The device was nothing more than an emerald embedded in a half-sphere of circuitry and attached to a chain. When the gem touched the skin on Scotty's chest, it began an intense brain scan. That data was then relayed to the *Door,* and a duplicate was created.

As Scotty slipped on the necklace, he noticed an additional square computer circuit attached to the back. "What is this?" he asked.

Spikey sighed, "I'll explain everything later. Right now, we have a major situation."

"So I gathered. What's wrong?"

"In short, a Stararockan vessel, the *Dragon's Blood*, was commandeered by an unknown hostile force. We have no word on the crew, and the hijackers are in possession of a computer virus that can neutralize any spacecraft in this system."

"Great! So, any ideas what to do?"

"We've already worked that out. I've been working on a vessel that will put the *Fire Cruiser* ships to shame. Shortstop,

Speedway, and Gloria are waiting onboard, and we've got to move fast." Spikey was already yanking Scotty toward the exit.

Scotty pulled back and asked, "What about Sparkey? I don't want to go on a mission without him!"

"Sorry, there isn't enough room onboard the *Zerubbabel*. Besides, this is not a mission for a kid!"

Scotty felt a flash of anger and disappointment at Spikey. A mere three months earlier, Sparkey Moonbeam, Spikey's seven-year-old son, had done what no other Starananian had done in thousands of years. He had gone to Earth, but not only that, he had brought back Scotty, a Christian and the fulfillment of the ancient *Blood of the Land* prophecy. That act had begun a chain of events that ended in the freeing of the Starananian people. As far as Scotty was concerned, the cub had proven himself, and he had thought Spikey felt the same way. So it was hard for him to understand this new attitude of the cub's father.

Because Spikey and the others were much older than he was, Scotty often submitted to their judgment, and he valued their counsel, but there were times he had to lay down the law with his God-given authority. He stopped in the hall and said, "I'm a kid, Spikey! And this kid wants you to get Sparkey to the ship immediately. Speedway will stay behind."

"But, Scotty…"

"That's an order, Captain. From what little you've told me, there is every chance we will have to put together a boarding party to save the crew of the *Dragon's Blood*. As much as I value the capabilities of the rest of you, I trust Sparkey with my life, and I want him along. That's the bottom line."

In the aftermath of the last confrontation with Seth and his horde, Spikey had become very much aware that he had almost lost his son. The years of the war had denied generations of cubs a proper childhood. With Seth now gone, Spikey had promised himself he would never put either of his sons in harm's way again. Even so, Spikey's faith still outweighed his fear. God had placed Scotty in charge of Staranana for a reason. He nodded, "I'll get him. The *Zerubbabel* is on the roof. I'll see you there in a few minutes."

Fifteen minutes later, Spikey faced the assembled crew of the *Zerubbabel*. They sat around a rectangular, conference table in the mid-compartment of the ship. Spikey was happy that, for the most part, everyone seemed pleased with the vessel. Its technology was state of the art, and though it was small and classified as a research shuttle, it was outfitted like a warship, which was exactly what they needed.

A bank of computer terminals and a 50-inch display screen was set up along the forward wall. Spikey brought a map grid up on the screen and then sat down. Shortstop took his place and reported, "This is a chart of our flight plan into the asteroid belt." The screen showed a small white dot, representing Staranana, and from it was a curving red line that went behind a large cluster of brown dots that represented the asteroid field.

Shortstop continued, "Assuming we can reach the projected velocity of one-half light speed, we should be able to get to the last known location of the *Dragon's Blood* in less than a minute."

"You've got to be kidding!" Scotty balked. "This is real life, not science fiction. That location must be at least a couple million kleps away."

Spikey growled under his breath, then said, "3.4 million to be precise, and with all due respect, I believe the engines will get us there in record time."

Scotty blushed a bit and apologized, "Oh, sorry, Spikey."

Gloria, sitting at the far end of the table next to Scotty, asked, "So, once we get there, what's our next step?"

Scotty answered, "We have to find a way to board the *Dragon's Blood*."

Spikey continued, "Yes, now, I've installed *Door* technology into this vessel, so boarding the *Dragon's Blood* should be relatively simple. The real question is, how do we retake the ship?" He turned to Scotty, "Can I see your necklace, Scotty?"

Scotty eyed him and said, "Spikey, if I take off the necklace, my duplicate back on Earth will vanish. It must be getting near bedtime. I'd hate to think what Noah would say if he saw me disappear. He'd probably think the Rapture had happened, and he'd been left behind."

Spikey conceded, "Right, well, this will only take a second. Just lift up your shirt."

Scotty was confused, but he did as he was asked. He lifted his shirt to reveal the necklace, the emerald glowing against the skin on his chest. Scotty fingered the new computer chip on the back and asked, "By the way, what is this, Spikey?"

Spikey held up a finger, indicating that he should wait. Then the bear removed an almost microscopic screwdriver from his pocket, and with it, he tapped four tiny controls on the surface of the chip. When he tapped the last control, the shuttle went dark.

"What's going on?" Gloria squealed.

"Patience, honey," Spikey soothed. Then he said, "TB, begin primary activation mode."

For a moment, there was nothing but silence, but then full illumination resumed, and the computer screen flickered back into life. A nasal pitched voice filled the cabin, *"Anything you say, Cap. Is everything working?"*

Spikey grinned, "Yes, TB, everything is fine. Okay, Scotty, you can put your shirt down now."

Sparkey, who sat next to his mother, chimed in for the first time since the briefing began, "Uh, is everyone as clueless as I am?"

"Sorry, son. The small device attached to Scotty's necklace is TB's self-awareness chip. In essence, it is the part of his inner workings that makes him more or less alive. It is equipped with all his memories, and fifteen backups of those memories, as well as all of his most vital programming."

Scotty suddenly felt ill at ease, "In other words, I have an alien computer hanging around my neck? Fun!"

TB sounded insulted, *"I'm not merely a computer, Your Majesty. I am a highly sophisticated, artificial intelligence that will…"*

"Easy, TB," Spikey said. "As I explained to the General, we have to run the ship in black mode during this mission. There can't be so much as one computer circuit online, or we're dead. TB, however, is sophisticated enough to eliminate the virus, so I have removed him from the *Door* and modified him to act as the computer system for the *Zerubbabel.* As soon as we find the *Dragon's Blood,* we will have to send in a team to attempt to retake it. TB will be able to use the same technology he uses to scan Scotty's brain to create a duplicate to create a telepathic link between all of us. We won't have to use communicators to keep in contact. In addition, no matter what their current state, TB can lock down the computers on the *Dragon's Blood* and assume control."

"That still leaves the hostile force that has seized the ship to deal with. What is your game plan for stopping them?" Scotty asked.

Shortstop tapped a few controls, and the computer image transformed into that of a *Fire Cruiser*-class vessel. "Captain Noble was kind enough to share the schematics of his ship with us after he rescued the crew of the *New Life* three months ago. The hope was that we could one day build ships like that of our own. Unfortunately, we are a good while from having such resources, but these plans are useful in another way."

"How?" Sparkey asked.

Shortstop tapped a few more buttons, and the image of the *Fire Cruiser* ship rotated to reveal its belly. Two green dots appeared, parallel with each other, near the belly's center. Shortstop explained, "Despite all the technological marvels of these vessels, their ventilation systems are fairly unsophisticated. These two green dots represent the only two external vents on the entire ship. Any toxic gases the ship produces must be dispelled from the ship through these ports. If we can seal the ports, the ship's air supply will become contaminated. When the toxins reach a high enough level, they will incapacitate whoever has taken control."

"Wait just a minute!" Scotty protested. "I'm no chemist, but I've heard of people getting trapped in their cars with the engine running, and the carbon monoxide killed them. Last time I checked, one of those ships has a crew of eight hundred bears. I don't want to risk hurting them."

"Not to worry," Gloria chimed in. "If we can get a time-delayed, gaseous bomb inside one of the vents, I can infuse it with a chemical agent that will retard the hazard of the carbon monoxide. Between the time the occupants of the vessel lose consciousness and the gasses become fatal, we will have about twenty-four hours. But it will still take several hours for anyone to start losing consciousness."

"They must have safeguards on the ship. What makes you think they won't detect the rising carbon monoxide levels?" Sparkey asked.

"Our only real hope rests in TB being able to take control of the main computer. We'll send in a covert team who will make their way to the primary computer core just above the engineering deck. Simultaneously, the *Zerubbabel* will attack from outside. We will target their sensor array. Once it's offline, we can fuse the vents. TB needs to be ready to take control the instant the sensors go offline. That way, their bio-alarms won't detect the rising toxins," Shortstop explained.

"Then you'll bring us back?" Scotty asked. "I say *us* because I assume I will be on the team."

"Yes, sir, and I'm afraid we have no choice either way. Spikey explained to me earlier that TB must remain linked to you for the telepathic communication link to work. Plus, we can't have your duplicate back on Earth vanishing, now can we? But besides you and TB, we can't risk sending in more than one other person."

"Then it will be Sparkey," Scotty said.

The young cub perked up, but Scotty swore he could hear Gloria's teeth grinding. Spikey began, "Sir, I think that…"

But Sparkey interrupted, "Dad! I can do this! And two small kids can sneak through the ship much easier than a couple of adults. And after all we went through with Seth, this should be easy work."

"Don't get cocky, cub. We still have no idea of who or what we're dealing with. But you're right; you're the best bear for the job. Besides, it will take both the General and me to carry out the attack."

"What will I do?" Gloria asked.

"Your role will come into play if and when we retake the ship. There will certainly be casualties. You'll have your hands full. But until then, you can come up on the flight deck and monitor Scotty, Sparkey, and TB's progress," Shortstop said.

That seemed to satisfy Gloria's motherly instincts. Scotty said, "Well, we've wasted a lot of time with all this planning. Spikey, let's put those engines of yours to the test. Everyone, prepare for launch."

Spikey nodded and said, "There is a station for everyone up on the flight deck. Follow me."

Everyone got up and followed Spikey. He paused momentarily at the hatch to the cockpit and took a deep breath. He felt like a kid who had just brought home his first drawing from kindergarten. This ship was the pride and joy of all his inventions. He hoped they would be impressed.

And they were! The flight deck was a technological marvel. In the front, before the forward viewport were the flight controls. Two chairs sat before banks of levers and switches, and each chair had a steering column and computer monitor before it. Many of the controls on the right-hand panel were devoted to the weapons array. Those on the left were devoted to flight control and engineering operations. Each of the two flight stations also had access to its own sensor array.

As everyone waited in the doorway, Spikey went to the pilot's chair and pulled back a lever. There was a clicking sound in both the port and starboard bulkheads, and then circuitry panels slid out, rotated, and connected together in the center of the room. Everyone, save Spikey, was surprised when three additional chairs rose from slots in the floor and locked in place before the rear control board.

"Take a seat, please, everyone," Spikey indicated. He and Shortstop took the flight controls, while Scotty, Gloria, and Sparkey took seats at the rear board. Those controls, though they lacked piloting and weapons access, were equally impressive. They each had their own sensor array and full computer access. There was also a pair of headphones and a microphone communicator for each crewmember. Spikey had slipped his on out of habit, but then he chuckled.

He said, "I guess I won't need these." And then, "TB, status report?"

"I've got control of everything, sir. You can run the ship as you

normally would."

"What about the brain link?"

"It's online. I promise I will use discretion, but I now know what each of you is thinking. Once we have boarded the Dragon's Blood, I will begin transmitting whatever is said out loud."

"Good. I'm initiating taxiing sequence. We'll build speed down the rooftop airstrip. Once we're airborne, I'll ignite the hydrogen boosters and launch us into space. Then we'll give my nuclear engines a try."

Scotty clenched the arms of his chair and squeezed his eyes shut. Gloria giggled and asked, "Are you okay, Scotty?"

Scotty dared to open one eye and whispered to her, "I haven't told anyone, but I've never been in outer space before. To be honest, I don't even like flying."

Gloria smiled and whispered back, "If it makes you feel better, the last time I was launched into space, my ship was being attacked by dragons."

Scotty gave her a slight grin and said, "Yeah, I guess the makes me feel better, I think!"

Gloria laughed and tapped him on the hand, "You'll be fine."

Scotty gulped and turned his attention to the front window. Spikey gripped his controls, "All right, everyone, this is it. Everybody, hang on!"

Chapter 4
Old Enemies

"*W*ake up!"

Toby Nakan gasped as a splash of ice-cold water brought him back to consciousness. He had no idea where he was. The room around him was dark, except for the flash of a red, emergency status light. The light was enough to reveal the silhouettes of two tall, hooded figures. His head was still throbbing, but from what he could remember, goons had invaded the ship. No doubt his guards were among them, but it didn't make sense. Hadn't the Starananians and Stararockans killed all the goons three months ago?

"What…Who are you?" he managed.

A third figure stepped forward and wrapped a hand around Toby's throat. He felt five claws sinking through his fur and stabbing into his flesh. The figure hissed, *"Turn on the lightss!"*

Another moment passed, and then Toby squinted as a painfully bright light flooded his eyes. When he was finally able to focus, he saw before him a very familiar, very evil, reptilian face. "You!"

"You know me, cub?"

"Everyone knows you. You're Lizard Face. You were Seth's second-in-command. You killed thousands of bears, and you even tried to kill Seth. But the *Blood of the Land* stopped you."

Lizard Face squeezed tighter. Only a few months earlier,

he had been mere moments away from killing Seth and assuming the throne for himself. Then, unexpectedly, a young cub had fallen from the ceiling of the throne room and knocked him to the floor. Seth had shot the human boy, Scotty, a moment later, and he too fell. Had it not been for a rescue by the goon, Captain Gakic, Lizard Face might have died that day. It wasn't until some time later that he learned that the human boy had survived and that he had defeated Seth.

"Don't believe everything you hear, boy."

"Where is my captain? My crew?" Toby asked.

"All of your *ssenior* officers are dead, along with much of your crew. However, we turned about three hundred of them into goons."

"No!"

"Yes!"

"Why haven't you done that to me then? I'm just an ensign. I'm of no value to you."

Lizard Face released his grip and said, "You are of more value than you know."

"What do you mean?"

"You are the only *Sstarananian* onboard. When *Sstaranana* ssends a rescue *sship*, you will be our bargaining chip."

"Staranana? This is a Stararockan vessel. What makes you think they won't send their own rescue ship?"

"They can't. Our virus will make *ssure* of that."

"Starananian vessels aren't as advanced as Stararockan vessels. They won't stand up against your virus either."

"Very true. But your people do have at least one computer that can vanquish our virus."

"Really?"

"Yes, the computer that operates Moonbeam's *Door.*"

"How do you know about that?"

"Do you think I don't have any friends left on *Sstaranana?*"

"Clearly you do, judging from that dazzling entrance you made. You somehow got your hands on *Door* technology, but who gave it to you? All the goons on Staranana are dead, and all the dragons, except one, are dead too. Hydro would never betray us. He betrayed you in the first place. And it is hard to imagine a bear turning against us. That hasn't been heard of since the time of Kelcott, so who's your spy?"

Lizard Face smirked, "Now, now, let's not get ahead of ourselves. You are alive, Mr. Nakan, for only one reason."

"What is that?"

"We want to trade you for your new Emperor."

"All this time in space must have made you crazy. Scotty and the others would never go in for that!"

"I have it on good authority that Emperor *Sscotty* detests the idea of killing."

"He won't have to kill you. I'll do it myself if I ever get out of here!"

"Temper, temper. We know very well that *Sscotty* won't make that kind of a trade even if it means he must *ssacrifice* your life. But he has no idea of all the intelligence we have on him. He will try and convince us that he will make the trade, but he will likely lead a boarding party to try and attempt to retake the *sship*. He will bring that Takillian computer along. He won't be able to purge this *sship's* computers without it. And then, while he and whoever else he brings are gallantly trying to retake the *sship*, we will capture him and make our escape."

"I'd be careful if I were you. He is no ordinary boy. He is a servant of the Hidden King, the Most High and Living God, and from what I saw a few months ago, I wouldn't want to be on God's bad side."

"Perhaps. *Sseth's* major mistake was that he underestimated the Hidden King. I haven't, but if my plans *ssucceed,* I'll have a major advantage over Him."

"Don't bet on it. Who are you kidding anyway? Are you going to try to go to war with the Hidden King?"

Lizard Face didn't answer. Instead, he turned to his goons and said, "Gag him, and take him to the communications terminal on level ten." Then he left the room.

~

"Well done, Spikey!" Scotty praised. The boy was now floating unrestrained through the flight deck of the *Zerubbabel.* It had taken almost five minutes for the engines to reach maximum velocity, but once they had, they had entered the asteroid field within less than a minute as predicted. Though the *Zerubbabel* did have an artificial gravity system, this being Scotty's first time in space, he had begged Spikey to let him experience floating. With the ship safe in orbit around a large asteroid, Scotty was having the time of his life.

Spikey smiled, "Thanks, Scotty, but if it's all the same to you, do you mind if I reactivate the gravity?"

Scotty maneuvered until he was able to strap himself back into his chair and then said, "Go ahead."

Spikey flipped a switch, and everyone felt themselves grow heavier. Gloria had clearly been focused on her controls because she reported, "I've spotted the *Dragon's Blood*. It is approximately one hundred thousand kleps from our current position. Their propulsion system appears to be on standby. They aren't moving. I can't tell why."

"Could the ship be damaged?" Scotty asked.

Sparkey replied, "My scanners are not detecting damage of any kind. It looks like they are waiting for something."

"This is odd. I'm picking up significant gravitational distortions about a million kleps deeper into the asteroid field," Shortstop reported.

"Eyes on the prize, General. The *Dragon's Blood* is nowhere near those distortions, so they don't concern us right now. We still know very little about what happened on that ship. This may be a trap. Can we still approach without being detected?" Scotty asked.

"I might have to get a little creative with my piloting skills, but I think I can get us there within the hour," Spikey said.

"Maybe there is a better way, Dad," Sparkey interjected. "Check your aft scanners. I'm picking up a large chunk of asteroid heading past us and right toward the *Dragon's Blood*."

Spikey asked, "What are you thinking, son?"

"If we set the ship down on the surface of the asteroid, it could carry us to the *Dragon's Blood* completely undetected. Plus, it would get us there in half the time."

Spikey turned to his son with a broad grin, "I'm glad we brought you along, Sparkey."

Scotty smirked at Spikey as if to say, "I told you so!" Then he gave a quick wink to Sparkey.

Spikey said, "General, if you wouldn't mind keeping an eye on the *Dragon's Blood*, I'll get us onto that asteroid.

~

"Any *ssign* of a vessel?" Lizard Face hissed. He was now standing on the bridge of the *Dragon's Blood*.

Captain Gakic, his chief goon, rose from the command chair and reported, "A small craft launched from Staranana fifteen minutes ago. We tracked them for a few minutes out of Staranana until they accelerated to an incredible speed, and we couldn't recalibrate our sensors in time. However, their last known trajectory had them coming in this direction."

"Excellent! Any idea what vessel they *ssent?*"

"Our source at the Palace reported that it was the *Zerubbabel*."

"Moonbeam's new *sshuttle?* That could be a problem. We have no access to the interior of that *sship*."

"Do you really think it will be a match for us?"

"Don't underestimate Moonbeam. The *Door* technology that we *sstole* is *sspectacular*. And the information we have gathered from our *ssource* indicates that Moonbeam is a genius. Take us to full tactical alert. The instant you detect them, open a hailing channel. The Nakan boy will be ready."

~

"How are you two coming?"

Scotty and Sparkey each clicked the last buckle on their supply belts. They now wore black jumpsuits, similar to Scotty's thermal suit, over their clothes. Each suit was equipped with an oxygen mask to help them avoid the effects of carbon monoxide poisoning. The belts had built-in toolkits, retractable grappling cables, and a new form of energy pistol.

Scotty answered, "We're just about ready, Spikey. By the way, what are these new ray guns?"

Everyone was now in the multipurpose room. The *Zerubbabel* was anchored securely inside a crater on the roving asteroid. Spikey took the pistol from Scotty and said, "Well, I wouldn't exactly call it a ray gun. It is what your people might call a stun gun, but a little more sophisticated. Notice the end here. Two razor-sharp micro-darts are expelled when you pull the trigger. They will cause a significant amount of pain to whomever they hit, but not enough to immobilize them. Then comes the good part. To reload a new set of darts, you have to flip this switch on the side, but if you don't, and you just pull the trigger again, the darts currently embedded in your enemy will send out an electrical charge and stun them."

"Wow, most stun guns I've seen have a wire attached," Scotty commented.

"These aren't exactly state of the art, but they'll get the job done. Hopefully, you won't have to use them, but we have no idea what to expect."

"Maybe we do," Gloria said.

"What?" Spikey asked.

Gloria had been accessing the mid-compartment sensor display. She wanted to ascertain the status of the *Dragon's Blood's* crew. From the look on her face, the news wasn't good. "The crew compliment of the *Dragon's Blood* was eight hundred bears, but I am detecting only three hundred ninety biosigns. Three hundred of those biosigns register as bears. All but one of them seem to be infected with some unknown viral agent. I can't be certain, but the virus seems to be transforming their cellular structures. Their bodies are now emitting a pheromone that I believe will disrupt the higher-level functions of their brains."

"Our sensors are that sophisticated?" Shortstop questioned.

"Stararockan technology," Spikey said simply. Then he asked, "What about the other ninety biosigns?"

"All I am picking up are heat signatures. Nothing more," Gloria reported.

"And the one uninfected life sign?" Scotty asked.

"It's definitely a bear. And judging from his blood temperature, I'd say he's Starananian."

"That has to be Toby. Is anyone thinking what I'm thinking?" Scotty asked.

"I'm afraid so," Gloria replied. "The *Dragon's Blood* must

have been taken over by goons. And it is a safe bet that Lizard Face is behind all this."

"But why is Toby uninfected?" Shortstop asked.

"I suspect we'll soon find out," Scotty said.

"But if the ship has been taken over by goons, and all the remaining crew, save Toby, have been *goonified*, do you think this is all worth it? Maybe we should rescue Toby and then do our best to destroy the ship," Shortstop suggested.

"Don't be hasty, General," Spikey cautioned. "Remember that God healed all the bears who had been *goonified* on Staranana. He can do the same again. We just need to get some people praying."

"We can certainly pray, but we can't contact home to rally a prayer vigil there. Our transmission would be detected, and we would be vulnerable to the virus," Gloria said.

"Maybe there is another way," Spikey suggested. "The *Zerubbabel* is equipped with four interplanetary robot probes. I can program one with a message and then launch it back toward Staranana. It should get there within an hour."

"Good, then…" Scotty began.

"Captain Moonbeam, I am detecting an incoming transmission," TB reported.

Spikey asked, "Any sign of the virus?"

"No, sir. In fact, it isn't a two-way signal. It is a video recording being continually transmitted on a broadband signal."

"Can you play it on the screen here?" Scotty asked.

"Yes, sir."

There was silence for a moment as TB processed the signal, and then the rear viewscreen flashed into life. On the screen was the image of a young Starananian, gagged and with several tears in his uniform.

A deep, unfamiliar voice spoke, *"The Stararockan vessel Dragon's Blood has been seized according to the laws of the Evilandian Empire. The vessel violated our territory, and we are within our rights to lay claim to it. We have executed most of the crew as criminals. However, we are prepared to negotiate for the return of the rest of the crew if Emperor Scotty Fields is immediately surrendered to us so that he may stand trial for their crimes. The bear in front of you, one Ensign Toby Nakan, is a citizen of your planet. If you do not comply, he will be executed before your eyes, followed by another bear every minute after that until Emperor Scotty is in our custody. You have fifteen minutes to comply."*

"That's the end of the transmission," TB reported.

Scotty's heart was aching in his chest. How could this have happened? If he didn't do as instructed, hundreds of bears would die - to say nothing of those who had already died. Part of him knew that it was impossible, but another part was ready to surrender.

Spikey understood the look on Scotty's face. He said emphatically, "You will not surrender yourself, Scotty! Every bear on that ship knows that, especially Toby. You are the last prophesied emperor of our people before the Lord establishes His Millennial Kingdom on Earth. If you're lost, we'll all be lost."

"Do you have any idea who these *Evilandians* are?"

"Lizard Face is a megalomaniac. If I had to guess, I'd say he found a few asteroids in the belt with atmospheres, or which could easily support a biosphere. He probably established a colony of goons and declared himself emperor," Spikey said.

"So what do we do?" Gloria asked.

Everyone looked to Scotty. He rubbed his chin, and then with a commanding voice well beyond his years, he declared, "We proceed as planned. Spikey, General, Gloria, get back to your controls. Bring us into an attack position with that ship and send Sparkey and me aboard. If there is going to be a fight, we're going to win."

No one needed to hear any more. Within moments, Spikey was back at the controls. A few well-timed bursts from the launch thrusters and the *Zerubbabel* was back in space and now less than one hundred kleps from her target.

Spikey reported through TB's communication link, *"We're ready, Scotty. Activate the Door!"*

Scotty tapped the necessary controls on the heavy base of the metallic door frame. As usual, the space between the energy crystals erupted with electrical discharges and then melded into a vortex. Scotty held out his hand to Sparkey and said, "Come on. Let's go help our friends."

Chapter 5

The Trap

"There they are, sir!" Captain Gakic had been staring at his tactical controls for the last ten minutes. Now, at last, a tiny spacecraft had appeared within the *Dragon's Blood's* sights.

Lizard Face ordered from the command chair, "Bring us closer, but make no hostile moves. Open a hailing frequency."

"I would happily comply, Master, but their vessel seems to be operating in black mode. None of their computers are online," Gakic reported.

"As I *ssuspected*. Transmit on a broadband frequency. That Takillian computer will pick it up."

"Ready, sir."

"*Sstarananian* vessel, this is Emperor Lizard Face, ruler of the Evilandian Empire. I assume you received our message. We are prepared to exchange hostages."

~

"Scotty, are you getting this?"

The sensation of hearing Spikey's voice inside his head was a bit unnerving, but Scotty was glad, at least, that TB's telepathic link was working.

"Yes, I am. We've arrived about two decks above the computer core. We're inside one of the maintenance tubes that extend throughout the ship."

"Sorry I couldn't get you closer. If I did, the energy from the Door

might have disrupted their computer systems and activated a security alert."

"No problem. Sparkey, TB, and I are on the move now. What are you going to do about Lizard Face?"

"We can't respond to his hails. If we used our regular system, we'd risk being attacked by the virus. And TB can't link with them without at least partially giving away our plans. Get in place as fast as you can. Then we'll begin the attack."

"Roger that, Spikey! We'll contact you shortly."

Scotty and Sparkey continued crawling through the maintenance hatch. Their target was only a few decks away, and if everything went according to plan, they would have control of the ship back within twenty minutes.

Sparkey said, "Hey, Scotty, I've been thinking. After that threat we received, one of us should probably go and try to free Toby."

"I agree that we can't leave him hanging, but we should focus on the mission first."

"Besides, it's too dangerous!" The voice inside their heads belonged to Gloria.

"Mom, I can do it!"

"No, little one. Stay with Scotty."

"Ugh! Stop treating me like a kid!"

"You are a kid!"

"Would you two be quiet! You're going to get us caught." Scotty's voice was insistent, but there was compassion in his tone. By Earth standards, at seven, Sparkey should still have been playing with toys and eating ice cream cones, but Scotty knew the cub was much more than that. Unfortunately, his parents were not convinced of the same.

"Fine! Let's just go!" Sparkey growled.

Scotty sighed and turned back down the shaft. A few minutes passed before Shortstop reported, *"Scotty, the Dragon's Blood just brought its weapons array online."*

"We've just arrived at the hatch above the computer core. We'll…" Scotty began.

"What's wrong?" Spikey asked.

Scotty looked all about him in the tiny maintenance tube. At first, he hoped he had been wrong, but he wasn't. "Spikey,

Sparkey is gone!"

"What! TB are you still linked to his brain?" Spikey asked.

"Yes, but that isn't exactly a homing beacon."

"Sparkey, are you there? Come in!" Gloria insisted.

There was nothing but silence for a few moments, and then Scotty said, "He must have gone after Toby."

"The Nakans are practically like Sparkey's big brothers," Spikey said.

"Should I go after him?" Scotty asked.

"No, we don't have time. Get inside that computer core," Spikey insisted. And then, *"Sparkey, if you can hear me, and I know you can, according to our scanners, Toby is being held in the auxiliary communications center on level ten. When you have him, make contact, and we'll bring you back."*

"Okay, Spikey," Scotty began. "I'm opening the hatch."

~

"Their time has elapsed," Gakic reported. "Should we kill the Nakan cub?"

"Not just yet. *Ssomehow*, I have a feeling that they have already *ssent* us what we wanted." Gakic wasn't sure what his master was getting at, but Lizard Face turned to his communications officer, "At my command, begin discharging 1,000,000 volts of electricity along our hull, and then tune each of our communications antennas to a different frequency. Transmit a different *ssignal* from each one."

The communications officer nodded, and Gakic asked, "What are you doing, Master?"

"Creating an interference field. I don't know how, but they have to be using that Takillian computer to communicate with each other. We don't know how to *sstop* that computer, but I figure a large enough disruption field *sshould* at least *ssomewhat* block its *ssignal*."

"The field is ready to be activated," reported communications officer.

"Good, let's *sstand by* for a moment. Captain, get our *ssecurity* teams in place, and then target that *sship* and open fire!"

~

"Report!" Spikey demanded.

"Minor damage to the titanium armor. I am bringing the energy repulsion shield online," Shortstop reported. Though technically he outranked Spikey, he knew better than to give Spikey orders on his own ship.

Gloria said, "I've locked onto Sparkey's biosigns. He's getting close to Toby's location."

"Any sign of guards?" Spikey asked.

"Only two, outside the entrance of the room," Gloria reported.

"Did you hear that, Sparkey?" Spikey asked.

No answer.

"All right, General, power the nuclear energy beams. Begin targeting their sensor arrays as planned."

"Aye!" Shortstop twisted a few valves, pulled a lever, and then took the targeting joystick in his hands and fired! In space, a beam of violent, purple energy ripped from the ship and cut through the icy vacuum. When the beam met with the port sensor array of the *Dragon's Blood*, the device was obliterated.

~

"All right, I'm impressed!" Lizard Face cursed. "Where did they get *ssuch* weapons?"

"I don't know. Chances are it's going to be one bloody firefight before either of our ships wins this," Gakic reported.

"Fortunately, this is not a fight we have to win. As *ssoon* as we have confirmed that the human boy is onboard, activate our disruption field, and *sset* a course for the vortex."

~

Sparkey Moonbeam stumbled as another barrage from the *Zerubbabel* pelted the *Dragon's Blood*. He was almost there. He hated disobeying his parents, but they just wouldn't listen. If he hadn't disobeyed them three months earlier, most likely his father would be dead, and he, his brother, and his mom would all be settling into their new life on Stararocka.

As far as he was concerned, that act of disobedience had been right, and so was this one. Toby had been awesome. Like his dad had said, the Nakans were as close to big brothers as

Sparkey would ever have. There was no way he was going to lose Toby. He hoped Scotty would be okay, but the kid had God on his side, and you can't get more secure than that.

Sparkey emerged from an access hatch into the open corridors of the tenth level. Everything seemed quiet enough. If his calculations were right, the communications room should be just around the corner. He took a peek. As his mom had reported, there were only two guards. Nothing two well-aimed shots couldn't take care of.

He took aim, and pull, click, pull, pull, pull. The guns worked exactly as expected. At first, the goons merely shrieked in pain as the needles dug through their already marred flesh, but with another trigger pull, their bodies pulsed with a violent shock of electricity, and they collapsed. Sparkey approached, his gun at the ready, but there was no point. The goons were down for the count. After he had removed their security access cards, he opened the door.

~

"Why is it so dark in here?" Scotty asked.

"I don't know," TB replied. *"According to the data I have on Fire Cruiser ships, this section isn't normally manned by the crew, but there are lights in the compartment for regular maintenance checks."*

"Do you need the lights to access the computer?"

"No. Hold on. This will only take a minute."

~

"Our shields are holding, Spikey. Only three sensor arrays to go," Shortstop reported.

"This is all moving too fast. I think our plan wasn't very well thought out," Spikey complained, even as he adjusted his own sensors.

"Why? We sent the gaseous diffusers into the air shafts after we sent the boys over. A few more arrays, and we can seal their air vents," Shortstop assured.

"Yes, but are we really willing to leave those boys over there long enough for the crew to be incapacitated?"

"We shouldn't have to. We can pick them up and then

withdraw. The *Dragon's Blood* will be adrift within a few hours."

"I hope so!"

"Spikey, take a look at this," Gloria said.

"What is it?"

Gloria tapped a few controls, and a new sensor reading appeared on Spikey's screen. She said, "I'm picking up a massive heat signature moving directly toward Scotty's position. I'm still not sure why our scanners can't distinguish them, but I'm willing to bet that they're goons."

"They know he's there!"

"That's my guess."

"Scotty, did you hear that?" Spikey asked.

"Yes, but we've got bigger problems."

"What?"

"According to TB, this computer core has been gutted. They must be processing the ship's data from another location."

"Can TB locate the other processor?"

"He's not equipped with sensors, Spikey, you know that. We were hoping you could help us."

"I'll get Gloria on it. In the meantime, get out of there!"

~

"Toby! Are you okay?"

"Sparkey?" Sparkey ignored his mother's pleading voice inside his head and rushed to Toby. The young officer was bound and gagged, but otherwise looked none the worse for wear. Sparkey removed his bonds, and the ensign ripped the gag from his mouth.

Toby wheezed, "Sparkey, it's a trap! They know you won't give up Scotty. They intended to capture him when you guys came to rescue me. Please, tell me he's not onboard."

~

"It's confirmed, Master. The human boy is in the computer core room," reported Lt. Kyak, head of security.

"Sseal the room. Let me know when you have him. I'm activating the disruption field."

~

"Why won't this stupid hatch open?" Scotty cursed. "Spikey, I'm trapped!"

"Hold on. We'll open a…"

"Spikey? Spikey, are you there? Spikey!"

~

"Scotty, can you hear me?" Spikey persisted. "I can't get through!"

"I think I know why," Gloria said. "They are emitting high-voltage electrical pulses across their hull, as well as random radio signals on every frequency across the band. They must be disrupting TB's link with us."

"Well, if they're disrupting his link, what about Scotty's duplicate on Earth?" Shortstop asked.

"It's very late at night on Earth by now. We can hope that everyone is asleep, and no one will notice, but we've got bigger problems. The ship must maintain a constant link with TB in order to run like this. When we lost contact, the ship reverted to gray mode. Our computer access is still minimal, but we are now vulnerable to the virus. We have to get out of here," Spikey insisted.

"What about the boys?" Gloria asked, panic in her voice.

Spikey slammed his fist into his console. "I'll go back to the *Door* and see what I can do."

Spikey was up from his controls in a flash. Before he left the flight deck, he said, "Gloria, take the helm." Her mouth dropped as he vanished into the rear of the ship.

~

Spikey arrived at the *Door's* controls, breathing heavily. It wasn't even like it was all that long of a trip. In fact, it was only about fifteen feet. His anxiety was more due to the fact that his son, to say nothing of Scotty, was now trapped on a ship filled with goons. If this didn't work, Staranana was in a whole lot of trouble.

He tapped a few buttons and then called out over the reactivated intercom, "I can't establish a lock on Scotty's coordinates. There is too much interference."

"Ah! Hang on everyone!" Gloria screamed.

Spikey lurched against the controls of the *Door* as the deck pivoted beneath him and cursed, "What's going on up there?"

"Nothing, Captain," Shortstop assured. *"Your wife is just engaging in a few clever evasive maneuvers. Can you cut through the interference?"*

"Are you kidding? This thing cuts through the fabric of space on a routine basis. Not even the disruption field they are creating should affect it. The only way this could be happening is if…"

"Captain?"

"Is if they are producing an inverse *Door* field. General, I think they have *Door* technology."

"How is that possible? We haven't even shared Door technology with the Stararockans."

"We can't worry about how right now! I can open a *Door* at Sparkey's position. I'm activating it now. Try to move us in closer. Maybe we can still get Scotty and TB out."

~

"I haven't heard from the ship in a while, nor Scotty and TB. Something must be wrong!" Sparkey was concerned almost to the point of guilt. Toby was now free, but Scotty was in mortal danger. He couldn't help but feel that it was all his fault.

"We should go after them," Toby suggested.

Sparkey nodded and got up, but then the air around them began to sparkle. A very familiar voice screamed over the roar that was now filling the room, *"Sparkey! If you can hear me, this is Dad! Once the Door is open, jump through quickly! We've got to get out of here!"*

The *Door* continued to form as Toby asked, "Should we leave Scotty behind?"

"I think I'm going to be in enough trouble for leaving him in the first place. I'm sure my dad has a plan. Come on, the *Door* is ready. Let's go!"

~

"Drop your weapon and put your hands on your head!"

Scotty was staring directly into the barrel of an energy rifle. The goon that had demanded his surrender, along with the twenty others with him, clearly meant business. He dropped his weapon and did as he was told.

TB, still in Scotty's mind, asked, "*Scotty, what should we do?*"

"*I don't know, TB. For now, let's hope they don't find out about you. And for both our sakes, let's hope you're as good a computer as Spikey says.*"

"*The necklace is concealed enough. Unless they go looking for it, they shouldn't find it. As for your latter statement, I'll do everything I can.*"

Kyak reported over the intercom, "Master, we have the human boy in custody."

"*Excellent! I'll meet you in the cargo bay.*"

~

Toby and Sparkey emerged from the *Door* and immediately fell to the floor as another enemy barrage struck the *Zerubbabel*. Sparkey began, "Dad, I…"

"Not now! Get back to your station!" Spikey raged. Sparkey retreated, downcast, toward the flight deck, and Spikey asked, "Are you okay, Toby?"

"Yes, sir. Just a few bumps and bruises."

"As I recall, you were the helmsman onboard the *Dragon's Blood*."

"Yes, sir."

"Would you mind taking the helm from Gloria? I think she would appreciate it."

"No problem, sir."

Toby turned toward the flight deck just as Gloria's frantic voice erupted over the intercom, "*Spikey, I've gotten as close as I can. Can you get Scotty?*"

"I'm working on it! Oh, and I'm sending you some reinforcements!"

~

"What does that mean?" Gloria asked as she lurched the shuttle forward to avoid yet another enemy attack.

"I think he means me."

Gloria turned to see Toby Nakan, and, to her relief, Sparkey. Sparkey was already back at his station, and Toby offered, "Doctor, I think I might have an easier time at those controls. Do you mind?"

"Not at all!" Gloria exclaimed and got up.

When Toby was at the helm, he took a quick glance at his scanner panel and said, "All but one of the *Dragon's Blood's* sensor arrays are offline."

"We were trying to seal the air vents to build up the toxin levels in the ship and incapacitate the goons," Shortstop said.

"Do you still want to go ahead with that mission?" Toby asked.

"Right now our priority is to rescue Scotty. I hate to say it, but we may just have to destroy the *Dragon's Blood*."

"There isn't much left on that ship worth saving anyway. Most of the crew is either dead or *goonified*. Oh, and Lizard Face is onboard."

"He sent us a hail," Shortstop said.

Toby tilted the helm controls slightly and then punched the intercom button, "Captain Moonbeam, we are as close as we are going to get. Any closer and their disruption field will start affecting us."

"Acknowledged, Toby!" Spikey returned. *"Unfortunately, they have a massive amount of energy to back up their Door. We're trying to fight it using a ship in gray mode. We need to bring the Zerubbabel up to full power!"*

"What about the virus?" Shortstop asked.

"We'll just have to take our chances," Spikey insisted.

Shortstop shook his head and turned back to Gloria, "Bring everything online. But if one of their radio arrays so much as twitches in our direction, cut main power immediately!"

"Yes, sir."

~

Spikey felt beads of cold sweat begin to form under the fur on his brow. The pulses from the *Door* were wailing at an incredible volume. Lizard Face's virus would be hard-pressed to do better. The unit was also starting to overheat, but the power of the *Zerubbabel* just wasn't enough to match whatever was resisting them.

Spikey had to yell to be heard over the intercom, "I CAN'T BREAK THROUGH! THERE IS ONLY ONE OTHER THING WE CAN DO. CHARGE THE NUCLEAR CORE TO FULL POWER AND SHUNT ALL OF ITS ENERGY INTO THE *DOOR*. IT WILL DESTROY THE SYSTEM, BUT WE SHOULD HAVE A TEN SECOND WINDOW IN WHICH WE CAN BRING SCOTTY OVER!"

Shortstop called back, *"We hear you, Spikey! Transferring power now."*

~

"Well, you have me. What do you want now?" Scotty asked.

Lt. Kyak rested his rifle across his chest. "The Master will explain everything when he gets…" The goon was cut off as the air began to crackle with electricity.

"I thought we had a *Door* repulser field on this area," one guard said

Scotty knew exactly what was going on. Leave it to Spikey to overcome any obstacle. He would have to be fast. As the goons looked at the forming field in confusion, Scotty landed a swift kick to Kyak's shin. The goon stumbled in pain, and Scotty seized his rifle and made a flying dart toward the glowing, blue vortex.

For a moment, there was nothing but chaos in the room, and Scotty thought he was home free, but then the heavy butt of a rifle slammed into the back of his head and sent him crashing to the floor. The vortex collapsed in a blinding flash of light.

~

Shortstop braced himself as an internal explosion rocked the *Zerubbabel*. He punched the intercom button and asked frantically, "Spikey, are you okay?"

~

In the mid-compartment, Spikey peeked up over the conference table at the now twisted and charred remains of the *Door*. He had jumped behind the table for protection. He replied, "It didn't work, General. The *Door* has been destroyed."

"Radiation levels?" Shortstop asked.

"Negligible. The cold fusion reactor can't produce deadly levels of radiation."

"Get back in here, Captain. The Dragon's Blood is heading deeper into the asteroid belt."

Spikey got up and headed back to the flight deck. When he arrived, he was met with the image of the aft thrusters of the *Dragon's Blood*. They filled the forward viewport. Spikey slid into Scotty's station and demanded, "Report!"

"The *Dragon's Blood* still has one functioning sensor array. We weren't able to seal the air vents, and they are increasing speed," Shortstop replied.

"Where can they possibly be going?" Toby asked. "This asteroid field is becoming far too dense for them."

"I think I can answer that," Gloria said. "They are heading directly toward those gravity distortions the General detected earlier."

Sparkey dared to ask, "Why?"

Spikey looked over at Gloria's readouts and instantly recognized the energy signature. "Oh, no! General, that's a spatial vortex. It is emitting high levels of gravity and several unknown forms of radiation."

"Is it safe?" Shortstop asked.

"In theory, such anomalies could serve as gateways to other parts of the Universe, but the only way to determine if it is safe is to go through it. Our scanners can't tell us anything from here," Spikey said.

"What should I do?" Toby asked.

"Maintain course, Ensign!" Spikey demanded.

"Wait!" Gloria shouted. "They are repositioning a radio array in our direction."

"Cut main power now!" Shortstop commanded.

"But they've got…" Sparkey started.

"Do it!" the General barked.

Gloria tapped her panel, and the entire ship went dark and fell still. They watched out the window as the *Dragon's Blood* drew further away, and then, in a ripple of gravitational distortions, it vanished.

Spikey hung his head, and Toby asked, "Orders, Captain?"

"We'll have to come back for Scotty and TB later. Bring main power back online. Take us back to Staranana."

Chapter 6

Scotty and Goliath

"Well, Your Majesty, it's been a while," Lizard Face smirked.

Scotty only glared at his captor. His hands and ankles were now bound with metal manacles connected by a chain. They were especially insidious in that if Scotty made the slightest move to escape, the cuffs would stab sharp needles into his skin. As such, after the first escape attempt, he had not resisted. The goons also took his jumpsuit and utility belt, leaving just his regular clothes.

He was now in a large cargo bay. The lights were down, except for a single spotlight in the middle of the room. In that spot, there was what appeared to be a replica of the throne at Cosmic Bubble Palace. Two lines of goons, not including those escorting Scotty, formed a path to the throne, and Lizard Face was seated upon it.

"I believe the human expression is, *has the cat got your tongue?*" Lizard Face asked.

Scotty shook his head and sighed, "No, I was just wondering how someone so stupid managed to accomplish all this?"

Lt. Kyak struck Scotty across the face, but Lizard Face held up a hand, "Take it easy, Lieutenant. This young man is royalty. He must be treated as *ssuch*."

"Oh, come off it!" Scotty balked. "You intended to assassinate Seth yourself. You don't care about royalty."

"*Sseth's* being alive was an obstacle to my plans. You, however, I need very much alive."

"Why?"

"All in good time, Your Majesty. We must return to our new home world first."

"New home world?"

"Evilanda. I think you will be impressed. It will take us a few hours to reach it. In the meantime, I will have you taken to *ssecure* quarters. There will be a hot meal of human food waiting for you, and you may bathe and *ssleep* until we arrive at Evilanda."

"And then?"

"As I *ssaid*, Your Highness, all in good time."

Lt. Kyak and another guard took Scotty's arms and turned him back toward the door of the cargo bay. They had barely taken two steps before Scotty asked, "Lizard Face, why are you being so…so nice to me?"

Lizard Face's stubby snout twisted into a wicked grin, "As I *ssaid*, Your Majesty, your life and your health are very valuable to me, at least for now. I *ssuggest* you take advantage of my hospitality."

~

A few minutes later, Kyak opened the doors to Scotty's quarters. Kyak removed his manacles, and as the door slid shut and locked behind him, Scotty couldn't help but be impressed. If he had to guess, he would have said that the room was a good twenty feet wide and about fifteen feet deep. On the right-hand wall was a doorway into a bathroom. In the center of the room, against the rear wall, was a king-sized bed with a soft-looking, green comforter and six large pillows at its head.

A thick and rich aroma met Scotty's nose, and he turned his attention to the left-hand side of the room. He saw there a large wooden table literally piled with food. It was enough to put any Thanksgiving dinner to shame. When he approached the table, he saw mountains of fresh fruits and crunchy vegetables. There were tomatoes, green beans, apples, oranges - everything he loved. A huge bowl of mashed potatoes, oozing with butter, and a gigantic pitcher of gravy sat in the center of the table. There was also a pot of stewed chicken and pastry, Scotty's favorite dish.

Several other human delicacies were also present, including iced shrimp and oysters still in their shells, along with many others that Scotty had heard of but never tasted. The best part was, there wasn't a fish in sight. Though, he would have gladly eaten an entire lake of that vile food if it meant he would escape from Lizard Face.

For the first time since he had left Earth, Scotty noticed that he was feeling tired, and now, with all this food to tempt him, his stomach was growling something fierce. Even so, it was not enough to keep him from enjoying the most impressive sight in these quarters, the expansive window.

It stretched the entire breadth of the room, and beyond it, swirls of colored gasses and purple sparks of energy moved past the ship. Wherever they were going, they weren't in normal space any longer.

"TB, can you still hear me?"

"Yes, sir."

"I suggest we continue to talk with each other using the mind link. My guess is they have this room bugged."

"Agreed."

"Any idea where we are?"

"I'm processing the visual images I'm getting from your brain. I encountered something similar about fifty years ago."

"What was it?"

"At that time, Lord Nimbus, of the neighboring solar system, had incorporated my circuits into his command vessel, the Icon. The ship was patrolling the outer reaches of their solar system when it was hit by what at first appeared to be a gravitational eddy."

"What was it really?"

"Well, the ship was drawn deeper into the anomaly. The sensors showed a series of tunnels at the center of the distortion field. The helmsman threw every ounce of power we had into the engines, but it wasn't enough. The Icon was shot down one of the tunnels, only to emerge back in space a few hours later. The anomaly was some sort of vortex. Less than a black hole, but more than a wormhole."

"Did you ever find it again?"

"No, in fact, the vortex ejected us into a completely unfamiliar solar system. There was another civilization there, but we couldn't make contact. They were too primitive. It took us over three months to get back home."

"Lizard Face must have found a similar vortex in our solar system. Judging from what he told us, he must have used it to either colonize or conquer another world deep in space. The question is, what can we do about it?"

"I think it is a little early to try and save another world, Scotty. The goons that left Staranana didn't leave with much in the way of technology. My guess is that they set up a biosphere on some asteroid or a dead planet."

"You're probably right."

"Scotty, we have no idea what to expect when we get to Evilanda, but I'm guessing you're going to need all your strength. You should eat and then go to bed."

"You don't think the food could be poisonous, do you?"

"To what end? Lizard Face could kill you a lot easier than that if he wanted to. I suspect the food is fine, and that we will be left undisturbed until we arrive at Evilanda."

"Shouldn't we try and escape?"

"My computer link is completely blocked. In fact, I am pretty sure your duplicate will have gone offline by now. If we can't access this ship's computers, I don't see how we can get out of here."

"Well, let's hope Spikey can deal with the duplicate problem."

"In the meantime, eat and go to bed!"

"You're right."

Scotty walked over to the table, his mouth watering. He bowed his head and prayed out loud, "Lord, to whom vengeance belongs, shine forth! Lord, I find myself in the nest of my enemies, cut off from my friends, and with very little hope. Come to my aid, Lord. But until You do, give me strength to endure this. Bless this food to my body and give me a good night's sleep, so that I might rise to fight tomorrow. In Jesus' name, amen." And then he filled a plate with as much food as it could hold and dug in. Thirty minutes later, he flopped onto the bed, still in his clothes, and was asleep before his head hit the pillow.

~

"Have you found the Takillian computer?" Lizard Face asked. Lt. Kyak had reported to the bridge and was standing before his master in the command chair.

"The boy has a jeweled necklace around his neck. We detected a mind scanner embedded in the necklace, and there is a small computer chip attached to it as well. According to our information, the chip is of Takillian origin."

"Excellent! Is *Sscotty* aware that we know about his little friend?"

"I don't believe so, sir. He has it well hidden under his shirt. Should I take it from him?"

"Not yet. The computer is not our real objective, and we don't have the means to alter its programming. I doubt even Moonbeam could do that. We could destroy it, but that would be foolhardy. Does the device have communications equipment?"

"I suspect the computer chip was once part of a much larger system. The necklace is equipped with a communicator, but it has a very limited range. The memory scanner has a far more extensive range, but our disruption field is blocking it from transmitting."

"We'll have to deactivate that field *ssoon* to conserve power *sso* that we can make escape velocity at the other *sside* of the vortex."

"Still, I don't believe the device's scanners can send a signal farther than a light year in distance."

"We'll *ssoon* be much further away than that. Very good, Lieutenant. Resume your *sstation*."

Kyak bowed slightly and then moved to the exit of the bridge. Captain Gakic reported, "We are approximately one hour from the threshold of the vortex. After that, we'll have another hour before we touch down on Evilanda."

"Is the launch facility prepared for our arrival, Captain?"

"Yes, sir. The southern strip has been cleared, and a boarding ramp is ready to be attached to our starboard airlock. Lt. Commander Nikit will be pleased with our capture of this vessel."

Lizard Face smirked, "Anything to please our Chief Engineer."

~

"Scotty, are you awake?"

Scotty wrapped his arms around a pillow and groaned. For a second, he almost let himself believe that everything that had happened was all just a bad dream. But as he opened his heavy eyelids and brushed the crusties out of them, he saw the starfield and sighed. It hadn't been a dream.

"Where are we?" Scotty asked.

"Back in normal space from what I can gather. The ship took quite a jolt about ten minutes ago. I'm surprised it didn't wake you."

"Oh, TB, I was dead to the world. I'm surprised you were able to wake me."

"It's an advantage of our mind link. I have the ability to terminate REM sleep."

"Are we at Evilanda?"

"I don't know. Take a look out the window."

Scotty got up on his knees and scanned the space beyond the window. "AH!" he screamed.

"What! What's wrong?" TB had never heard the human boy scream before, and the sound of it sent a jolt through his emotional circuits.

"I look a fright!"

"What?"

"I can see my reflection in the window. I look terrible. My hair is messed up, and how did I get dirt on my face?"

"Oh, my goodness, Scotty! We have more important things to worry about!"

Scotty giggled, *"You're right, of course. But I need to take a shower if I am going to be fully functional today. Are your systems waterproof?"*

"Waterproof, fireproof, and clumsy-proof."

"Good. And do you have a copy of the Bible in your databanks?"

"Yes, Spikey programmed one in a few months ago."

"Great! I'm in the mood for the story of David and Goliath. Can you read it to me while I shower?"

If TB had had a mouth, he would have been grinning ear to ear. He said, *"I think I can do you one better."*

Scotty crawled from his bed and stumbled into the

bathroom. The shower was much as those on Earth were. Lizard Face clearly went to a great deal of trouble to prepare these quarters for him. What he couldn't figure out was what Lizard Face wanted. Killing him would have accomplished a great deal for the lizard, but for some reason, Lizard Face wanted him alive. Which could only mean Lizard Face wanted to exchange him for something far more valuable. But what did the Starananians have to offer? They would never surrender their world, and there weren't enough goons left to secure it even if they did. The location of Stararocka was also a closely guarded secret. So what did he want? Oh, well, as Lizard Face had said, "All in good time."

Scotty undressed and adjusted the water temperature of the shower. It took a second to reach a comfortable temperature, and then he stepped inside. He asked, *"Are you okay down there?"*

"No problems whatsoever."

"Okay, well, I'll take that story whenever you're ready," Scotty said, but as he waited for TB to begin, something he had not expected happened. The shower, the bathroom, and everything around him, vanished.

He found himself standing in the middle of a vast field. There were large hills in front of him and behind him, and from those hills, he could hear roaring chants. From behind him came the call, "God go with you, David!" and in front of him, "Kill him, Goliath!"

Though he had been naked in the shower, he now wore a simple wool covering about his waist. His chest and torso were still bare and boasted a deep tan. He had crude sandals on his feet, and on his left hip was strapped a heavy pouch that he discovered held several smooth stones. And then, there was the giant!

About a hundred meters off stood an enormous man. He was easily nine feet tall, and even from that distance, Scotty could tell he was ugly. He had a helmet of brass and a coat of mail. He also had a form of brass shielding on his legs and shoulders, and he had a spear in his hand that looked like it had been forged from the entire trunk of a small tree. Scotty didn't notice at first, but there was also a smaller man running ahead of the giant with a shield.

"TB, what's going on?"

"You wanted to hear the story of David and Goliath."

"Yeah, hear it, but from what I can tell, I am now in it. How is this possible?"

"The mind link. I can project images into your brain, and thanks to your very developed imagination, you can also participate in those stories."

"And am I supposed to kill Goliath? TB, I can't do that! David was a master of the slingshot."

"If I'm not mistaken, Sparkey is quite the shot, and he has taught you a thing or two, hasn't he?"

"Well, yes, but…"

"Besides, all David really had was his faith. You have that too, plus the added advantage of knowing this isn't real. So have fun, and let it jazz you up for the real battle that lies ahead."

Scotty took a deep breath and nodded, "Okay!"

Seeing Scotty, Goliath came forward and raged, "Am I a dog that you come at me with a mere sling? And a boy yet! Oh, may the God of fools lament and be shamed by the blood that will be on His head. Rot in a dog's vomit, God of the Israelites."

Scotty didn't have to be the real David to feel rage bubbling up inside him at this giant's words. Like David, he wondered who this Philistine was that he should defy the armies of the living God!

Goliath further mocked, "Come to me, and I will give your flesh to the birds of the air and the beasts of the field."

Hatred flashed in Scotty's eyes, and words that were not his own came from his mouth, "You come to me with a sword, with a spear, and with a javelin. But I come to you in the name of the Lord of hosts, the God of the armies of Israel, whom you have defied! This day the Lord will deliver you into my hand, and I will strike you and take your head from you. And this day I will give the carcasses of the camp of the Philistines to the birds of the air and the wild beasts of the earth, that all the earth may know that there is a God in Israel. Then all this assembly shall know that the Lord does not save with the sword and the spear; for the battle is the Lord's, and He will give you into our hands."

At those words, Goliath's gaze narrowed, and he charged, screaming curses all the way. Scotty really didn't feel like himself. In fact, he felt possessed by some holy force, but it was a good feeling. He ran toward the giant and slipped a single stone from his pouch along the way. The stone was in the sling before Scotty had a chance to think, and then he was spinning the sling, and the stone shot forward.

For one timeless moment, the stone hung in the air. But then, with a thundering smack and the crushing of bone and the ripping of brain tissue, the stone sunk into Goliath's forehead. The giant stood still for a moment, as if in shock. But then, with a thud the entire area could hear, he fell to the ground, dead.

Scotty walked over to the fallen Philistine heaving, "I...I did it, TB!"

"*Yes, you did. But if I recall correctly, there is still something else you have to do.*"

"*I know!*"

Scotty held his nose at Goliath's foul stench. The flies were already gathering. It didn't take long to find the giant's sword. It was enormous, to put it mildly, and heavy. It took more than one attempt for Scotty to lift it over his head, but when he had, he stood over the giant's neck and said, "Glory be to the Lord God of hosts who leads His troops in war!" Then he swung forward and sliced through Goliath's neck. When the head was severed, he kicked it away from the body and raised the sword over his head again. And as he heard the Israelites' shouts of victory and the Philistines' screams of terror, the entire valley vanished. He was back in the shower. But more than that, he was ready for whatever Lizard Face had in store for him.

Chapter 7

Evilanda

S cotty had just polished off two apples, an orange, and a huge glass of milk when a rap came at his door. He didn't even have time to answer before the door slid open, and Lizard Face and two goons stepped inside.

"Did you *ssleep* well, Your Majesty?" Lizard Face asked.

Scotty smiled, "Yes, very well, thank you. And the food was delicious. Where did you get it?"

"Your Chef has become quite *sskilled* with human dishes. Our new world has animals and plants *ssimilar* to Earth. We only had to follow Berry's instructions, and we had this wonderful feast."

"Wait a minute! Are you telling me Chef Berry has had contact with you?"

"That's a discussion for another time, Your Majesty. In the meantime, we've arrived. Come with us, please."

Scotty stood and approached the door. The tallest goon secured his hands in the manacles again, and they headed down the corridor.

"How will we get down to the surface?" Scotty asked.

"We'll land the *sship*," Lizard Face replied. "I think you'll be impressed with what we've accomplished."

"Lizard Face, I'm still your prisoner. And I would sooner see your world destroyed than be impressed by it. My friends are probably working on a way to rescue me right now."

"I wouldn't count too much on that. Your people will find

it impossible to track our course through the vortex. And even if they could, our virus would neutralize their technology immediately."

Scotty bluffed, "Don't bet on that! Spikey has an alien computer that can neutralize your virus!"

"You mean the alien computer hanging around your neck?"

Scotty's eyes grew wide, and he couldn't say anything. Lizard Face continued, "Do you honestly think we're *sstupid?* We detected it around your neck the minute we took you into custody. Without it, Moonbeam will accomplish nothing against us."

"Don't underestimate Spikey. You'll recall we all escaped from Cosmic Bubble Palace right under your nose three months ago. He also created the *Door* technology that brought me to Staranana, and he was one of the deciding factors in helping me defeat Seth. He also built the *Zerubbabel.*"

Lizard Face sneered, and Scotty asked, "So, are you going to take the computer away from me?"

"Not just yet. As it is, it poses no threat to us. But the moment it does, we will destroy it. And if we *sshould* discover a way to commandeer it for our purposes, we will take it from you immediately. And now, let me *sshow* you our world."

They walked down the corridor and boarded an elevator. Seconds later, they stepped out onto the bridge. Scotty had only seen schematics of the *Fire Cruiser* ships, but seeing the bridge of the *Dragon's Blood* was truly impressive. In some ways, it reminded him of the bridges of spaceships he had seen on various sci-fi programs. There was the central command chair, the forward helm, and the rear tactical and engineering stations.

The only problem was the happy crew of Space Age explorers was nowhere to be found. In fact, the bears that once crewed this ship were nowhere to be found, except for a few bloodstains that marred the otherwise well-shampooed carpets. Lizard Face must have been keeping his new goon recruits under lock and key.

"Captain Gakic, bring our planet up on the forward viewer for our young emperor," Lizard Face said.

The goon tapped his console, and a gorgeous planet appeared on the screen. It had three continents, all bathed in green, four ocean-like bodies of water, and a canopy of swirling white clouds. It put both Staranana and Earth to shame.

"Scotty?"

"Yeah, TB."

"Well, I don't know if this matters, but that image is being processed from their computer banks, not their sensors."

"You have access to their computer banks?"

"Not exactly. By now their systems are probably alarmed and heavily encrypted. I could break through, but not without getting caught. That would give Lizard Face plenty of reason to carry out his threat to destroy me. But I did a flash scan of Gakic's brain. He'll never know, and he accessed the computer banks, not the sensors."

"Maybe we're not close enough to Evilanda yet."

"I'd agree, but I scanned the helmsman's brain too. We entered a standard orbit five minutes ago."

"What do you think it means?"

"Only that this is not, in fact, Evilanda. I mean look, that planet is a little too perfect. And you know Lizard Face would corrupt it in a heartbeat."

"What can Lizard Face be trying to accomplish?"

"Who knows? He's a megalomaniac trying to hold onto what he already lost. That throne in the cargo bay looked exactly like yours. The planet on the viewscreen could very well be an image of Staranana in Iren's time. He's probably just trying to impress you."

"Yeah, we're learning a great deal about our lizard friend."

"Scotty, I can read your mind. You're worried about Chef Berry, aren't you?"

"Kind of. You don't think Berry could be helping them, do you?"

"Berry lived in the Palace when Lizard Face was there. He knows exactly what kind of evil he is capable of. Plus, Berry isn't exactly a treasure trove of tactical data. And if all he was stealing was a list of your favorite foods, that isn't exactly a crime."

"Yeah, but something is up at the Palace. Maybe…"

"*Sso* what do you think of our planet, Your Majesty?" Lizard Face asked.

Scotty shook his head and said, "It's nice. I was just

thinking, though, that if you dumped down several billion tons of snow, and threw in a seismic event or two to smash some of the continents together, it would look a lot like Staranana."

Lizard Face's eyes narrowed, and he opened his mouth to speak, but his helmsman beat him to it, "Master, we have been cleared for landing."

Lizard Face turned from Scotty and gestured toward Gakic. The Captain flipped a switch, and Lizard Face began, "Attention all hands, we are preparing for landing. *Ssecure* your *sstations*."

One of his goon escorts placed Scotty in a seat near the outer wall of the bridge. He asked, "What are you going to do with me once we reach the surface?"

Lizard Face did not respond. Instead, he commanded Gakic, "Remove the image of the planet from the viewer. We operate on *ssensors* from here."

Gakic nodded, and the image of the planet vanished, and the screen went dark. Scotty could feel the trembling of the deck plates beneath him as the ship began its descent. But somehow, even with a ship this sophisticated, he expected the vibrations to be more intense when traveling through a planetary atmosphere.

"TB, I know you said you couldn't access their computers without them knowing, but there has to be something we can do."

"I'm way ahead of you. I've been keeping tabs on Gakic and the helmsman. I have only collected a few seconds of data, but I think I've learned a few significant details that might be to our advantage."

"Let's hear them."

"Right! Well, first, the planet we saw is not Staranana, but neither is it inhabited by Lizard Face and the goons. At least, not exactly."

"What do you mean?"

"According to Gakic's memories, the planet was once the home of a race called the So. They had thousands of ships and highly advanced technology. Their planet was actually a rogue planetoid. Its core produced so much heat that they didn't need a sun to sustain life on their planet. Somehow, a highly luminescent comet got trapped in orbit and provided the light they needed."

"I see, but you said that's not the planet we're approaching?"

"No, I had to stop my probe of Gakic. But from what I can tell from

what I learned from the helmsman, we are approaching a large asteroid in a field of many other asteroids."

"We were just in an asteroid field."

"I suspect this field was created by the breakup of a planet."

"Do you think they destroyed the So's planet?"

"I highly doubt it. Before they took the Dragon's Blood, they didn't have the means, not even with their virus. The planet was probably wiped out by a natural disaster. I've analyzed the debris field, and from the drift patterns and fragmentation, I'd say the So's orbiting comet struck and destroyed their planet around one hundred years ago."

"You got all that from just a few seconds linked to their brains?"

"Hey, remember I'm no ordinary computer, buddy. I can process four trillion terabytes of information per nanosecond, and I have enough memory capacity for ten thousand years of such computations. And to top it off, from your sensations of the ship vibrating, I have also determined that we are not traveling through a planetary atmosphere."

"So the question remains, what does Lizard Face really want? He as much as said he couldn't use you to his advantage, and he is obviously taking good care of me to barter for something. Any idea what?"

"No clue."

Scotty lurched forward as the ship thudded to a stop on the landing platform, and Lizard Face said, "Welcome to Evilanda, Your Majesty."

Scotty got up, and his goon guards wrapped their hands around his arms. Lizard Face stood from the command chair, and the goons directed Scotty to follow the lizard onto the elevator. Within minutes, they had arrived at the airlock.

Scotty asked, "I don't suppose you'll tell me your plans now?"

"After a brief tour, you will be taken to a detention cell," Lizard Face replied and tapped the control to open the airlock. Scotty caught a whiff of the air beyond. It had a wet, earthy aroma, almost as though it had been processed through damp soil. Beyond the airlock was an illuminated boarding ramp, but Scotty couldn't see anything past it.

Lizard Face waved the goons off and drew his own pistol. "I don't think the Emperor will be able to escape now. I'll escort him through the city and then to the detention center.

Tell Captain Gakic to begin the modifications to the *sship*."

"What modifications?" Scotty asked. Lizard Face did not answer. Instead, he sent the goons away, took Scotty by the arm, and led him down the ramp.

Scotty had only flown a few times in his life, but it was enough to recognize the similarities between aircraft boarding ramps and the one he and Lizard Face were walking down now. There was one distinct difference, though. This ramp was on a definite decline, which meant it wasn't connected to a building. Rather, it was leading into the ground, which explained the earthy aroma.

Something else also struck Scotty. Since his mother had been born in North Carolina, he had flown there from Oregon a couple of times. North Carolina's climate was significantly more humid than that of Oregon, and that fact had been immediately noticeable once he had stepped onto the boarding ramp. This ramp, however, seemed to be airtight. And there were no windows by which to look outside onto this supposedly lush and paradise-like planet.

Scotty halted in his tracks, "All right, enough is enough, Lizard Face. I want to know why you are taking me underground!"

"Our capital city is *ssubterranean*."

"A subterranean city on your beautiful planet?"

Lizard Face's answer wasn't immediately forthcoming, but it was TB who interjected into Scotty's thoughts, *"Uh, sir, until we have a greater tactical advantage, I suggest we not provoke Lizard Face, nor reveal what we know about this planet. If he finds out what we know, he might make good on his threat to have me destroyed."*

"Agreed!"

Lizard Face replied, "This location is of a greater tactical advantage."

Scotty nodded, and they continued down the ramp. When they were finally at the bottom (though, Scotty swore it took about twenty minutes), they were standing in a large room carved directly out of stone. The floor was covered in damp soil, and a ring of hand-lit torches circled the room. A single workstation, with a single goon operator, sat in the center of the room.

Lizard Face walked to the officer and said, "I would like to give Emperor *Sscotty* a tour of our city. Would you please arrange a transport vehicle?"

The goon officer nodded and then opened a communications link. Scotty said, "I'm impressed, Lizard Face. You are most gracious to your subjects. I doubt Seth would have been caught dead using the word *please*. You have also been very kind to me."

"I *sserved* under *Sseth* for two thousand years. He was arrogant and cruel. I will not deny that I possess those qualities. However, I have learned that you can accomplish much more with happy *ssubjects*. Thus, I treat them generously. That way, I need not fear rebellion. Besides, when my plans are complete, I doubt very *sseriously* there will be anyone in the Universe who will be able to oppose me."

Scotty felt his stomach clench, "And what exactly are those plans?"

"All…"

"Yeah, I know. All in good time."

"The transport has arrived, sir," the goon reported.

Lizard Face led the way to a pair of metal doors at the end of the room. The doors opened automatically at the detection of their presence to reveal what looked like a roller coaster car on a track.

Scotty gulped, "Uh, this isn't going to be like a real roller coaster, is it?"

"What's a roller coaster?" Lizard Face asked.

"A form of Earth entertainment, but let's just say, I'm not too fond of them."

"Well, our city is another klep beneath the *ssurface*. The car will take us there at an accelerated velocity. Get in."

Scotty hesitated until Lizard Face pushed him forcefully toward the car. He sat down and immediately noticed something. "There are no seatbelts!"

"What?" Lizard Face asked as he sat beside the human boy. Before Scotty could frame an answer, the car lurched forward, propelling itself down the virtually vertical tunnel at a speed that quickly shoved Scotty's stomach into his throat. He was glad that he had eaten a light breakfast, but he doubted he'd be ready for lunch anytime soon. When the car finally came to a stop, he was certain he now looked as green as Lizard Face.

Lizard Face helped Scotty to his feet and said, "Just in case you were thinking about escape, I must tell you there is only one way in or out of this city, and that is this tunnel. *Sshould* you attempt it, I will have fifty goons waiting for you, and they will kill you."

"Now, that's the Lizard Face I know!"

Lizard Face grumbled, then said, "Follow me."

They stepped from the car into another large room of stone, though this one had metal support beams and several computer terminals. There were also about ten goons. They were chatting casually. In a way, this place seemed nothing like a military base.

Lizard Face led the way across the room, then through another tunnel, and then Scotty saw the city, and his mouth dropped. Lizard Face had led him onto a ledge overlooking an enormous cavern. Scotty couldn't help but be reminded of Black Eye Canyon in the aqueducts on Staranana, but this place was fully illuminated. There were literally hundreds of buildings, the smallest of which was at least five stories high. Each one was carved out of stone and had dozens of windows. There was also a network of roads, though no motor vehicles, and a wide and rapid river snaked around the perimeter of the city acting as a natural moat. It also appeared that, in the distance, there were acres and acres of farmland. Whatever the reason Lizard Face had lied about the actual condition of the planet, Scotty was still impressed.

And, in fact, the most impressive two sights of all were directly in the center of the city. The first was a building easily the size of Cosmic Bubble Palace. Scotty guessed it was the headquarters of the Evilandian Empire. At least, he couldn't imagine what else it might be. Far above it, on the ceiling of the cavern, he saw an enormous crystal with hundreds of jagged spires extending from a spherical base that was embedded deep in the rock. The crystal was shining brightly, and thus, illuminated the entire city. However, the intensity was as gentle as moonlight.

"I can see why you want to have your city here," Scotty said. "And I will admit that I am impressed. But what I can't understand is, how did you do all this in less than three months?"

Lizard Face pointed his pistol at him and then waved him toward a narrow path that led down toward the city. "Proceed, and I'll explain."

"You're not leading the way this time?"

"This trail is rather narrow. I am *ssorry*, but I don't trust you enough to let you proceed behind me. You might try and take advantage of the *ssituation*."

"Not before I learn the mystery of this place."

"Go!" Lizard Face directed. Scotty started down the trail, and Lizard Face explained, "Three months ago, after we escaped from *Sstaranana*, my three hundred goons and I had no idea where to go. We thought of *ssearching* for *Sstararocka*, but after the encounter with the *Fire Cruiser,* we decided against it. We opted to *sstart ssearching* for an asteroid in the belt where we could establish a colony and rebuild our forces. We were charting a particularly dense pocket of asteroids when a gravitational *ssurge* hit our *sship*. We were badly damaged, and before we knew it, *sspace* had dissolved around us. We had no clue what was going on, but our hull was breaching, and we were losing life *ssupport*.

"My *sscience* officers *ssurmised* that we were trapped within a *sspatial* vortex of *ssome ssort*. We managed to *sstabilize* and reinforce the hull. With barely an hour of life *ssupport* left, we came to an abrupt *sstop*. We couldn't explain it. We were in empty *sspace*, no *sstars*, no gasses, and very little radiation. However, beyond the perimeter of this null *sspace*, we detected literally dozens of event horizons."

"Event horizons?"

"It appears Moonbeam hasn't taught you as much as I had hoped."

"I'm only in the fourth grade! Now go on."

"An event horizon is the gravitational field that forms around a collapsing *sstar* as it is becoming a black hole.

Vortexes and wormholes also have event horizons. Our *ssensor* readings were *sso* distorted that we could not find the vortex from which we had come, *sso* I ordered my helmsman to take us through the closest one. We emerged back in normal *sspace* a *sshort* time later, and we found this planet. Because of our extensive damage, I ordered the *sship* to land on the *ssurface*."

Scotty took a chance, "Are you ever going to tell me that we aren't actually on a planet?"

"SCOTTY!"

"How do you know that?" Lizard Face asked.

"It's easy enough to figure out from your story. If this planet really were the paradise you showed me, the last place you would have started to search would have been the underground."

"I take what I *ssaid* earlier back. You clearly are very *ssmart*. You're right, we wanted to put on a little *sshow* in the hopes that it would break your *sspirit*. You are, after all, God's chosen one, and all He gave you was a frozen wasteland of a planet. If you had believed we had this planet as it originally was, we hoped it would *sshake* your faith."

"I can assure you, that will never happen. Now, go on with your story."

"We found the *ssurface* barren and lifeless, exposed to the vacuum of *sspace*. I led a team of goons out in *sspace ssuits*. Quite by accident, we discovered an airlock buried under a *sshallow* layer of *ssoil*. We managed to open it, and followed the tunnels to this city. The place was amazing; it had hundreds of buildings, computers, water, and farmland. I ordered the rest of the crew to disembark, and we *ssearched* the city. Captain Gakic found a library that had books that explained everything.

"This asteroid was once part of a planet called *Ssoal* inhabited by a race call the *Sso*. Even with their immense library, it appears they weren't much for taking pictures, *sso* we *sstill* have no idea what they looked like. From what we were able to learn, they were a highly *ssophisticated* race, millennia old. Their entire *ssociety* was geared toward the attainment of absolute knowledge. Their planet was rogue, it had no *ssun*, but an orbiting comet provided all the light they needed, and perfect amounts of heat emanated from its core. Their records also indicated that they had built a fleet of thousands of *sspacecraft.*"

"So what happened to them?"

"From what we have gathered, they were a very proud race. They considered themselves the *ssuperior* race of the Universe. In time, they even believed themselves to be greater than God and *ssought* to destroy the first world, *Earth.* As I am *ssure* you are aware, the *Text of Iren ssaid* that all life in the Universe began with God's creation of Earth. The *Sso* felt that if they destroyed Earth, they would take the dominant place in the Universe. However, even as their fleet prepared to make the journey to Earth, *ssomething* terrible happened. Millions of their people began to die *sspontaneously.* It took their *sscientists ssome* time to figure out that their comet was dumping massive amounts of radiation down onto the planet. A few thousand escaped underground and built this city. However, they had to abandon their *sspace* fleet and all their plans. Within a century, the comet's orbit decayed completely. It crashed into and *sshattered* the planet. A *ssmall* fragment, that crystal overhead, penetrated the *ssurface* above the city. Any *Sso* who weren't killed in the planet breakup died from the comet's radiation. And that was the end of the *Sso* race."

By this time, they had reached a bridge that crossed the river. The entrance to the bridge was sealed off by a gate with two goons guarding it. Lizard Face approached one and said, "Have you arranged transport?"

"Yes, Your Majesty. It will be here shortly."

"I didn't see any vehicles from above. What will we be riding in?" Scotty asked.

Before Lizard Face could answer, something roared. And from the sound of it, it was something huge. The gate opened and there, sitting on the bridge, was a huge, long, black reptile. In many ways, it reminded Scotty of a dragon, though it had no wings. It had four stubby legs and an equally stubby snout. There were dozens of spikes running down its back to the tip of its tail. The three largest spikes on the top of the reptile's back had two saddles between them. The creature hissed as Lizard Face approached him, but Lizard Face only hissed back.

Then the creature became very docile. It even shot out its forked tongue and gave Lizard Face a loving lick.

Lizard Face patted it on the head and said, "Let me introduce Blackie."

"Blackie!" Scotty laughed.

"Is there *ssomething* wrong?"

"Oh, no."

"Blackie and a few others wandering the farmlands were the only animals we found alive. Get on."

Scotty had ridden on Hydro the Water Dragon's back before, but that had been altogether different. Hydro would have never let anything happen to him, but Scotty wasn't about to trust this creature. Still, he didn't seem to have a choice. When he was secure on the front saddle, Lizard Face climbed on behind him.

"Take us home, Blackie!" Lizard Face called, and the lizard roared again and then turned and waddled toward the city.

Scotty continued their conversation, "So, God destroyed the *So*?"

"Oh, please, it was probably just a natural disaster."

"The people who heard about the destruction of Sodom and Gomorrah probably said the same thing. You can't possibly be arrogant enough to think God had nothing to do with the destruction of these people?"

"To be honest, I don't care if God killed them, or they all jumped into the river and drowned themselves. What they left behind has been very useful to me. Our transport *sship* had to be dismantled. However, Gakic took a few goons in maintenance pods and found their *sspace* fleet. The *sships* were adrift in the thickest part of the planetary fragment field, *sso* they hadn't been lost to deep *sspace*. They are both impressive and powerful, but *sstill* no match for *Fire Cruiser sships*. Gakic got one online. The *sship's* databanks had full records on the vortexes. Apparently, the *Sso* used them to explore *sspace*. The vortexes extend into thousands of *sstar ssystems*. They also had a most useful weapon they had planned to use on the humans."

Scotty nodded in understanding, "Your virus?"

"Yes, unfortunately, all records of a course to Earth were lost, but the way back to *Sstarananian sspace* was well charted.

Evidently, they considered our *ssolar ssystem* not worthy of conquest. In any case, after we understood their virus, it proved a most useful weapon."

"And five hundred bears lost their lives," Scotty sighed.

"Yes, it was wonderful, wasn't it?" Lizard Face smirked.

Up until now, Lizard Face had been almost cordial, but now Scotty felt his hate boiling. He wanted to whip around and rip the throat out of this pathetic lifeform, and he wasn't thinking of Blackie. All he could do, though, was grip tighter to his saddle.

Scotty asked, "What about that comet fragment? Aren't you concerned it could kill you?"

"We've run extensive tests. It's no longer dangerous. In fact, its radiation has increased our crop production and the health of my *ssoldiers*."

"I don't suppose it can cure *goonieness*?"

"There is only one person who can do that."

Blackie had reached the edge of the city and was now moving down the main street of town. There were dozens of goons walking about. The street was lined with shops and restaurants, which Scotty assumed were left over from the *So*, but he was surprised to see that the goons were operating them. In fact, there seemed to be too many goons.

"I thought you said only three hundred goons left Staranana. There have to be at least a hundred in this area, plus those on the *Dragon's Blood*, and from above it seemed like the entire city was alive with goons."

"One of the multiple advantages of the *Sso* technology. They were quite *ssophisticated* at cloning. The city is less populated than it *sseems*, but I now have close to five hundred goons at my command."

"I'm surprised you are being so open with all this information."

"It is of no consequence. Once our plans are complete, it won't matter if I have fifty goons or fifty thousand."

"I don't suppose you're ready to tell me what those plans are?"

"*Sscotty, Sscotty, Sscotty*, I can't *sshow* you all my cards. We are nearly at my palace, where you will be incarcerated, and I will transmit my demands to your people. Then I will explain my plans."

Scotty was beginning to get tense. Whatever Lizard Face wanted, there was no way it was going to be good. He had the building blocks here to establish an actual empire that could blow Staranana, maybe even Stararocka, out of the galactic pond. He had to escape, but how?

The palace loomed closer and closer. Unlike Cosmic Bubble Palace, this palace had no surrounding wall, nor courtyard. However, there were several statues, mostly of animals, carved out of colorful gems leading up a pathway of actual gold to a gigantic set of wooden doors. The palace went up and up and up to the point where it made Scotty dizzy to look up. He had often had that feeling looking up at his Palace from the ground. Though this palace was carved from a single slab of stone, it had been milled and smoothed, and it had many interesting animal forms carved along its various ledges. Scotty could not identify all of them, but some appeared to be wolves, eagles, and even gargoyles.

Lizard Face pulled back on the reins, and Blackie roared. Subsequently, the doors began to drag open across their stone base. When they were open, Blackie leaped through and wailed in triumph.

Lizard Face smirked, "Easy, boy! You just brought us home."

A goon approached and spread a red carpet along Blackie's side. Then he helped his master down. Scotty hopped down too. He started looking around the room, but Lizard Face's next words horrified him.

"Thank you, Blackie. You may eat him."

"What?" Scotty screamed. He thought Lizard Face had meant him, but he was surprised when the goon attendant bowed and then walked around in front of Blackie. Blackie ripped the goon apart, and Scotty had to cover his eyes as the attendant's blood began to ooze all over the floor.

Scotty was outraged, "I thought you said you treated your people well!"

"Relax, Your Highness. It was just a clone, one of our

earlier experiments with *Sso* technology. I don't do that with my original goons, nor with any of the clones that prove themselves. This one had not."

"And that makes it right?"

"Don't forget who you are talking to."

Scotty growled in anger. He could hear Blackie crunching on the attendant's bones. Despite the fact that he had been a goon, and a clone at that, Scotty couldn't help but feel sorry for him.

Two more goons approached, and Lizard Face said, "Remove the manacles. He can't escape now." Scotty was disgusted to have the goons' fungus covered hands touching his skin, but they managed to get the devices off his wrists without too much resistance. Then Lizard Face said, "Now, let's go."

With the goons' weapons trained on Scotty, Lizard Face led the way through the palace. The boy asked, "Do I get a tour of this place too?"

"No! You have entered the headquarters of the Evilandian Empire. The most you will *ssee* right now is your cell. There are *ssecrets* here that would be deadly in your hands."

"Really? Do tell!" Scotty smirked.

Lizard Face did not comment further. He led the way through some very winding hallways, still all carved from this single section of cavern rock. Scotty had to give credit to the *So*. They were certainly excellent engineers.

Lizard Face continued through the palace, but he turned so many times, Scotty thought he must be lost. When they came to a halt at a dead end, Scotty was convinced of it.

Lizard Face turned to him, "As much as I have enjoyed the pleasure of your company, here is where we part ways and where you lose any respect you have had. According to our laws, I hereby *sstrip* you of the rank of Emperor and *ssentence* you to imprisonment until *ssuch* time as our requested ransom is paid. If it is not paid by the day you call Christmas, we will kill you." He turned to his goons, "Throw him in."

Scotty was confused. *Throw him in where?* But his question was soon answered. One of the goons stepped to a control panel embedded in the wall. The other pulled up the rug on the floor in front of them to reveal a metal trapdoor. The first goon pushed a few buttons, and the trapdoor slid open. The pit below was black and ominous, and Scotty's heart began to throb.

Lizard Face gestured toward the hole, and Scotty screeched, "NO! Wait! Not in there!"

One of the goons slammed the butt of his rifle into the back of Scotty's head, and the next thing he knew, he was flailing through the trapdoor. He fell for only several seconds and then came to an abrupt stop on the stone floor. He felt some of his ribs snap, and blood was pouring from his nose. The door slid shut above him, and then it was dark, and he was alone.

Chapter 8
Grounded

"**C**onfirming all stop, Captain. Thrusters are offline, exhaust vents are sealed, and parking brakes have been engaged. I am opening the hatch and taking main power offline," reported Ensign Toby Nakan.

The *Zerubbabel* had returned to its port on the roof of Cosmic Bubble Palace. The whole trip back, which due to a lack of nuclear power had taken almost a day, Spikey had uttered not so much as a word. He just sat at his control board staring into space, or he hid in the rear compartment fixing things. And if Spikey was silent, Sparkey was just the opposite. He kept talking, trying to make jokes to cheer people up. He didn't say it, but he felt desperately guilty and wanted, above all, for someone to tell him it wasn't his fault that Scotty was gone. But no one ever did.

When the cockpit lights faded, Spikey finally spoke, "If you will all excuse us, I would like to have a word with my son."

Sparkey felt a lump form in his throat, and his heart began to race. This couldn't be good. Gloria kissed him gently on the top of the head and then left without a word, and Shortstop and Toby both gave him a sympathetic look. Then they were all gone, and Sparkey was left to face the wrath of his father.

For a moment, Spikey only stared at him, and try as he might, Sparkey could not meet his father's gaze. Finally, Spikey said, "Well, I'm waiting."

"So am I," Sparkey muttered.

Spikey growled, "So you have no apology, no defense? I knew it was a mistake to bring you on this mission! I told Scotty that, but he insisted that you come along. So I gave in."

"Scotty outranks you, Dad. You didn't have a choice."

"Shut up, cub! The point is, I decided to trust in your abilities, and you let me down. Scotty is gone! No doubt his double on Earth has vanished, which means his parents are probably worried sick by now, and for all we know, they are going to lose their son. And none of this would have happened if you had stayed with him like you were supposed to!"

Sparkey had tears building in his eyes. "You're the one who sent him to that ship!" he yelled. "Toby told me the whole thing was a trap! If I had stayed with him, I would have been captured too!"

"At least he wouldn't be alone!"

"DAD!"

Spikey turned from his son, heaving. He had no idea what he was saying. Of course, he didn't want Sparkey in the clutches of Lizard Face. He could have been killed or *goonified*. But he and Scotty had turned the tables on Seth together. Who was to say they couldn't have done it again? He took a deep breath and turned back around.

"I have to get to my workshop. I have to find some way to create a temporary duplicate of Scotty to send to Earth. I have no idea how I'm going to do it, but I have to try. In the meantime, you will go back down to our apartment and shut yourself in your room. And assuming we get Scotty back, I don't care what he says, you are never going on another mission again. Now go!"

Sparkey got up, the fur on his face drenched with tears, and left the *Zerubbabel* without another word. Spikey prayed, "*Oh, God, what now?*"

~

"Report!" demanded Shortstop as he stepped onto the CD of the Palace with Toby Nakan.

Colonel Speedway swiveled in the command chair and

reported, "We received your probe. I have Garlan, Sam, and several others in the Palace chapel holding a twenty-four-hour prayer vigil."

"Tell them not to stop until Scotty is back."

"Aye, sir," Speedway replied. Then he said, "Welcome back, Toby."

Up until that moment, Cak had been focused on his station, but when he heard his brother's name, he turned around quickly, and his face exploded in a smile. "Toby! Toby! You're alive!"

Cak abandoned all propriety and raced across the room to embrace his twin. Toby managed under his brother's tight embrace to say, "Yeah, I'm alive! But I'm about the only one."

Speedway snapped, "As you were, Ensign Nakan!"

Both teens straightened to attention, and Cak said, "Yes, sir. Sorry, sir." Then he returned to his station.

Speedway continued, "We got your report about Scotty and TB. Is there any hope of a rescue?"

Shortstop assured, "There is always hope, so long as we have the Lord on our side. But it isn't going to be easy. First, we must find a way to neutralize the virus, and we need to learn all we can about that vortex."

"I've been in contact with Captain Noble. They've been studying their sample of the virus. They are close to understanding how it functions, but they still have no idea how to stop it. He is bringing the data here on the *Fire Cruiser*. Spikey should take a look at it."

"Noble is coming here himself? Why doesn't he just transmit the data to us?" Shortstop asked.

"Well, many of the Stararockans aren't too happy that this task has been left up to us. It's not that they don't trust us; it's just that it's their families who are in danger, and they want to help. Without TB, we have no way to stop the virus, and we're all vulnerable. However, if we pool our resources, we might have a better chance of success."

"All right, here is the plan," Shortstop began. "Cak, could you come back up here?" The teen smiled and hurried back to his General. Shortstop continued, "Spikey installed a deep space sensor array on the roof of the Palace last month. I want you two boys to use it to collect as much data on the vortex as you can. I am specifically interested in whether or not we can track the *Dragon's Blood* through it. Also, Toby, a report on anything you learned while you were captive would be of great interest."

"Aye, sir."

"Colonel, there is every chance that Lizard Face will try and attack Staranana. Get every ship we have in orbit. I know it isn't much, but for now, it will have to do. Also, tell each ship's commander to find a way to modify their vessels so that they can be run without computers."

"Without computers, sir? How is that even possible?"

"I don't have the slightest idea, but tell them to find a way to make it possible."

"Yes, sir. Should we launch the *Zerubbabel* too?"

"It still needs to be repaired. Plus, that ship is out of my jurisdiction. You will have to ask Spikey. Even so, we will have to send both the *Zerubbabel* and the *Fire Cruiser* on the rescue mission."

"Aye, sir. I'll get those ships in orbit."

"Good, I'm going to go talk to Chef Berry."

"Chef Berry, sir?"

"Yes."

~

"Yes, I've got it. It will be ready on time! Oh, wait, I have to go. Someone is coming in." Chef Berry quickly tapped the termination button on his video communications terminal and turned to face General Shortstop.

"Who were you talking to?" Shortstop asked.

"Oh, uh, Ensign Shallow, sir. Poor girl has a terrible cold. She was sending down her request for dinner. As if I weren't busy enough!"

Shortstop nodded, then said, "I suppose you heard what happened to Scotty."

"Yes, sir. Is there any chance of rescuing him?"

"We're working on it."

"Is there anything I can do?"

"Yes, actually. I plan to have Scotty back safe and sound in time for his Christmas party. That is now only six days away. I'm putting you in charge of having the party ready, and I want it to be the best Christmas party Scotty has ever had. You can use his personal computer in his chambers to get any more information on Christmas that you need."

"You can count on me! It will be a great party."

"Good, and give Ensign Shallow my regards."

"What? Oh, right, I will, sir."

~

"How's it going, honey bear?" Gloria Moonbeam began to rub her husband's shoulders. Spikey had the control panel of his Palace-based *Door* open, and he was twisting a screwdriver around inside of it. For a moment, he said nothing, but then frustration flashed across his face, and he threw the screwdriver across the room and slumped into his chair.

He buried his face in his hands and began to sob, "This is all my fault, Gloria! All my fault!"

"What are you talking about, Spikey? None of this is your fault. And as much as you might want to believe it, it wasn't Sparkey's fault either."

"No. I am angry with him, but he was just following his heart. Sparkey has always been good at that."

"So has his father."

"But don't you see, Gloria? This is my fault. Lizard Face had *Door* technology, and he used it to help him capture that ship and to kill all those bears. I analyzed the readings we took. Their technology was identical to mine. That means, somehow, they stole it from me."

"Spikey, that's like saying you were guilty of murder because someone stole your gun to commit the crime. It's not your fault."

"But how did they steal the technology?"

"Can't you think of any way they might have done it?"

"No, not unless they had a spy on Staranana. But even if they did, I keep most of my inventions under lock and key. And besides, the possibility of there being a spy, especially after we were liberated, is ludicrous."

"I'd hate to think of another Kelcott in our midst."

"The worst part is Kelcott only got himself and one hundred bears killed. Well, unless you count those Seth killed using the information Kelcott sold to him. Either way, this spy could get our entire race annihilated."

"Which is why it is hard to imagine a bear in that role," Gloria sighed. Then she asked, "You don't think it could be Hydro, do you?"

Spikey thought a moment, then shook his head, "No, Hydro risked everything to help us three months ago."

"But we also had all the other dragons on the planet destroyed. We left him alone."

"Considering Hydro helped us with that effort, I doubt he is harboring a grudge. Besides, I think he believes he will one day find his brothers, the *Noble Dragons*. Seth turned them into stone and sent them into space. If he finds them, he won't be alone anymore. Plus, he has one other major alibi in his favor."

"What is that?" Gloria asked.

"He returned to his ancestral brooding grounds in the Melec Mountains on the other side of the planet. He is engaged in a dragon burial ritual that takes over a year to perform. I doubt we'll be seeing him for a while."

"Well, let's just hope we're both being paranoid, and there is no spy. Right now, the important thing is that you do not blame yourself, and we focus on how to rescue Scotty. Now, what's going on with his duplicate?"

Spikey took a deep breath, "Well, some good news. Time on Earth seems to be frozen."

"What?"

"Do you remember I once told you that there was a difference between Earth time and Staranana time?"

"Yes."

"When we first met Scotty, I assumed time would pass slower on Earth while he was here. But it didn't. He was here for two weeks, and two weeks passed on Earth. I was very confused. I mean, we have 1,005,018 years of well-documented history. Yet a biblical view of Earth shows it to have less than ten thousand years of history."

"And since Earth was created first, something is out of whack," Gloria commented.

"Right. Then I looked at these readings. The instant that Scotty's signal to the *Door* was broken, everything on Earth froze. As near as I can figure, it was the *Door* all along that linked time on both our worlds. Now that nothing is passing through the *Door* on a consistent basis, we see the difference between our two times. The best I can figure is that because the creation of our world was based on God's perfect understanding of the human imagination, our time moves at the speed of the human imagination."

"This is all a lot to take in, but at least with time on Earth frozen, you won't have to create another duplicate of Scotty."

"I don't know about that. This is the first time we have observed this phenomenon. We can't predict what will happen."

"So can you create another duplicate?"

"I can create the image of Scotty. But without the brain scanner, it won't act like him."

Gloria thought for a moment, and then her eyes sparkled, "What about Sparkey?"

"What?"

"Well, they've spent a lot of time together. If you could link his brain to the duplicate, he could at least make it act something like Scotty."

"Yeah, except I told him I wasn't going to let him go on any more missions."

"Oh, Spikey, for goodness sake, let the boy do what he's good at. Besides, when Scotty gets back, you know he is going to have a thing or two to say about your punishment of him."

"Ugh! A child telling me how to deal with my own son."

"A child chosen of God to rule our planet."

Spikey grumbled and then surrendered, "Okay, I'll make a deal with you. I'll rig up another brain scanner and get the *Door* ready. You tell Sparkey."

Gloria smiled, nodded, and then left the room.

~

Sparkey Moonbeam wiped one last tear from his eyes and folded his hands behind his head. He was on his bed, on his back, staring up at his starry ceiling. His entire room had been painted to look like a star cluster, and he had gotten into the habit of counting each star whenever he was upset. He had never counted them all, but this time, he was up to 599 when a knock came at his door. He didn't answer, and the knock came again. Finally, he growled, "What!" And the door slowly opened. His mother was standing on the other side.

He sniffled and said, "Have you come to yell at me too?"

Gloria walked over and sat down on the bed next to him. She tapped his leg and said, "Sit up, Sparkey." He did so, but reluctantly. He had had enough lectures for one day.

Gloria got right to the point, "Your father and I have a mission for you, Sparkey."

"A mission? Dad said he would never let me go on another mission."

"Look, both you and your father said and did things that I am sure you regret. But you have to understand, Sparkey, that he is only mad because he loves you, and you let him down. Plus, he feels responsible for Scotty. The Emperor is only nine, and your dad and I are the Starananian equivalents of his parents. I have never met his real parents, but I know they would be horribly upset if we ever let anything happen to him. Now Scotty is in very real danger, and we are not sure if we can do anything about it."

"I didn't want that to happen, Mama. But Toby was in trouble, and I had to save him."

"Your dad and I both understand that. And the truth is, Scotty probably would have been captured either way. But we are going to do everything we can to get him back. Now, there is a mission that has to be done, and you are the only one on Staranana who can do it."

Sparkey perked up, "What is it?"

"Your dad thinks he can create a temporary duplicate of Scotty to send back to Earth, but we have no brain to operate it. You know Scotty better than anyone else. We want to link your brain to the duplicate so that you can pretend to be Scotty."

Sparkey sniffled again, wiped his nose, and said, "But Scotty's duplicate is only controlled by his brain on a subconscious level. If the same thing were done with my brain, the duplicate would act like me, not Scotty."

"I'm not sure how it will work, but I know your dad thinks he can do it. So, will you help us?"

Sparkey sniffed, "Of course!"

~

"All right, let's see if this will work." Spikey Moonbeam fastened the new mind scanning necklace around his son's neck, then flicked a switch on the *Door*. Energy began to pulse between the frames, and then it projected out into the room. One by one the molecules solidified, transformed, and took shape and color. After a few moments, a perfect replica of Sparkey Moonbeam was standing silently in the middle of Spikey's workshop.

Gloria began, "Ah, Spikey, I thought…"

"Just a second," Spikey said. He tapped a few more controls, and the duplicate cub began to shimmer and vibrate, and with another flash of light, it transformed into the image of Emperor Scotty Fields.

Spikey directed, "All right, Sparkey, your mind now has full control of this duplicate. Try and make it scratch its nose."

"How?"

"Just scratch yours."

Sparkey complied, and just as his hand moved to his nose so did the duplicate's. Sparkey was intrigued. He lifted his right foot; the duplicate did the same. Then his left, and again, the duplicate copied him. He made a funny face, but to his surprise, the duplicate's face remained motionless.

"Its facial functions will not be activated until it reaches Earth, nor will its memory banks," Spikey explained.

"Dad, each time I have gone to Earth, no one could see me. How will they be able to see the duplicate if it is not Scotty controlling it?"

"I have only one solution to that problem. I prayed and asked God to let them see you. Hopefully, He will, because there is nothing else I can do about it."

"So exactly how am I supposed to control it all the way from Staranana?" Sparkey asked.

Spikey reached under his workbench for a box. He opened it and pulled out a small helmet, similar to a motorcycle helmet, with a thick, black visor. Gloria said, "I haven't seen that in a long time."

"Is that what I think it is?" Sparkey asked.

"Yes, it's my virtual reality helmet. I invented it when you were a baby as a form of entertainment that could help us escape, at least temporarily, from the world of Seth. General Shortstop got a hold of me, though, and convinced me to use my skills for more practical purposes. Now, however, I can hook this helmet up to the *Door*, and it will let you see through the duplicate's eyes. That, along with your body's control over it, will help you operate the duplicate on Earth. There is a gym on the 45th floor. Once you put the helmet on, you will only be able to see Earth, so you will need a large space to walk around. You might occasionally bump into a wall, but you shouldn't too often."

"What about things like sitting in chairs, or riding in cars?" Gloria asked.

Spikey sighed, "It's not a perfect plan."

Sparkey suggested, "I have an idea. We can have a few of the servants with me in the gym. I can work out a signal so that if I need to sit down, they can rush a chair out to me."

"I like it," Spikey smiled. Then he touched his son's arm, "And, Sparkey, I'm sorry. You'll do great."

"I'm sorry too," Sparkey replied, his head down. He looked up, and they exchanged a smile and then embraced each other. Gloria joined in, a few tears forming in her golden-brown eyes.

Finally, Spikey said, "Okay, let's do this. Gloria, take Sparkey up to the gym and get a few servants to help him. When I contact you, activate the helmet."

"Right!" they both chimed.

~

Minutes later, Sparkey, Gloria, and two servants with

several chairs and even a folding cot, stood in the center of the Palace gym. Spikey's voice piped over the intercom, *"Everyone ready up there?"*

"Ready!" they all called back.

"Okay, put on the helmet."

Sparkey inhaled deeply and then slipped the helmet onto his head. For a moment, there was nothing but black plastic in front of his eyes. One of the attendants eased him gently down onto the cot, because at last report, Scotty's duplicate had been asleep in bed. Gloria flipped the activation switch on the top of the helmet, and the next thing Sparkey knew, he was waking up on Earth.

Chapter 9
United Front

General Henry Shortstop stood at the head of the 75th floor conference room table and noted the bears around him. Captain William Noble of the *Fire Cruiser*, along with his brother and first officer Commander Josh Noble, were on his right. Gloria and Spikey were also on his right. Toby and Cak were on the left, along with one other unfamiliar officer, and Colonel Speedway was at the far end of the table.

He asked, "So, would anyone like to go first?"

Spikey began, "Well, the duplicate situation is under control for now, but I doubt Sparkey can keep the pretense up very long. He has none of Scotty's memories, and he is being asked to act correctly in a human environment. He has never done that before. I have full confidence in him, but we can't leave him down there forever. We need to find Scotty and fast."

"He may have to make do for a few days. This could take a while," Shortstop said. "Will, your report?"

William Noble began, "We have completely analyzed the virus. It involves literally billions of lines of code, and each of those lines of code is encrypted, so we can't tell exactly what each line does. However, as a whole, the codes are designed to overload a ship's computer processor. The virus can reproduce itself so that it takes up every free bit of computer memory. It is also highly adaptable so that it can change itself to function through any kind of electronic medium. The virus can override any command code, delete any database, and assume control of any ship's function."

"We already knew most of this. Is there anything new you can tell us?" Speedway asked.

"Yes, Colonel," replied Josh Noble. "We have successfully identified the single line of code that controls the sonic attack subroutine. Our computer technicians haven't been able to develop an anti-viral program to take out the entire virus, but they were able to create a program to delete that single line of code."

"That's good news," Gloria chimed in.

"Yes," Josh continued. "But that still leaves the rest of the virus to deal with. Sonic attack or not, it can still cripple any of our ships."

"We know the *Dragon's Blood* was infected. But Lizard Face seized control of it, so we can assume he has a counter virus," William said.

"No, we can't," Spikey began. "Scotty reported that the *Dragon's Blood's* computer processor was gone. Lizard Face must have replaced it with another one after the original was infected. He kept the location of the new core hidden as part of his trap to catch Scotty."

"Why would Lizard Face create a virus he couldn't stop?" Speedway asked.

Spikey said, "I think it is becoming more and more clear that Lizard Face did not create this virus. I mean, come on, the only thing that could stop it was an alien computer, centuries more sophisticated than we are. Lizard Face left this planet in a horribly under-equipped transport vessel. The virus has to be alien in origin."

"Agreed," Shortstop said. "And if Lizard Face didn't create the virus, he is probably vulnerable to it. Is there any way we can use the virus?"

"We'll need to study it a great deal more," Captain Noble reported. "I think we should focus on stopping the virus first."

"Any ideas, Spikey?" Shortstop asked.

"I've reviewed their data, and there may be a way. Like

Captain Noble said, the virus reproduces itself to fill up an entire computer core. If we install multiple computer cores in our ships, we could instantly switch to another core if the first was infected."

"What's to stop them from sending out the virus again, and infecting the other computer cores?" Josh asked.

"Have you ever heard of a *data dump*?" Spikey asked.

Josh shook his head, and Spikey explained, "Computers are extremely vulnerable to magnetic disruption. A little magnetic field can erase an entire database. We have taken great precautions to shield our computers, but I can create a device that will generate such a field. I don't care how sophisticated the virus is, it is still just computer code. If exposed to a magnetic field, it will be deleted. Normally, that would cripple our ships too, but with multiple cores, it won't."

"That still doesn't answer my question," Josh broke in.

"Patience, Commander," Spikey assured. "Consider this scenario. We're on the *Zerubbabel,* and one of the cores gets infected. The ship instantly reverts to the auxiliary core. The magnetic field activates and wipes out the memory of the first core. Once the first core is clean, the second core instantaneously transmits a copy of all its data back to the first. That way, if the virus is transmitted again, and the second core is infected, the first is ready to go. The two cores will only be connected by a radio link, and then only if the *data dump* is activated. Lizard Face could try and try, and we would always have computer control. Eventually, he will get tired of sending out his virus, and he'll have to come up with something else."

"I like it," Shortstop smiled. "But what's to stop them from sending out multiple copies of the virus at once?"

"Only one core will be connected to our receiving antennas and communications equipment at a time. If the virus can't get to a core, it can't infect it," Spikey replied.

"Good," Shortstop said. "How long will it take to get multiple cores set up?"

"In the entire Starananian fleet, at least three days," Spikey sighed. "But who knows what will have happened to Scotty by then?"

"Focus on the *Zerubbabel* and the *Fire Cruiser* for now. We are working on something else for the rest of the fleet," Shortstop ordered.

"Aye, sir. Then we can be ready to go first thing in the morning."

"Excellent!" Shortstop turned to the Nakans, "Toby, Cak, your reports?"

Toby began, "Well, first things first. For the brief time I was with Lizard Face, I learned that he still has at least one contact on Staranana, most likely in the Palace."

"What!" Speedway cursed.

Gloria continued, "Spikey and I came to the same conclusion, Toby. Do you have any idea who it is?"

"No clue, but we have to assume that nothing we do or say won't go unreported to Lizard Face. The spy could be anywhere or anyone."

Shortstop's shoulders slumped, "Just what we need! I'm willing to bet that the spy isn't anyone in this room, but we're stretched thin as it is. We can't spare many resources to find them."

"What about us?" Cak asked.

"What was that, Ensign?" Shortstop asked.

"After we deliver our report, Toby and I could take command of the search. We both have security training, and Toby here is just great at finding things," Cak beamed.

"Consider the project yours, and now, let's have the rest of your report," Shortstop said.

"Right," Cak continued. "The gravity field you encountered was indeed a vortex. According to our calculations, the event horizon is approximately one klep in diameter. Gravitational readings measure only about 10 Gs. Any of our ships could easily survive that. We detected various forms of radiation, dust particles, and photons. You know, the usual, but the one thing we did not detect was helium, and there were only trace amounts of hydrogen."

"What's so unusual about that?" Gloria asked.

"Most vortexes, wormholes, and black holes are formed by a collapsed star. Stars are made up of helium and hydrogen, so those gasses should surround any such phenomenon. But other than the smallest amounts of hydrogen, these gasses were completely absent," Toby explained.

"What do you think it means?" Shortstop asked.

"The best Toby and I have been able to conclude is that this vortex was not created in the normal fashion. It is almost as if someone took a giant finger and poked it right through the fabric of the Universe. This was very confusing to us, so we had the *Fire Cruiser* launch a sensor probe into the vortex. If I may use the viewscreen, I'll show you what I mean?" Cak requested.

"Please!" Shortstop gestured.

Toby and Cak both got up. Cak activated the screen. At first, it was nothing but a black field, but then a sparse and twisting trail of orange dots appeared on the screen. Toby explained, "The probe detected these ionized hydrogen particles. They could have only come from a spacecraft's propulsion systems."

"The *Dragon's Blood!*" Spikey proclaimed.

"Yes, but that's not all." Cak tapped another control and two circles appeared at each end of the hydrogen trail. Each circle had four smaller circles inside it, making them look like bull's-eyes. The tap of another control made the inner circles move outward, gradually taking the place of the larger circles around them. A new circle replaced the smallest one in the center.

Toby reported, "Cak and I believe the *Dragon's Blood* traveled through the vortex and exited through this event horizon."

"Good, then we can follow them," Speedway interjected.

"For now anyway," Cak said and tapped another control. The entire screen filled up with the pulsing circles, save a cross-shaped area of black extending through the middle of the screen. The hydrogen trail was in this crossroads.

Cak went on, "The vortex leads to a subspace crossroads filled with thousands of identical event horizons. Essentially, we have a gateway to almost anywhere in the galaxy in our backyard. The problem is the hydrogen particles are dissipating quickly. In time, our trail to Evilanda will be gone. We have left the probe in place, but the readings in there are so chaotic, it may not be enough to chart the vortex. Until we find a way to successfully chart the vortex, all we have are those hydrogen particles. We have to act fast."

"It's settled then," Shortstop began. "We will leave as soon as the *Zerubbabel* and the *Fire Cruiser* have been modified. Will, Josh, Spikey, make sure you're ready."

"Excuse me, General, but I don't believe any of us have had the pleasure of meeting this officer here," Captain Noble gestured toward the unfamiliar officer who, so far, hadn't said a word.

"Ah, yes, forgive me. Allow me to introduce Lt. Commander Trevor Hull. Mr. Hull has been studying spacecraft design for several years. He was one of the key designers of the *New Life*," Shortstop reported.

"That's right! I remember treating you for radiation sickness on the *New Life* when we were attacked by the *Space Shark*," Gloria chimed in.

Shortstop continued, "The Lt. Commander will be receiving a field promotion to captain if his plans succeed. I contacted him earlier today, and in short, he has come up with a way for our ships to operate completely on manual power."

"Really?" Spikey perked up. "Please explain."

"May I?" Hull asked.

"Please," Shortstop said.

"We are going to equip our fleet with solar sails and explosive decompression thrusters. The designs are still coagulating in my head, but with a few dozen cables, levers, pulleys, and what you might call a space rudder, we will be able to maneuver our ships without so much as one computer command. We won't get anywhere fast, but the explosive decompression thrusters will give us an edge in maneuverability. We will augment the solar sails with high-intensity photon projectors, so we will be able to build up pressure on the sails quickly."

"I'm not familiar with solar sails," Gloria said.

Hull explained, "On Earth, seafaring vessels, especially in centuries past, were propelled by catching the wind in canvas sails. In space, using a reflective fabric, we can use light, namely photons, like the wind. When the photonic pressure gets high enough, it will move the ship, and thanks to the projectors, we can build that pressure up quickly. In addition, I am replacing all of our intercom systems with an ancient human device called the telephone."

"Ancient?" Spikey quipped. "People still use phones on Earth today."

"Ah, but they don't use the very first version of the phone created by Alexander Graham Bell in the nineteenth century. It didn't require a computer. As far as communicating between ships is concerned, we will be adapting a form of human communication called Morse Code. We can use the searchlights on the ships to send signals to each other. The laser cannons already have a manual control function. With all these modifications, we shouldn't be vulnerable to the virus."

"I hate to be grim," Captain Noble began. "Even without the virus, the *Dragon's Blood* could blow all your ships to dust."

Shortstop nodded, "Well, let's hope our rescue attempt succeeds, because if the *Dragon's Blood* makes it to Staranana, these ships will be our last defense."

Hull continued, "General Shortstop has given me command of the *New Life* for this mission. I'll take her up and begin modifying the fleet. If I have a large enough engineering crew, we should be in position by the time that you leave in the morning."

Spikey was giddy, "You can use all of my engineers, and I'd love to talk about your other ideas."

Gloria giggled, "Mr. Hull, I think you just made a new friend."

"All right, here is the game plan," Shortstop said. "Toby and Cak will begin an immediate investigation for the spy. Spikey, you and the Nobles will begin preparing the *Zerubbabel* and the *Fire Cruiser*. Lt. Commander Hull will begin his modifications. Gloria, study the scans you took. See if you can find a medical cure for *goonieness*. Drop that request off with the prayer vigil, and if you don't have any fruitful results by morning, join the vigil. Colonel Speedway and I will begin working on a way to chart the vortex. This is going to be an all-nighter people. Let's get to work!"

Chapter 10

Goon Omega

Scotty Fields felt his shoulders slump in defeat. *"Well, TB, here we are."*

"Yep, here we are. Wherever here is?"

Scotty sighed. He was now in the darkest room he had ever been in. It was exactly like being blind. To make matters worse, his ribs felt like they were on fire, and he was growing insanely hungry. According to TB, eight hours had passed since they had been thrown in this dungeon.

For the first hour, Scotty had felt his way around the room trying to find some means of escape, or a dish of food, or even some form of bed, but there was nothing. When Seth had captured him, he had at least had hay to sleep on and a window. Now, it seemed Lizard Face's civility was at an end.

Scotty had never been claustrophobic, but then again, he had never been enclosed in such a small, dark space before. If it weren't for TB's distractions, he might have lost it by now. He was quite certain several of his ribs were broken. TB had suggested tearing his undershirt up into bandages, but that barely helped. TB had also suggested a nap, but with the pain, he had only gotten a few minutes' worth. All they could do now was wait.

Scotty asked, *"TB, have you thought about what Lizard Face may want?"*

"Constantly."

"Any ideas forthcoming?"

"*Nothing realistic. Starananian history is very thorough, but it is also filled with mysteries. The location of Emperor Iren's first son's grave is one example. Even after tens of thousands of centuries, no one has come close to finding it. Also, the disappearance of the Time Dragon is a particularly enticing mystery.*"

"*Time Dragon?*"

"*No one knew much about it. It was an idol of sorts. Seth kept it in his vault. According to one legend, if used correctly, the bearer could use the dragon to manipulate time. If used incorrectly, the idol could, well, let's just say, be very deadly. But, very early in Seth's reign, it vanished with no explanation whatsoever.*"

"*Well, I've never seen it, so I doubt he wants that.*"

"*There was also the Kodyax Turtle.*"

"*Kodyax? I've heard that word. It indicates the time Iren opened his human eyes for the first time, but what is the Kodyax Turtle?*"

"*It's silly really. According to records from the time, a huge amount of energy surged from Iren's eyes when he opened them. The energy caused a shockwave that shook the entire Palace. In the process, a statue of a turtle on the ledge outside Iren's chambers broke free and fell into the energy surge. Now, scientifically, the energy should have blasted that statue to bits, but legend has it that the statue absorbed the energy and then was pushed out of normal space-time. Any sane person would have believed it was destroyed, but there have been about five reports throughout the centuries of a strange turtle-like statue appearing in various parts of Staranana. The people who had it gained instant wealth and power. But they say the turtle vanished after spending only a short time in their possession.*"

"*Ha! Those people probably just made the story up,*" Scotty balked.

"*Maybe so. Regardless, no one has even claimed to have had the turtle since Iren died. If it ever did exist, who knows if we will ever see it again?*"

"*Maybe Lizard Face has it?*"

"*No, if he had it, there would be no reason to hold you captive. If the legends are true, he could take Staranana back with no resistance.*"

"*Just a bunch of nonsense!*"

"*Let's hope so.*"

"*I guess we won't know what Lizard Face wants until he tells us himself. Now, any ideas on how we can get out of here?*"

"If Lizard Face is correct, it will be very difficult to get back to the surface. And even if we did manage that, we'd still need a ship to get through space."

"From what Lizard Face told me, the So had plenty of ships. Maybe we could steal one of those?"

"There might be an easier way," TB suggested. *"If we could get hold of a transmitter, I could send a signal through the vortex to the Door on Staranana. We could use it to get home."*

"I thought you had a transmitter in the brain scanner. Isn't that connected to the Door all the time?"

"Yes, at least, it was until the signal was blocked. Plus, the signal is far too weak to fight its way through the vortex. We need to amplify it somehow."

"Let's hope we get the chance. First, we have to get out of this cell."

Scotty had no sooner thought the words than there was a hiss above him, and a piercing light shone down from the ceiling and cut into his eyes. When his vision had adjusted, a rope was hanging down through the trapdoor, and a goon was looking down on him.

"Take the rope," the goon commanded. To Scotty, every goon looked alike, but he thought he recognized the voice as belonging to Captain Gakic. He took hold of the rope, and Gakic pulled him up. At the top of the pit, Scotty grabbed onto the stone floor and pulled himself out onto the ground, an act which sent several sharp jolts of pain through his ribs. Gakic grabbed his arm and pulled him roughly to his feet.

"Hey! Watch it!" Scotty cursed.

"Shut up, human!" The goon captain began pulling Scotty back down the hallway they had originally come from. Gakic seemed to have no interest in being polite to him. He even acted a bit disgusted to have to touch the boy.

Scotty tried to make some casual conversation, "So how are the modifications to the *Dragon's Blood* going, Captain?"

"They finished three hours ago."

"Going back out soon?"

"What concern is that to you?"

"Just trying to get to know the ship's new Captain. At least, I assume that is what you'll be. Lizard Face does hold you in such high regard, and…"

Gakic whirled around and slammed him into the wall. Scotty wailed from the pain in his ribs, and Gakic wrapped his fungus-covered hand around the boy's throat. He growled, "Let's clarify something, human. I am not Captain Gakic. I am a clone of him, and I have no interest in talking with you!"

The clone Gakic let go of his neck, and Scotty gasped, "Oh, sorry. I don't suppose you're the Blackie feeding variety of clone?"

The goon lifted his arm to backhand Scotty, but then he thought better of it. He took the boy by the arm and continued down the passage. Scotty asked, "So where are you taking me?"

"The Master has something to show you."

"Does he know how badly you're treating me?"

"He doesn't care."

"What about my ribs? I need to see a doctor."

"Soon that won't matter at all," the goon chuckled. "Now, shut up!"

Gakic led Scotty back out into and across the main chamber of the Evilandian Palace. When they reached the opposite side, they came to the base of a winding case of stone stairs. The clone ushered Scotty up the stairs, and they climbed forever! Obviously, the So, as advanced as they had been, had never heard of an elevator. Scotty guessed they were on the 60th or 61st floor when they finally stepped off the stairs and into a bare stone passageway. At the end of the passageway was a set of sliding metal doors.

The clone rapped at the doors, and they swished open. Scotty was hit with the stench of bleach and ammonia, along with a wave of heat easily ten degrees higher than that in the passage. The clone said, "Go in!"

Scotty walked into a scene straight from a horror movie. The room was lined with tall, glass tubes filled with green liquid, bubbling, and shot through with light. At the base of each tube was a mechanical box with various smaller tubes going from it into the larger tube. There was also a separate workstation before each tube.

The room itself extended back two hundred feet, though it was only about twenty feet wide, and it was made out of solid metal, not stone. There were several goons present, and *Gakic* started Scotty down the long line of tubes. However, Scotty did a double take, when, after he had passed the first set of ten tubes, he saw a goon inside one of them. A quick look around revealed dozens of goons in tubes each at varying stages of development. There were some infants, and some were almost fully grown. They were all naked, but their bodies were covered by a thick collection of soapy, green bubbles. The bubbles were especially thick around their faces. Lizard Face stood at the end of the room.

"Ah, *Sscotty*, I trust you are enjoying your *sstay*?"

Scotty sneered and said, "I'm in a lot of pain."

"I do apologize for that, but it will not be an issue much longer."

It was then that Scotty noticed that the two tubes on either side of Lizard Face were dark. They still had liquid in them, and he could make out a form in each one, but he couldn't tell what they were.

"What do you want?" Scotty asked.

"You're going to help me with the next *sstage* of my plans."

"Don't bet on it!"

Lizard Face snickered and turned to the tube on Scotty's left. He tapped a single control, and the tube's lights turned on. Scotty's eyes grew wide. Inside the tube was not yet another goon clone. Instead, floating in the bubbling, green brew was an exact duplicate of Lizard Face himself.

"So, your ego is so big you need two of you to hold it now, is that it?" Scotty asked.

Lizard Face only smiled and explained, "Not quite. Though this creature looks just like me, it is actually very different. Allow me to introduce the first in a long line of *ssoldiers* in my imperial army, the *Goon Omega*."

"*Goon Omega*?"

"The ultimate fighter. You *ssee* the *Sso* knew more than how to just copy existing DNA. They knew how to manipulate that DNA, how to alter it at will. They were working on a way to change their own DNA to give their race the ability to *sshape sshift*. They believed the dominant race of the Universe *sshould* not be limited to a *ssingle* form. Their data was incredible, but their *sspecies* was destroyed before they could implement their plans.

I combined their research with *ssamples* of my DNA and the best portions of goon DNA to create this prototype. This *Goon Omega* can transform into any organic form I command it to. However, the *Sso* research also indicated that in time, clones could be created that could turn into inorganic objects as well. Imagine a race that could turn into *sspacecraft* or even weapons at my command."

Scotty grew sick at the thought. Whoever these *So* had been, they had been a twisted and evil race, and the Universe was fortunate God had destroyed them. Unfortunately, all of their power was now in the hands of one of the most dangerous villains ever known.

In an attempt to distract Lizard Face, if only momentarily, Scotty asked, "What is in this other tube?"

"Ah, yes!" Lizard Face grinned and turned to the other tube. He switched on the lights, and Scotty saw inside another lizard, but this one was much smaller, an infant. Lizard Face said, "Allow me to introduce Leif, my *sson*."

"Your son?"

"Yes, an exact replica of me. Leif will be the heir to my empire. All my subjects will obey him, and when my time is over, he will rule."

"And ultimately, because he is your clone, he will be exactly like you. You'll be immortal in your own way."

Lizard Face's grin threatened to jump off his face and dance around the room. Scotty supposed even villains wanted children to carry on their legacy. If he had had the ability, Scotty was certain Seth would have cloned himself. Especially after every spirit woman in Katana rejected him.

Scotty asked, "Do you plan to leave him in the tube until he is fully grown?"

"No, in fact, he will be released by the end of the week. But he'll reach adulthood twice as fast as I did."

"Lizard Face, you're over two thousand years old. Will Leif live that long?"

"Unfortunately, no. His accelerated growth will cut his life in half, but that will *sstill* give him centuries."

"And how exactly did you manage to live so long? I know human blood on Staranana is practically immortal, but every other kind isn't. How have you survived?"

Lizard Face hissed, "Don't assume that we are friends that I *sshould* tell you my *ssecrets*, human!"

Scotty changed the subject, "So what do you plan to do with this first *Goon Omega?*"

Lizard Face whipped out his forked tongue in delight and hissed, "I'll *sshow* you!"

He maneuvered a few controls on the *Goon Omega's* tube, and a strong sucking sound began at its base. All the liquid inside was drained into the metallic base. Lizard Face pushed another few controls, and the glass tube slid up into the ceiling. The *Goon Omega* was left dripping and heaving on its knees.

Lizard Face ordered, "*Goon Omega,* on your feet!"

The creature shot out its tongue and then obeyed its master. It gazed intently at Lizard Face with large yellow eyes, unconcerned with anything else going on in the room. Lizard Face looked at Scotty, and then commanded the creature, "*Goon Omega*, carry out your orders."

The creature's head instantly snapped in Scotty's direction, and it bared its teeth. Scotty was afraid the thing was about to rip him apart. Had not the clone Gakic been holding him, he would have run. The *Goon Omega* stepped closer to him, and Scotty felt like his heart was going to break through his already destroyed ribs. The creature extended a hand and wrapped it around the boy's wrist.

"Ah! What the heck are you doing?" Scotty cried as something like acid burned into his skin. Was this how Lizard Face was going to kill him? But after only a moment, the creature released its grip, and Lizard Face's true intentions became clear.

The creature stepped back and instantly began to contort. Its green scales started to flake away to reveal pink skin beneath. Its razor-sharp teeth became flattened and smaller. Earlobes formed, its eyes shrank, and hair began to grow. Its nose moved away from its snout and grew slender, and the snout shrank into a small mouth. A belly button formed, as well as several other things, and before Scotty knew it, the *Goon Omega* had completed its transformation. Scotty saw standing before him, albeit naked, an exact copy of himself.

Lizard Face said, "And now, *Sscotty* Fields, you are no longer of any use to me."

Gakic asked, "What about the Takillian computer?"

Lizard Face smirked, "Destroy it!"

"WHAT!" Scotty screeched.

Lizard Face turned back to him and said, "It has been nice having you here, *Sscotty*. But now, I am afraid, it is time for you to die!"

Scotty's heart sank. His copy was now grinning wickedly at him. Lizard Face nodded at the clone Gakic, and the next thing Scotty knew, he was being dragged from the room. Was it over for he and all his friends on Staranana? Had evil finally won? No! Oh, dear Lord, no!

Chapter 11
Demands

"**S**hortstop to Captain Noble, come in please."

"Noble here, sir."

"Confirm your status, Captain," requested Shortstop, once again onboard the *Zerubbabel*, along with Spikey, Gloria, and Speedway. Both the *Zerubbabel* and the *Fire Cruiser* hung in a stationary orbit over Staranana, flanked by the fifteen-vessel Starananian fleet. Computer modifications had been made to the two rescue vessels, and for the most part, Hull's modifications had been made to the fleet. Shortstop had his doubts about the ragtag armada. Ancient sailing vessels on Earth had been better equipped to fight, but if this rescue didn't work, those ships would be Staranana's last defense.

"Multiple computer cores are online, sir. Weapons are at the ready, and we are standing at condition red," replied Noble over the communication link.

"Excellent, Captain. We're ready as well. What's your top speed?"

"We can reach 75% of your top speed. I have to commend Spikey. Out doing our ships in such a short time is quite the accomplishment."

Spikey, at the helm, smiled and replied, "Thanks, Will."

"No problem, buddy. I knew you'd be a great engineer from the time we were kids."

Spikey grinned, reminded of the brief but happy times of his childhood. William and Josh Noble had been his best friends on Stararocka. At least until that fateful day when he had accidentally struck Staranana's polar icecap with an ultra-powerful laser beam. After that, he had been exiled from Stararocka, and Staranana became his home.

Shortstop said, "Please standby, *Fire Cruiser.*" Then he tapped another control, "Shortstop to Hull, come in please."

"Lt. Commander Hull here, General."

"Status?"

"Thanks to the manufacturing capabilities of the Fire Cruiser, all of our vessels have been equipped with solar sails. We have also reconfigured the airlocks and environmental vents into explosive decompression thrusters. We can raise the sails using a winding cable system and steer ourselves using an old-fashioned wheel and rudder. I have to have an officer stationed at each ED thruster, but they'll get the job done. Internal communications have been replaced by the ancient phone system. Laser cannons are standing by, as is the Morse Code lighting system. Once we terminate our communications, we'll take our computers offline."

"Good job, Mr. Hull. I hereby promote you to the rank of captain. Please take command of the fleet."

"Aye, sir! Captain Hull, out."

"*Fire Cruiser*, are you still there?" Shortstop asked, readjusting the frequency.

"Yes, sir," Captain Noble replied.

"We'll maintain your speed, Captain. Set a course for the vortex and hold position one hundred kleps from the event horizon. I want to take a few more scans before we go in."

"Understood, General. Our ETA will be in about ten minutes. See you there."

"Thank you, Captain. Shortstop out."

~

"You can't possibly be planning on killing me!" Scotty pleaded.

The clone Gakic had escorted him back down the stairs, across the main chamber, and into a small room to the left of the corridor that led back to his dungeon cell. In the room, there were two more goons, a chair, and a computer monitor. The clone ordered, "Hold him!"

Gakic's fellows stepped forward and took hold of Scotty's arms. *Gakic* grabbed the collar of Scotty's shirt and ripped the shirt straight down the middle. Even through the makeshift bandages he had fashioned, Scotty could see that the majority of his chest and torso were now purple. But the clone had not ripped his shirt to tend to his wounds. He had something far more sinister in mind.

Gakic saw what he wanted, an emerald embedded in a mesh of circuitry and fastened to a golden chain. The clone took the jewel in his hands, and he ripped it from Scotty's neck. The chain broke and fell away, and *Gakic* stared at the microscopic computer resting in his fungus laden palm.

"What are you going to do to him?" Scotty demanded.

The clone said, "Bind him to that chair. Then take this and have it scanned." He turned back to Scotty, "Don't worry, human. You'll get it back before you die. But this is a hard world for a clone to survive in, especially with the *Goon Omega* project. If I can figure out how the Takillian technology works, Lizard Face will let me join the ranks of the original goons."

"Best of luck to you," Scotty mocked. "Why don't you just kill me and get it over with?"

"Your means of death is being prepared even as we speak, but the Master wanted to be present for it. He also wanted you to hear his demand of your subjects."

"They are not my subjects! They are my friends."

"Then you were a weak emperor indeed. No wonder you fell so easily into our trap. The message will be brought online shortly."

Gakic waved the goon with TB out of the room, and Scotty's mind raced. How could Lizard Face do this? And how could God let him die? It was one thing to die on Earth, for his faith, but to die here on an asteroid a thousand light years from Staranana and thousands more from Earth, where no one would ever know what really happened to him, seemed unthinkable.

"You're not going to die, Scotty."

"What!" Scotty jumped at the voice in his head.

"What's wrong?" *Gakic* asked.

Scotty shook his head, but inside his head he beamed, *"TB, is that you?"*

"Yes, Scotty."

"But they took the necklace; how can we still communicate?"

"I lost contact with the others because of the interference field, but when I was touching your skin, I had direct access to your brain. They must have turned their field off. As long as I stay on this asteroid, or immediately in orbit, I should still be able to talk with you. But I have to admit, I'm scared."

"I know, but the clone said we would die together. TB, learn whatever you can. Scan their brains. Probe their computers. Crash their cloning system, if possible. We have got to try and stop them. I have a feeling that the mystery of what Lizard Face wants will be solved once I see this transmission. And whatever he wants, we have to stop him if we can."

"Understood."

~

"Sstatus report, Captain," Lizard Face hissed, stepping back onto the bridge of the now space-borne *Dragon's Blood*. *Scotty* was standing next to him, now in the real Scotty's original black jumpsuit.

"See for yourself, sir," Captain Gakic said, directing his master to a computer terminal. On the screen was an image of the *Dragon's Blood*, with one notable difference. Attached to the belly of the ship was a gigantic, metal claw. Had he been human, the claw would have reminded Lizard Face of the crane and claw machines children played to win prizes in video game arcades. Each titanium finger was well over a hundred feet long and had two adjustable knuckle joints. There were five fingers in all. The entire claw almost doubled the size of the ship.

Gakic reported, "The claw is ready, sir. We can leave at any time."

"Excellent!" Lizard Face snickered. He turned to his helmsman, "Lt. Manken, lay in a course for the vortex. Hold us twenty kleps out from the event horizon. Then he turned, "Communications officer, ready a radio probe to be launched into the vortex. We'll use it as a relay to transmit my message."

Gakic questioned, "You don't plan on taking the ship back into Starananian space, sir?"

"Not just yet. Not until we have what we want. Besides, I'm willing to bet that Moonbeam has come up with *ssome ssort* of defense against our virus."

Gakic gestured toward *Scotty*, "Is that...?"

"The *Goon Omega*, yes. Excellent, isn't he?" Lizard Face replied.

Gakic hesitated, then lied, "Yes, sir. He is." It wasn't that he wasn't impressed. It was just that he was a little too impressed. Rumors had been circulating since Lizard Face started this project that their Master planned to replace all the goons with *Goon Omega*. The lizard had quickly lost any real interest in his goon cloning. He was no longer providing the clones with the enhancements he had promised. All his brewing chamber was spitting out was the normal run of the mill variety of goon, even defective ones. He had a feeling that in time, those same tubes would only be spitting out *Goon Omega*.

The helmsman reported, "We're on our way, Master. Now that I have had a chance to get to know this helm configuration, I can have us there in five minutes."

"Very good, Lieutenant," Lizard Face said, then he slid into the command chair, his creation beside him.

~

"We're in position, General," Spikey reported from the helm of the *Zerubbabel*.

"I'm beginning scans," Speedway reported from the right rear station. "The *Fire Cruiser* has confirmed they're doing the same."

"What are you hoping to find?" Gloria asked.

Shortstop replied, "Any clue as to how this vortex works, and how to chart it."

"Well, we had better get what we need fast," Spikey commented. "The hydrogen trail is almost completely dissipated. I estimate that in approximately sixty-nine minutes there won't be enough left for us to follow."

"We won't need that much time to complete our scans. But we'll need more than that to analyze them," Speedway reported. "I suggest we go through before the trail is gone."

"Not so fast," Shortstop cautioned. "We need to take this one step at a time. Chances are we won't be able to save the *Dragon's Blood*. I've discussed this with Captain Noble, and he agrees that once we confirm Scotty's location and have the means to safely free him, we will destroy the *Dragon's Blood*."

"What about the crew?" Gloria asked.

"That's where you come in," Shortstop said. "How did your research for a cure for *goonieness* go?"

Gloria replied, "Not too well. We are dealing with a satanic curse not a virus."

"But if it's satanic, how can people in the charge of Christ be affected by it?" Speedway asked.

"It's not exactly demon possession, Colonel. Satan can hurt followers of Christ in many ways. The curse rewires the brain, causing temporary insanity so that the original individual can no longer function. When the brain is rewired, a new personality is created. The soul of the original person is still there. It has just been trapped and suppressed. It's the same way a Christian could suffer from Alzheimer's disease or bipolar disorder. The Holy Spirit won't let demons into His temple, but He is willing to contend with human weaknesses. It's part of what makes our God so awesome.

"I have also been able to confirm that the belief that looking at a goon will turn you into a goon is just a myth. Goon bodies are covered in fungus. Somehow, the fungus on the face emits a pheromone that begins the rewiring process. I have no doubt that goon faces are horribly grotesque, but they aren't as dangerous as we thought. I believe the pheromone has to be inhaled at an extremely close range in order to be effective. Their faces constantly emit it, but it dilutes too quickly in the air to be harmful over large distances. Their face masks probably absorb the pheromone, otherwise if you got close enough, even those wouldn't protect you."

"What about the *Faces of Light* incident?" Spikey asked, recalling the invasion of the Palace three months earlier. "God lit up their faces like light bulbs. Why would He do that if their faces weren't as deadly as we thought?"

"To be honest, I'm not sure. The light gave you the confidence to fight. It was also a holy light, so it no doubt blocked the pheromone. Regardless, at present, I have no cure for *goonieness*. Unless God does what He did again, I'm afraid there is nothing I can do for the crew."

Shortstop wasn't at all pleased with that report, but he didn't have much time to worry about it. Speedway reported, "Sir, we're being hailed by the *Fire Cruiser*."

"Put them through."

Captain Noble's voice spilled through the *Zerubbabel's* speakers, *"General, we have detected our original probe. It's still operational, and Josh has an idea."*

"By all means, Commander, what's your idea?" Shortstop asked.

"We have our entire astronomy department studying our scans of the vortex. The department head is very confident that within a few weeks, they will be able to fully chart the vortex."

"That's excellent news, Commander. But that doesn't address the current problem," Shortstop said.

"Aye, sir, but that is where my plan comes in. The probe can emit a trail of plasma along the original trail of hydrogen. If we then send an electrical charge through the plasma trail, it will cause the plasma and hydrogen molecules to bond. That kind of trail wouldn't dissipate as quickly. By my estimates, we would have three full days to find Scotty and get back through the vortex."

"Excellent work, Commander. How long will it take?"
"Just a few minutes."

~

"We're in position, Master," Lt. Manken reported.

"The probe is ready," said the communications officer.

Lizard Face stood and faced the forward viewscreen. On the outer edges of the screen, stars rippled like a reflection in a lake disturbed by a stone. In the middle of the screen, however, there was nothing but black. Lizard Face turned to *Scotty* and said, "On your knees, please."

The *Goon Omega* complied, and Lizard Face waved two security guards over. The guards leveled their rifles on *Scotty's* head. Lizard Face said, "As long as they believe their precious Emperor is *sstill* alive, and that we will hurt him, they will do whatever we ask."

"Do you still plan to kill the human?" Gakic asked.

"Unquestionably! As long as he lives, *Sstaranana* will fight to the last bear."

"But, sir," Gakic protested, "In many ways, our empire is superior to theirs. What possible value could Staranana be to us?"

Lizard Face replied, "After we get what we want, very little. Call it a personal *sscore* to *ssettle*. We will exchange the *Goon Omega* for our ransom. Once he is in place, we can begin the next phase of our plans."

"Are you sure the bears won't know the significance of what we ask for?" Gakic asked.

"Yes! It is a legend that has not been taught for centuries, but if it proves accurate, I will be like God. If not, the *Goon Omega* is *sstill* in place, and *Sscotty* is *sstill* dead. Gakic nodded, and Lizard Face commanded, "Launch the probe. When it is in position, begin transmitting."

~

"The new trail is in place," Commander Noble reported over the communications channel.

"Excellent work, Commander. Please, standby," Shortstop acknowledged.

"I'm picking up the trail," Spikey reported. "Shall I take us in?"

"Yes, Captain. Put us in front of the *Fire Cruiser* and set a course to follow the trail at ten thousand kleps per hour," Shortstop replied.

"Wait a minute, General," Speedway broke in. "I am receiving an urgent hail from the *Fire Cruiser*. Captain Noble is standing by."

Shortstop tuned his transmission frequency and asked, "What is it, Captain?"

"General, our sensors have just detected another probe in the vortex. Have you got it too?" Will asked.

Speedway manipulated his controls and reported, "Aye, sir, it's there. I can just barely make it out."

"According to our sensors, that probe is Stararockan. It is identical to the first, and according to the registry number, it was assigned to the Dragon's Blood."

"Lizard Face is in there!" Spikey cursed.

"The probe is moving toward us. I recommend extreme caution," Noble said.

"I'll do you one better, Captain. All stop!" Shortstop ordered. The respective helmsmen of each vessel halted their engines until each ship hung still in space. For a short time, nothing disturbed the empty void of the vortex, but then, barely noticeable at first, something moved, a light pulsing rhythmically. It was the beacon light of a Stararockan probe.

"The probe is transmitting an audio-visual message," Noble reported.

"Any sign of the virus?" Shortstop asked.

"No, sir. I believe it is safe."

"All right, Captain. You watch from your ship; we'll watch from here."

Shortstop had no sooner finished speaking than Spikey flipped a switch, and a large, flat screen rose from between the helm and weapons stations. Shortstop was surprised, "Another hidden secret of your ship, Spikey?"

"I just thought this way we could all watch it together," the inventor replied.

"Very good. Put the transmission on screen, Captain."

Spikey complied, and the image of a *Fire Cruiser*-class bridge appeared on the screen. In the middle of that bridge was the undeniable reptilian image of Emperor Seth's former second-in-command, Lizard Face. Most disturbing, however, was the sight of a small, human boy on his knees, gagged, with two rifles pointed at his temples.

Lizard Face began, *"Attention Sstarananian authorities, approximately one day ago, as of the Earth date December 18 of the Sstarananian year 1,005,018, the Evilandian Empire took*

Sstarananian Emperor Sscotty Fields into custody for crimes committed against our sstate. The charges are as follows. First, that he did knowingly and willfully murder Emperor Sseth of Sstaranana. Ssecond, that he helped incite rebellion among the Sstarananian people and was the cause of the deaths of many goons, dragons, and bears. Third, that he illegally usurped the throne. Fourth, that he did banish or murder any of those members of the former and rightful Sstarananian government. And finally, that he and a party of his ssubjects violated territory currently under the jurisdiction of the Evilandian Empire.

"For these crimes, there can be only one punishment and that is death. I can assure you that our current method of execution is both painful and long. However, in as much as we recognize that our two empires must coexist, hopefully in harmony, we are willing to offer a ransom for the ssafe return of Emperor Sscotty Fields. Our demands must be met without reservation or negotiation. They are as follows."

~

Scotty leaned forward in his chair and stared more intently at the monitor. This was what he had been waiting for, the secret to this puzzle and what Lizard Face really wanted. He hoped the bears would figure out that the boy on the *Dragon's Blood* was not him, and that they would not be foolish enough to give in to Lizard Face.

~

"The Sstarananian Empire will ssurrender to us the Cosmic Bubble of Cosmic Bubble Palace. If the Bubble is ssurrendered to us, we will return your emperor unharmed. Up until this moment, he has been treated well. He has been fed and given comforts worthy of his sstation. However, if you do not comply, he will be tortured and killed without mercy. Due to the massive undertaking removing the Bubble from the Palace will be, we will wait three days for you to comply. We are transmitting with this message sschematics for a grappling claw ssystem that will allow you to transport the Bubble through sspace. These designs must be applied to a Fire Cruiser-class vessel.

"And on that note, we will not negotiate for, nor ssurrender the Dragon's Blood. It has been impounded, and its command crew has been executed for violating our sspace. The ssurviving crew has been goonified. They are ours. When you are ready, bring the Bubble to the threshold of

the vortex. We will allow one Fire Cruiser-class vessel ssafe passage into our sspace. All other vessels will be fired upon. When you arrive at the vortex, the Dragon's Blood will emerge. You will release the Bubble, and we will ssend Sscotty over in an escape pod. You will then take possession of him, and we the Bubble. Both our vessels will then part company. As of now, you have sseventy-two Earth hours to comply."

The video signal terminated, and Spikey reported, "We have the schematics, General. Orders, sir?"

Shortstop squared his shoulders and stared directly into the void, "Take us in, Captain!"

"Belay that!" Speedway interrupted.

"What?" Shortstop asked.

"The probe is transmitting another signal."

Spikey activated the screen again, and Lizard Face declared, *"Be it also known that we are aware of the plasma trail you have created to track our sship through the vortex. In ten sseconds, this probe will sself-destruct and ignite your trail, eliminating it. I ssuggest you don't waste time trying to find our new home world. Lizard Face out!"*

Speedway reported, "The probe exploded, General. The trail is gone."

Shortstop slammed his fist into his panel and succeeded in cracking his display monitor. Spikey was a bit chagrined, but Speedway reported before he could comment, "Captain Noble is asking for orders, sir."

Shortstop slumped in his chair, "Take us home."

Chapter 12
Crew Meeting

"*A*re you sure about this, Captain?"

Captain William Noble responded to the image of General Shortstop on the viewscreen of his bridge, "Yes, General, you need to dock the *Zerubbabel* in our shuttle bay, and we need to talk in person."

"But we'll be back on Staranana soon. Can't it wait?"

"No, General, it can't! Look, Stararocka has cooperated with this mission, and so far, I have submitted to your authority out of courtesy. But the truth is, your planet has been compromised by a spy, your rescue attempt failed, and we are left with few options. However, we do have some important information I think you will want to hear. But I am not willing to transmit it to you, nor will I share it on Staranana. You need to come here."

Shortstop sighed, *"All right, Captain. We'll be right there."*

~

Twenty minutes later, General Shortstop, the Moonbeams, and Colonel Speedway were sitting with Josh Noble at the conference room table of the *Fire Cruiser*. Will Noble was at the head of the table, and he got right to the point, "You cannot surrender the Cosmic Bubble!"

"What?" the entire *Zerubbabel* crew resounded.

"Captain, I will admit the Bubble is pretty, and the Palace will look odd without it, but it's not worth Scotty's life. If that's all Lizard Face wants, I say we give it to him," Gloria commented.

Noble growled, "Ugh! It is worth more than Scotty's life, way more! And if he knew about the Bubble, he would agree. Besides, do you think Lizard Face would even ask for it if it didn't give him some sort of tactical advantage?"

"Slow down," Shortstop soothed. "Tell us what you know."

"Well, have any of you ever heard about the Snow Phoenixes?" Noble asked.

Shortstop, Gloria, and Speedway shook their heads, but Spikey was quick to speak up, "I have!"

"That's because you were born on Stararocka."

"What?" Shortstop asked.

Noble took a deep breath, "It's a side effect of the war with Seth. Our ancestors suffered from it too. During the war, the Starananian people focused on teaching their children things that were practical for survival. Toward the end of the war, many had even abandoned the *Text of Iren*. However, when my ancestors left Staranana and established a safe world on Stararocka, they were able to take the time to study many of our ancient legends. Spikey, would you care to go on?"

"Well, if I am following your line of thinking, the Snow Phoenixes were among the most mysterious creatures God created on Staranana. They dwelt in the icy regions before our planet was completely icy. They were also said to have incredible powers that would make dragons look like common houseflies. According to legend, the Snow Phoenixes sing just before the dawn, and if you were ever to see one, they would take you to their secret city, where you would be free from Seth."

"Fascinating, but what does all this have to do with the Cosmic Bubble?" Speedway asked.

Josh Noble went on, "According to another legend, the phoenixes gave Emperor Iren the Cosmic Bubble as a gift at

Nana's birth celebration. They created it from the dust that forms naturally beneath their wings and with their own fire. Because Satan crashed that party, Iren never investigated the gift of the phoenixes. He simply added it to the roof of his palace as a decorative item. But if it contains even a fragment of phoenix power, it would be extremely dangerous."

"It can't possibly be as powerful as the *Fire Cruiser* or the *Zerubbabel*," Shortstop boasted.

"I wouldn't bet on that," Captain Noble cautioned. "It is said that the phoenixes were once birds in Heaven. They voluntarily surrendered their heavenly place to watch over the Starananians after Iren sinned. Their powers are said to rival those of the angels."

"Regardless, we, at least, need to still give the show that we will comply with Lizard Face's demands," Shortstop decided. He turned to Spikey, "Captain, you'll stay on board the *Fire Cruiser* and help their engineers build the claw."

"I'd like to stay too," Gloria said. "I can use their medical facilities to continue my research for a cure."

"Very good. Colonel Speedway and I will see if we can find the city of the Snow Phoenixes," Shortstop said.

"How are you going to do that?" Spikey asked. "No one ever has."

"We'll have to find a way, or Scotty will die."

Captain Noble said, "We will be better able to construct the claw at our spacecraft construction facility on Stararocka. I'll take the *Fire Cruiser* there."

"Agreed, we'll meet back in orbit of Staranana in sixty hours. If we can't find the phoenixes by then, we'll have no choice but to surrender the Bubble. We'll just have to deal with the consequences later," Shortstop said.

"We should hurry and get underway," Noble urged.

Despite the dire situation, Spikey's grin was ear to ear as he said, "Well, I guess, I'm finally going home!"

Chapter 13
The First Trial

S cotty Fields sat back and sighed. It seemed utterly ridiculous that everything he had suffered had all been for the sake of a stupid ball of pink glass. He had always felt a little corny with the thing on top of his Palace. Despite the fact that the place had once been known as the Palace of Death, the Cosmic Bubble gave it a kind of girly look. Once he had taken over the Palace, he had considered having it removed, but in the end, he had concluded that the Palace was an important part of Starananian history. The building had survived for countless millennia and changing it in such a major way seemed wrong. Now, however, if that was all Lizard Face wanted, he was tempted to give it to him. But the fact that Lizard Face was still intent on killing him, and replacing him with a shape-shifting abomination gave him pause.

"TB, can you still hear me?"

"Aye, Scotty."

"I know what Lizard Face wants. He wants that giant ball of glass on top of the Palace. Do you have any idea why?"

"Spikey was planning on downloading a complete copy of every historical text on Staranana into my databanks, but he hasn't gotten around to it yet. There are only a few references to it in the Text of Iren. The Bubble was a gift to Iren from the Snow Phoenixes on his first son's birthday. Satan cursed his son, and after that Iren had the Bubble put on the roof of the Palace and pretty much forgot about it."

"There isn't any other reference to it?"

"None."

"What about these Snow Phoenixes? What can you tell me about them?"

"Not much more. Many have relegated them to a myth. Like the Earth phoenixes of legend, they are mystical birds who live for centuries and then burn to death in their own flames. They are then reborn from their own ashes. However, the Snow Phoenixes prefer colder climates. Rumor has it that they once dwelt in Heaven. And there is one, and only one, legend that says at the end of time, they will be responsible for whatever change Staranana undertakes when the humans enter their eternal state. I think we can assume at least one thing; they are very powerful creatures, and if they created the Cosmic Bubble, Lizard Face having it is a very bad thing!"

"No kidding. Well, I'm praying our friends are smart enough to figure this all out. In the meantime, it's a good thing Lizard Face has such a huge ego. I have a feeling he'll be bragging about his plans before he kills us."

"How are you feeling about that, Scotty? The killing part, I mean."

"I'm trying not to think about it, but I can't. My mind keeps going back to the moment when Seth shot me in Cosmic Bubble Palace. I thought I was going to die then too, but God saved me. There was also the time when I was all alone with Hydro before he turned good, and also when I had to fight that gator in the aqueducts. I've survived so many horrible things in so short a time that I can't help but think God is going to get me out of this too. Besides, I've only been emperor for three months. You would think the Blood of the Land of prophecy would have more staying power."

"You would think so, wouldn't you? Well, don't lose faith. As long as we're alive, there is still hope."

"Have you learned anything?"

"Nothing valuable, unless we can escape."

"What do you mean?"

"The goon that has me made an effort to avoid all computer terminals. I barely got in range of one for a split second."

"Well, that should have been plenty of time for you."

"Not really. It was heavily encrypted. But I did manage to find out that there is another docking port deep below the asteroid, almost two kleps

below the city. There is a tunnel from the palace straight to the port, and six So vessels are docked there. I even managed to get the access code to one of the ships."

"That's great! If we can escape, we can take the ship back to Staranana, assuming we can figure out how to fly it. Where are you now?"

"That's the good news. The goon took me to a small room on the twenty-third floor. There was nothing but stone in there. He used a portable scanner on me, but I am betting it could take decades before they even come close to duplicating my technology. Now we're on our way back downstairs. I scanned the goon's brain, and it appears they were telling the truth about returning me to you."

"Good, I'm still in the same room. I'm tied to a chair, but only the clone Gakic is still here. Enough time has passed for Lizard Face to have returned. Wait…I hear someone coming. I'll talk with you soon."

The room Scotty was in, the best he could tell, was a common area where anyone could access the high-powered transmitter. It was never designed for secret meetings, and as such, it had no door. So when Lizard Face, along with two goons, appeared on the threshold, it wasn't much of a surprise.

Scotty asked, "So where is that thing?"

"If you are referring to the *Goon Omega*, I left it on the *Dragon's Blood* with Captain Gakic. How is everything here?"

The clone Gakic reported, "Excellent, sir. The boy saw your transmission, and hasn't said much since."

"And the Takillian computer?"

"It's on its way back here, sir."

Lizard Face tensed and said, "I don't understand?"

"Begging Your Majesty's pardon, I felt that if we scanned the device, we might one day be able to duplicate it and use it for our own purposes. I fully agree the current computer is a lost cause, but I would have been negligent in my service to you if I lost such a valuable opportunity."

Scotty felt like he was going to be sick. He wanted to blurt out, *"Can you say butt kisser?"* But that was a bit beneath him. And Lizard Face obviously didn't mind being kissed up to. If this clone continued to play his cards right, he was certain to survive.

Lizard Face smiled and said, "Very good, Lieutenant Gakic. I admire your forward thinking. Consider the project yours. Let me know what you learn."

Despite the fact that he couldn't see the clone's face, Scotty was positive he had to be beaming. Lizard Face then turned and addressed him, "Well, Your Majesty…oops, that title no longer belongs to you. Well, *Sscotty*, I'm afraid our time together really has come to an end. My goons have prepared *ssomething sspecial* for your execution, but we must return to your cell."

"Your people promised TB and I would die together."

"And you will!" Lizard Face turned back to Lt. Gakic, "*Ssignal* the goon that has the computer to meet us at the cell."

Lt. Gakic nodded and headed out of the room. The remaining two goons untied Scotty and pulled him to his feet. Then they all headed out of the room and down the passage to the dungeon. Scotty asked, "Since I'm going to die anyway, I don't suppose you want to tell me your plan? I mean, you've succeeded so far. You're obviously far cleverer than I thought." Then he thought, *"Time to try a little butt kissing of my own."*

Lizard Face's tongue slurped out and a razor-toothed grin consumed his face, "You have a point, *Sscotty*. My plan is *ssimple* enough. What do you know about the Cosmic Bubble?"

"Very little. It was given to Iren by the phoenixes, but he lost interest in it after his first son was cursed."

"Yes! What he did not realize was that the gift of the Bubble was for more than just *sshow*. It was a guarantee of *ssafety* for all *Sstaranana*. The phoenixes were, after all, the guardians of *Sstaranana*. They created the Bubble and embedded the powers of fifteen phoenixes in its glass."

"Fifteen!"

"It was really a *ssmall ssacrifice*. Fifteen phoenixes died, but they were immediately reborn from their ashes. Regardless, the combined power of fifteen phoenixes, especially when one phoenix rivals an angel in *sstrength*, is immeasurable by our *sstandards*. A person with that much power would be a *god* in his own right."

"And all this time, all that power has been hanging right over my head," Scotty mused. Then he shook his head, "You can't possibly believe that ball of glass will make you as powerful as God? That is the height of arrogance. That is the very lie that got Adam and Eve kicked out of the Garden of Eden. That Bubble is not going to give you the power to speak things into existence, or give you the power to overcome death, or exalt you above the entire Universe. There is one God and one God only. Try as you might, you will never be Him, and just like the *So*, eventually, God will destroy you!"

Lizard Face stopped in the corridor, and the goons halted Scotty with him. The reptile sneered, "I am not interested in your love for your God. The fact is power belongs to those who are *sstrong* enough to take it. Regardless of whether you believe in me or not, all the galaxy will worship me in fear. I will overthrow *Sstaranana* and *Sstararocka*, and maybe *ssomeday*, even Earth. The entire cosmos will belong to me."

Scotty rolled his eyes. The fact was, like the ancient pre-Flood Earth, and the future depravity of the Great Tribulation, God would not allow evil to go on indefinitely. Even so, Lizard Face could still do a whole lot of damage before the time of his inevitable downfall. If Staranian history proved true to form, that time could still be thousands of years away.

Scotty asked, "What are you going to do with the *Goon Omega?*"

"We will trade him for the Bubble as we *ssaid*. He will take your place, and for a while, the bears will breathe easy. Months will pass, and no *ssign* of an attack will come. In the meantime, I will continue to build my empire. The *Goon Omega* will gradually begin to act more and more evil until the bears despise him. However, their belief *ssystem* will not allow them to overthrow him. When they are finally in as desperate a position as they were under *Sseth*, my people will *sswoop* in for the kill. By then, I will have legions of goons and *Goon Omega*.

We will plunder the planet. Then we will use the Bubble to destroy it."

"The entire planet!"

Lizard Face laughed, "That is only the beginning of the Bubble's power. We will do the *ssame* to *Sstararocka*, but we will incorporate their *sships* into our fleet. In time, we will chart the vortex that leads to Earth. We will conquer it, and finally, colonize it. When the planet belongs to us, God will realize He has lost."

"Oh, my goodness, I don't think I have ever heard such deluded ramblings in all my nine years. What is it about you bad guys that makes you think you can so easily overcome the Creator of the Universe?"

TB quoted, *"For this reason God sends them a powerful delusion so that they will believe the lie and so that all will be condemned who have not believed the truth but have delighted in wickedness,' 2 Thessalonians 2:11-12."*

Scotty smiled, "Oh, yeah!"

"Oh, yeah, what?" Lizard Face demanded.

"I was just reminded of something from the *Bible*. God let's those who want to do evil do it. That way, when He overcomes them, it is all the sweeter, especially for those who truly serve Him!"

Lizard Face backhanded him and spat, "Your God will not overcome me. I have *ssurvived* for two thousand years. Even your Christ cannot make that claim!"

Scotty wiped the blood from his mouth and preached, "My Christ pre-dates Creation itself. Not even death could hold Him, and now, He sits on the right-hand of the power of God. And one day, He will cut you off like the rotten branch you are!"

Lizard Face's eyes narrowed, but he did not speak again. They continued down the passage until they came to the trapdoor. The door was shut, and Lt. Gakic along with another goon was waiting there. The second goon walked over to Scotty and placed TB back in his hands.

"Thank you!" Scotty said, though there was more than a little sarcasm in his tone.

Lizard Face addressed his captive, "In your *Bible,* it *ssays* that Christ will baptize with the Holy *Sspirit* and fire!"

"You've read the *Bible*?"

Lizard Face did not answer. Instead, he continued, "We are going to help Him keep that promise."

Lizard Face gestured toward the two goons who had escorted Scotty, and they walked over to the computer panel that controlled the trapdoor. The taller of the two goons tapped a button, and the door swished open, and before the goons had a chance to react, they were engulfed in flames and fell face forward into the pit screaming, as a plume of fire raged toward the ceiling.

Lizard Face stepped boldly closer to the flames, "You have been a worthy adversary, *Sscotty*. But here it ends. Tell your God to beware!"

"You don't expect me to walk into those flames?"

"Of course, not."

"I'll do it," Lt. Gakic offered.

"Thank you, Lieutenant, but you are more valuable to me alive," Lizard Face said. He turned to the other goon, "You'll do it."

Scotty thought he saw the goon shudder. Lizard Face said, "There is one last way out of this for you. In as much as my godhood is guaranteed, fall down and worship me, *sswear* to *sserve* me, and I will *sspare* you. I will have you *goonified*, of course, but you will live a long and full life."

"Why haven't you *goonified* me already?" Scotty asked.

Lizard Face suddenly became very quiet and started looking at his feet. Scotty was struck with a realization, and he was excited when he proclaimed, "It's because you can't, isn't it? Humans can't be *goonified*! God made sure of it, and that's why Seth was able to use them for so long. Well, let me tell you something, *Lizard Breath*, my God is fully able to deliver me from these flames. He has done it before, and He can do it again. But even if He doesn't, like my ancient brothers

Shadrach, Meshach, and Abednego, I will never bow the knee to you, nor worship you. There is only one God, and I serve Him alone."

Lizard Face bared his fangs and hissed. The goon then pulled Scotty forward. Its stained and rotting robes quickly caught fire, but it proceeded toward the flames without hesitation. When it reached the threshold of the pit, it was little more than walking ash. The last thing it did before collapsing into fiery death was throw Scotty into the pit. The human boy never said a word.

"Orders, Master?" asked Lt. Gakic.

"Let the fire burn for a few hours just to be *ssure*, and then cut off the gas *ssupply* and wash the place out. I'm going back to the *Dragon's Blood*. Contact me when you have confirmed the human's death."

"Aye, sir!"

~

"Scotty, can you hear me?"

Scotty Fields was on his knees, head cupped in his hands, eyes closed tight. He had imagined what it might be like to burn to death. The agony of the flesh searing flames, his eyes melting in their sockets, his blood boiling, and the inconceivably horrible pain, but none of that had happened. To be honest, if anything, he felt better. In fact, he felt great!

"TB! You're okay!"

"Yes, at least, I think I am. You don't suppose we are dead, do you?"

"I don't know. Can computers go to Heaven?"

"I've always hoped my eternal fate would be the same as the bears, whatever that may be."

"Well, I know what my fate is, and burning in fire is not it. We must still be in Lizard Face's pit."

"How do you feel?"

"Fine. Great in fact!" Scotty looked down at his torso. In the intense light of the flames, he could see that the purple bruises

had all vanished. *"I think my ribs have been healed! What I can't understand is, how are we still alive?"*

"I would think that would be fairly obvious, young one!"

The deep and mysterious words were no sooner spoken than Scotty found himself prostrate on the floor. He recognized the voice and the absolute confidence that came with it. The light from the flames was absolved, although the flames didn't vanish. Scotty could still feel the heat. The light was replaced by a purer, brighter, white light, which tingled Scotty's skin. He could only describe the sensation as love mingled with power.

Scotty looked up into the face of a man dressed in white, a gold band about his chest, and a well-trimmed, red beard on his face. He asked, "Joshua, is that you?"

"You sound surprised, young one."

"Well, it's just, the last time I saw you, you said I would never see you again."

"Actually, young one, I said I would never be on Staranana again. This is not Staranana, and the Lord has sent me to be with you in this trying time."

Scotty remembered something he had heard in Sunday school, "Shadrach, Meshach, and Abednego had Christ with them in the flames. At least, that's what most people believe."

Scotty had been sheepish when he said that. After all, one shouldn't look a *gift angel* in the mouth. So he was surprised when Joshua knelt, placed his hand over Scotty's heart, and said, *"You have the Lord Jesus with you every moment of every day of your life. You don't need to be in these flames to know that. He wanted me to remind you that He loves you, and that He is with you, and that He is very pleased with how you treat the bears. You are restoring Staranana to what He always intended it to be."*

Scotty had to ask, "Joshua, am I going to die?"

"It is given to men to die once, and then the judgment."

"Yes, I know, but will I die on Evilanda?"

"That is not given me to tell you. Only know that the Lord will not abandon you."

"Well, what about my friends? Lizard Face is going to trick them into making a devastating mistake! They need to be warned! You have to…"

Joshua placed a single finger against Scotty's lips and whispered, *"Be still and know that He is God."*

"Well, then what am I supposed to do?" Scotty asked. "I obviously can't help my friends from in here."

"Praise him, Scotty. Thank Him for rescuing you from these flames. Pray for your friends. As you said, they need it. Above all, remember that He is God, and He is bigger than any situation you are in."

Scotty pleaded, "But, Joshua, you saved me twice before on Staranana, and you fought in the battle to take over the Palace. Why can't you blast us out of this place?"

Joshua stood and exclaimed, *"I will do only as I am commanded to do, young one! You would do well to remember that! Do not tempt the Lord your God! He does according to His will, not yours."*

Scotty shrank back against the wall and cried, "I'm sorry! I'm just scared."

Joshua's tone became gentle again, *"Young one, have faith. There are more trials you must endure here. Just remember, you will never be alone."* Then the angel vanished.

"So, um, Scotty," TB began, *"What do we do?"*

"You heard the man, TB. We pray!"

Chapter 14
Investigations

Ensign Toby Nakan rubbed his eyes and sighed. Still nothing! He had been staring at literally hundreds of pages of communications readouts on his computer monitor for more than five hours, and he had yet to find any clue as to who the spy might be. As a matter of security, every transmission into and out of the Palace was recorded and documented. Out of courtesy, each transcript could only be accessed with the personal security code of the individual who made it, or one of the senior officers. Though neither Toby nor Cak fit into that category, General Shortstop had given them access to a temporary senior officer code, but even that had turned up nothing.

That, of course, meant either the spy had a separate transmitter that wasn't connected to the main system, or he/she knew how to override the recording function on the Palace transmitter. If that were the case, the list was narrowed quite significantly, for only a handful of people had such expertise, among them Captain Spikey Moonbeam, an idea both ensigns dismissed immediately. Spikey had been key in the process of freeing Staranana. It seemed inconceivable that he would betray them.

The other suspects all had excellent alibis, so the possibility that someone had overridden the system was growing more and more unlikely. The only way it could have happened was if there were an expert in the Palace who had thus far kept their abilities a secret. For now, however, the Nakans were leaning toward the alternate transmitter theory.

Toby switched off his monitor and slumped back in his chair. Just then Cak entered their shared Palace apartment. Toby turned to his brother and asked, "Any luck, bro?"

Cak shook his head. "I used the Palace scanners on every inch of the building. From the private apartments to the lift tubes to the crawl spaces to the officer's offices and workstations, even the garbage compactors showed absolutely nothing. Whoever this spy is, they're good. Any luck on your end?"

"I read every – and I do mean every – transmission transcript that has gone out of the Palace in the last month. Most of them were family messages to the bears that returned to the cave villages in the Nana Forest after the war. There were a few technical messages to Stararocka and several dozen communiqués between the Palace and our fleet. However, none of it was classified information, nor did it explain how Lizard Face got his hands on *Door* technology."

"Well, that's the next place we should look, the Moonbeam apartment and Spikey's workshop. Both Spikey and Gloria are on their way to Stararocka, and Sparkey is in the gym pretending to be Scotty," Cak said.

"What about Tommy?" Toby asked.

"The baby is staying with Dorothy Shortstop at the moment."

"Okay, well, General Shortstop and Colonel Speedway are up in the library. We'll need to get clearance from them to enter the Moonbeam apartment. I'll contact them, and then we can get started," Toby offered.

Cak gripped his brother's shoulder, "Wait, I think we have time to grab a quick bite first. I don't know about you, but I'm starving. What do you say we go see Chef Berry?"

Toby smiled and said, "I'm right behind you, bro."

~

"So what exactly are we looking for, General?"

"Anything that can tell us about the Snow Phoenixes and where to find them, and anything about the Cosmic Bubble."

General Shortstop and Colonel Speedway were standing in the entryway of the immense library of Cosmic Bubble Palace. There were literally tens of thousands of books from authors throughout Starananian history. The majority of them were from Iren's era, but a few had managed to be published during Seth's reign. The library consisted of five levels and almost an entire wing of the Palace.

Most of the books had fallen into disrepair, as Seth had no love of reading. When the new library staff had taken over at the start of Scotty's reign, they had had to clean literally inches of dust off the shelves and books. To date, the Palace librarians had only cataloged one percent of the manuscripts into the Palace computer. None of those manuscripts had anything to do with the phoenixes or the Cosmic Bubble.

"Where do we start?" Speedway asked.

"One of the librarians said they found an ancient copy of the *Text of Iren* in here when they were cleaning. It was handwritten and quite possibly the original manuscript composed by Iren himself. It might have something in it the modern versions don't."

"What should I do?"

"Look for any books you can find on the Snow Phoenixes."

"Where should I start?"

"I don't have a clue."

"Ensign Nakan to General Shortstop."

"Go ahead, Toby. What is it?"

"Cak and I need to get into the Moonbeam apartment to continue our investigation. We need your authorization."

"What do you hope to find?"

"We're not sure. We've searched all the communication records and come up with nothing. The stolen technology did come from Spikey's workshop. It seemed the next logical place to continue our investigation."

"I agree. Add the numbers 37729 to your current senior officer code, and that should get you in. Keep me informed of what you find."

"Aye, General!"

~

"Ugh! Your demands are getting to be a little more than I can handle. I will get to you when I have the chance, but I'm a little busy right now. The Emperor's Christmas party, remember? Just standby. You'll have what you need soon!" Chef Berry once again terminated his communication link just in time for two new visitors to enter his kitchen.

"Toby! Cak! What can I do for you?" Berry asked.

Both teens rubbed their bellies. "We're hungry! The General has us on an important assignment, and we need a little fuel," Toby explained.

"I've been concentrating on the Christmas Party, so I'm afraid lunch will be a little late today, but I think I can find you two something."

"Oh, please, we don't want to be any trouble. If you'll let us into the pantry and the icebox, we'll take care of ourselves," Cak said.

"That's not necessary. I think I have just the thing. How do fresh fish and oboca rabbit stew sound?"

"Great!" the teens beamed.

"The stew is in a pot on the stove. Please help yourselves," Berry said, and then he opened the door to the icebox. It often amused the Nakans that as advanced as the Starananian race was, they still preferred to keep much of their primitive equipment. Berry's kitchen had five potbellied stoves, fueled by open flames, and the icebox really was an icebox. A twenty-pound block of ice sat at the bottom of a tall wooden box. Inside the box, above the ice, were several wire shelves where food was kept. On some levels of the Palace, the only light available came in the form of hand-lit torches. Most of the bears agreed that the reason they kept the primitive technology around was that there was no need to replace something that worked and worked well. However, Scotty had once suggested that the real reason was that the human imagination had an equal fascination with its past and its future, and in a way, Staranana was a reflection of the human imagination.

Chef Berry had a tiny wooden table against the far wall of his kitchen. He set two plates with two fishes each on the table. Then he poured honeysuckle apple cider into mugs for the teens. When the Nakans sat down at the table, their mouths were already watering.

Berry poured himself a mug of cider and sat down with them. Toby prayed, "Lord, thank you for this wonderful meal, and for the chef who prepared it. Chef Berry is a wonderful cook and friend. Please help us with our investigation. Amen!"

"Amen!" Cak and Berry repeated.

The prayer had no sooner ended than the teens began shoveling food into their mouths. Cak had already slurped down half his stew, and Toby was crunching into his first fish to which he had added a light amount of seasoning. Berry sipped his cider and asked, "So, what are you investigating?"

"Well, we actually can't…" Cak began.

"Oh, I think it's okay, Cak," Toby interrupted. "Everyone trusts Chef Berry."

Berry grinned and took another drink of cider as Toby explained, "When the *Dragon's Blood* was taken, Lizard Face used *Door* technology. Spikey analyzed it, and it was identical to his own, which means someone gave Lizard Face the plans for the technology. That can only mean that we have a spy in the Palace."

"A spy!" Berry shouted.

"Shh! Would you keep it down!" Cak cursed. "Toby and I are in charge of the investigation, but we have to admit, we are getting nowhere fast. And to make matters worse, we're on a deadline. Lizard Face has threatened to kill Scotty in less than three days. Hopefully capturing this spy will give us an edge."

Berry tensed. He didn't like the thought. He changed the subject, "So, Toby, if you don't mind my asking, how did you feel when you were captive on the *Dragon's Blood?*"

Toby sighed, "Well, it was pretty scary, but I think I was more concerned for the crew than for myself. I wasn't on the ship long enough to make many friends, but I did respect a lot of them. Captain Turrock was a good bear. He had a wife and three sons back on Stararocka, and Lizard Face killed him in cold blood."

"Someone has to make Lizard Face pay!" Cak cursed. "And if he had killed you, Toby, it would have been me."

Toby put in, "If he kills Scotty, Staranana and Stararocka will fight to the last bear."

Berry said, "I see your cups are empty. How about a refill?"

"Sure!" the teens exclaimed. Chef Berry's cider was famous planet wide. Rumor was even the Stararockans enjoyed it, and that was saying a lot. Hot drinks were nearly unheard of on a planet whose standard surface temperature could reach up to 150 degrees.

Berry shook the kettle he had brought to the table. It was empty. He got up and said, "Just a second, let me get some more." The Nakans continued eating, and Berry stepped over to the icebox and opened it. There actually was no more cider, but he had the perfect thing for these two *investigators.*

He stared at the tall bottle of purple liquid on the second shelf. He took it and walked back to the table. This would do the trick. He said, "Sorry, boys, I'm all out of cider. But how about a refreshing mug of plume berry juice?"

Neither teen could answer, as their mouths were stuffed, but they nodded enthusiastically. Berry poured the juice, but did not fill up his own mug. Toby took his and had the mug halfway to his mouth when...

"Shortstop to the Nakans!"

"Here!" They both replied.

"How's it going?"

"Um, actually, General, we stopped for a bite of lunch," Toby replied.

"We don't have a lot of time, Ensigns! I suggest you get back to work!"

"Aye, General!" Toby complied.

Both bears set down their mugs without drinking. Toby said, "Thanks, Chef. We can always count on you for a good meal. Oh, don't tell anyone what we told you."

Berry nodded, "Of course, not." Toby and Cak smiled at him, and then left the kitchen. Behind them, Chef Berry frowned.

~

"Colonel, take a look at this!"

Speedway set down the twentieth dusty manuscript he had sifted through. Ancient Starananian books were all handwritten, and thus were often difficult to decipher. To make matters worse, these books had survived longer than any book had a right to, so they were very fragile. Three had already collapsed into dust in Speedway's hands.

"General, I haven't found anything, and to be honest, I would feel better if an expert were handling these books. I mean, some of them have to be a million years old at least."

Shortstop continued staring into the huge dusty copy of the *Text of Iren* he had found, but he said, "That's little likely, Colonel. Although God gave us the gift of writing at the dawn of time, all of our writing was done on scrolls until the last hundred years of Iren's time. All of those were then copied into books, so you see, none of these books could be older than 6,000 years old."

"Very funny, sir. What do you have?"

"Something significant, I hope." Shortstop pointed to a picture of a bird in the *Text of Iren*. Speedway was no art connoisseur, but the picture he was looking at was definitely the most beautiful painting he had ever seen. The bird on the page was both breathtaking and proud. Its feathers were orange, flaked with specks of white and black. Its wings spread out powerfully, and its head was crowned with a plume of purple feathers that, if the image had been real, might have been two feet long. Its talons and its beak were solid black, and its piercing brown eyes seemed to cut into them even from the page.

Shortstop allowed his first officer to be dazzled by the painted phoenix for one instant longer, and then he flipped the page. The next page was covered with details about phoenixes, and he explained, "Iren may not have written much about the Cosmic Bubble, but he was incredibly detailed about the phoenixes."

"I don't remember reading that in the *Text of Iren*," Speedway said.

"We've never really had a complete manuscript. Iren had only just finished the original manuscript when he was killed.

His servants fled the Palace with whatever notes, or rough drafts of the *Text* they could get their hands on. Those we later cleaned up and recopied, but only this copy has the complete writings of Iren. It would take more study, but I wouldn't be surprised to find additional prophecies in here. I mean, think about it, Colonel, we know next to nothing about a Starananian afterlife. This book could answer those questions."

Speedway thought, "It's kind of like the *Text of Iren* we had was the *Old Testament*. This version is the *Old* and *New Testaments* combined. That is if we were to set the *Text of Iren* on the same level as the *Bible*, which would be wrong."

"You're right, but just having this complete manuscript could change our entire society, again."

"We should have Garlan begin studying it, but for now, what does it say about the phoenixes?"

"Well, Iren visited their secret city often. Only, at one time, it wasn't so secret. When Iren received the prophecy of his death, he told the phoenix king to shroud his city in mystery, so that his killer would never find it. The King, whose name was Thimble, was grieved that his friend was going to die, so he gave Iren a promise. He said that he and his fellows would watch over Staranana forever. At the time, they passed back and forth between Heaven and Staranana as easily as angels. King Thimble loved Emperor Iren so much that he asked the Lord to make he and the other phoenixes planet-bound so that they could watch over the bears in the coming times of evil.

"Only Christ Himself voluntarily gave up His Heavenly place to save people, so the Lord was very pleased that Thimble made such a Christ-like request. He did make one requirement, though. The birds could not directly interfere with the goings on of Staranana. They were allowed to sing only just before the dawn, and if a bear ever saw one of the phoenixes while they were singing, they were allowed to take them to their city, where they would be able to live in safety."

"Did any bears ever see a phoenix?" Speedway asked.

"I don't know. I've never heard of it, but it is certainly possible. And there is more. The Phoenix City is made out of something called *fire glass*."

"*Fire glass?*"

"A substance of enormous power. The *Text* says that the glass is created by passing the sand, which forms naturally under the wings of the phoenixes, through the death flames of the birds. Phoenixes have an eternal resurrection cycle, but Iren said that each of the ten thousand phoenixes would have had to die several times over to create their city."

"What exactly does this *fire glass* do?" Speedway asked.

"Well, for the one who wields it, it emits energy, immeasurable amounts of energy. You replace a ship's weapons array with this stuff, and it could blow away a planet with absolutely no drain on the ship's energy reserves."

"Wow! I'd love to get my hands on some of that stuff."

"We already have."

"What?"

"Colonel, the Cosmic Bubble is made out of *fire glass*. It has to be, and judging by Iren's estimates of how many birds it took to create the city, I'd say it took close to twenty phoenixes to create the Bubble."

"So that's why Lizard Face wants it! What are we going to do?" Speedway asked.

"We're going to give it to him."

"With all due respect, General, are you insane!"

Shortstop snapped the book shut and said, "Come with me, Colonel. I'll explain on the way."

"Where are we going, General?"

"To the Nana Forest, back to our home village. We have to see one of those phoenixes when the morning comes." Speedway was thoroughly confused, but he obeyed his General. This would no doubt turn out to be a very interesting few days.

~

"All right, we're in. Now, remember, be quiet!" Toby cautioned.

Cak balked, "What in the world are you talking about? We have permission to be here. Plus, except for Sparkey and Tommy, the Moonbeams are over five million kleps away on Stararocka by now."

"I know. I was just being funny. Scotty gave me a detective novel just before I was assigned to the *Dragon's Blood*. That's how those Earth-type investigators always talked."

"Never mind. Let's get to work."

As was typical of the Moonbeams, the area Gloria was responsible for was neat and orderly. They had entered through the main door that led into the Moonbeam's spacious living room. Most of their furniture were antiques, some of it dating from Iren's time. They had a large cotton stuffed sofa. The sofa had flowers designed on it and a thick patchwork quilt draped over the back. There were also two hand-carved rocking chairs, a love seat, and believe it or not, two beanbags. The pride of the room was the hearth with cherubs carved into each end. Usually, there was a fire, but right now all that remained were a few charred embers and some ash.

Off the living room, there were three bedrooms, a small kitchen, and a bathroom. However, the Nakans' particular purpose in being here involved the largest room in the Moonbeam apartment, Spikey's cluttered workshop. With a bay window across its twenty-foot length, the workshop had the best view in the whole apartment. Down the center of the room, there were three long tables littered with books and countless inventions, most of which didn't work and never had. During the years of the war, Spikey's obsession with gadgets of any kind had nearly broken his marriage apart. At one point, Gloria had given him the ultimatum that he either give up his life on Staranana and come to Stararocka with her, or she would leave without him. In the end, she had left without him, but they had separated on good terms and under the belief that Spikey was about to be killed on a mission to help she and many others escape. Things did not work out that way, and after Scotty defeated Seth, Spikey had quickly risen in fame and authority.

This was primarily because of the invention that sat at the far end of the room, the *Door*, and ironically, the cause of all this mess. Spikey's personal computer was set up next to the *Door*. It would be the first place they should look.

Toby slid into Spikey's chair and switched the computer on. The machine began to boot up, and Cak asked, "So, do you have the password to get onto Spikey's system?"

"Our senior officer code, along with the access code the General gave us, should get us through. I'm betting Spikey's schematics for the *Door* will be encrypted, though. I highly doubt we'll be able to look at them."

"Well, if we can't, how could anyone else?" Cak asked.

"I see only two possibilities. One is that whoever the spy is, is a computer genius. However, I tend to doubt that because it is likely that TB came up with the encryption code for the file. It is next to impossible that anyone in known space could have cracked any code he wrote."

"And the other possibility?"

"Someone may have come in here when the plans were displayed on the monitor. They could have taken a picture of the screen, or if Spikey left the room, they could have copied the plans onto a disk. What we need to figure out is who was in the workshop at that time."

"But, Toby, the Moonbeams have dozens of friends. Not the least of which is Scotty. Should we add him to the list of suspects?"

"Assuming we had a list of suspects, of course not. I've run every bear I know through my mind, and even in my wildest dreams, I can't imagine any of them wanting to hurt us."

"That's what everyone said about Kelcott, and we all know what happened then. Chances are, if this spy succeeds, things will be much worse this time."

"It's just frustrating!" Toby cursed. "We've only been free for three months. Why would anyone want to betray us?"

Cak shook his head, then pointed at the screen. "The computer is booted."

"Oh, right." The login prompt was on the screen. Toby typed his password, and an instant later, Spikey's custom desktop, with a picture of Earth in the background, was displayed on the screen. Toby brought up the file access command.

"All right, we want to find any files relating to the *Door*," Toby said.

"If they are encrypted, how will that help us?" Cak asked.

"We don't need the file opened. We just need a list of each time it was accessed. We then cross-reference that data with the entry logs on Spikey's workshop."

"Entry logs?"

"Honestly, this is your post, and I know more about it than you?"

"Oh, Toby, just tell me!"

"The Palace computer records where each individual is at any given time. We just figure out who was in this room other than Spikey at a time the file was accessed. We should then have a list of suspects."

"Well, wait, maybe this is all pointless. Couldn't somebody have scanned the *Door* itself?"

"No, the *Door* is equipped with a scan inhibitor. Plus, TB would have detected any scan when he was still part of the system. TB stopped being a part of the system only a few days ago, and even with Spikey's expertise, it would have taken someone weeks to construct a duplicate *Door*."

"Okay, let's see what the computer says."

"Right, if TB were here, I could do this all by voice command, but let's see what I can do," Toby said. Then he typed, **"Computer find: Access all times of files pertaining to the Door. Cross reference with all entry logs of people in Spikey Moonbeam's workshop at any of those times."** He then tapped *enter*.

"It can understand all that?"

"It's a very sophisticated system. Wait, here it is." They both glanced down the list. It was fairly unremarkable. In the last month, the file had been accessed twenty times. For most of those times, Spikey was the only one in the room. Once Scotty was there, another Gloria, and another Sparkey, all people with legitimate reasons to be there, and absolutely no potential gain in betraying Staranana.

Cak pointed to one name and declared, "There we go! We've found the spy! That Tommy Moonbeam, I knew he was no good from the start!"

"You have to be kidding?"

"Yes, I am," Cak giggled. Tommy was barely over a year old. He couldn't read, much less comprehend computer schematics.

"Wait, what's this? There is another name here," Toby said and scrolled down to the last entry.

Cak's mouth dropped, "It can't be!"

"I don't believe it either! But we have a duty, a duty that we betrayed by spilling our guts at lunch. Come on, we have to go."

Cak could barely move, but after a moment, his rage propelled him upward. If this bear was guilty, he was responsible for hundreds of deaths and the abduction of Scotty and TB. He stared at the name on the screen for one final moment before he and his brother hurried out of the room. The name on the screen was *Chef Berry*.

Chapter 15
Homecoming

"**N**ervous?"

"About what?"

Gloria glared at her husband. He knew very well about what. It had been twenty-two years since Spikey had last set foot on Stararocka. Most of that time, he had everyone on Staranana convinced that he was as much a Staranananian as any of them. His secret had only recently been revealed when Gloria spilled the beans to General Shortstop during their aborted mission to Stararocka.

"All right, maybe just a little," Spikey confessed. "Who knows if anyone will remember what I did?"

Both Gloria and Spikey were sitting in chairs off to the side of the *Fire Cruiser's* bridge. Captain Noble was in the command chair, Josh Noble was at the helm, and there were other bears at the various different posts, none of which they knew. Gloria took Spikey's hand and said, "Don't worry. What you did didn't cost any lives, and we have adapted to it. Besides, the shifting of our planetary axis affected Staranana, not Stararocka. These people have no reason to hold a grudge."

"Yeah, I know, but I was banished, and being the first child – in fact, the first bear ever – to be banished from Stararocka was no doubt a huge news story. I'm sure my grandparents were devastated."

"Did you have a chance to say goodbye?"

"It wasn't much after my parents' deaths that I ran away from them. After I misfired the weapon, I was arrested. I was taken to trial and sentenced less than a day later. The evidence against me was solid. My grandfather did call me at the holding facility, but the Stararockans' rather strict adherence to their own laws would not allow them to visit me. I can remember feeling scared, lonely, even enraged. I didn't even get to go to my parents' funeral. When they blasted me into space, I was so filled with hate towards the Stararockans that I swore never to forgive them. When I got to Staranana, I did everything I could to become a part of your culture. After the first few years, I pretty much stopped thinking about Stararocka. My feelings toward them were a large part of my desire to stay on Staranana three months ago."

"Do you still have any of those feelings of hate?"

"I'd be lying if I said no, but meeting Scotty has changed me. But most of all, the *Bible* has changed my feelings. Don't get me wrong, I love Iren's writings, but the *Bible* is a far more complete text. What Jesus said about our having to forgive those who sin against us or God will not forgive us our sins, caused me to take a hard look at my feelings toward Stararocka."

"Well, we won't be there long. It will give you a chance to put some more of those old feelings to rest. And also, remember that the generation currently governing the planet is not the one that banished you. Things will no doubt be different. Plus, Scotty has granted you a full pardon. Stararocka may not be legally part of Scotty's empire, but they recognize his authority."

Spikey nodded and turned his attention back to the image of Stararocka on the viewscreen. He had to draw in a deep breath at the beauty of it. Stararocka was not, in and of itself, a planet. It was an asteroid nearly three-fourths the size of Staranana, with an atmosphere thick with oxygen and carbon dioxide. Its shape was more of an oval than a sphere, and its sides were jagged. Not with the mere jaggedness that mountains might produce, but with huge rock projections that extended beyond the atmosphere and out into space. Much of the surface was comprised of red and barren deserts. However, there were several jungles whose thick, green vegetation was visible even from space.

The planet had two deep purple oceans, which made up only fifteen percent of its entire surface. The water in the oceans was purely fresh and not exactly purple itself. Rather, it was the thick, purple algae that blanketed both seas, preventing excessive evaporation, which gave the water the illusion of being purple. There were no other rivers or lakes on Stararocka, so water could only be harvested from the oceans and from what few underground sources there were.

The planet's three biospheres had been built over those underground sources. The Capital Biosphere was only a few kleps from the Rocka Jungle, but the other two were in the middle of the desert. Thus, large irrigation pipes had to be set up to bring extra water in from the oceans. The birth of the civilization had taken nearly a year of space travel and almost fifty years of construction that cost many lives due to the excessive heat. Now, however, Stararocka boasted a population of over 100,000 bears – a scrawny number compared to Earth, but still far more than Staranana.

The planet's moon population varied from year to year. Staranana's moon had been destroyed by Seth, which had plunged the planet into an eternal winter. Stararocka, however, had anywhere from two to ten moons at any given time. Lazy asteroids wandered into orbit from time to time, but rarely stayed longer than a year before their orbits destabilized, and they veered off into space. The two dominant satellites, which were each barely one hundred kleps in diameter, had remained in orbit for just over a century. They were called Mama and Papa Bear.

"Commander, secure all stations and begin landing sequence," Captain Noble ordered.

Josh complied from the helm, and Spikey stood and rounded the bridge. "So what's next?" he asked.

Captain Noble replied, "We sent a message ahead. Our engineers should have the materials for the claw ready by the time we land. With your help, we should have the thing built and attached within fifteen hours. I want to get underway again at least twenty hours before Shortstop's deadline of sixty hours. That's more time than we need, but I want to make certain we don't have any problems hauling that thing through space. That should give you more than a day to reacquaint yourself with Stararocka, perhaps see a few old friends."

Spikey smiled, "I wasn't too worried about that. But do you know if my grandparents are still alive?"

"They moved away from the Capital about ten years ago, but as far as I know, they are."

"Well, I'll definitely want to see them. We have a lot of catching up to do."

Captain Noble grinned and leaned toward his friend, "Do you remember that sleepover we had when we were seven?"

"Do I!" Spikey chuckled. "We got in so much trouble. We took apart every kitchen appliance in my parents' quarters, crashed my father's computer, and caused the entire eastern wing of the biosphere to be evacuated when we set the sofa on fire. Boy, those were the days!"

Noble giggled, "Yeah, those were the days. We got in so much trouble, but looking back, we had so much fun, I wouldn't change a minute of it."

"We're on landing approach, Captain," Josh reported.

"Very good; put the station on the screen."

Josh tapped his board, and the image on the viewscreen changed. It was now a swirl of red dust blowing in the wind. Barely visible was a huge white dome punctuated with exhaust tubes and ventilation fans. That was the Capital Biosphere. Extending from the back of the dome was a huge, gray pipe. Spikey guessed that was the docking port. He later learned that he was only partly right. From their present altitude, the tube looked large, but not large enough for a spacecraft to enter. So he was surprised when, a few minutes later, the ship stopped at the end of the pipe before two gigantic, interlocking, metallic doors. The hatch was three times the size of the *Fire Cruiser*, which in and of itself was huge. It would easily accommodate the ship and the claw.

Spikey cocked his head, "Well, some things have certainly changed."

Josh responded, "These docking bays were just set up about five years ago. Originally, the *Fire Cruiser* sat on the open surface. It was constructed under the cover of the Rocka Jungle. However, when the angel Joshua ordered us to build four more ships, we needed the resources of our cities. Obviously, building ships in 150-degree temperatures would have been difficult, if not impossible, so we built these docking bays. The *Volcano* and the *Dragon's Blood* were both built here."

Captain Noble ordered, "Josh, transmit the access codes, and then put the ship down." He complied, and almost instantly, the metallic doors began to slide apart. Inside the doors was an open bay with another wall beyond. That wall protected the bay's personnel when the outer doors were opened, exposing the hellish environment outside.

Josh set the ship down with a thud, then reported, "All systems are secure, sir. Docking Control reports that the claw materials are ready. They are waiting for you and Captain Moonbeam in the control center. Commander Honeytub requests the evacuation of all personnel from the ship. They have a super crane ready to lift the ship so we can attach the claw, but they don't want anyone onboard. If the crane doesn't hold, well, let's just say, the crew could be a little shaken up."

Will nodded and flipped the intercom switch on the arm of his chair, "Attention all hands, secure your stations and quarters. The ship needs to be evacuated within the next thirty minutes. All engineering officers, report to Commander Samuel Honeytub of Docking Control for a claw construction assignment. All remaining personnel are on leave for the next thirty-six hours. Go home and see your families. Noble out."

Gloria joined Spikey, and Noble said, "We can head down to the airlock. It's only a short walk to Docking Control. Commander Honeytub will want to meet you."

"Honeytub? I remember that name," Spikey said. "There were two of them. They were older than you and me. I remember them watching me a few times when I was little."

"Yeah, that was no doubt Elijah," Will said. "He was the first officer of the *Dragon's Blood*. He's dead now. Sam is his younger brother. Don't be surprised if you detect a hint – oh, heck – a lot of passion in his work today. And don't be surprised if he seems a little rude. He's naturally very focused on his work, but after his brother's death, he has become even more so."

Gloria suggested, "Not that I don't enjoy your company, but I would probably be in the way in Docking Control. I was hoping to stay onboard to use your medical facilities to work on a cure for *goonieness*."

"That won't be necessary. I've asked Dr. Grizz, the highest-ranking doctor on our planet, to join you at the Capital hospital, *Rocka Memorial*. You'll have access to all the resources you need."

Spikey could tell his wife was doing all she could to keep from breaking into song and dance. During the war, despite her vast medical knowledge, her experience and resources were limited. Her resources had increased exponentially when Scotty took over, but even that could not compare with the resources Stararocka offered.

The Nobles led the way off the bridge, down the elevators, through several busy corridors, and finally to the airlock. Will said, "I'll take Spikey to Docking Control. Josh, will you take Gloria to the hospital?"

The fur on Josh's face bristled, the bear version of a blush. There was no denying he was attracted to the female Starananian. When he had first met her three months earlier, he had entertained the idea of asking her out, for the brief two minutes he didn't know she was married. After Scotty had taken over Staranana, he had not seen her again until this crisis. Even so, those same feelings came rushing back. Spikey was unaware of these feelings, and fortunately for all concerned, adultery was an unheard-of concept on both Stararocka and Staranana. Josh would never do anything to harm Spikey and Gloria's marriage, but he had to admit, he was glad to be able to spend even a little one-on-one time with her.

"I'd be happy to!"

"Okay, well, let's get to it!" Will ordered.

~

"Ensign Brown, where are those power cells?"

"They're on the way from storage, sir!"

"They were supposed to be here an hour ago, Ensign! Consider yourself on report! Ugh! Lt. Black, I said size L85 joints not L58. Those will be too small. Honestly! The life of the *Blood of the Land* and an entire ship's crew hinges on what we accomplish here, and I have the most incompetent staff in the solar system!" Commander Samuel Honeytub raged. To put it mildly, he was having a bad day. Typically, he was a reasonable commanding officer, but his was not the post most bears preferred. As such, most of the bears assigned to him were, at best, average engineers. Usually, that got the job done, but not today. To make matters worse, his parents were screaming for him to resign and return home. The loss of Elijah had been horrible, and they didn't want to lose Sam too. Unfortunately, when it came to grieving, Sam was clueless. He preferred to bury himself in work, which meant his staff would suffer more than he did.

"That's a little unkind," someone said from behind him.

"I don't recall asking for an opinion," Honeytub snapped, still staring at his control panel.

"Well, you got one anyway."

"Look, I…" Honeytub turned, and his eyes widened at the captain's bars on the shoulder of the newcomer. When he saw Captain Noble standing next to the stranger, he snapped to attention. "My apologies, Captain Noble. Understandably, I am having a bad day, but that is still no excuse for my actions."

"Quite all right, Commander. Though I do expect you to apologize to your staff. For now though, allow me to introduce Captain Spikey Moonbeam, Chief Engineer of the Starananian Space Fleet, commanding officer of the spacecraft *Zerubbabel,* and the Starananian guardian of the *Blood of the Land.*"

Honeytub extended his hand, "That's very impressive, sir. Pleased to meet you."

Spikey took his hand and smiled, "You don't remember me, do you?"

Honeytub shook his head, "I'm sorry, I…Wait! Yes, you were the kid who was banished!"

Spikey frowned and grimaced, "Yeah, I was! At least I was remembered for something. I was also friends with your family. Your brother used to watch me."

"Oh, yeah. That's right, I was five years older than you. I'm surprised you made it to captain so quickly."

Spikey huffed, "Things work a little differently on Staranana."

"Yeah, and I'm sure being friends with the *Blood of the Land* doesn't hurt either. Look, *Captain,* we were never really friends, and I'm not much interested in a reunion. Can I suggest we get to work?"

Spikey wanted to smack Honeytub! *Surprised he got to captain so quickly, indeed!* With this bear's attitude, he was surprised he had made it past ensign at all.

Captain Noble quickly interjected, "What do you have, Commander?"

Honeytub turned back to his computer. He brought up a diagram of the claw and said, "We've analyzed Lizard Face's designs. They are fairly straightforward. We have all the materials we need to begin construction. Most of those are here now, with a few more on the way. With all due respect, sir, I don't know why we need the help of the Starananians."

Noble opened his mouth to speak, but Spikey had heard more than enough. The inventor exclaimed, "Understand this, Commander, the most important person in this solar system is in very real danger! We have a chance to rescue him, but there is no room for error. We have no time for bad moods or hurt feelings. I would appreciate having your expertise in this matter, but I will have you removed if necessary. Is that understood?"

Spikey's eyes were locked dead on Honeytub's. For a moment, the Commander did not so much as blink, but then he replied in a dry, yet respectful tone, "I understand, sir. You'll have my full cooperation."

Noble clapped his hands together. "Good! Well, I'll leave you both to your work. Spikey, would you mind giving me an update in a few hours? You can contact me using one of the communication terminals."

"Of course, Will. Talk to you later." When Captain Noble had left, Spikey turned back to Honeytub. "Commander, the *Fire Cruiser's* engineers are waiting on the landing deck. If you could have your bears join them, we should get this show on the road."

~

"Dr. Grizz, allow me to introduce Dr. Gloria Moonbeam, Chief Medical Officer of Staranana, former rebel patriot, and one of the Starananian guardians of the *Blood of the Land*," Josh Noble introduced, with perhaps a little more pride than was necessary. Their trip in a subway from the docking bay to the hospital had been great. Gloria's beauty was only enhanced by her compassion and intelligence. Josh wanted to ask if she had a sister, but never quite got the nerve.

Gloria held out her hand, but she was too awestruck by her surroundings to make eye contact with Dr. Grizz. Josh had been kind enough to take her on a tour of the hospital (though, for him, it was just an excuse to spend more time with her). The hospital was twenty stories high, and had literally dozens of doctors and nurses walking the halls. There were signs leading to neurology, pediatrics, and emergency care. There were other signs as well for medical fields Gloria had never even heard off. The pharmacy comprised an entire floor of the hospital, and many of the medications were well beyond Staranian pharmacology. She almost felt herself regretting the fact that the original crew of the *New Life* had been turned back to their home on Staranana. From what she had seen so far, she and her family would have thrived here.

"Pleased to meet you, Doctor. I've read a few of your papers. Your work is brilliant," she said, finally drawing her attention away from her surroundings.

The plump bear, with his shaggy facial fur and bright blue eyes behind silver-rimmed spectacles, glowed, "Oh, you flatter me, Doctor. It is I who am impressed with your work."

Gloria chuckled, "Surely you're joking? Your facilities are amazing, and your research is decades ahead of ours."

Grizz waved her compliments off like they meant nothing, "Research and technology are one thing, but the compassion to save lives during a war is much more important. I've read your triage reports from your cave hospital on Staranana. You saved more lives there than I'll ever come close to, even if I should work for another 100 years. And you did it with virtually no support staff. And your invention of *ice blood*, with only the most basic supplies, was genius!"

Gloria smiled. She was going to like working with this doctor. She said, "Well, Doctor, as much as I'd love to continue exchanging compliments, I think we should get to work." She turned to Josh, "Oh, Josh, thank you for everything, and I'll see you later."

Josh hesitated. He wanted to think of some excuse to stay, but finally, he nodded and said, "Of course, Doctor. I think I'll take advantage of that leave my brother gave everyone. Best wishes to both of you."

Both doctors smiled, and Commander Noble left. Gloria said, "I've brought my data on the goons. We were operating under a misconception all these years. Looking at a goon will not make you insane. Seth must have come up with that rumor to make them seem all the more deadly. Their power actually comes from a pheromone the fungi on their faces produce. I wasn't able to come up with anything on Staranana, but perhaps with your resources, we can create a serum that will reverse the effects of the pheromone."

"I agree. We'll have full access to the pharmacy's lab and any medications we may need. The director of the pharmacy also offered to help us. If you'll follow me please, we'll get your data entered into the computer."

"By all means, lead the way!" Gloria waved.

~

"There! Stop! Yes, that's good! How are the cables doing? All right, stay in position and monitor the stress levels." Commander Honeytub pulled his headset off and reported, "The ship is secure, Captain Moonbeam."

Spikey looked out through the control room window down into the docking bay. The *Fire Cruiser* was now suspended like a Christmas ornament from the ceiling of the bay by seventy, eight-foot thick, metal cables. Technically, the ship's maneuvering thrusters could have held it aloft, but then the fumes would have filled the bay, and with limited ventilation, that wouldn't have been pretty.

"Great, let's get those parts out on the floor and put together," Spikey ordered. Honeytub nodded and put his headset back on. So far, they had managed to be cordial to one another. Spikey felt a little bad though. He had been right to take a stand, but Sam had lost his brother, and in any normal situation, he would have been relieved of duty so he could grieve properly. That hadn't been possible in this case.

Gloria had encouraged Spikey to be more sensitive, so he decided to try on Sam, "You know, Sam, I always looked up to your brother. I guess it was just your typical little kid/big kid worship. I remember begging my parents to go out just so he would come over and watch me. He must have been a great brother."

Honeytub turned back toward Spikey, "With all due respect, sir, I would prefer it if you called me Commander, or Mr. Honeytub. And as much as I know you want to help, I really don't want to talk to you about my brother. I don't know you, nor do I wish to know you. So can we just stick to business?"

Spikey huffed and nodded. So much for sensitivity! He said, "Well, *Commander*, according to these plans, you've made some modifications to Lizard Face's original designs."

"Yes, I added padding to the inner side of the fingers. It should cushion the Bubble and keep it from getting scratched."

"Good thinking, but I doubt it will be necessary. The Cosmic Bubble has survived over a million years without so much as a scratch. I don't know if it is even possible to damage it."

"You people are fools to even consider giving it to Lizard Face! Surely you know the phoenix legends?"

"I do, Commander, and we are trying to prevent it. But I promise you, Scotty is infinitely more important than that pink ball of glass."

"If he's so important, why hasn't he visited our planet yet?"

"He's only known about Staranana for three months! Most of that time he has spent on Earth. He only made his first spaceflight two days ago."

"Well, maybe he should show his face after this. After all, Stararockans will have played an important role in his rescue."

Spikey clenched his fists and bit his lower lip. He grumbled, "I'll suggest it to him the next time I see him!"

Honeytub said, "All the parts are in place."

Spikey turned back to the window, "Okay, let's get this thing put together."

~

"*Repilldiffium*, *Niogbellium*, *Gewtingiolum*, what are they?" Gloria asked. Dr. Grizz laughed, "They're stomach medications, and somehow, I doubt they'll be of any use to us." Both he and Gloria had been sifting through the shelves of the pharmacy for the last hour. This was mostly to satisfy Gloria's curiosity while the hospital's computer analyzed her data. Grizz had said she could take samples and formulas back for every kind of medication the hospital had. She now had two large paper bags filled to overflowing.

Gloria said, "This is more than generous of you, Doctor. My hospital will make good use of these."

"I'd love to see your hospital sometime."

"Oh, I don't think you'd be very impressed. It is only one story of the Palace. I have a small pharmacy, an emergency room, surgery and recovery rooms, a lab, and an examination room, but not much more. My staff is small. My assistant, Jesse Nova, and I are the only doctors, and there are several trainees. It's not like here."

"Nevertheless, with you in charge, I am sure it is a stellar facility."

Gloria dropped a few more medications into her bag and said, "Thank you, Doctor. Still, I'd love to have full time access to facilities like these."

"We could always use a doctor like you. You could transfer from Staranana," Grizz suggested.

Gloria allowed herself to entertain the idea for an instant, then shook her head, "No, Staranana is still recovering from the war. Besides, I'd have to convince Spikey. He was dead set against it three months ago. Obviously, we would also have to take our sons, and without Sparkey, Scotty would be lost. Our family is kind of the bridge between our world and his."

Grizz was curious, "Have you conducted any medical examinations on Scotty?"

"Nothing major. I treated a few cuts and bruises right after the war ended, but I haven't run a complete physical. That would be best left to human doctors."

"Still, I'd love to examine him. On a purely scientific note, he would be a fascinating specimen."

"He's not exactly a lab rat, Doctor."

"A what?"

"Oh, nothing. Human scientists conduct experiments on little animals called rats."

"Sounds barbaric!"

"I agree. Computer models are much more useful and accurate."

"In any case, I meant no offense. It's just, I have only had the chance to study bear physiology. Human anatomy would be a great challenge. Who knows, we might be able to develop a few treatments that might be beneficial to Earth."

"Well, Seth had to have had doctors when he ruled. There must be records of it somewhere in the Palace. I'd be happy to send you the data, after I copy it for myself, of course. But I wouldn't plan on creating anything that will work on Earth. Humans can't see us."

"Why is that?"

"I don't have a clue. That's just what Sparkey told me. I assume it has something to do with God, but we haven't learned why yet."

Grizz was beaming, "Oh, Doctor, I do envy you. Our medicine has been fairly mundane for a hundred years. Just after we built our biospheres, we advanced quickly, but in the last century, our technology has pretty much leveled out. The last significant medical advance was over twenty years ago.

Having the chance to study the human race would certainly change that."

Gloria grinned, "Maybe you should be the one to transfer to Staranana. It's a little more backwoods than you're used to, but it would be an excellent challenge."

"I may just look into that, Doctor," Grizz said.

"Do you have any family?" Gloria asked.

"Yes, indeed, a beautiful wife and two gorgeous babies. They're fraternal twins actually, Lydia and John. My wife's name is Elisabeth. Like your family, it would take some convincing to get them to move off-world."

"Well, you should bring them for a *working* vacation anyway," Gloria offered.

"I just might. I just might!"

Gloria and Dr. Grizz were just finishing up with the last cabinet of medications when an attendant came up to them. She reported, "Excuse me, Doctor Grizz. The computer has finished analyzing Dr. Moonbeam's data. It is waiting for you in the lab."

"Thank you, Mary," Grizz said.

"Well, Doctor, shall we get to work?"

"By all means," Gloria replied. Grizz waved her toward the lab, and they entered together.

~

"Ugh! Here, let me do it!" Honeytub cursed.

"Sir, I can do it!"

"Yes, I am sure you can, Ensign, but you are doing it too slowly!" Honeytub pushed the young ensign from the control seat of one of the operating cranes that was moving the fingers of the claw into place. So far, two of the five fingers had been secured. The third finger was latched to the crane, and the last two were still in pieces on the ground.

Spikey Moonbeam was talking with one of the construction teams on the other side of the docking bay, but he overheard Honeytub. He shook his head. *Great, just great!*

"Commander, could you come here for a moment?" Spikey called.

"I'm busy right now, Captain!" Honeytub shouted over the twisting grind of the crane's motor.

Spikey flexed his claws and started toward Honeytub. Clearly, the Commander was not used to taking orders. Why Honeytub was given this command, any command for that matter, was beyond him. So far, he had relieved two officers from their duties because he felt he could do their work better. Spikey had his doubts about that. This last officer was one of the *Fire Cruiser's*, who, thanks to Will, were directly under Spikey's authority. If Honeytub was going to interfere with the duties of Spikey's officers, the Commander was going to be relieved himself.

Spikey climbed up and tapped on the window of the crane door. Honeytub ignored him, so Spikey yanked open the door and pulled the keys from the ignition. "What do you think you're doing?" Honeytub screamed.

"We need to talk!"

"About what?"

"Commander, you have now dismissed three officers from their work. You are slowing things down. Frankly, I don't think you have any business commanding anyone or anything. I realize you lost your brother, but so have a lot of people. I was just talking with Ensign Peril. She lost her sister, and Lt. Pine lost his wife. Captain Turrock had a wife and three kids, so don't act like you're the only one grieving around here. Everyone is hurting over this, but everyone is willing to do the work necessary to rescue Scotty and what's left of the crew. Right now, these people need a solid leader, and if you can't be competent in that role, it's time for you to step down."

"What are you saying?"

Spikey stiffened, "Commander Samuel Honeytub, you are hereby relieved of any and all of your duties. You are ordered to return to your home and remain there until further notice. I assume there may be a hearing to determine whether you are fit to continue as an officer."

Honeytub raged, "You can't do that! You're not part of our military chain of command."

"Guess again! This is a joint operation between Staranana and Stararocka. Our peoples have agreed to work in concert, which means for the duration of this operation, our two militaries are one, and thus, I am your superior officer. You will leave the docking bay immediately!"

Honeytub growled and pushed his way past Spikey. *Who did that arrogant Starananian think he was?* Some stupid human boy didn't give him the right to barge in here and take command. And now Moonbeam had robbed him of any chance he had to help stop Elijah's killers. He would get even! He would!

Spikey sighed. He had never been much of a leader. Before the arrival of Scotty, his suggestions were tolerated at best, but no one really took him seriously. For a while, not even his wife had. Scotty had changed all that by giving him a position of authority and respect. It had taken some time to get used to being a captain and to being in charge of an entire core of engineers. However, this incident had reminded him of what a great feeling being in charge was. Though his heart was pounding, and his breathing heaving, he was exhilarated. He was in charge, and people had to do what he said.

"Look out!" someone from the floor shouted.

Spikey looked out from the cockpit of the crane. The finger that the crane held aloft was swinging back and forth. A born engineer, Spikey's eyes instinctively locked on the problem. The cable attached to the finger was splintering. It would snap within seconds, and Commander Honeytub, obviously lost in his own rage, was heading right for it.

The next few moments were a blur. Spikey couldn't be sure, but it felt like he flew across the floor, or ran at speeds that no bear had a right to reach. Before he knew it, he was wrapping his arms around Honeytub and slamming the Commander to the floor. The finger crashed to the ground an instant later, barely missing Spikey and Sam.

Commander Honeytub was lying flat on his back, staring up at the *Fire Cruiser* dangling overhead. *What had just happened?* He hated to admit it, but the plump bear lying across his belly proved only one thing. Spikey Moonbeam had just saved his life.

Spikey pushed himself up. "Are you okay, Commander?"

Honeytub looked up and smiled; he actually smiled. "Yes! I am! You saved my life, Captain."

"All in a day's work."

They both stood, and Honeytub said, "Captain, I'd like to apologize for my attitude today. I've been out of line. I was mad about Elijah, but my behavior certainly hasn't helped to stop Lizard Face. I realize I've been relieved of command, but if I apologize to *our* officers, could I stay and help? I'll obey any order you give me. I just want to help."

Spikey looked down and shook his head. Then he met the Commander's gaze, "Are you sure?"

Honeytub nodded enthusiastically, "Yes, sir!"

"Well then, Commander, I'd love to have your help. Please return to your *original* station."

"Yes, Captain. And, sir?"

"Yes."

"You can call me Sam."

Chapter 16
The Second Trial

Scotty Fields awoke to blackness. Quite odd since he had fallen asleep in the blinding light of a blistering inferno. The fact that he was alive at all was a miracle. But miracles had become a common occurrence on Staranana, as well as all the other extraterrestrial places Scotty had visited. He didn't know what to expect now. Lizard Face and the goons thought he was dead, so they had no reason to come back to his cell to check on him. He could be trapped down here for days, even weeks, with no food or water.

"TB, are you okay?"

"Yeah, but I was more worried about you."

"We survived the fire. That's a good sign. But we have to figure out a way to get out of here. Any ideas?"

"You always ask that like I'm smart or something."

"TB, are you sure you're okay? Because you are the smartest machine I've ever met."

"Yes, I'm fine. I was just kidding you. There is only one thing I can think of. If we had some rope and could get that door open, we could climb out."

"Well, just two problems with that. First, how do we get that door open? In case you didn't notice, it's a little over my head, and more than likely, it's locked."

"Do you think I didn't consider that? The flames blocked my computer probes, but I might be able to establish contact with that control panel on the wall next to the trapdoor."

"Why didn't you do that before, when they first threw us in here?"

"The computers were being watched too carefully then, but chances are, if they think you're dead, they've lowered their guard."

"Great, so what about rope?"

"I don't know. You could rip your clothes up and tie something heavy to the end. Then throw it, and hopefully, it will catch on something."

"Let me think about that. Ah, not a chance, pal! I am not running around Evilanda stark-naked."

"Do you want to get out of here or don't you?"

"Well…Wait, what's this?" Scotty had been steadily pushing himself up against the wall. He still couldn't see, but his hand moved across something both soft and greasy.

"What is it?" TB asked.

Scotty pulled the large fabric into his lap. It stank of smoke, and he could feel its greasy covering all over his hands. He said, *"It's some sort of cloth. I didn't notice it here before. I can't imagine where…oh, yes! Thank you, Lord!"*

"What! What! What is it?"

"TB, this can only be the cloak of a goon. It must be from one of the goons that fell into the fire."

"How could it have survived?"

"TB, how could we have survived? Obviously, God did it."

"Is there a body?"

"I don't think…oh, yuck!"

"What!"

"Well, unless I missed my guess, I'd say I just put my hand through the eye socket of a skull."

"Yuck!"

"Yeah, and I think I feel a lot more bones. TB, this cloak could be what we need to make a rope. Then we can fashion some sort of grappling hook with the bones."

"As grisly as it sounds, it's a great plan."

"Yeah, but even if we do get out of here, we're going to have to find a ship and then pilot it back to Staranana."

"One problem at a time, Scotty."

"You're right. Well, can you open the trapdoor just a crack? I could use a little light."

"No problem!"

Scotty waited for a moment for TB to open the door, and then the door swished open, and a sharp, white light stabbed his eyes. *"TB, I said just a little bit!"*

"I didn't do anything!"

"But…"

"Oh, no! No! NO!" The scream came from directly overhead, and it belonged to Lt. Gakic. Scotty was directly under the trapdoor, and when something heavy smacked him on top of the head, he saw Lt. Gakic's original rope.

"I don't know how you survived, human," *Gakic* cursed, "…but you won't much longer. Take the rope!"

Scotty exhaled and then complied. *Gakic* pulled him up. When he was at the top, the clone grabbed him by the arm and yanked him to his feet. He pushed Scotty down the hall.

"Where are we going?" Scotty asked.

"To see Lizard Face."

"Are you sure that's safe? I've seen what he does to your clone fellows."

"It's safer than lying to him. Besides, I've earned some clout with my research about your computer."

"Well, don't say I didn't warn you!"

As far as Scotty had been able to ascertain in his now almost two-day captivity, the Evilandian Palace was almost as big as Cosmic Bubble Palace. So he was not surprised to be taken to yet another section of it. This time, he and Lt. Gakic climbed even higher than they had before to the eightieth floor. Oddly enough, Scotty had a renewed energy while climbing the stairs. He could only remember feeling as energetic one other time, and that was right after God had healed him before his final confrontation with Seth. It must have been some sort of post-miracle adrenaline rush.

Once on the eightieth floor, *Gakic* led him to another sliding metallic door. It appeared to be the only door on the entire floor, and the walk down the hall to it was barely worth mentioning. The hallway was plain stone. *Gakic* tapped a panel next to the door, and a chime sounded. A moment later, the door opened.

"How is this possible?" The stunned question had come from the person who greeted them at the door, Lizard Face. He gestured them inside. The place was obviously the reptile's quarters, and it put Seth's former quarters to shame. It was clearly designed for a reptile, and it was huge, easily the size of the throne room at Cosmic Bubble Palace. Instead of a bed, there was a large, bubbling tub of water in the center of the room. There were dozens of palm trees, making the place look like a mini jungle. The ground was covered with a smooth layer of sand, and there were several large sunning rocks dispersed throughout the chamber. The lights, which towered probably twenty feet overhead, had increased the temperature to at least twenty degrees higher than the rest of the palace. Scotty could see how Lizard Face would find all this appealing.

Lt. Gakic reported, "I'm sorry, sir. He was in the fire all night. We only extinguished the flames twenty minutes ago. I have no idea how he survived."

"I do," Scotty said. "I told you God was fully able to deliver me from your trap."

"You're *sstill* in our custody, human, and our plans are underway. The bears will deliver the Bubble tomorrow night."

"Don't count on that!"

"What should I do with him, sir?"

"*Sshoot* him!"

Gakic pulled his pistol from its holster and pointed it at Scotty's head. Scotty could feel his pulse racing. "You…you don't think that thing could kill me if your fire couldn't?" Scotty wailed.

"We'll see," *Gakic* said. The goon pulled the trigger, and Scotty closed his eyes. Nothing happened. Not a sputter, not a spark, the energy pistol was completely dead.

Lt. Gakic examined the weapon and said, "My apologies, Master. The energy cell is dead. I can find a replacement."

Lizard Face waved him off, "No need, Lieutenant. I have a better idea. Do you remember the *original* idea I had to get rid of the boy?"

"Yes, Master, but you favored the fire more."

"Well, I think I've changed my mind. Take the boy back to the communications room and hold him there. Then prepare the *ssecond* trap. I have a feeling this one will work."

"What's the second trap?" Scotty asked.

Lt. Gakic pulled him from the room. Scotty begged, "What is the second trap!" But *Gakic* said nothing. Obviously, the time for courtesy had ended. In the back of his mind, Scotty knew God could get him out of whatever horror Lizard Face had in mind for him, but that pesky fear was there, nonetheless. He was beginning to believe that for the glory of God or not, he was not going to leave this place alive.

"TB, scan the Lieutenant's mind. What are they going to do to me?"

"Something is wrong, Scotty."

"No kidding!"

"No, I mean wrong with my brain scanner."

"What are you talking about? You're using it on me."

"Yes, but when I try to scan anyone else, I get back a single, repeating message, and then one additional word. The brain waves are not goon, lizard, or human. In fact, I don't think they're brain waves at all."

"What's the message?"

"How is it that you have no faith – Daniel?"

"Daniel? My name isn't Daniel."

"I know. Regardless, I think we know where this message came from."

"Ya think? Obviously, God sent it, but I must confess; I'm worrying that my faith won't be enough to get me through this. I may be an emperor of an alien planet, but I'm still just a little boy, TB. And I want to go home!"

"I know, Scotty. I know. God is with you, and remember what Jesus said. Faith as small as a mustard seed can move mountains. All you have to do is trust Him, and God will take it from there."

Scotty had tears welling in his eyes when Lt. Gakic returned him to the communications room. The boy wiped them away as the Lieutenant said, "You'll wait here while we prepare your cell. I will have the guards bring you something to eat. It will make you tastier."

Scotty wanted to ask what *Gakic* meant by that, but he didn't figure he'd get an answer. A few minutes later, two guards arrived with a plate of brown, dried biscuits. Scotty wouldn't have been surprised if they were dog food, assuming they once had some version of a dog on this world. To drink was a green liquid that looked like thick milk tainted with food dye. It also had a most repulsive odor.

"Eat, human!" one of the guards demanded.

Scotty pushed the plate away. "I think I'll pass."

The goon leveled his rifle on him. "Eat!"

"Look, why don't you just shoot me? I'm going to die in a few hours anyway. But then again, maybe I won't. Your master's fire couldn't hurt me. What makes you think you could? My God is with me, and He will most certainly destroy you!"

"Now that's the Scotty I know!"

The goon lowered his weapon and cursed, "Fine, if you don't want to eat, that's your business! We just thought you might be hungry."

"So you give me smut to eat! Not that this matters, but if you were in my place, you would be treated much better."

"You murdered Seth and slaughtered all the remaining goons on Staranana, and you expect me to believe that?"

"I don't even know why I'm arguing with you, but I executed Seth according to the will of God. It was Lizard Face who tried to murder him. This newfound sympathy for a ruler you all hated so much is shocking. As for the goons you left behind, we were at war, and I didn't personally kill any of them."

"Worthless details, human!"

Scotty flung up his hands. There was no point in arguing. These beings had lost whatever goodness they might have once had. The clones had no doubt been bred purely evil. Except for Lt. Gakic, though. His actions were evil to be sure, but Scotty could sense something more. *Gakic* was a thinker, willing to do anything to ensure his own survival. The other clones walked willingly into fire or allowed themselves to be eaten by giant lizards, but Lt. Gakic didn't. Scotty hadn't spent much time with the original Gakic, but he assumed this sense of self-preservation was a quality both goons shared. Perhaps that could be useful.

Lt. Gakic had barely been gone fifteen minutes before he returned and reported, "Your cell is ready."

"Yippee!" Scotty mocked.

"Let's go." *Gakic* took Scotty's arm and led him out of the room.

Scotty decided to try his luck as they walked back to the cell. "Lieutenant, I have appreciated how well you have taken care of me."

Gakic balked, "You have to be kidding?"

"No, granted, you have tried to kill me on several occasions, but you don't appear to be the same as the rest of the clones. I'm impressed with you. You would have been a great good guy."

"Human, nothing you say is going to influence me, so why don't you just shut up?"

"Ah, but don't you know it is God who works in me to will and to do for His good pleasure? You may be able to resist me, but not Him. I just want to give you fair warning. One way or another, God is going to end this situation, and you had better believe, He is going to come out on top."

"What are you trying to say, human?"

"You don't have to serve Lizard Face. God got through to one of Seth's minions already; why not you? I'm betting my doctor could figure out how to cure your *goonieness*. If not, God has already cured others. Maybe He'll do it again."

"I will not betray my master!"

"Then you will die in vain and spend the rest of eternity burning in the Black Lava Pits!"

Gakic tensed, and Scotty could tell by the vise-like grip on his arm that he had struck a nerve. Perhaps this wasn't so useless after all. They arrived at the trapdoor moments later. *Gakic* opened the door. This time, there was just blackness, no fire. As the Lieutenant dragged Scotty toward the pit, the boy said, "Just think about it! You don't have to live or die like you most likely will. If I survive this trap, at least consider giving God a chance."

"You won't survive! But even if you do, even if I will burn for all eternity, I will never betray my master."

"There is none so blind as him who will not see! I'm sorry, Lieutenant," Scotty said, and there was nothing but sorrow in his eyes as he fell back into the pit. But the sorrow was not for himself. It was for Lt. Gakic.

~

Scotty had been thrown into this pit enough times now to know to bend his knees when he fell in. This allowed him to absorb most of the impact of the fall, and subsequently, he landed on his feet. The room was still dark, and when the trapdoor shut, it was even more so.

"So what do you think, TB?"

"I don't…"

TB was cut off by a low menacing growl coming from deeper into the cell. Scotty gulped, *"Uh, TB?"*

"Yeah."

"I think I know what -Daniel- means."

"I know. It just came to me too."

"Do you think God will deliver us?"

"Do you even have to ask?"

"Can you still open that door?"

"I think so, but we don't have time to make a rope."

"I just want to be able to look into the face of my would-be killer. If I'm going to be eaten by a lion, I want to do it with my eyes open."

TB got the door open, and the light shone down like a spotlight on Scotty. The boy knelt down and picked up one of the leg bones from the unfortunate goon that had died in the flames. He would die fighting if he had to die at all. The creature in the shadows growled again, and oddly, it hissed. Scotty took it to be like the hiss a cat makes when it is backed into a corner. How Lizard Face had managed to get a lion there was a mystery.

For a moment, the darkness was still, save for the heavy breathing of the creature it concealed. Scotty stepped back against the wall out of the light and waited. There was a scratch and a thump as something moved closer and closer, menacing and deadly. The creature roared again, and Scotty's heart leaped into his throat. Was this it? Did this adventure end here?

Was God really willing to let him become kitty chow on this distant asteroid, where no one he loved would ever find him? No! No, he wouldn't accept that! And with that determined stance, he raised his arms for the fight and faced the darkness.

A single claw emerged into the light. However, it didn't have the soft tan of a lion's fur. It was black and scaly, with five razor-sharp claws. This was no lion. The creature had to be Blackie. This was confirmed seconds later when the beast's stubby, reptilian snout emerged into the light. It roared again, baring its knife-like fangs. Scotty didn't wait for the creature to attack first.

With the bone in his hands like a baseball bat, he charged at the lizard and lashed out. The first blow landed squarely on Blackie's snout, and the creature erupted, lashing its tail in Scotty's direction. Scotty leaped over the tail with ease and landed a second blow. The bone broke over Blackie's spiky back, producing a sharp tip. Great! He would gut the miserable reptile!

Scotty took another swing, severing Blackie's front spike. The giant animal wailed and spun and smacked Scotty full on in the stomach with its tail. Scotty went flying into the wall and crashed to the floor. He couldn't move. Were his legs broken? No, something very heavy was on top of him. The hot, putrid breath in his face confirmed it was Blackie.

Sparkey had once told Scotty about how the gators in the aqueducts ate their prey. Chewing off a limb or two, but leaving their victims alive to rot in their nests for perhaps weeks. It would have been a horrible way to die. He expected no less from Blackie.

"Lord! Where are you?" Scotty screamed, but nothing.

Blackie lifted Scotty's right arm into his mouth. This was it. Scotty braced himself for the pain. He took comfort in the fact that he would soon be in Heaven, which meant none of the pains of growing up, none of the responsibility. Even only for these short few months, God had granted him a life of both faith and adventure. What Christian could ask for more? He prayed the Starananians would make it, and that someday his parents would find out what happened to him. With these last thoughts, he surrendered to eternity and closed his eyes.

And Blackie's teeth sank in. Flesh ripped, bones snapped, and the room was filled with a blood-curdling cry. Blackie waddled off of Scotty and retreated into the shadows. Scotty sat up. His arm was just fine. There wasn't so much as a tooth mark.

Above them, the door shut, plunging the entire room into black again.

"TB, what are you doing?"

"I didn't do anything. Are you okay?"

"Yeah, I'm great. How…" Scotty threw his arms over his eyes. The cell had filled with light again. That could mean only one thing.

Scotty slowly lowered his arms. Blackie was huddled in the far corner, blood pouring from his back and his mouth. Scotty looked to his left and right, no angel. "Joshua?" he called.

"Here, young one."

Scotty turned to find the angel towering over him. The boy sank to his knees, exhausted from his fight, and Joshua knelt with him. ***"Well done, young one."***

"What? What did I do?"

"You faced death preferring the life God offers to the one you now live. Most people cannot see beyond the day they find themselves in. It is a true servant of God who is willing to abandon this life at any moment the Lord calls."

"I was still scared."

"But you fought with the courage of God, and you faced this pit as bravely as Daniel did."

"Daniel in the lions' den? So that was what God's message meant? Though, I fought a giant lizard, not lions."

"Daniel did not fight at all. He waited on God. In that, you are different, but because you fought with the passion of one of God's holy ones, it will not be held against you. And you shall fight no more. The creature's jaw has been broken."

"How? Well, I mean, I know God could do it, but Blackie was about to rip off my arm, and then he wailed and ran away. Why?"

"The Lord made your flesh as iron to that beast. It will not trouble you again."

"Is it time to go?

"The Lord has already provided you a means of escape. Use it, but know this. You will glorify the Lord one last time before you leave here, and you will turn many to righteousness."

"What does that mean?"

Joshua only smiled, and then faded away, taking the light with him. TB asked, *"What do we do now?"*

"I don't know about you, my friend, but I say it's time to get out of here!"

Chapter 17
Spies and Phoenixes

"Are you sure about this, Toby?"

"Of course! Listen, Cak, so far, Chef Berry is the only possible suspect. You know, now that I think about it, it all makes sense. How eager he was to help us when we infiltrated the Palace. His willingness to give up his life of luxury for the life of a fugitive. I bet he was a trained spy all along. He could have been one of the traitors working under Lizard Face."

"Yeah, but what possible advantage could having a chef on your side be?"

"Are you kidding? Everyone has to eat, and Chef Berry is the best cook on the planet. Lizard Face would have been hard-pressed to replace him. A cook can also poison food. It's a great way to assassinate someone."

"Poison! Oh, my goodness, Toby, do you remember that plume berry juice the chef gave us? I bet that was poisoned. Remember, he didn't offer it to us until after we told him about the spy?"

"How could we have been such idiots? General Shortstop will demote us for sure."

"We can't get any lower than ensigns. We'll probably be sent back home to live with mom and dad!" Both teens shuddered at that idea. Though their parents were great people, after a taste of freedom, it was hard to imagine giving it up.

They approached the kitchen, blocked from the main chamber of the Palace by only a heavy, purple curtain. "We're here," Cak said.

"Wait, listen," Toby hushed. Two people were arguing in the kitchen. One of the voices clearly belonged to Chef Berry. The other was muffled.

"You are demanding too much…I am going to get in trouble…Well, I'm sorry you feel that way…I've given you enough…Fine, if you want more, come and get it yourself!"

"Put your hands on your head, sir!" Toby and Cak burst into the kitchen, their stun guns aimed at Berry.

"Toby! Cak! What's going on?"

"On your knees, sir!" Toby ordered.

"Listen, Ensigns, I don't have time to play around. I have a very big party to get ready for, and I am running out of time."

"I'm afraid you won't be attending that party, Mr. Berry. You're under arrest," Cak said.

Berry looked at the teens wide-eyed, "What in the sweet name of Iren are you talking about?"

"On the ground now!" Toby shouted.

Berry hesitated only a moment longer, then lowered to the ground. When he was on his belly, Toby pulled a pair of handcuffs from his pocket and secured Berry's hands. Cak said, "Chef Berry, you are hereby charged with espionage. You will be held in the Palace dungeon for questioning, likely to be conducted by General Shortstop. The important thing is, you won't be able to leak any more information to Lizard Face."

"What are you talking about? I'm not the spy!" Berry protested.

"Oh, yeah? Well, who were you talking to?" Toby asked.

"Ugh! It was Ensign Shallow! She's sick, and she keeps asking me for things every ten minutes. I'm not her personal servant, but she seems to think I am!"

"Well, we'll see how true that is later. In the meantime, we have evidence that shows you having the chance to steal the schematics for the *Door* technology. No one else had the chance. A little questioning might just turn up a motive," Toby said.

"You boys are insane! Spikey is my friend. I would never steal from him. Besides, I have no technical expertise. How could I have stolen the schematics?"

"We'll find out later," Toby said. He addressed his brother, "Take the plume berry juice to Dr. Nova. Have him test it for poison. Then come back here and review the Chef's communication logs. I'll take him up to the dungeon."

"Right, good luck!" Cak said.

Berry struggled as Toby pulled him to his feet, "I am not the spy! You boys are making a huge mistake!"

"I'm sorry, sir. We can't take any chances. If you are innocent, which I am sorry to say seems unlikely, you'll be free to return to your duties once we have Scotty back safe and sound. If not, I honestly don't know what will happen to you. We've never had to deal with prisoners before. If we follow Stararockan law, you'll probably be executed." Toby was incredibly somber. Despite all this, he still liked Berry, and the idea of an execution seemed unthinkable. But what choice did they have?

Berry sobbed, "Please, please, it's not me! Toby, you have to believe me!"

Toby said nothing more as he led Berry out into the main chamber. Their confrontation had obviously been loud enough to attract some attention. There were several bears standing around. When they saw Chef Berry in cuffs, they all stared.

"As you were," Toby called. For a moment, none of the bears moved, so he shouted, "GO NOW!" The bears scurried away, and Toby led Berry to the lift tubes. General Shortstop was going to love this.

~

"How are you doing, Andy?"

"Sir?" Colonel Speedway looked at his commanding officer, stunned.

"I was wondering if you were cold?"

"Well, no, sir. I'm fine. But, well, in the many years we've served together, you've never called me by my first name. Sometimes I forget I even have one."

Shortstop smiled and said, "Well, neither of us is technically on duty. I think we can let the formality drop for a while."

"Well, *Henry,* how much longer do you think we'll be waiting?"

At the moment, they were sitting on a snowy bluff overlooking the cave village of Moonville, their former home. Beyond the village, a powdery field of trees stretched to the horizon. If any birds took flight in the first light of the day, they would be sure to notice. To make things easier, Shortstop had brought along a pair of infrared binoculars.

"Sunup is around 6:30 a.m. That's just under an hour from now."

"Do you really think this is going to work, sir?"

"It has to."

"What do you want to get from them?"

"I suppose it wouldn't hurt to tell you. I want to negotiate for more *fire glass*. If it's as powerful as the ancient *Text of Iren* says, we can arm our ships with it."

"Exactly how much are you going to ask for?"

"Just enough for the *Zerubbabel* and the *Fire Cruiser* for now."

"But Lizard Face will have the Cosmic Bubble. It will be a hopeless fight."

"Only if Lizard Face gets the Bubble."

"What do you mean?"

"The way I see it, we take the Bubble to the rendezvous, and we release it into space. The *Dragon's Blood* releases Scotty, and while they close in on the Bubble, we blast them. They won't stand a chance."

"What about the original crew?"

"If Gloria finds a cure or God heals their *goonieness*, we'll do everything we can to rescue them. If not, I'll destroy them with the ship. They'd understand. Who'd want to live out his life as a goon anyway?"

"I guess you're right."

"Say are you hungry? I'm hungry!"

"Actually, General…*uh, I mean Henry*…I'm famished!"

"Let's just see what good old Chef Berry prepared for us." Shortstop pulled two thermoses from his duffel bag. One was long and slender. The other was more like a pot. He then pulled out two bowls, and two cups, and a fork each.

He opened the slender thermos and took in the aroma of its piping hot contents. He said, "Nothing hits the spot like Chef Berry's honeysuckle apple cider!"

"Oh, oh, pour me a cup fast!" Speedway said, thrusting his cup toward Shortstop.

The General poured the sweet, amber-colored liquid into Speedway's cup. The Colonel gulped it down in less than a second. One had to do it that way because in the sub-zero temperatures of the forest, even boiling liquids would quickly freeze. Speedway asked, "Tell me again why we can't have a fire?"

"We can't let the phoenixes know we're waiting for them. It might scare them off if they saw our fire."

"So how are we supposed to get their attention if we do see one?"

Shortstop scratched his head, "I hadn't thought of that. Hopefully one will show up close enough to us that when we hear it singing, we can call out to it."

"Well, that might work. Let's just hope this phoenix stuff isn't just a legend."

"That's what we used to say about the *Blood of the Land*. God proved us wrong there. I'm willing to bet the phoenixes exist, and if they do, they have sworn to protect our people."

"I can think of at least one way to get their attention," Speedway said.

"How is that?"

"We pray and ask God to send them to us."

Shortstop nodded, "Good idea. We can bless the food too. Let's pray."

They both bowed their heads, and Shortstop prayed, "Lord, we are in need. Our friend is in danger, and we need to find the great phoenixes to help him. Lord, for You, nothing is impossible, and so we ask if it is Your will that You allow us to see a phoenix when the morning comes. We thank You and love You, Lord. Please bless this food to our bodies. Amen!"

Speedway began scooping large helpings of the oboca rabbit stew Berry had prepared into their bowls. The stew was hot and bubbling. Both officers began spooning bite after bite into their mouths. Shortstop raved, "This is so good! I love that Chef Berry."

"Yeah, so do I, but you know, I think it's making me sleepy," Speedway yawned.

"I know what you mean," Shortstop said.

"Do you think…think…?" Speedway slumped into the snow, and his eyes rolled back into his head.

Shortstop panicked. *What was going on?* He wanted to help his friend, but his own vision was beginning to blur, and the strength was oozing from his body. This was not simple fatigue, nor anything the stew might have brought about. *Unless?* He had to find help. He had to! He dug his fingers into the snow and pulled himself up the bluff, hoping against hopelessness to see a phoenix before whatever was happening overtook him. But he was too late. The entire world around him faded to black.

~

Toby Nakan pushed the door to Chef Berry's tenth story dungeon cell closed behind him. Berry sat weeping in the hay. The dungeon hadn't changed much since Seth was in control of the Palace. Honestly, it hadn't been a priority, and no one was expecting prisoners anytime soon. For the moment, however, the mildew, wet hay, and rodent remains would have to do.

Toby asked, "How long have you been supplying Lizard Face with information?"

Berry took in a deep breath, "I have never supplied Lizard Face with information of any kind. I only ever spoke to him once when he lived in the Palace."

"I find that hard to believe."

"What, you think the Palace chef and the second-in-command of an evil empire would become best buddies?"

"Mr. Berry, stranger things have happened. I wouldn't be surprised if your coming on the *New Life* with us was all just a ruse. You get to Stararocka and then transmit its coordinates back to Lizard Face."

"Are you insane, Toby? You're making up worthless theories. And you were there! The Stararockans would have blown Lizard Face away no matter what size fleet he sent after them. You saw what they did to the *Space Shark*."

Toby knelt next to Berry, "I was also on the *Dragon's Blood*. Lizard Face murdered my captain and crew in cold blood! Obviously the Stararockans couldn't stop that! If I find out you really were responsible, being accused of being a spy will be the least of your worries."

It was unbecoming of any bear to express hatred, but it was a character trait they had all learned well from Seth. When Scotty took over, and Garlan's Christ campaign began, they had learned hatred was contrary to God's will. Even so, Toby's blood was boiling. But if he took any action against Berry, guilty or not, it would mean the end of his career.

Berry balled, "Toby, please, you know me. I'm not a killer, and I certainly didn't give or sell *Door* technology to Lizard Face."

Toby stood, "You are the first bear we have ever had to take into custody. If you're found guilty, your crimes will have been worse than Kelcott's. Only one hundred bears died because of him. You've killed hundreds, and you might just find a few families who'd be willing to take revenge on you for what Kelcott did. After all, one traitor is as good as another."

"Who are you?" Berry raged. "You're only fifteen. You have no right to speak to me this way, guilty or not!"

"We'll see about that." Toby turned and opened the cell door. Outside, he locked it behind him. One way or another, he would get his answers. And if need be, Berry would burn.

~

"Computer Find: Recent transmissions sent from this station. Time frame: The last 24 hours."

Ensign Cak Nakan finished typing his request into Chef Berry's console. He had no idea what to expect, but somehow, he suspected it wouldn't be a list of messages to Ensign Shallow *if there really was an Ensign Shallow*. He had certainly never met her, and he had served in the Palace since Scotty took control.

"How's it coming?" Cak turned to see his brother.

"Well, Dr. Nova is testing the plume berry juice, and the computer is processing my request. It should just take another minute."

"Good. Chef Berry still claims he's innocent. I don't get it."

Cak hesitated, "Um, Toby, did you ever consider the possibility that he might be?"

"What do you mean?"

"Well, we just jumped on him and arrested him. I mean, it's not like we found the schematics on him."

"You saw the computer records. He was the only one who could have copied that file."

"Scotty once told me that on Earth they have a saying, *innocent until proven guilty*. The evidence we have against Berry is all circumstantial. Granted, if the juice proves poisonous, and these transmissions prove to be what we think them to be, it will have been a good call to arrest him. But I think we took him down way to fast."

Toby shook his head, "I don't like it any more than you do. I just have a feeling he's guilty."

"Uh, excuse me," someone behind them sniffled. They turned around to see a petite, female bear, wrapped in a blue, cotton blanket.

"Can we help you?" Toby asked.

"Ah...ah...choo!" the bear sneezed. "I'm looking for Chef Berry. He was supposed to have sent me some soup thirty minutes ago."

"Well, I'm afraid, Chef Berry won't be available for a while."

"*Sniff*...That's okay. I'll just grab some soup for myself."

"No problem. Oh, by the way, I'm Ensign Toby Nakan. I don't think we've met before."

Toby extended his hand, but she waved it away. "I'd shake your hand, but I don't want you to get sick too. My name is Martha, Ensign Martha Shallow."

"What!"

Cak grabbed Toby's shoulder, "Toby, you need to look at this."

Dumbstruck, Toby turned back to the computer screen. Scrolling down the monitor were over twenty entries made between the Palace kitchen and the quarters of Ensign Martha Shallow.

"Dr. Nova to Ensign Cak Nakan!"

"Go ahead, Doctor."

"Cak, I finished analyzing the plume berry juice. There is not a trace of poison. In fact, I'd say it was the best juice in Berry's stock. It's over fifty years old."

"Um, thanks, Doctor."

Toby's mouth was dry, "Cak, I think we owe someone an apology."

~

"Strange creatures these bears."

"Yes, indeed."

Shortstop heard the high-pitched, nasally voices, but comprehended them only as if in a dream. Something had happened, but he had no idea what. In fact, he was having enough trouble remembering his own name, let alone what had happened. His eyes were only taking in blurred colors, and though his ears worked, the sounds they brought in seemed distant. The one thing he did notice for sure though was that he was warmer, much warmer. Not uncomfortably so, but it was clear, he was no longer on the bluff. Was this what it was like when you died, a hazy tunnel eventually to be replaced by the glories of Heaven? Did Starananians even go to Heaven? That question had not yet been answered. All anyone knew was that whatever happened to the *Blood of the Land* would happen to them in one way or another.

A pinch on his arm brought everything screaming back into focus, "OWE! What in the world is going on?"

Shortstop was ready for a fight, but he felt his courage vanish when he looked straight into the brown eyes of a gigantic bird. He pushed himself up on his hands and was startled by a second bird. The first was orange with white and black spots, just like the picture. However, its plume of purple feathers was tied like a ponytail with a long golden chain. The second bird was solid purple and had a plume of orange feathers flapping freely and no spots. Both birds had the trademark black talons and beaks of the phoenixes, and they stared at him with the curiosity of children.

"Where am I?" Shortstop asked.

The orange bird ruffled its feathers in delight and replied, "You are in Cololot, city of the Snow Phoenixes."

"The city actually has a name?" Shortstop pondered. "We always just called it the Phoenix City."

"I suspect that there is a great deal about us that you do not know," the purple bird replied.

The orange bird said, "I am Davic, and this is my companion Shella. She is my mate."

"Pleased to meet you both, but how did I get here? I never saw a phoenix in the forest, and according to the legend, you have to see a phoenix to come here. The last thing I remember, I fell asleep on the bluff overlooking Moonville. The stew must have been poisoned."

"It was not poisoned. Trust me, we enjoyed eating what you left," Davic chirped. "The Lord of Heaven alerted us to your dilemma. Rather than take the risk that you wouldn't see us, we sent a sleeping wind upon you. When you and your companion had fallen asleep, we brought you here."

"Speaking of my companion, where is he?" Shortstop asked.

"He awoke a few minutes ago," Shella replied. "He is waiting for you in the garden. Come, we will take you to him."

Shortstop pushed himself to his feet and immediately knew why they called the city Cololot. There were rainbows everywhere. As the stories had said, the roads, the buildings, and almost every other object in the city was formed out of the pink *fire glass*. Light refracted through the glass, painting the city in color. Breathtaking spires, that seemed to scrape the sun itself, stretched from the heights of temples and cathedrals. Crystal cherubs spouted water from their mouths into pools and streams of water so clear you couldn't tell it was there unless you disturbed the surface. And everywhere there was the music of bells ringing and birds singing.

Scattered all along the road were perches made from the glass, and many of them had phoenixes on them. The birds were of every assortment and color, from green with black plumes to red with white plumes and every color combination in between. Shortstop particularly enjoyed the blue phoenixes with the white plumes. All the birds looked on with curiosity. Shortstop couldn't know for sure, but it was possible none of these birds had ever seen a bear before. If so, he probably looked as strange to them as they did to him.

Shortstop had awoken on the street up against a wall at the back of a small courtyard. Davic and Shella, who waddled on their feet rather than fly, led him out onto the main road and a few blocks away to another courtyard. This one was much larger, and it was filled with hundreds of varieties of plants. Roses, lily pads, blueberry bushes, and orchids were everywhere. Many of the plants he saw had been assumed extinct for millennia. After Seth destroyed the moon, the only plants that survived in the wild had to be rugged enough to endure the harsh winter conditions. Unfortunately, that was very few beyond the trees. The only delicate plants to survive were those in the Palace gardens and those few private greenhouses scattered across the planet.

Speedway was sitting on the ledge of the fountain at the center of the garden. Vines hung down all about him, and he was running his fingers back and forth through the cool water. Shortstop asked, "Colonel, are you all right?"

Speedway stood at the sound of his commanding officer's voice. "Yes, sir. The phoenixes have been very kind to me."

"It would be dishonorable to do otherwise," Shella said.

Shortstop walked to the side of his officer, then turned and addressed the phoenixes, "Davic, Shella, I want to thank you for bringing us to your city. It was a long shot for us, but we desperately need your help. We must speak with your king immediately."

"Of course, the Lord of Heaven has also told King Thimble about your plight. He is waiting for you in the Fiery Palace," Davic said.

"Wonderful!" Shortstop smiled. "Can we head there now?"

Both Shortstop and Speedway began moving toward the exit of the garden, but Shella said, "Please, my friends, you haven't much time. Your friend is in danger. We must hurry. We will take you to His Majesty."

"But *hoooooooooow*!" Shortstop's question had barely been framed before Davic scooped the General's arms into his talons and lifted Shortstop into the sky beneath the beat of his powerful wings. Within seconds, the icy chill of the sky replaced the warmth of the city, but Shortstop didn't mind. Beneath him, Cololot radiated color like a giant prism, and for a moment, Shortstop thought that must be what Heaven looked like.

Beyond the city was an endless field of ice and snow. Not one tree and not one mountain littered the landscape. It was like the White Desert magnified a thousand times over. Shortstop glanced back long enough to see Speedway squirming in the grip of Shella. He laughed and then asked, "Where is this Fiery Palace?"

"On top of the world!" Davic shouted back.

Shortstop was confused. According to legend, the Phoenix City was on the top of the world. However, a few more seconds of flying revealed what Davic meant. Beyond the nearly endless plain of ice towered a mountain. Tall and powerful, it looked to be carved from pure diamond, and at the top of it, which was well above the cloud line, was a palace.

To say it put Cosmic Bubble Palace to shame was an understatement. Like the city, it was made of solid *fire glass*. Unlike the city, the fire was alive in the glass. Flames danced in harmony through each sheet of pink glass. The palace had nine spires on top of nine towers, and each tower was two hundred stories high. There was also a vast courtyard filled with beautiful plants. Shortstop couldn't tell which kind from his altitude, but he figured he would find out soon enough.

Davic began his descent toward the courtyard, and Shortstop asked, "How could we have missed all this? Your kingdom is huge!"

"You could have walked every square inch of this planet, turned over every stone, and uprooted every tree, and you would never have found our city. It was hidden by the Lord Himself, and only those who we wish to come here can come here."

"It almost looks like Heaven, at least, what I imagine Heaven to be like."

"If you believe that, you have no conception of what Heaven is like. The home of Almighty God makes our kingdom seem rather plain."

When Shortstop's feet touched down on solid ground again, he found himself perspiring. At first, he thought it was from the exhilaration of the flight, but it wasn't. The garden they had landed in, which was ripe with fruits and vegetables of every kind, was humid and pulsing with heat. The fire in the walls clearly had the effect of heating the entire palace.

Speedway pulled at his collar, "Is it this hot all over the palace?"

"I am afraid it's worse," Shella replied. "Most of the palace is ninety degrees, but King Thimble prefers 110 degrees in his throne room. You will have to bear it if you want to speak with him."

"I thought you birds were *Snow* Phoenixes?" Speedway complained.

"We don't have much time. Please take us to King Thimble," Shortstop said.

Shella waved her wing in the direction of a large entryway. They all went inside, and as Shella had predicted, the heat only got worse. Speedway imagined the Stararockans would have been right at home here.

As Shortstop had no doubt it would be, the interior of the Fiery Palace was stunning. There were hundreds of statues, all made of *fire glass*, and most of them were of bears. However, they passed one Shortstop had to stop by. It was of a human man. He had on royal robes and a crown. He had a very thick beard, a cutlass in his right hand, and a book under his left arm.

Shortstop asked, "Who is this?"

Davic replied, "That, my friend, is a statue of your very first emperor. We keep Iren's tomb here."

"I had never really thought about where Iren was buried," Shortstop said. "Seth stabbed him and threw him out a window on the 100th story of the Palace. After that, there is no mention of what happened to his body."

Shella explained, "In the chaos that followed Iren's assassination, King Thimble sent two phoenixes to ferry his body back here. It is kept in a place of high honor on the top floor of our palace."

Shortstop gulped and asked, "Is his tomb, uh, transparent?"

"Yes, of course, but the cosmetic damage to his body was repaired. Thanks to the *fire glass*, his body has been preserved for over 5,000 years," Shella said.

"And what about his spirit?" Shortstop asked, hoping to get some answers about a Starananian afterlife.

"Unfortunately, there is little I am allowed to say on that matter. But you will find the answer in the *Bible*. Iren's fate was the same as that of the *Old Testament* saints," Davic said.

"I believe I'll ask Minister Garlan about that as soon as we get back," Shortstop said.

Speedway pushed on his General's shoulder, "With all due respect to the opportunity we have here, sir, I can't handle this heat much longer."

"Of course, Colonel, let's keep going."

"His Majesty's throne room is just at the other end of this chamber," Davic said leading the way.

"I would have thought a king would have taken a throne room on a higher floor," Speedway said.

"Have you never read that he who exalts himself shall be humbled, and he who humbles himself shall be exalted? The government in Heaven is unlike any other in the Universe.

King Thimble took a lowly place as a representation of his servitude of you and your people," Shella explained.

Speedway smiled. These truly were birds of Heaven. What kind of creatures must they be to so willingly surrender their heavenly positions to watch over a few thousand bears? If the situation weren't so dire, and the heat so intense, he would have been glad to spend much more time in the company of these birds.

Davic and Shella paused before a huge entryway. Apparently, doors were not the norm for these creatures, as they had yet to see any, which was understandable. Creatures without hands might have had a difficult time opening them. Davic said, "His Majesty awaits you. We must part company with you here."

Shortstop nodded and stepped into the throne room. Unlike the rest of the palace, it was simple. Well, as simple as anything got in this extraordinary place. The walls and floors still shone with their own internal fire, but there were no statues, no fountains, no decorations of any kind. Of course, when they got their first look at Thimble, they realized why they weren't necessary.

At the other end of the throne room was an enormous perch, and on top of it sat a gigantic phoenix. The other phoenixes were large enough, but this one was at least twice their size. It had snow-white feathers, and blood red spots from head to talon. Its long tail feathers stretched out over ten feet behind it, and on its head, it wore a crown of pink glass. Like the other *fire glass* in the palace, it had fire dancing inside of it. The King's talons and beak were black, an obvious trademark of his people, but his eyes were deep emerald green. The bears hesitated, overcome by him.

"Please, come closer!" Thimble's voice boomed like thunder across the throne room. The other phoenixes had chirpy, almost nasally voices, but the King's voice was deep and commanding.

Shortstop and Speedway approached cautiously, and when they had come near to the King, they knelt. Shortstop said, "We are honored to be in your presence, Your Majesty. My name is General Henry Shortstop, and this is my attaché,

Colonel Andrew Speedway. We are members of the Starananian Space Force."

King Thimble hopped down from his perch, an act that shook the ground more than a little, and took Shortstop's shirt in his beak. After both officers were pulled to their feet, he said, "Please, you need not bow to me. It is my people and I who are your servants."

"Apologies, Sire, but it is we who are humbled by your presence," Shortstop said.

Speedway pulled at his collar. It felt like 210 degrees, not 110. Either way, he wasn't going to last much longer. Thimble noticed this and said, "Forgive me, friends. I know the fire of my home must be a bit much for you. Please, we will continue this discussion on the balcony. I believe you will find it much cooler."

King Thimble led the way across the throne room to the balcony, and the bears followed. When they were outside, Speedway closed his eyes and absorbed the cold in delight. Though they were only on the first floor of the Fiery Palace, Shortstop was still in awe of the view down through the clouds and onto the Diamond Mountain.

Once it was obvious the bears were more comfortable, Thimble said, "Now, my friends, please tell me why you have come."

Shortstop explained, "Sire, the *Blood of the Land* was taken captive two days ago by the former second-in-command of our empire, Lizard Face. We have no idea where he took him, but he demands that we give him the Cosmic Bubble in exchange for Scotty's safe return."

"YOU CAN NOT!" Thimble's voice shook the mountain, and Speedway had to brace himself against the ledge of the balcony to keep from falling.

Shortstop was not fazed, "We know that, Your Majesty. We have learned of the power of the glass, and we have a plan to save both Scotty and the Bubble. We have come here to request more *fire glass*."

"More?"

"Yes, sire. You see, we do not believe Lizard Face will surrender Scotty unless he believes we have surrendered the Bubble. We plan to take it into space to our assigned rendezvous point. We'll release it, and then, once Lizard Face has released Scotty, we will attack him from our ships with the *fire glass* we hope to get.

"If everything goes according to plan, we will destroy Lizard Face and his ship and crew. However, if he gets the Bubble, there is no chance that will happen."

Thimble shook his head, "I am sorry, but the spread of *fire glass* is strictly controlled by the Lord Himself. We were allowed to give Iren the Bubble as a gift in the hopes that Satan's curse on his son would not cause him to abandon his faith. He never did learn its full potential. If you knew it, you would never give Lizard Face the opportunity to seize control of it."

"Sire, we are a people hardened by war. Before Iren was killed, there were millions of us. Now there are barely ten thousand of us left. We know the risks of offering evil power. But, sir, we are willing to take that risk by faith. The *Blood of the Land* is worth far more to us than *fire glass*. He is one boy, but he is a boy backed by God. I dare say that all the *fire glass* in the Universe could not stand against God."

Thimble pondered this, "You are right, of course. But creating more *fire glass* would cost the lives of at least two of my phoenixes. I cannot ask them to do that."

Shortstop persisted, "Sire, your lives are an unending circle. Though you die, you rise from your own ashes an instant later. And besides that, it must have taken hundreds of deaths to build your kingdom."

"My people are weary of death. When the *Blood of the Land* came, we believed none of us would have to die again until we were allowed to return to Heaven at the coming of the Lord Jesus Christ."

"Is death that painful for you?" Speedway asked.

"After we surrendered our heavenly places, we had to endure all the pain of living flesh. To be sure, burning to death is painful. So, you can understand what a great deal creating *fire glass* is."

Speedway suggested, "We do, Sire, but you have plenty of *fire glass* already made. Perhaps you could give us some of that?"

Thimble ruffled his feathers, "*Fire glass* cannot be broken, and since most of the glass in the kingdom is interlaced, it would be impossible to give it to you."

"Well, we could take a statue or a perch, anything not fastened down," Shortstop offered.

Thimble sighed, "I am afraid not. In order to do what you ask, you will need two small globes of *fire glass*. Statues and perches would be incompatible with your weapons arrays."

"Are there no globes in all your lands?" Shortstop asked.

Thimble surrendered, "Even I do not know everything. I will beseech the Lord. If there are such globes, and you can find them, and the Lord allows it, you may take them."

Speedway pleaded, "Thank you, Sire, but we don't have time to search your entire kingdom. We have less than two days before Scotty will be killed if we don't comply with Lizard Face's demands."

Shortstop's shoulders slumped. They had been brought to the top of the world into a land thought only to exist in legend. They had spoken with a creature that once held a prominent place in Heaven, and they had seen sights and glories that would never be topped unless they lived to the coming of the Lord. And yet, they had been turned away. Now they had to weigh the survival of Scotty with the survival of all Staranana. Either way the story turned out, the bears were doomed.

Shortstop said, "Please beseech the Lord, Sire. Perhaps He can give you wise counsel. My officer and I will need to be taken home soon, as we are running out of time. However, before we go, we would like to pay homage to Emperor Iren."

"Of course, Davic and Shella can take you there. I will pray." Thimble no sooner finished his sentence than he beat his wings and leapt into the sky. He vanished within seconds. Apparently, he preferred doing his praying while flying. Either that, or he was going to beseech God in Heaven itself.

"We will take you to Emperor Iren." Shortstop and Speedway turned to see that Davic and Shella were standing just inside the palace.

"How long have you been there?" Speedway asked.

"We came in at the King's request," Shella said.

"We didn't see him speak with you," Shortstop said.

"He did not need to. With all respect to King Thimble, his voice carries better than thunder. It is one of the reasons why his palace is so far from the city. Otherwise, our entire land would be filled with his voice constantly," Davic explained.

"We understand. Please take us to Iren," Shortstop said.

Shortstop and Speedway found themselves in the phoenixes' talons again. Then it was out over the balcony and straight up. Shortstop often got dizzy looking down from the roof of Cosmic Bubble Palace, and that was only 100 stories over level ground. This palace was 200 stories high and was built on an already incredibly high mountain. As they climbed higher and higher, the clouds became fewer and fewer until all that remained was the vast star field and the long expanse of asteroids.

Shortstop expected to be gasping for breath. Even if the top of the Fiery Palace didn't scrape the edges of space, the air in this layer of the atmosphere would be far too thin to breathe. Yet he felt fine. The air in his lungs was rich and deep. The icy temperature, though probably deadly to humans, felt wonderful. When they finally reached the top, the ground had been completely obscured by the clouds, and even those were far, far below.

The phoenixes released them on the balcony of the 200th story and Davic said, "This entire floor is devoted to your first Emperor. Please enjoy it. We will wait for you here."

The two officers headed inside, relieved that the temperature, though not typical for bears, was much cooler than the rest of the palace. The balcony led into a hallway. Like the rest of the palace, the place was made of *fire glass*, but it was also unique. There were real swords and suits of armor. Not that they knew what they were there for, as there were no wars before Seth's time. Perhaps Iren had them to defend against Satan.

There were also many pictures on the wall, and they kept changing. One minute, there was the image of Iren with a baby boy on his knee. The next, a rip of flames shot across the picture frame, and the image was transformed into something entirely different. There were many pictures of Seth, most of which must have been taken before he fell. In his youth, he had been a beautiful child. His smile was hypnotic, and the pictures of him embracing his parents showed that, at least at one point, he knew what it was to love.

Perhaps the most dazzling of all were the pictures of Iren's wife. As the only human on Staranana, Iren could only take a wife from the spirit people of Katana, a city on the far side of Staranana. Little was known about her. Apparently, not even her name mattered to historians. Or perhaps she didn't have a name. Speedway recalled the story of when Moses asked God His name. The concept and restriction of a name seemed unimportant to heavenly beings. Thus God had given Moses the only name that would fully encompass who He was, *I AM.*

Iren's wife had the shining countenance of an angel. Though her appearance was human, she radiated a holiness Shortstop had only experienced when the angel Joshua had crowned Scotty emperor on the steps of Cosmic Bubble Palace. In most of the pictures, her hair flowed loose and red about her shoulders, though in some it was braided with a bit of gold lace. Her skin was milky white, and it appeared transparent. She wore a simple white dress, and she had small emeralds hanging from her ears. In every picture, she was smiling. Why Iren had wanted to give up such a perfect existence for a life of flesh and blood, Shortstop would never know.

At the end of the hall was another entryway that led into a large room. When Shortstop and Speedway reached the threshold, their jaws dropped. It was a room fitting of any royalty save God Himself. There was a throne formed from pure gold and with red velvet cushions. Two *fire glass* phoenixes sat on either side of the throne as an eternal honor guard. The room was also littered with treasure. Thousands of gold coins, silver goblets, jewels, and spools of silk were everywhere, and in the very center of the room was Emperor Iren.

Staranana's first emperor was laid out in a *fire glass* coffin. The bears approached in awe. Iren was a legend, almost a saint.

He had established Starananian civilization, and even now, over five thousand years since his death, his teachings continued to influence the populace. Shortstop rubbed his hands over the top of the coffin and stood silent.

For all intents and purposes, Iren looked merely asleep. His hair and beard were thick and gray, and his flesh still looked pink and alive. The wrinkles on his face and the slight curve of his lips gave him a gentleness that transcended his centuries-long sleep. His robes were green, and he wore a coat of chain mail. His hands cupped over his chest held a well-polished, silver cutlass. Across the blade, something was written in an ancient Starananian script that neither Shortstop nor Speedway could translate. On his head, he wore a golden crown with a single orange jewel in its center. Shortstop recognized the jewel as brillium amber.

The General had to hold back the tears as he said, "I never imagined I would see this, Andrew."

"I know, sir. It's amazing. I don't think anyone will ever believe us."

"Do you ever wonder what life would have been like if Seth had never overthrown his father? I mean, imagine living in Iren's day. We had a lush, beautiful planet, and really, no sin. If Seth hadn't betrayed everyone, our people would have spread well out into the galaxy by now. We could have been a world very pleasing to the Lord."

"I agree, sir, but despite all the hardship, things turned out all right. Scotty serves the Lord, and assuming we get him back, he will until Christ comes. I don't know about you, but that sounds pretty good to me."

"Yes, but how many people had to die before the *Blood of the Land* came? Our population once numbered in the millions."

"Yes, General, but none of those people lived or would have lived during our time. Begging your pardon, sir, but it makes no sense to mourn for bears we would never have known anyway. God knows what He is doing."

Shortstop smiled, and he allowed a single tear to begin fighting its way down the fur on his face, "This from the bear who three months ago wanted nothing to do with God."

"People change."

Shortstop nodded, and he lowered his head, his hands gripped around the handle of the coffin. Almost absentmindedly, he began rubbing his hands over the spherical knobs at either end of the long handle. He hoped, he prayed, Thimble would be able to get permission from the Lord to give them some *fire glass*, and that they would be able to find the right sized globes.

"Henry."

Shortstop looked up, "Did you say something, Colonel?"

"No, sir," Speedway replied.

"Henry."

Shortstop perked up again. Someone had definitely said his name. It wasn't Speedway's voice, nor Davic's or Shella's, and it definitely wasn't Thimble's. This voice was still and small, and yet powerful, and it was coming from inside of him. It could only be…OH!

"Lord!"

"Yes, Henry. Let him who has eyes to see, see!"

"Lord?" Shortstop asked, but the voice did not speak again.

He sighed. Maybe he had imagined the whole thing, and then it hit him like the entire Fiery Palace had been slammed on top of him. "Colonel, come look at this!"

Speedway hurried to the other side of the coffin, and Shortstop began screwing off the spherical ends of the coffin handle. When he was finished, he held up two small globes of *fire glass*.

Speedway gasped, "General, is that…?"

"Yes, they are just what we need! For some reason, the handle wasn't one solid piece, lucky for us!"

"I highly doubt luck had anything to do with this, but do you think we can take them? Who knows, we may be defiling Iren's tomb?"

"I don't think His Majesty would mind, especially in our current situation. I just hope Thimble let's us take them."

"Of course, I will!" The thundering voice ripped through the tomb. Even despite their short conversation, they knew it well.

Shortstop and Speedway turned and faced the King of the phoenixes. The General said, "Your Majesty, we believe these globes will help us. Have you asked the Lord if it's all right?"

Thimble pranced into the room and replied, "You already know the answer to that, General. You may take the globes. Use them well to save your friend."

"We would be happy to return them," Speedway offered.

"That won't be necessary. My conversation with the Lord led me to believe you have many more perilous times ahead. You may need them, but I am afraid, other than these globes and the Bubble, I can never again offer you any *fire glass*."

"We understand," Shortstop replied. "By the way, Sire, how do we use it?"

"It merely needs to touch your hand or be attached to something that can transmit the heat of your hand. Then you simply think of the amount of energy you want it to expel, and the glass will do the rest. Be warned, though; once one person has used the glass, it will only work for that person. It will be useless to everyone else. Therefore, it is imperative that Lizard Face not even touch the Cosmic Bubble. If anyone touches and uses it, it must be the *Blood of the Land*."

"We understand, sir, and thank you!" Shortstop said. "And now, begging Your Majesty's pardon, we need to be getting home."

"Of course," Thimble thundered, and almost instantly, Davic and Shella appeared at his side.

Thimble said, "I do hope we will meet again. I am glad you had the faith to find us." Shortstop smiled in response, and then Davic and Shella scooped them up. They flew down the hall, out the balcony entry, and dove down toward the planet. Within minutes, and with Cololot once again shrouded in mystery, they were on their way back to Cosmic Bubble Palace.

Chapter 18
The Real Spy

"How much time do we have left?" Cak asked. "We have thirty hours before the *Fire Cruiser* is supposed to be back. I have no idea when the General and the Colonel will be back. And right now, we have no spy to show for our efforts," Toby said.

"We still have Chef Berry in custody, and we do have evidence against him."

"Not enough. Like you said, the fact that he was in Spikey's workshop when the computer file was active is circumstantial evidence. We need to know more. Nothing adds up here. Even if Berry did steal the plans, he would have had to send them at some point. I have gone back over the scanner logs on Chef Berry's locations over the last month. Other than the time he was in Spikey's workshop, there was nothing suspicious."

"So what are we going to do?"

Toby cupped his forehead in his hands, "We only have one choice. For now, we have to let Berry go."

Cak sighed, "Well, let's get it over with."

~

"Oh, Lord, what have I done to deserve this?" Chef Berry cried. He had spent an entire night in his cell, in the cold and with the rodents crawling all over him. Was this what the reign of the *Blood of the Land* had brought about? An innocent bear was likely to be condemned to death! *Oh, Lord, why!*

Berry started at a creak from outside the cell. When the cell's wooden door began scraping over the stone floor, he stood. No doubt the firing squad, or perhaps General Shortstop had arrived to seal his fate. However, the two he saw were the last bears he ever expected to see, or really wanted to see. They were the ones who had put him in here, Toby and Cak Nakan.

"What do you want?" Berry spat.

Both bears looked at their toes, and Toby said, "Sir, we came to apologize. We examined some additional evidence, and we are not totally convinced you're guilty."

"NOT TOTALLY CONVINCED! I'll have both your heads for this. I am not guilty, and when Scotty hears about this, you'll pay for sure!" Berry was shaking with rage, and the Nakans couldn't really blame him. He had had to spend an entire night in a rank dungeon cell crawling with bugs and freezing cold for what might turn out to be false charges.

"We're sorry, sir," Toby continued. "But you have to realize, there is a spy in the Palace who is indirectly responsible for the murder of hundreds of Stararockans, the theft of a Stararockan vessel, and the kidnapping of Scotty and TB. We're sorry we arrested you so foolhardily, but all the evidence we currently have still points to you."

"So what are you going to do?" Berry asked sarcastically, though a bit calmer.

"We're going to give you the benefit of the doubt. We'd be negligent in our duties if we let you wander free, so you'll stay with us until General Shortstop gets back. We'd like you to join our investigation."

"Me? I'm just a cook."

"Come on, clearing your name has to be a pretty good incentive. Someone took that technology. Don't you want to prove it wasn't you?"

"Well, yes. Where do you want to start?" Berry asked.

Toby shook his head, and Cak suggested, "What about the scene of the crime?"

"The Moonbeams' quarters, why?" Toby asked.

"It should be obvious," Berry snorted. "Whatever you're looking for will be there."

"But we already checked the computer files. What more could we find?" Toby asked.

"Well, we won't find out if we just hang around here," Cak said.

Toby asked Chef Berry, "So are you with us?"

"Yes. I am not happy about what you did, and you can bet both Scotty and General Shortstop will hear about it, but I will help you." Toby and Cak weren't exactly thrilled about that, but it would have to do. They only hoped that this investigation would not turn out to be their last official act as officers in the Starananian Space Force.

~

It was quiet in the Moonbeam apartment in the early hours of the morning. This was not at all typical. Usually, Gloria was fussing over a hot stove, arguing with Sparkey about his homework, and reviewing her daily appointment schedule, all at the same time. Sparkey, though an excellent student, always complained about having to go to school. A small school had been set up on the fiftieth floor of the Palace. At first, Gloria was worried about Sparkey's complaints, but after listening to Scotty talk about his school, she realized a child's dislike of school must be a universal constant. Spikey, of course, would be in his workshop, or mulling over some technical manual at the breakfast table. And Tommy would still be sleeping. Needless to say, with the family gone, the apartment seemed rather dull.

The two young ensigns and the suspected traitor moved through the main living area and back into Spikey's workshop. It was as they had left it, cluttered, disorganized, and oh, so Spikey. Toby sat in the computer chair. He started to switch it on, but Berry said, "You as much as told me there isn't any more to be found on the computer."

"So what are we looking for then?" Toby asked.

"I don't know!" Berry bellowed. "But if the choice is between finding something, and me being branded a traitor, I'll tear this apartment to pieces."

Cak began rummaging through the tables down the center of the workshop. He laughed at some of the inventions. There was the toothbrush/communicator, the fishing pole that contracted and then folded out into the perfect fish cleaning gear, and, of course, there were dozens of models of spacecraft engines.

A stack of papers drew his attention. Countless new inventions had been designed on them, and Cak wondered, "You don't suppose Spikey wrote the plans on a piece of paper, and then that was stolen?"

Toby shook his head, "Spikey is smarter than that. Besides, I'm willing to bet TB was his main source of information for the *Door*."

"So we have nothing!" Berry slammed his fist down onto the table.

"Don't give up so quickly," Toby soothed. "We'll find what we're looking for. We just need to spread out. Cak, you and Berry keep looking around in here. I'll start going through the rest of the apartment. Report anything unusual, no matter how small."

The two nodded and the search began. Cak tore through every paper written plan in Spikey's workshop. Berry examined every invention, and he even took a few apart. Toby emptied every drawer and moved every piece of furniture. Yet, after an hour of searching, they had still found nothing.

Toby wandered back into the workshop, frustrated, and asked, "Any luck?"

Both Berry and Cak shook their heads. Berry said, "We've gone over every inch of the place. Obviously, there is no more evidence here."

"We might as well stop for breakfast," Toby suggested.

"Breakfast! What time is it?" Berry shrieked.

Cak looked at the clock over the bay window, "0730 hours, why?"

"Why? WHY! Ugh, I would have been cooking for two-and-a-half hours by now. Breakfast is ruined! Everyone will be starving."

Toby held up his hand, "Easy, Chef, I canceled breakfast this morning. All the Palace residents were instructed to fend for themselves. Cak and I were going to set out a salad bar for lunch, and Dr. Nova offered to take care of dinner."

"Jesse Nova in my kitchen!" Berry bellowed.

"We've eaten in his quarters a few times. He's no Chef Berry, but he's a pretty good cook."

"Nevertheless, I don't like the idea of…" Berry paused.

"What is it?" Cak asked.

"That clock, I've never noticed it before."

"Maybe Spikey put it in recently," Cak said.

"Maybe, but look at it. The numbers are human, not Starananian, and it's twice as thick as any clock I've seen around here."

"Scotty probably gave it to Spikey," Toby offered.

Berry ignored him and climbed up on a chair and pulled the clock from the wall. It was much heavier than he expected. He set it on the table. Cak asked, "What do you hope to accomplish?"

Berry ignored the question and ordered, "Get that computer online."

Toby switched it on, but asked, "Why?"

"When you thought I was the spy, you must have checked the Palace scanner records to figure out that I was in the room when the file was open."

"Yes," Toby admitted.

"Well, how accurate are those scanners? I mean, do they record when every object was placed in every room?"

"That would be a little cumbersome," Toby said. "But I honestly don't know. Anyway, what are you getting at?"

"All I need you to do right now is access whatever you need to access to find out when this clock was put in place and where it came from. Try the inventories of the things Scotty brought back from Earth. I am going to get this clock open."

Toby turned around to the computer and typed, **"Computer Find: Inventory manifests that include Earth clocks."**

Then he turned back to Berry, "Chef, I have no idea what you are up to. I mean, that clock is really irrel…"

"There!"

"What?" both brothers chimed.

"Take a look at this." Berry had the back of the clock open exposing all its gears. When Toby and Cak looked inside, they saw a pulsing red light.

"What is that?" Toby asked.

"I don't know, but how many mechanical clocks do you know of that have red lights inside of them?" Berry asked.

"Toby, I think you should take a look at this." Toby turned back to his brother who was facing the computer screen. It read, **"NOT FOUND."**

"So either Scotty never mentioned this clock or someone else put it here without following protocol," Toby said.

"This puzzle just keeps getting more and more complicated," Berry said.

"Well, I think we can rule out Scotty never mentioning the clock. Spikey is the only one who has operated the *Door* each time Scotty has come through it. And Spikey is meticulous. He records everything. He would have cataloged the contents of any package Scotty brought over, and even if he didn't, TB's scanners would have," Cak said.

Berry wiggled his screwdriver inside the clock, "I think I can move some of these gears out of the way and get to that light. Maybe it's some sort of recording device. I can…"

Berry had no sooner moved the first gear out of place than a shrill whine erupted from the clock. Their hands were over their ears in an instant, and Toby couldn't help but feel a pang at the memory of the virus's sound and the deaths of his crew. However, nothing could have prepared them for what they saw next.

The clock on the table began to shimmer and sparkle. Its very substance was dissolving, and then in a flash, the clock was gone. All that remained was a half-sphere of mechanical circuitry, with the red light glowing at its front like a menacing eye. It became more eye-like a second later when eight spidery legs sprouted from its sides, and it scrambled off the table and out of the room. As soon as the thing was gone, the sound faded.

"What the heck was that?" Cak cursed.

Toby answered, "I don't know, but I think we found our spy."

Chapter 19
Reunions

"**S**cotty, will you get up!"

Sparkey Moonbeam started at the agitated female voice. He remembered the voice from three months ago. It was Scotty's mom. Which meant, he was on Earth. At least, that was what his senses were telling him. In reality, he was still on Staranana, controlling Scotty's duplicate through virtual reality. Even so, it was an odd sensation. Everything looked and felt so real. Now he just had to play his part.

He pushed himself up from the bed and stretched. He was shirtless and wearing a pair of blue athletic shorts. Scotty's Earth room was far from glamorous. There were toys everywhere, as well as dirty laundry. One particular pile, next to a soccer ball, reeked! The curtains and the carpet were green. And there was also a set of bunk beds. On the top bed, there was a very large, bare-chested, human boy.

That was Noah as Sparkey recalled. Three months earlier, Sparkey had had the unfortunate opportunity to have Noah sit right on top of him in the Fields family's minivan. In three months, the boy had barely changed. His exposed muscles gave him away as an athlete, obviously, a good one, and the stubble on his face beset his age. He was probably rolling toward seventeen by now. And at the moment, the whole muscular package was dead to the world.

Mrs. Fields burst into the room, "Scotty, are you ready yet?"

Yes! So God had answered their prayers, and Scotty's mom could see him. Sparkey decided to play this thing right from the start, "Well, Noah's not up yet!"

"Noah doesn't have a dentist appointment in an hour. Now, get dressed! You slept too late for breakfast. I don't want the dentist to have to clean all that gunk out of your teeth!"

Sparkey scratched his human head, which felt like plastic because of the virtual reality helmet. What was a dentist? Obviously, it had something to do with cleaning teeth. Was that even possible on an energy matter duplicate? Sparkey remembered his dad telling Scotty that the duplicate had to periodically discharge energy into the ground. If the dentist started poking around with metal tools, he would be in for a shock, literally. He could even possibly deactivate the duplicate. There had to be a way out of this, but what?

"Scotty!"

"Ah, coming, Mrs…Mom!" Sparkey walked over to the window. The last time he had been here the temperature had been unbearable at sixty degrees. Likely, he would not suffer the same ill effects only controlling this duplicate by remote, but still, he detested the idea of excessive heat. However, that fear was laid to rest when he pulled back the curtain to reveal beautiful, white snow.

"Hey, brat, close the curtain!" It was Noah that had spoken. The light from the window had hit him in the eye, and he now had his pillow pulled over his head.

"Sorry," Sparkey said, but then he got an idea. "Hey, Noah, are you cold?"

Noah groaned, but before he could answer fully, Sparkey grabbed the edge of his *big brother's* blanket and yanked hard. Noah crashed from the top bunk to the floor, and Sparkey held the blanket in his hands, laughing. Noah, now fully awake, looked up at his brother wide-eyed, "What are you doing, you little runt?"

Sparkey winked at him, "Catch me if you can!" Then he darted out the room, blanket still in hand.

Sparkey dashed down the hall and into the living room. Samantha was there with one of her friends, and at first, they were only annoyed with the blanket-clad nine-year-old jumping up and over the couch. However, the Fields' daughter was mortified when her big brother came running into the living room in only his boxer shorts.

Noah was more than secure in his own body, so he didn't notice Samantha's friend, Katie, turn beet red, when he asked, "Where did he go?"

Samantha hesitated before answering, "He's behind the couch."

Noah was about to jump right between the two girls and over the couch to his brother, but Sparkey beat him to the punch, literally. With the blanket wrapped around him, Sparkey leaped from behind the couch, over the heads of the two girls, and slammed his fist into Noah's overly muscled torso.

Noah fell to the ground and gasped as he tried to catch his breath, "What's gotten into you, Scotty?"

But Sparkey didn't answer. This whole game of cat and mouse was all a ruse. His real objective was the snow and an excuse to skip the visit to the dentist. When he reached the front door, he forsook the blanket and charged barefoot and bare-chested outside. And there, he saw just what he was looking for. It was a good thing he would be impervious to the cold, despite how little the duplicate was wearing. When he heard Noah again behind the closed front door, he charged toward a sheet of ice on the ground and went sliding, coming to a very abrupt stop on his head.

~

"Well, Commander, I would say that is a good job, well done." Captain Spikey Moonbeam took a moment to admire their completed project. True, the thing they had just built was intended to serve Lizard Face and plunge Staranana back into an era of slavery, but nonetheless, completing a project always made him feel good. The *Fire Cruiser* now had a fully Cosmic Bubble-compatible grappling claw attached to its belly.

Commander Honeytub said, "Sir, I know it has been a long night, and I gave you a hard time. You probably want to grab some sleep, but if you're up to it, I'd like to buy you dinner, or eh, breakfast, depending on your point of view."

Spikey smiled, "Thank you, Sam. I'd appreciate that. But actually, I've been drinking honeysuckle apple cider all night. I'll be wired for a while. Hopefully, I can catch a few hours of sleep before we head back to Staranana, but right now, I have something else in mind. I could use your help."

"Of course, sir, anything."

"Well, first, I want to go check on Gloria, but then I would like to look up my grandparents. You wouldn't be able to help, would you?"

"I don't remember meeting them, but we can easily look them up in the population database."

"Captain Noble told me they moved away from the Capital some years ago."

"It doesn't matter. They'll still be listed in the database. Why don't you go check on your wife? Then meet me back here, and I'll have a transport ready to take us to whatever biosphere your grandparents are currently living in."

"That is certainly very generous of you."

"Consider it just another part of my very humble apology for everything I put you through last night."

"Gosh, you save a guy's life, and suddenly, he's your best friend!"

Honeytub said, "You had best get moving, Captain. We don't have much time left."

"Right, well, thank you, Commander."

"Don't mention it."

~

"Let me guess, not good news." Dr. Gloria Moonbeam had been leaning over microscopes and burying herself in simulated experiments for hours. Now she looked up at Dr. Grizz who held the latest test results in his hands.

"All negative. It would be more helpful if we had actual blood samples and not just computer scans."

"Somehow, I doubt even that would help. How do you stop an infection that has its roots in Hell itself?"

"Maybe we should be thinking less like doctors, and more like ministers."

"How do we do that? Hold a prayer vigil? We've already got a bunch of people doing that back on Staranana. But the bottom line is, this is a physical infection. It should have a physical cure."

"You know, maybe we are looking at this the wrong way altogether?"

"You just said as much," Gloria sighed. Though Dr. Grizz was a brilliant physician, she was beginning to see that he had the problem of stating the obvious. Once more, they had now worked all through the night and come up with nothing. All she wanted to do was collapse on her soft feather bed back at home. This cure was going to take years to find if it could be found at all.

"No, I mean, we've spent all this time looking at computer simulated samples of infected tissue, but not once have we looked at samples of cured tissue."

"But there is no cur…OH! How could we have been so stupid? God cured hundreds of bears on Staranana three months ago. I took blood tests from all of them, but I never thought of using their blood in the development of a cure. Honestly, I didn't think I'd see another goon in my lifetime."

"Can you access your data from here?"

"Yes, I'll set up a datalink. But this may just be another wild goose chase. Maybe God and God alone can cure this thing."

"For the sake of the three hundred Stararockans who were *goonified* on the *Dragon's Blood*, I hope the Lord allows us to find the cure."

"I couldn't agree more."

"Am I interrupting?" Gloria and Grizz turned to see Spikey standing in the entryway to the lab. He looked a little sheepish, almost as if he were afraid to step inside. Spikey would never admit it to Gloria, but her job gave him the creeps. Oh, sure, he could deal with battles and blood, but when it came to surgery and everything else doctors had to do, he became rather queasy. His trips to Gloria's hospital, simply to visit her, could be counted on one hand.

"Not at all, honey," Gloria replied. "In fact, I was just going to make a trip down to the computer room. I noticed the cafeteria is just down the hall from there. Care to join me for a light breakfast?"

Spikey grinned, "I'd love to. Though, I have Commander Honeytub waiting to take me to see my grandparents, so we had best not be long."

Gloria beamed. She was so glad Spikey was going to have the chance to reconnect with his family. She turned to Dr. Grizz, "Will you excuse us?"

"Of course, of course, you two lovebirds be on your way!"

Gloria giggled slightly, then led Spikey out of the room. Spikey said, "He seems like an interesting fellow."

"You have no idea," she whispered, and he didn't quite know whether she meant that as a good thing or a bad thing. "Dr. Grizz is a great doctor, but I am so tired right now. Mostly, I'm tired of seeing his face. I just need a bit of a break."

"How is the cure coming?"

"Well, if having absolutely nothing to show for the last fifteen hours is *coming*, it is coming along nicely."

"That good, huh?"

Gloria rubbed her temples. "Spikey, I'm telling you, it is going to take years to find this cure if we can find it at all. I am going to call up my data on the bears that God already cured, but even starting the analysis will take months. I'm afraid the only hope for the bears on the *Dragon's Blood* is God."

"That's as it should be. If there is going to be a cure, I am sure you'll find it. But you won't find it until God wants you to."

"You're right. So, what are you feeling like this morning?" Both Spikey and Gloria had made their way down to the hospital's cafeteria. Only a few patients, most of them elderly and in bathrobes, were present, but a lovely buffet of fruits and cereals had been set up in the center of the room. Gloria took two hot buns of bread and smeared a green jam on top of them. Then she filled a mug with a thick, purple liquid she hoped would be similar to grape juice. Spikey was reveling in forgotten fruits from his childhood. He filled his plate with several fruits that were the size of oranges, but they were blue, red, and green. Surprisingly, he did not take a cup of honeysuckle apple cider. Rather, he took a tall glass of cold water. He later confessed that he had drank so much cider through the night, he was considering giving it up. Plus, he added that Stararockan water was an experience in and of itself.

Gloria sat at one of many circular tables and asked, "So how did the night go for you?"

"It started off pretty rocky. I was ready to belt Commander Honeytub. But then one of the claw's fingers almost killed him. I saved his life, and he's been a gem ever since. We finished the claw a little while ago. The *Fire Cruiser* is ready when Captain Noble wants to leave."

"Are you looking forward to seeing your grandparents?"

"I think so. Actually, I'm a bit nervous. I was just a cub when I left them, and I was also a criminal. It will definitely be an interesting reunion."

"It'll be fine," Gloria assured, and she squeezed her husband's hand. "I wish I could come with you."

Spikey shook his head and said, "No matter how much or how little you accomplish, your work here is more important. Besides, after all this is over, what do you say we come back with the boys and have a little family vacation? We can bring Scotty too."

"Sounds nice."

"To me too." Spikey leaned across the table and kissed his wife.

Gloria said, "I had best get back to work. See you soon?"

"Count on it!"

~

"Scotty…Scotty, oh, easy now! You've got a fairly nasty bump on the back of your head." Sparkey sat up slowly. He had been lying on the Fields' couch with a hand-knit blanket pulled up over him. Mrs. Fields was pressing a cool cloth on the top of his head.

"What happened?" Sparkey asked, though he knew exactly what had happened. He had fallen on purpose so that he could use any injury as an excuse not to go to the dentist.

"You slipped on some ice and hit your head," Mrs. Fields replied. "What were you doing?"

"Just having a bit of fun with my big brother," Sparkey answered.

"You okay, bro?" a deep voice asked. Sparkey saw Noah, now in his trademark baggy pants and hoodie, standing over him.

The Starananian replied, "Yeah, sorry, Noah. I just wanted to have some fun with you. I don't get to spend much time with you these days."

Noah tousled Sparkey's human hair. "No big, bro. I'm just glad you're okay."

Sparkey pushed himself up further and winced in pain. He hoped his act would be convincing. He said, "Oh, no, the dentist! I'll get ready fast, Mom."

Mrs. Fields pushed him back down on the couch, "You're not going anywhere. I've already called and canceled your appointment. The only thing you are going to do is lie here and watch Christmas movies. If your head still hurts tomorrow morning, I'll take you to the doctor. I don't think you have a concussion, but it never hurts to be cautious."

Sparkey asked, "So, what's on first?"

Noah held up a small, slender box. It was a DVD. The teen said, "How about *Rudolph the Red-Nosed Reindeer?*"

Sparkey laughed, "What kind of stupid name is that?" Then he slapped his hand over his mouth. The way Noah had presented it, the movie was probably one of Scotty's favorites. Of course, TV was nonexistent on Staranana, and Sparkey had never watched one (though he had played video games on the one in Scotty's chambers). Perhaps he should give this *Rudolph* a try.

"I thought it was your favorite Christmas movie?" Noah questioned.

Sparkey corrected, "Oh, yeah, I guess I just hit my head harder than I thought. Go ahead, pop it in."

Noah did so, and before long, the animated reindeer was dancing across the screen. It wasn't exactly an adventure like he was used to, but it was enjoyable. Later, Mrs. Fields brought him some soup and juice. If this was what it was like being sick, it was great!

~

"Your grandparents live in the *Red Fire* biosphere about one hundred kleps from here in the middle of the desert," Commander Samuel Honeytub reported.

"How fast can we get there?" Spikey asked.

"Five minutes sound good?"

"Really, that fast? It would take us at least a few hours to travel that distance on Staranana in a land vehicle, and that is pretty good considering the conditions of most of our roads."

"Well, there are no outside roads on Stararocka, or land vehicles. We'll be taking an inter-sphere shuttle. It's leaving in just about ten minutes. It's a brisk walk from here. Shall we get going?"

Spikey gestured that Honeytub should lead the way, and they headed from the docking bay's control room back out into the main biosphere. The morning hustle and bustle had shuttles and sky trains whizzing overhead, and the pathways were filled with bears. Though he had just walked through all this when he went to see Gloria, Spikey couldn't help but be impressed at the magnificence of the city. There were buildings as tall as Cosmic Bubble Palace, streams of water rushing over red rocks, and streets filled with smiling faces. For all intents and purposes, after twenty-two years, Staranana was his home now, but after seeing the Capital again, Spikey was beginning to feel homesick for Stararocka.

The transport arrived right on schedule, and they were soon zooming across the desert plains. Spikey found himself wishing that Scotty could have been with him. The boy loved astronomy, and visiting Staranana had only intensified that love. These fiery red plains reminded Spikey of pictures of the planet Mercury Scotty had shown him. He hoped the boy would live to have the chance to visit here.

Minutes later, the spires and arc of another dome appeared on the horizon. Honeytub said, "This biosphere is obviously smaller than the Capital. *Red Fire* is mainly a farming community. Only about one percent of the sphere is devoted to the city. The rest is all farmlands."

"How well do the crops grow in the desert sand?" Spikey asked.

"Actually, they brought in a lot of the soil from the jungle areas, and they also discovered that only one hundred meters beneath the surface there is a very fertile soil deposit."

"So my grandparents are farmers now? I honestly don't remember what they did when I was a kid."

"According to the records, your grandfather, Titus, was an environmental biologist by trade. And your grandmother, Naomi, was a veterinarian. They oversaw the health and vitality of all the crops and livestock in their community. That is, until they retired about five years ago. According to the last available records, they still maintain their own twenty-acre farm in the northeastern corner of the biosphere. We'll be docking in the southwestern corner, so it will give you a chance to see the community."

"I'd like that, but we can't take too much time. Now that the claw is ready, I imagine Captain Noble will be prepping to leave."

The transport continued for another minute until the entire biosphere came into view. What it lacked in size, it made up for in natural beauty. The sphere itself had a twenty-klep diameter with the usual white color, communications spires, and ventilation fans. However, behind the dome, stretching beyond sight into the sky, were the most breathtaking rock formations. They shot upward like jagged daggers, piercing space itself. The red dust swirls sifting down through the cliffs dripped like blood from these heavenly blades, and here and there all the way up were crystal deposits of red, green, and blue that glittered like stars in the morning light.

When the transport finally docked, and the hatch hissed open, Spikey was ready to see the rest of the place. The docking center was tiny. In addition to their transport, there were only two others, and a staff of only three bears manned the port. Sam led him out into the biosphere, and Spikey immediately caught the scent of sweet corn. He hadn't had corn since he left Stararocka, so he was surprised he remembered what it smelled like. Fields of the stuff stretched out for acres to the tiny community about a klep away.

"So, if my estimates are correct, it is at least twenty kleps to my grandparents' quarters. You don't expect us to walk all that way, do you?" Spikey asked.

"Of course not, Captain. We'll catch a sky train in the village. Unfortunately, we'll have to walk at least that far."

Honeytub began leading the way down a narrow path right through the middle of the cornstalks. After several minutes, Spikey asked, "Why did they start these corn fields right outside the docking port?"

"Farming is survival here. They have to make use of every square inch of land. Plus, this place isn't exactly a tourist trap. To stay competitive, they have to pump out enough crops for all the other biospheres."

"I guess I understand that. Makes me wonder what it must be like to live and work here. The Capital was overwhelming after all these years, but I have a feeling this place would be even more so. I mean, actually digging into the soil with your own fingers, feeling its dampness and texture, and then seeing the seedlings sprout and grow. It must all be very satisfying."

"You must have some version of farming on Staranana?"

"Yeah, we have greenhouses, and we harvest honeysuckle apples from the wild. Seth also left behind some impressive gardens at the Palace, but it is nothing compared to all this."

"We all have a lot to be proud of on our world. And this is only 500 years' worth of work. Imagine what Staranana could have accomplished if Seth had never come to power, or, at least, never been cursed by Satan."

"It boggles the imagination. Hey, isn't this where we're going?" Spikey asked, pointing to a small, but official looking building at the edge of the local village. They had actually traversed the klep from the docking bay to the village rather quickly. Spikey felt like his blood had been completely replaced with adrenaline. It was a shame he was in the middle of a crisis.

He would have loved to spend a great deal more time reacquainting himself with every wonder this planet had to offer.

"Yeah, that's it," Sam replied. Though the building itself was small, from its roof extended an incredibly long track, similar to that of a roller coaster. The track rose beyond sight toward the high ceiling of the biosphere, looping the entire environment before connecting back at its starting point.

"Let's get tickets," Honeytub said, and he led the way inside.

~

"Don't tell me you found something already?" Gloria asked in shock. A mere ten minutes earlier, her data had arrived from Staranana. Five minutes later, Grizz had entered it into his bio-analysis computer, and now, another five minutes later, he was back in the lab, a smile beaming across his face.

"Well, it's no cure, but it's a start. It's almost as if God encoded this cellular data with a readable computer program. My computer came up with two things. First, only the goons' epidermis is infected. Essentially, beauty, or in this case ugliness, is only skin-deep. The fungus and the mucus sacks that grow on the skin do not infect the subcutaneous tissue. According to the data on the cured bear-goons, the uninfected tissues received a jolt of energy that increased the division of cells to an exponential level. It literally pushed the infection right out of the skin."

"That's one thing. What's the other?"

"The energy also disrupted the synaptic pathways in the brain. In a normal brain, it would cause a complete wipe of the short-term memory. I can't verify this, but I suspect *goonieness* alters the short-term memory storage centers of the brain. The pheromone that causes temporary insanity can't genetically alter the brain to create its own memory banks, so it suppresses the long-term memory and expands the short-term memory to act as a long-term memory. But if those banks are wiped, and the pheromone is forced out of the body, the victim's brain will rewire itself according to its original genetic coding, and the victim's long-term memory will return."

Gloria smiled, "So we do have a cure? I didn't realize your computer could do all that! This is great!"

"Uh, I hate to burst your bubble, but my computer only got that because, like I said, the cell samples have been encoded with information. I believe God wanted us to find it. Unfortunately, what He didn't want us to find is the type of energy that was used. There is no data to determine if it was electrical, biochemical, or even radiation. My guess is that it is unique to Heaven. We're still a long way from a cure."

Gloria stood, "Doctor, what are you doing for the next few days?"

"I'm on duty here. Why?"

"Because I need you to come with me. There might just be a type of energy that can get the job done, but I'll need your help and Spikey's too."

"What kind of energy?"

"I'll explain on the way. We need to get to the *Fire Cruiser*."

~

"All right, I can do this." Spikey stood before the front door of a small country cottage, the likes of which had never been seen on Staranana, and it was surprising to see here. Everyone in the Capital lived in cookie-cutter apartments. There were no houses, but this one was beautiful. The wood was finely milled, and it was painted sky blue, save the trim of the roof, which was white. There were Stararocka's famous green roses hanging in pots from a log deck, as well as a porch swing. On the front door was a sign that read simply, *"Welcome to our home. May God bless it and you!"*

Spikey lingered, his hands trembling, and Honeytub said, "You know, if you want to talk with them, you're going to have to knock."

Spikey rubbed the back of his neck, "Yeah, um, Commander, thanks for all your help, but would you mind heading back without me? I'd kind of like to do this by myself."

Honeytub nodded, "No problem. I'll see you back at the Capital. God bless."

"Thanks," Spikey smiled. Honeytub wandered away, and Spikey took a deep breath. All right, this was it. He just hoped that twenty-two years and over five million kleps of space wouldn't change the way they felt about him. He knocked.

Someone beyond the door grumbled something inaudible. Though Spikey could have sworn it had something to do with having to get up so early in the morning *to answer the blasted door.* When the door opened, Spikey's eyes filled with tears.

Standing there, slightly hunched, fur flaked with gray, and a pair of dirty spectacles halfway down his snout, was Titus Moonbeam. "Well, what do you want?" the elder Moonbeam asked.

Spikey wiped his eyes. "You don't recognize me, do you?"

"Should I?"

Spikey was slightly disappointed when he said, "Well, yeah, I'm…"

"Oh, no, not another one of those environmental biology majors. Look, son, I told the last professor who sent one of you my way I'm not…"

"Sir, I'm thirty years old, and honestly, I've never set foot inside a university or college. I'm not a student. I'm your grandson."

Titus's eyes grew wide and he gasped, "Spikey?"

"Yeah, Granddad, it's me!"

Spikey wasn't sure what would happen next. He thought maybe a hug or a shout of joy. Instead, Titus disappeared inside the house without another word. Spikey felt more than a little awkward just standing on the porch, but he didn't know if he should go inside. This was not the home he knew, and maybe these were not the grandparents he had known. They had obviously gotten on with their lives without him. At one time, Spikey had even been angry that his grandparents hadn't come to Staranana to find him. He didn't know at the time that Stararockan law forbade it. No one could assist a criminal in such a way that it might lessen the intensity of their punishment. Laws like that were among Stararocka's few evident flaws. Since technically Stararockans were of Starananian descent, that put them under the authority of the

Blood of the Land. Hopefully Scotty would make it here one day and set things right.

Titus returned a moment later, accompanied by a petite female bear, clearly elderly, but not altogether unattractive. She was wearing a soft white, cotton dress, and a blue apron, perfectly matched with the house. Spikey assumed who she was and was about to introduce himself, but never got his chance. The instant she saw him, she shouted and threw herself at him. Before he knew it, he was locked in a hug. *Now, that's more like it!*

"Uh, hi, I'm…"

"Spikey! Yes, I know, dear one! Let me look at those sweet cheeks."

She proceeded to grab his cheeks, and Spikey managed to say, "You're my Grandma Naomi, I take it?"

"Yes, yes! Oh, I don't blame you for not remembering. You were so little when they sent you away."

"How long can you stay?" Titus asked, clearly in a better mood, despite having been woken up early.

"Actually, probably only for a few minutes. I'm here on an urgent mission. Scotty – *the Blood of the Land* – was kidnapped by Lizard Face. My wife and I are here trying to help rescue him."

The expressions on the elder Moonbeams' faces transformed from joy to concern, and Naomi said, "Come, let's go inside and talk a bit."

"Okay, but really, it can't be long. I imagine everyone is getting back to the *Fire Cruiser* by now. Gloria and I are planning a trip back here soon, once Scotty is safe again."

Titus said, with a bit of gruffness in his voice, "We'd love to get reacquainted as much as you would, Spikey, but there is something more important you have to hear. It concerns your rescue mission."

Spikey furrowed his brow, "What?"

"Come inside. We'll explain," urged Naomi.

Spikey was confused, but he complied. They all went inside, and Spikey was met with the sweet aroma of baking apple pie and flowers. The house was simple, with a small living room decorated with antique vases and a tan loveseat draped by a patchwork quilt. The kitchen was adjacent to the living room with only an island countertop separating the two rooms. A hallway beyond the two rooms led back to what appeared to be the only bedroom in the house.

Titus and Naomi pulled chairs from the kitchen table and gestured for Spikey to sit on the loveseat. When they were all seated, Titus began, "You need to know something about Lizard Face."

"How do you know about Lizard Face?" Spikey asked.

"He is over 2,000 years old. That was long before our ancestors left Staranana. People still tell horror stories about him that have been passed down through the generations," Naomi said.

"So what is it you have to tell me?" Spikey asked.

"It has to do with his origins, and why he has lived so long," Titus explained.

"I'm listening."

Titus went on, "During the first three thousand years of Seth's reign, he held dominion over the people through intimidation and a little satanic assistance. When it was first created, Staranana had a moon. At the beginning of Seth's reign, a demonic horde went to the moon and blew it apart. As a result, Staranana's orbit was shifted."

"I know all this. That is why Staranana is more or less a winter wonderland eleven months of the year."

"Yes, but at the time, Seth's space travel ability was eliminated – at least temporarily. The moon could not have been destroyed without the demons."

"So, what does this have to do with Lizard Face? As you pointed out, he didn't come around for another three thousand years."

"Spikey, you never change. You were such an impatient little cub as I recall," Naomi scolded.

"Why do you think I became an inventor? I like making things happen faster than they might otherwise. I mean, it got the *Blood of the Land* to Staranana. Impatience can't be all bad."

Titus smirked and continued, "As you know, Staranana exists in what you might call a different time continuum than the Earth. For most of its history, time has moved more quickly on Staranana than it has on Earth. In fact, according to ancient records smuggled off the planet when the first Stararockans left, at one point nearly a million years passed on Staranana when only about one thousand passed on Earth. Our scientists have never been able to figure out exactly why. Now, some temporal differential remains, but it is less severe."

"Yes, I know, we've observed that since Scotty came to us. Though as long as he is with us and his duplicate is online, the times of our two worlds seem to be bridged. When Scotty's duplicate recently went offline, we saw that time more or less freezes on Earth."

Titus continued, "Be that as it may, our scientists discovered the differentials between our two time streams have become increasingly more synchronized in recent centuries."

"How could they know that?"

"They measured it using temporal scans of Earth."

"What! Uh…we'll get back to the temporal scans thing in a minute. What I want to know is how you know where Earth is? No astronomer on Staranana has ever located any planet that matches its description. Even my *Door's* scanners only found it by chance. How did you find it?"

"One of the many advantages of not being hindered by Seth. The original colonists brought data from the library at Stony City. Part of that data described the journey the original Staranananians made to Earth to collect DNA samples. It included the coordinates of the planet. The long-range telescopes on the *Fire Cruiser* ships are able to detect it. Earth is one thousand light years from Staranana."

"All right, I'll buy that. And that explains why no Staranananian has ever located it. Stony City was destroyed centuries ago, and its library along with it. But let's get back to that temporal scanners thing, and while we're on the subject, how do two farmers have all this scientific data?" Spikey asked. He wasn't exactly suspicious. After all, these were his only living blood relatives (with the exceptions of his sons). But their knowing all this did seem a bit odd.

"Your grandmother and I are students more than farmers, especially since we retired. And all the information we have shared with you is a matter of public record. Temporal scanning is not as advanced as it sounds. You do a few computations with distance, gravity, and planetary rotation, and you can usually get the data you're after. But please, Spikey, hear me because this story is far more important. For three thousand years, the demons helped Seth wage war with the bears. They wrestled dragons into his service and all but obliterated the entire Starananian population. Then, with no explanation, for a period of time about 2,000 years ago, all the demons on Staranana simply vanished. Seth was left with only his dragons to contend with the bears. Some demon hordes did eventually return centuries later in the decades leading up to the Nimbus invasion and Seth's 50-year exile in that solar system. However, upon his return, the goons replaced the demons as Seth's chief horde. They are cursed version of a race called the Kodi from the Nimbus solar system."

"I know about the goons, but as for the rest, there is no record of any of it left on Staranana that I know of. Did it all come from the libraries of Stony City?"

"Yes, in its day, Stony City was the pride of the bears. It was well protected and productive. It probably only survived as long as it did because its distance from the Palace made it an inconvenient target. Lizard Face tried once with an army of mongrel dragons, but he was stopped by our ancestor Splash and a young dragon tamer named Rys Noble."

"I remember the story. But back to the demons; do you have any idea what happened to them"

"They left."

"Obviously, but why?"

"Can you think of no reason?" Naomi interjected. "Come on, think, Spikey. What was important about 2,000 years ago?"

Spikey scanned his brain, but try as he might, he could think of nothing. There had been minor skirmishes back then, but no mass killings or anything that merited more than a footnote in Staranana's obviously incomplete historical texts. What could it be?

"I'll give you a clue," Titus said. "It has nothing to do with Staranana or Stararocka."

Spikey smacked his forehead. How could he have been so stupid? Scotty and Garlan would have been very disappointed in him. He said, "That is approximately the time when Jesus Christ was on Earth."

"Yes! That's it!" Naomi clapped her hands.

Titus continued, "I believe the human expression is *the gloves were off* at that time between God and Satan. With Christ working toward human salvation, Satan and his minions no longer had time to mess around with Staranana. Seth was frustrated and angry that he was being abandoned by his god, and for some unknown reason, Satan, the father of lies, made a covenant with him. First, he gave Seth some of his own power, so that Seth might curse any that did not know God. And second, he created a horrific beast you have come to know as Lizard Face."

"How did he do that?" Spikey asked.

"It's ghastly even to think of," Naomi said. "Satan instructed a demon to mate with a dragon. From that hellish mix came six eggs. The first hatchling to emerge was already strong and filled with evil. It crushed the other five eggs. Seth was pleased with this, and he took the hatchling as his own *son*. He trained it to be lord over all dragons, and though it never grew any larger than Seth himself, it was a powerful master for the beasts. Over time, the father/son relationship fell apart. Even so, the hatchling, whom you know as Lizard Face, became Seth's second-in-command."

"That explains a lot about him, but how is it relevant to my mission?"

Titus said, "The fact that he has dragon and demon blood means he is virtually immortal. He will die one day, but at the rate things are going, that may not be until Jesus returns to Earth. And because Seth raised him, he sees himself as the rightful heir to the throne. You may get Scotty back, but Lizard Face will not stop until he kills the boy and reclaims Staranana."

"What can I do?"

"For starters don't let him have the Bubble."

"Boy, you know about that too?"

"Trust me, Spikey," Titus assured, "if there is one thing Stararockans know, it is how to keep a secret. We share information freely with each other, but it never leaves this world if it is considered classified."

"Well, let me assure you, we have no intention of giving him the Bubble."

"That's good for the short term, but if you want to stop him once and for all, you must destroy him, and by destroy, I mean *destroy*. There can be nothing left of him; not one cell of his body, not one strand of DNA can survive. At the very least, his people will clone him, but more likely, Satan will reanimate his carcass with a demon far eviler than he is now. If Scotty is to survive, Lizard Face must die."

Spikey took a deep breath at that. He had killed before in the war, but he still didn't like thinking about it. Lizard Face didn't have an ounce of good in him, but he was no Seth, and he had never been as hated as the former emperor. Spikey said, "If we are going to kill him, the best way would be to blow up the *Dragon's Blood*, but that would mean sacrificing the crew."

"As grim as it sounds, do what you have to do, Spikey. You can't put Scotty at further risk."

Across the room, the elder Moonbeams' computer terminal chirped. Titus rose and tapped the terminal control. He then spoke into it, and a voice from the other side responded, but Spikey couldn't make out what it said. Titus turned back to his grandson and said, "It is a Commander Honeytub. He says Captain Noble is ready to get underway."

"Please tell him I'm on my way," Spikey replied.

Titus did so, and then he rejoined his wife and grandson. They all stood, and the silence was awkward for a moment. Finally, Spikey said, "I'm sorry I couldn't stay longer."

Naomi smiled and apologized, "We're sorry our conversation had to be about something so dire."

"It's okay; we'll have other conversations. I promise," Spikey grinned. Then he hugged them. Even after all these years, it felt so good to be back in their arms again. Naomi was sniffling by the time he finally let go. He shook Titus's hand, then turned and left. It was time to go home.

Chapter 20
Escape Attempt

"*I*t's taken all night to fashion this rope, TB. It had better work."

"*It will work. Now, are you ready?*"

Scotty felt the long, greasy piece of fabric in his hands. He gave it a few good yanks. It felt strong enough, but his tiny, nine-year-old muscles didn't present it with much of a challenge. The real question would be, could it hold his weight? It had been hours since Joshua left, and TB had said the trapdoor needed to remain closed until they were ready to leave. Leaving it open too long might have set off some sort of alarm. As such, fashioning the rope and a grappling hook of bones had been quite the challenge in the dark. But now, finally, they were ready to give it a try.

"*Okay, TB, let's do this. Open the door.*" The trapdoor whooshed open, and Scotty squinted at the light that washed over him. He gripped the rope in his hands and asked, "*Can you tell if there is anyone around?*"

"*My brain scanners aren't picking up anything, but be careful.*"

"*I will,*" Scotty replied. Then he began to spin the rope over his head. Its arc became wider and wider, and, in the back of the cell, the still moaning Blackie had to duck to avoid being hit. Finally, Scotty released the rope to fly up through the trapdoor. The skeletal grappling hook landed, and there was the distinct scraping sound of bone scraping on stone. Scotty gave the rope one final yank and said, *"I think it's secure. Let's go."*

He pulled himself up inch by inch, only slipping a few times on the greasy and rank rags of the rope. He was glad Sparkey had gotten him into rock climbing. He just hoped he would see his friend again. After only a few moments, he reached the top.

"We're out, TB. Now what?"

"We need to get to that docking port I told you about. The passageway should be somewhere on this floor. We just have to find it and then head down."

"Before we do that, I need some sort of weapon."

"We don't have time to search for a sword, Scotty."

"If there is one thing I learned from my treks through the aqueducts, it's that the weapon doesn't have to be complex to be effective. Look, there is a table over there. I'll just break off one of the legs. That should work well."

"All right, but get it done fast. We have to go!"

Scotty nodded and grabbed hold of the tiny table that was sitting up against the hall wall. He then smashed it along the edge of the trapdoor so that the remains fell back into the pit. He was left with a single, slender, but strong table leg with a twisted nail extending from its head. *"I'd like to see a goon mess with me now,"* Scotty chuckled.

"Yeah, yeah, now get going!"

Scotty rolled his eyes, *"You know, you can be so demanding!"*

"Scotty, I…"

"Okay, I'm going!" He held his makeshift club at the ready and started down the hall. Thanks to the several trips he had made back and forth from the cell, he at least knew his way back to the main chamber. Getting to the subterranean docking port would be another challenge altogether.

He asked, *"TB, when we first got here, you said you could use a transmitter to contact the Door and have it open to take us home. Wouldn't that be easier than stealing a ship?"*

"Don't think I haven't tried with all my trips through the palace. I can't gain access to their transmitters. Plus, I remember reading something about a Door repulsion field in the minds of the goons that were guarding

us on the Dragon's Blood. I'm willing to bet they have something similar in place here."

"Dang! Well, did anything you scanned from the computers tell you how to get down to the port?"

"Unfortunately, it did. There is a security checkpoint leading to a tunnel on the other side of the main chamber."

"Well, that should be easy to get by," said Scotty sarcastically. *"Is there any kind of ventilation shaft, or something we could sneak through?"*

"None near enough to let us into the tunnel."

Having moved all the way down the hallway, Scotty stepped to the edge of the main chamber and said, *"There has to be some way to get in. Maybe I can find a goon cloak and disguise myself."*

"Like they would ever fall for that! Most goons are twice as tall as you are."

"You know, Sparkey is a lot more supportive during a crisis. He usually likes my ideas!"

"Well, Sparkey…"

"WAIT!" Scotty exclaimed, still inside his head.

"WHAT! What?" TB shrieked.

"It is so obvious! Why didn't you think of it?"

"Listen, you…" TB protested.

Scotty interrupted him, *"TB, you can speak into people's minds and scan people's brains. Can you affect what people see and hear?"*

"I've never tried, at least, not beyond creating a complete mental environment like I did with you on the Dragon's Blood. This would be altogether different. I suppose I could send a disruption signal into their visual cortex. That would disrupt the optical signal to their brain. Then I could just transmit my own images, but why?"

"TB, all you have to do is make the guard think it's a goon he's speaking with. Then he'll let us by."

"But I'm pretty sure you need a clearance code to get through there. How are you going to manage that?"

"You said you had the clearance code to one of the ships. Can't we just use that?"

"It's a risk. If the code doesn't work, but the guard finds out you have security clearance for one of the ships, he is likely to kill you no matter what you look like."

"Well, aren't we Mister Sunshine?"

"Scotty, this is serious."

"After all I…we…have been through, don't you think I know that this is serious? I guess the only solution is that we make the guard think that I am someone who should be granted access without a code."

"Who would that be?"

"Why, Lizard Face, of course!"

"Scotty, you can't…"

"TB, just do it!"

~

"Wake up, Ensign!"

The young goon dozing at his post jumped at the sound of the agitated voice. When he looked up into the masked face of his superior, he snapped to attention, "My apologies, Lt. Clak. It's been a slow night."

"We've just executed the Emperor of Staranana, Lord Lizard Face is preparing for an invasion, and the goon people are on the verge of being replaced, and you think this night has been slow?"

The ensign apologized further, "I merely meant, sir, that no one has needed access to the docking port."

"Yes, well, it's morning now, and I'm here to relieve you."

"Thank you, Lieutenant," the ensign piped and stood up to leave.

Clak took hold of his arm as he was moving away. "You're a clone aren't you, Ensign?" Clak asked.

The young goon nodded, almost shamefully. Clak said, "Don't be ashamed. I'm one too. Just be careful. This is not going to be a good time for our people. The Master is convinced that his new soldier will ensure his victory. He sees the clones as a failed experiment. If we are to survive, we must prove ourselves."

The ensign dared to ask, "How long are we going to have to put up with this?"

"Until we're killed, or the bears kill Lizard Face."

"Not very pretty choices."

"There is nothing about being a goon that is pretty. Now, go get some sleep."

The ensign nodded, and Clak sat down at his post. There wasn't much to it, an old wooden stool backed up against the wall and a computer terminal. A simple accordion fence sealed the passage beyond, which led to the subterranean docking port. Usually, no more than four or five goons went to the docking port per day. The ships had been set up as escape pods for the palace, so usually, only maintenance teams went down to them.

Clak settled in and entered his login code. He then began reviewing the previous few nights' entries. He became so involved that he did not notice someone walking up to his station.

"Um-hum!" the visitor growled.

Clak was about to look up, but a sharp pain shot through his head. He grabbed his temples and managed to take in a fuzzy pink image before he closed his eyes. When he opened them again, *Lizard Face* was standing in front of him.

"Master, my apologies!"

"Great job, TB. It's working."

"Yeah, now hurry up and make him open the fence. I can't keep this up forever. It is causing considerable strain on his brain. Unless he threatens you, I'd rather not kill him."

"Agreed. Don't worry, I'll get us in."

Scotty, with his best imitation of Lizard Face's voice, asked, "Are you all right, Lieutenant?"

"Yes, sir. I just had this sudden sharp pain in my head. I'm sure it will pass. How can I help you, Master?"

Scotty continued, "With the human dead, I am interested in how the *Sso sships* might help us invade *Sstaranana*. The *Dragon's Blood* will provide the firepower, but we will need to land troops and have access to information to *ssubdue* the people. The *Sso sships* will provide that."

Clak was rubbing his temples incessantly, but he said, "Of course, sir. I'll open the gate."

"Wouldn't you like my access code, Lieutenant?"

"That is–ah-owe!" Clak stumbled, the pain in his head nearly unbearable.

Scotty asked, "Can I get you *ssome* help, Lieutenant?"

"Scotty, no! Lizard Face would never ask that!"

"Well, I can't just kill him like Lizard Face would, and besides, we're the ones causing his pain."

Clak didn't seem to notice his *Master's* generosity. He merely said, "Begging your pardon, sir, I'll open the gate for you without your code if that is permissible. I don't think I could see well enough to enter it anyway."

"Very well. Please proceed, Lieutenant."

Clak managed to get the key in the lock. He turned it, and then he pushed the two halves of the accordion fence apart. Scotty stepped through and said, "Thank you, Lieutenant. I hope you feel better."

Clak nodded and returned to his station. As *Lizard Face* moved down the tunnel, the pain in his head began to ebb. Soon his vision came back into focus. He punched the communication pad on his terminal, "Lt. Clak to Lt. Gakic, please report to the docking tunnel access station. We have an intruder in the tunnels!"

~

"What is it?" General Henry Shortstop asked. He was staring at a strange mechanical spider with a single red eye on the front of its half-spherical body. Toby, Cak, and Berry had managed to capture the former clock before it could escape from the Moonbeam apartment. It was now being restrained by two steel bars that were screwed into the tabletop of the conference room. Shortstop and Speedway were back from their excursion to Cololot and were waiting to be briefed.

Chef Berry took the initiative and explained, "General, this is your spy."

"Really? That's interesting. And why are you involved in this investigation?" Shortstop asked. He liked Berry, but when it came to Palace security, he didn't like putting the job in the hands of a civilian.

"Well, you see, Gen…" Berry began.

"It's our fault, General!" Toby broke in and confessed. "Our first investigation led us to believe that Chef Berry was the guilty party. I am afraid we arrested him before we had all the facts. Later, when we got more evidence, we released him, and he agreed to help us with our investigation. We are willing to take whatever consequences you feel would be appropriate, sir."

The General rubbed his furry chin. To be honest, the whole thing was rather comical. He could just imagine these two foolhardy teens jumping on Berry and slapping him in the dungeon. In addition, he was still on cloud nine over what had happened in Cololot. He had no real desire to punish them right now. Berry probably wanted their commissions revoked, or at least suspended. That was out of the question, but he had to at least do something. Then a very delicious idea came to his mind.

He squared his shoulders and addressed the boys formally, "Ensigns Toby and Cak Nakan, I hereby sentence you to wait until December 26th to open your Christmas presents."

"What!" Berry exclaimed, but Toby and Cak were ecstatic.

Shortstop turned to Berry, "And you, Mr. Berry, I sentence you to learn what it means to have the Christmas spirit. In short, you need to forgive them. Yes, what they did was wrong, but they only did it because they care about Scotty, and right now, he is all that matters. Now, you should set your focus back on the party. I suggest you get back to your kitchen."

Berry was dumbstruck, but he nodded and excused himself. Shortstop had to smile. Had he been in Berry's place, he would have probably felt the same way, but there was no time for hurt feelings right now. He turned back to the teens, "So, tell me about this thing."

Cak continued, "I've been analyzing it for the last several hours. It has a sonic defense system, which I imagine is similar but not as intense as the virus. Needless to say, I disabled, or rather, I destroyed it."

"Yeah, he stabbed it with a screwdriver!"

Cak shot Toby a cold glance, but went on, "Anyway…humph…the device is a combination scanner/computer/transmitter. It also has the ability to create a particle duplicate of whatever it wants around its circuitry, so it can become whatever it wants."

"Where did it come from?" Speedway asked. "I thought only the *Door* could create particle duplicates?"

"Lizard Face is the chief suspect," Cak said.

"I don't think even Lizard Face has that kind of technology. Even if he did steal the *Door* schematics, this thing would have to have been in place before he did it," Shortstop speculated.

"With all due respect, General," Toby put in, "that virus was beyond Lizard Face's capabilities too. He must be getting advanced technology from somewhere else."

"Hopefully we'll find out where that *somewhere* is soon. In the meantime, what else can you tell me about this device?" Shortstop inquired.

Cak went on, "Only that we would be fools to believe it is the only one in the Palace. I think that with the data from my analysis, we can reprogram our scanners to search for them. The Palace needs to be fumigated, so to speak."

Shortstop sighed, "Is this thing still transmitting?"

"To be honest, I don't know. I disconnected what looked like a battery, but this is alien technology. It could still pose a threat."

"Then we have no choice," Shortstop surrendered and turned to Speedway. "Colonel, begin evacuating the Palace. We'll leave behind a skeleton crew to start searching for these things."

"What about your trip, General?" Toby asked.

Shortstop held a finger to his lips and whispered, "I'd rather not talk about that here. We'll continue this conversation aboard the *Zerubbabel*. Have all the bears go to the meeting cave in the Nana Forest. Tell them to watch out for any animal or object that they suspect might be a spider probe in disguise."

Speedway said, "We only have four hours until the *Fire Cruiser* should be back. The evacuation process will take longer than that."

"I know, but the less information these things get the better. Now, get going!"

Speedway headed out, and the rest of them made their way up to the roof and the *Zerubbabel*. Those who were to remain behind included Colonel Speedway, Cak, Dr. Nova, and a handful of others. Chef Berry was also permitted to stay, but he was to be in either his kitchen or his quarters or in route to either one. The rest of the bears evacuated surprisingly orderly and quietly. It would have made any overseer of a fire drill very proud. It only took a whisper of treachery to switch their survival instincts, which had helped them survive during Seth's reign, back on. Despite Speedway's estimation, within an hour and a half the Palace was evacuated.

~

"You have to be kidding, sir!" Toby exclaimed. He and General Shortstop were now hovering over the Palace in the *Zerubbabel*.

"No, I'm telling you, it was the most amazing experience of my life. The Phoenix City, they call it Cololot, was breathtaking, and the phoenixes themselves were…well…amazing!"

"And they just let you take the knobs off of Emperor Iren's coffin?"

"Yes, once Spikey gets back, we can install the *fire glass*. I just hope this scheme works."

"How do you plan to get the Bubble off the Palace?" Toby asked.

Shortstop pointed out the window to the massive pink glass dome that rested on top of the Palace. The bottom half of the sphere extended down inside of the Palace to the 95th story, making the entire Bubble ten stories in diameter. Extended over the top of the Bubble was a curved beam that stretched from one side of the roof to another. Shortstop explained, "Inside the Palace, the bottom of the Bubble rests inside a transparent fiberglass dish. However, only that beam secures the top. It should be fairly easy to remove. I just hope the bolts aren't rusty after all these centuries."

Another hour passed, and Colonel Speedway contacted the *Zerubbabel*, *"We've searched and scanned the Palace, General. There weren't any other spider probes."*

"Are you sure?"

"Positive, sir. Unfortunately, we had to break a few things we suspected, but take my word for it, sir, the Palace is clean. We know the first one was mobile. Lizard Face probably didn't want to risk sending any more. Oh, and, General, the Fire Cruiser has made contact. They'll be in orbit in another hour-and-a-half."

"Very good, Colonel. Signal everyone that they can come back to the Palace, and then meet us on the roof. We have work to do."

~

"Which one, TB?" Scotty asked. He was staring at six circular hatchways. Each was metallic with a single circular window at its center. Next to each hatchway, embedded in the stone, was a numerical keypad.

"It should be the fourth ship. The code is 7668921."

Scotty stepped up to the appropriate hatch, punched in the code, and to his great relief, the hatch hissed and then slid open. He was just stepping over the threshold when an alarm sounded, and the lights in the stone corridor transformed into blood red.

"What's going on?" Scotty screeched, forgetting to speak inside his head.

"You must have tripped some sort of alarm. We might as well expect company pretty soon. Quick, get inside and get that ship fired up!"

"I assume you know how to do that?"

"Well…uh, I'll figure it out. Now go!"

~

"What do you mean there is an intruder in the tunnels?" Lt. Gakic asked.

"A few minutes ago, Lord Lizard Face asked to be admitted to the tunnels. The strange thing was, the instant he approached me, I had this overwhelming headache. I can't explain it. When I expressed my pain, he asked if he could help me. When was the last time you heard Lizard Face offer to help a clone? Killing us means nothing to him now that he has the *Goon Omega*."

"That is odd, but you said you saw him. Who else could it have been but him?"

"I don't know. The human boy is dead. Maybe it was the *Goon Omega*."

Gakic shook his head and said, "Perhaps, but Lizard Face left him on the *Dragon's Blood* last I heard. The exchange is in less than twenty hours. I wonder if perhaps…?" And then he paused as a dreadful thought entered his mind. Could it perhaps have been the boy's God again? He did, after all, deliver him from the fire and the energy weapon, to say nothing of all He did on Staranana. And if He was somehow behind this, that meant only one thing for Lt. Gakic and his fellow clones.

He addressed Clak, "Contact every clone you can. Have them meet in my quarters immediately."

Clak was confused, "Why, sir?"

"I will explain when I see you there. In the meantime, open the gate."

"You're going down there alone?"

"All alone! Deactivate the alarms and send word to security that the situation is under control."

"But, sir, I can't just lie!"

"Best get used to it! Your life may depend on it. Now, open the gate!"

Clak clearly wasn't happy, but he unlocked the gate. Lt. Gakic withdrew an energy rifle from the locker next to the gate and said, "Twenty minutes, Lieutenant Clak. Have everyone in my quarters in twenty minutes." Then he turned and sprinted down the tunnel.

~

"I can't understand any of this!" Scotty cursed. He was sitting in one of several rather uncomfortable, triangular chairs in the cockpit of the *So* vessel. The controls were a combination of circles, squares, and triangles in various colors. But there was no helm column as there was on the *Zerubbabel*.

And there were also no display monitors, only a bank of flashing lights in every color of the rainbow. Whoever these *So* had been, they were obviously very strange.

Scotty asked, "TB, can you link up with their computers?" He had given up speaking inside his head.

"I already have, but their language is highly complex. It will take me a few seconds to translate it. I just wonder how Lizard Face managed to do it?"

"He used the translation module under the console."

"Thanks, that could be…ah!" Scotty shrieked at the sound of the new voice. He turned to find the heavy, black barrel of a goon rifle pointed at his head. From the goon's size and the sound of his voice, he assumed it was Lt. Gakic.

"I have no idea how you survived again, human, but I assure you, it will be the last time! Get up!"

Scotty lifted his hands slowly away from the control panel, but said inside his head, *"TB, can you do what you did to the other goon to him?"*

"I'll try!"

For a moment, *Gakic* only glared at the human boy as he stood, but then a knife ripped through his brain, or at least, it felt like a knife. The goon dropped his rifle and grasped his head wailing.

Scotty wasted no time. He grabbed his club and slammed it across the goon's back. The clone slumped to the floor with a thud, and Scotty twisted back toward the control panel. He was just about to reach it when he felt his legs pull out from under him, and he too was on the floor. Lt. Gakic had grabbed his leg. Scotty kicked him in his masked face and reached for his club, which had clattered away across the cockpit.

The boy let out a mental wail, *"TB, are you still doing it!"*

"Yes! But he isn't giving up! You were right; he's a fighter!"

"I wish he was a little less of a fighter right now."

Try as he might, Scotty could not reach his club, and *Gakic* was not letting go. In fact, he now had his arms around the boy's waist. Scotty flailed and kicked, but to no avail. *Gakic's* grip was like a vise despite his obvious pain. They wrestled further toward the control panel, and Scotty braced his feet against the base bulkhead and pushed as hard as he could. He and the clone went flying back into the bottom of one of the chairs, and Lt. Gakic finally let go.

Scotty was up and over the chair before *Gakic* had a chance to react. He jumped toward his club hoping to end this fight and launch the ship before more goons showed up, but he never got the chance. Still in mid-jump, his hip caught fire, and he slammed into the deck unable to move his right leg. He twisted his torso to see *Gakic* still lying on the floor, but with his now smoking energy rifle back in his hands.

Scotty slumped back on the floor and breathed heavily. He said, *"TB, I guess God didn't want to save me."*

There was no response.

"TB?"

Still no response!

Scotty felt his bloodied hip in horror. The energy blast had melted his buttons, seared his flesh, and burned that part of his pants so that the three were now melded together. He couldn't get into his pocket. What was most horrifying was that TB had been in his right pocket. The tiny computer had been there ever since Lt. Gakic had broken the necklace. If TB wasn't responding now, that could only mean one thing.

Lt. Gakic stood and leveled his rifle on Scotty. "Get up!"

"I can't!"

Gakic cursed, and then he knelt and grabbed Scotty by the arm. The boy stood with no small amount of pain, but at least his leg still worked. Scotty asked, "Why don't you just kill me? Obviously, your rifle works now!"

Surprisingly, *Gakic* replied, "The time for killing is over."

Scotty wondered what that meant, but *Gakic* did not comment further. Instead, he dragged Scotty back toward the hatch, and the boy did not resist. He limped along in extreme pain, finally surrendering to the fact that getting out of here would take a direct act of God.

As *Gakic* brought him back out into the tunnel, he wailed inwardly one last time, *"TB, please, are you okay?"*

Still no response.

Chapter 21
Goon Medicine

"Let me get this straight; you think the *Door* can cure *goonieness*?" Spikey Moonbeam was more than a little skeptical of his wife's suggestion. They were now all back onboard the *Fire Cruiser* preparing for launch. Including launch time and orbital establishment time at Staranana, the entire trip would take only fifteen minutes. From there, they would have just shy of twenty hours to remove the Bubble from the Palace and then return to the meeting point. As of yet, there had been no word on how things were going back on Staranana, but when Gloria declared that she had a cure, it was the first good news any of them had had all day.

Gloria, along with the Nobles, Spikey, Dr. Grizz, and even Commander Honeytub were in the conference room of the *Fire Cruiser*. Gloria held in her hands an electronic pad, which Spikey had given her. On it were the technical schematics for the *Door*. She explained, "We have learned that God cured the *goonified* bears on Staranana three months ago by subjecting their bodies to a form of holy energy that pushed the infection from their bodies and reestablished their original minds' control over their bodies."

"What exactly does this have to do with *Door* technology?" Captain Noble asked.

Gloria deferred to Spikey, "Spikey, can you tell us how the *Door* functions? Specifically, how is the gateway between locations created?"

Spikey sighed, "Well, the technology generates three types of energy. First tachyons, which are faster than light particles, are used to cut through the fabric of space. It helps if you think of the fabric of space as sand or water. If you put something like a tube through it, the sand or water will make way for it, but if you remove the tube, the water or sand will instantly rush back in and fill the space. So really, no damage is caused to the fabric of space. After that, a stream of beta rays, which are essentially very fast electrons, pulses through the middle of the tachyon field expanding it into a sizable passage. Then the passage is flooded with a form of bio-electric plasma, which allows a biological life form to travel safely through the portal."

Gloria asked, "What would happen if that plasma field was gone and someone went through the passage?"

Spikey answered, "Their bodies would be subjected to harmful radiation. The tachyon radiation would cause their cells to start dividing at an exponential rate. The outer layers of their epidermis would be crushed, only to be replaced instantaneously. The beta radiation would overwhelm the bioelectric systems of their brains, wiping out their short-term memories. The process would be extremely painful."

"But not fatal?" Gloria asked.

"Maybe not on the first trip, but there is no way they could make the trip twice. That's why I originally added the plasma field. What are you getting at, Gloria?"

"Isn't it obvious? What you just described is exactly what is required to force the goon infection out of our people."

"But God healed the bear-goons on Staranana with no ill effects. If you do what you're suggesting, the Stararockan-goons will need massive amounts of time to recover, and likely, they will never be the same again."

"Regardless, this plan will save their lives."

Dr. Grizz broke in, "We still have twenty hours. Maybe we can refine the idea, but I've had a chance to look over the data, and I believe it could work. I am still praying God will do the job, but if He doesn't, it is better to get our friends back damaged than dead."

Captain Noble rubbed his forehead. It wasn't a pretty prospect, but enough people had already died during this crisis.

He didn't want to lose anyone else, and if this plan could save them, he would take it. He said, "Fine, we'll go with it. Gloria, you, Grizz, and Spikey start working on a way to implement it and get those people back safe and more or less sound."

"We'll have to install *Door* technology on the *Fire Cruiser*. Assuming you have the components and the engineers, I can have a *Door* online for you by the deadline," Spikey said.

"Good, set it up in one of the cargo bays. We can lock them down, and if necessary, vent them into space in case there is trouble," Captain Noble suggested.

"Good idea, but let's hope there is no trouble," Gloria quipped.

Noble asked, "Spikey, I believe you had a report?"

Spikey replied, "Yes, my grandparents were able to give me a very disturbing report about Lizard Face. Essentially, we are not dealing with a normal being here. He was bred through a satanic mesh of dragon and demon blood. That is why he has lived so long. My grandparents warned that we must destroy him utterly and completely. Otherwise, there will be no end to the trouble he will cause, and Scotty will always be a target."

"The only way to do that is to destroy the *Dragon's Blood*," Josh Noble put in.

Will nodded, "Very well. Josh, go up to the bridge and take us to battle stations. Prepare a tactical scenario of how we can best destroy the *Dragon's Blood*. Have a report ready for me within the hour."

"Aye, sir!" Josh piped, then he got up and left.

Captain Noble turned back to the rest of them, "Here is the game plan, people. Commander Honeytub, you'll remain onboard to operate the claw. Dr. Grizz and the Moonbeams, you'll begin immediate work on your plan to cure the bear-goons. Spikey, as of this moment, I am putting you in charge of the engineering section. Use all the resources you need to create a *Door*. I'll see you all when we get to Staranana. Dismissed."

~

"Haven't you people ever heard about elevators?" Scotty

complained. *Gakic* had dragged him up the palace stairs, and with every step he took, it was like a new fire erupted on his skin. *Gakic* did not answer him, so he asked, "Where are you taking me?"

To that, the goon replied, "To my quarters."

"Why?"

"Because the time for deception is over."

Scotty wanted to know what that meant, but never got the chance. Lt. Gakic pulled him off the stairs around the twentieth story. Scotty continued to limp down the hall, and then the last person he expected to see appeared from around the corner. Judging from his reaction, Lt. Gakic wasn't expecting to see him either.

"L—Lord Lizard Face, what are you doing here?" *Gakic* asked. Lizard Face was there along with another goon. Scotty soon learned it was the original Gakic.

"I have a better question! Why is he *sstill* alive?" Lizard Face hissed.

"I don't know. I found him in a *So* ship trying to escape. I shot him, and my rifle worked this time."

"Where were you taking him?" asked Captain Gakic.

Lt. Gakic hesitated and replied, "Uh, to Master Lizard Face, of course."

"Really, because you are nowhere near his quarters." Captain Gakic had his hand on his weapon, but Lt. Gakic quickly recovered.

"With all due respect, I know what I am doing, Captain. It just so happens I was heading to my quarters to meet with several of the clones first. It seems that my scans of the alien computer yielded something useful that might be of value in the current mission."

"Indeed," Lizard Face perked up. "Well, we have discovered *ssomething* too." He turned to Captain Gakic, "Take the boy and complete your orders, and then dispose of him. I will take the *Dragon's Blood* to the meeting point."

"What are you going to do to him this time?" asked Lt. Gakic.

"That doesn't concern you, clone," Captain Gakic snapped.

Lt. Gakic was chagrined, but he said nothing. Captain Gakic pulled Scotty away back toward the stairs, and he was far rougher than the Lieutenant had been.

Lizard Face addressed Lt. Gakic, "Please proceed to your meeting, Lieutenant. Let me know what you find out." Then, the lizard headed for the stairs himself.

Lt. Gakic continued toward his quarters. When he arrived, he entered the access code and stepped inside. Clak and a dozen other clones were waiting for him. Clak asked, "Okay, Lieutenant, what is this all about?"

Lt. Gakic took a deep breath and said, "It's about being on the right side."

Chapter 22
Preparations

General Henry Shortstop was beginning to despise the conference room, but hopefully, this would be the last time he would have to be there until this crisis was over. All the major players, with the exceptions of Scotty, TB, and Sparkey, were present. Will and Josh Noble were there. As were Spikey and Gloria, Dr. Grizz, Captain Hull, Commander Honeytub, Colonel Speedway, Toby and Cak Nakan, and even Chef Berry had been invited. The *Fire Cruiser* had returned about five hours earlier, leaving fifteen hours until the deadline. Currently, the ship and the claw were in a stationary orbit one hundred kleps above Cosmic Bubble Palace.

General Shortstop said, "I'm sure we all have something worthwhile to report, but let's take this in stages. First, Spikey and Gloria, your reports?"

Spikey went first, "The *Door* on the *Fire Cruiser* has been installed and is online. I've done it enough times that I can do it rather quickly with the right bear-power and supplies."

Gloria went on, "We have programmed the *Door* to shut down its plasma field when the infected bears are halfway through the passage. They will then be exposed to the tachyons and beta rays. It's not going to be pretty. We have expanded the power of the *Door* so that we can take all the bears at one time. The aperture of the *Door* on their side will also act as a vacuum and suck anything not fixed in the area it opens into it. Assuming this works, the bears will need immediate medical attention once they board the *Fire Cruiser*. I would like to request that everyone we can find with any medical experience, from first aid to neural surgery, be assigned to the cargo bay of the *Fire Cruiser* under Dr. Grizz and me."

"Agreed, but what if it doesn't work?"

Gloria held up a small, white, plastic mask with a long tube extending from it. She explained, "Given what we now know about contracting *goonieness*, these masks will keep us from inhaling the *goonieness* pheromone. Everyone in the cargo bay should wear one until we have confirmed the health of the bears. Even then, I am recommending a 72-hour quarantine on all those who were infected until we can run complete physicals on them, and anyone who comes in contact with them should be run through the decontamination showers. In addition, in the event the bear-goons are hostile, I would like to request that a full security team be assigned to the cargo bay."

"Done," Shortstop said. Then he moved on to Captain Noble, "Will, install this in the firing chamber of your forward weapons array." He held up one of the tiny, pink globes of *fire glass*.

Will took it and cupped it gently in his hands. "I can't believe you actually convinced the phoenixes to give you these."

Speedway broke in, "It wasn't easy, but since we got back, we have managed to develop a method for integrating the glass into our systems. I'll come aboard and work with your engineers to install it."

Will nodded, and General Shortstop turned his attention to Captain Hull. "Captain, your report?"

Hull replied, "We've installed multiple cores in the entire fleet, so we no longer have to run on manual power. We've also been conducting a few weapons tests. We have our lasers up to 120% of maximum. It's still not much against a *Fire Cruiser* ship, but we should be able to hang in a firefight a bit longer."

"Excellent, we need every edge we can get," Shortstop

said. He turned to the Nakans, "Toby, Cak, have you learned anything new from the spider probe?"

Cak's grin was all-consuming, "As a matter of fact, we have, and it's more than we ever hoped for. Toby and I have been able to access the spider's programming center. It was sent to Staranana with a single objective, to steal the schematics for the *Door* technology. Then it was to deactivate and wait for further orders. And we were right; there are no other spider probes in the Palace."

"That's good news. I was…" Speedway began.

"Wait, sorry, Colonel, that's not all." Toby continued where his brother left off, "The probe was created by a race of people called the *So*. The probe's databanks didn't have much information about them, but I see only two possibilities regarding their involvement in this crisis. One is that Lizard Face has forged an alliance with them, or two, that Lizard Face stole technology from them. Either way, the *So* have technology far more advanced than ours."

"That's encouraging!" Spikey quipped.

Toby went on, "There is some good news, though. The probe's redundant files contain a flight plan that Cak and I believe leads from the *So* home world to Staranana through the vortex. We'd appreciate it if Spikey could reinterpret the data, but from what we can tell, it shows the exact aperture in the vortex we have to go through to get to their world, *Soal*. It also gives its spatial coordinates; their planet is approximately 1,000 light years from Staranana. If the vortex weren't there, there would be no way they would pose a threat to us."

"Could we destroy it? The vortex, I mean," Josh Noble asked.

General Shortstop shook his head, "That would be foolhardy. Lizard Face is coming here one way or the other, and once we have Scotty back, we have no choice but to destroy the lizard. But I think it is too early to declare these *So* our enemies, whoever they are."

"Besides, if we can chart the vortex, it would be a great opportunity for space exploration," Spikey smiled.

Cak finished the report, "The last thing of value that we discovered was an old copy of the virus in the redundant files.

It has only half the coding of the virus we dealt with, but there is an attachment at the end of the coding labeled *cure*."

"You're kidding!" Shortstop shrieked.

"I wouldn't kid about that, sir. Maybe Captain Moonbeam can take a look?"

Spikey nodded his head, "Of course, I'm sure I could work something out of it. I can't promise it will be effective against the virus, but we can at least test it."

"See to it as soon as we are finished here," Shortstop ordered. Then he addressed Captain Noble, "Will, as soon as the *fire glass* is installed, you must keep a few things in mind."

"Of course, General."

"First, the glass can produce as much energy as you want. The Colonel and I have spent every moment since we got back designing arrays for the glass. I won't bore you with the technical details. In brief, though, the resistors we've installed in the arrays can handle up to one quadrillion joules, and they'll last for at least 10,000 shots. I am essentially handing you the deadliest weapon known to exist."

"We'll use it wisely," Will assured.

"Oh, I'm not worried about that, Captain, and I don't think the phoenixes will be either."

"Why?" Noble asked.

"Because the first person to use the glass will be the only person it will ever work for. So I must insist that, for the duration of this mission, you personally man the tactical controls of your ship."

"Not a problem, sir."

Spikey broke in, "Wait a minute, General. I have to stay onboard the *Fire Cruiser* to operate the *Door*, but you said you were going to install the glass in the *Zerubbabel* as well. I don't want to seem petty, but the *Zerubbabel* is my ship, and it would seem pointless to have a weapons array installed that I can't use."

Shortstop growled under his breath. *Not petty indeed!* Spikey was not usually selfish, but then again, he could be pretty particular when it came to his inventions. Even so, one would think he would be willing to make some concessions when

Scotty's life was at stake. The human boy was, after all, closer to the Moonbeams than anyone else. The array could always be removed after the mission if need be, but it made sense to have it on Staranana's most advanced ship. The General simply didn't see a way around Spikey's pettiness.

"I'm, sorry, Captain, but…" Shortstop began.

"Wait a minute, General," Speedway interrupted. "Spikey's right. Likely, he'll be going on a lot of missions for Scotty, and the array could come in handy."

Shortstop crossed his arms, "What exactly do you suggest, Colonel?"

"Well, there is one person that could help us?"

"You mean God?" Gloria asked.

Speedway smiled. Only a few months earlier, he had given up all faith in God. Gloria had been a big part of his turning back to his Creator. Still, in this case, God was more the inspiration than the answer. He continued, "We can always use His help, and maybe it was God that gave me this idea, but I was thinking about Sparkey."

"Sparkey!" Spikey and Gloria sounded at once.

"Well, yes, we installed molecular scanners from the hospital on the access ports of the arrays. The scanners will transmit the thermal energy of the operator's hand to the glass to activate it. In addition, each scanner will imprint that person's DNA on the glass, putting it forever under their control."

"Let me get this straight," Gloria broke in. "You stole my molecular scanners?"

Speedway shook his head, "Don't lose focus, Doctor! My point is, Sparkey's DNA is made up of Spikey's DNA and your DNA. A simple adjustment to the scanner would make it think Sparkey was Spikey. If we take him onboard the *Zerubbabel*, he can run the weapon, and Spikey can stay on the *Fire Cruiser*. Then afterward, the glass should still work for Spikey."

"Clever thinking, Colonel," Shortstop quipped. "So what do you say?" Shortstop asked the cub's parents.

They both hesitated for a moment. Were they willing to put their son in danger yet again? After the incident on the *Dragon's Blood,* Spikey and Sparkey had exchanged more than a few sharp words with each other. They had worked past that, of course, but they were beginning to wonder how many more times they would have to put their son in jeopardy. Spikey looked at Gloria, and her eyes said it all. As long as Scotty was around, their lives would never be normal, and since the boys were so close in age, it was likely Scotty would want the cub along on many more adventures.

Spikey surrendered, "He's still in the gym controlling Scotty's duplicate. I'll check on him. If he can get away without disrupting things on Earth, I'll have him report to you." Gloria squeezed his hand; nothing more needed to be said.

Shortstop stood, "All right, if there is nothing else, here is what we're going to do. I will take command of the *Zerubbabel* and Toby, Cak, and Sparkey will come with me. We'll leave an hour before the *Fire Cruiser*. I want to take us in around the far side of the asteroid belt. We'll find a large asteroid and set down. With a prayer, hopefully, Lizard Face won't detect us. He did tell the *Fire Cruiser* to come alone after all. The Nobles, Spikey and Gloria, Dr. Grizz, Commander Honeytub, and Colonel Speedway, along with the Staranian medical detachment will head out on the *Fire Cruiser*. You should be at the meeting coordinates two hours before the exchange, just to be safe. Captain Hull will stay in orbit of Staranana with his fleet, just in case things go south. At this moment, I have a team working on the roof to remove the Bubble. The *Fire Cruiser* will have to descend into the atmosphere and grab the Bubble from the top of the Palace, but that shouldn't be any problem. As planned, once we are at the coordinates, we will release the Bubble into space. Once Lizard Face sends Scotty over, and we confirm his safety, the *Zerubbabel* will come out firing, and the *Fire Cruiser* is to follow suit. Our objective is not simply to cripple or even destroy the *Dragon's Blood;* we have to annihilate it. I don't want so much as a pile of ash left. Any ideas how to accomplish that, Captain Noble?"

Will sat up in his chair, "If the glass is as powerful as you say, we could generate a beam wide enough to vaporize the ship. But since this is our first time using the glass, I recommend something a little less extreme. Our engines exhaust ionized hydrogen particles, as you know. Usually, it's not enough for an enemy to take advantage of, but if we can blow off the nacelles, we could create a hydrogen leak. If that caught fire, it would cause a chain reaction back into the engine core and blast the ship to atoms. We can then incinerate any remaining debris with the *fire glass*."

"Excellent! Above all, we must make sure that neither Lizard Face nor any of his people get a chance to touch the Cosmic Bubble. From what I understand, the glass is indestructible. If we have to force it down onto an asteroid to keep it away from Lizard Face, so be it. We can retrieve it later. In conclusion, this mission has two objectives: get Scotty back and destroy Lizard Face. Neither is optional because failing to achieve either one is going to mean the end of both Staranana and Stararocka sooner or later. Are there any questions?"

Everyone shook their heads, and Shortstop said, "Okay, you have your orders. Spikey take about an hour to check out that virus cure, but with the dual-core defense, it is not a priority. After that, get some sleep. That goes for all of you. I need you all awake for this one. It is 2:00 p.m., Palace time, right now, and we are fourteen hours from the meeting. That is 4:00 a.m. tomorrow. The *Zerubbabel* will be leaving at 9:30 p.m., and the *Fire Cruiser* should leave at 10:30 p.m. Take about five hours to sleep, and then get everything ready. God go with us all, dismissed!"

As everyone was filing out, Shortstop asked Chef Berry, "How's the party coming?"

Berry smiled, obviously, at least somewhat over what had happened with the Nakans. He replied, "Trust me, sir, Scotty will have a homecoming he will never forget."

Chapter 23
Brotherly Charge

Everyone else in the Fields' home had been asleep for nearly an hour before Sparkey dared to return to Scotty's bedroom. It had been an event-filled day. After faking a head injury to get out of a dentist appointment, *Scotty* had enjoyed a few hours on the couch in front of the television watching Christmas movies and drinking a human beverage called hot chocolate. Sparkey had worried about that at first. He wondered what happened to the food inside the duplicate once the duplicate was turned off. Thankfully, Spikey had designed the duplicate to reproduce Scotty's body down to the cellular level. Before long, the duplicate had to go to the bathroom.

When lunchtime rolled around, things had heated up. Samantha's friend Katie, who had proved herself a bit of a ditz, had been helping Mrs. Fields and Samantha baking cookies in the kitchen. When the first batch had been finished and Mrs. Fields took it out of the oven, Katie had accidentally laid her oven mitt on the hot oven door. Before anyone realized it, the glove caught fire. Though no serious damage was done before the fire was put out, Mrs. Fields was seriously annoyed. That, in turn, made Samantha mad, and she and her friend had stormed out of the house, not to be seen again for hours.

Noah, on the other hand, had kept to himself most of the day. For the early afternoon, he had been working out in his bedroom. Sparkey made the mistake of going in there once, only to get yelled at. Noah was "pumping iron" as the human expression went and had thrown a sweaty towel in Sparkey's face. It was unfortunate that the duplicate's sensations were processed back into Sparkey's brain. After a day with Noah, he had learned that human sweat was very smelly.

In the late afternoon, Noah had left to go swimming at the indoor pool in nearby Redmond, Oregon. That had given Sparkey a few hours to explore in Scotty's bedroom. He hoped it would give him a little more knowledge to keep up this act, but he honestly was beginning to wonder when he would be able to go back to Staranana (at least mentally, since he was literally still there physically).

Noah returned around 6:30 and went into the kitchen just long enough to grab a few cookies and a sandwich. Then he disappeared again, throwing Sparkey out of the room, and then blasting his music for the entire house (and no small percentage of the neighbors) to hear.

When Mr. Fields returned around 7:00 p.m., it was only long enough to grab his *Santa Claus* suit, a character and concept that Sparkey really didn't grasp, and then he headed out again. Mr. Fields was well known for playing Santa at Christmas time in homes around Prineville. Sparkey had to stifle a giggle at Mr. Fields in his red coat and hat, and flowing white, artificial beard. Perhaps it was just his Starananian mind, but why did humans dress up to give presents away? He had learned enough from the Christmas movies to get an idea of who Santa was, but the man seemed almost imaginary in nature. He would have to ask Scotty if there really was such a person. At the very least, the man had many people who loved to imitate his spirit of generosity.

Mrs. Fields had spent the evening in the kitchen continuing to bake, and then she curled up on the couch with a good book until she fell asleep. After a brief nap, she had gotten up and retired to her bedroom. Samantha, who had returned some time before, was also shut up in her room, and soon Sparkey had been left all alone.

That had actually been advantageous. The last time he had been here, the Fields' home had not been decked out like this. There was, of course, the tree, which was far smaller than the one they were raising in Cosmic Bubble Palace. Beneath it was a cache of presents wrapped in an assortment of colored papers. This being Sparkey's first Christmas, just what was under the tree looked wonderful, but Scotty had told him the really good presents came with *Santa's* arrival.

Around the hearth, behind the Fields' wood stove, hung five colorful stockings. Scotty had said those would be filled with goodies as well. And there were holly leaves, paper snowflakes, and strings and strings of lights all over the house. It was only when things got quiet in Noah and Scotty's room that Sparkey dared to venture back inside. Noah was once again a hulk of snoring flesh on the top bunk, and he had thrown his dirty laundry right on Scotty's bed. Sparkey wondered how the boy put up with the walking muscle mass.

Sparkey shoved the clothes off the bed and laid down, staring at the *alarm clock*. When would his dad signal him? And more important, would he be allowed to go along to rescue Scotty? He desperately wanted to. Though he was glad he had rescued Toby, he was being eaten alive by guilt for abandoning his best friend. Would Scotty still like him? Could he forgive him? And the most painful question of all, was Scotty even still alive?

He stared at the clock for about an hour, watching each minute drum by slowly. Then his eyes began to feel heavy, and he drifted off to sleep.

~

"Scotty! Wake up and turn off that stupid clock!" The enraged voiced belonged to Noah, but Sparkey barely registered it. This had been the first time he had been able to sleep for almost a day and a half. But the next moment, he was wide awake.

"AHHHHHHH!" Sparkey sat bolt upright in his bed and saw the panic-stricken Noah slammed against the end of the bottom bunk. He was in his underwear, but his hair was smoking, and there were burns on his chest and arms, and his hands were bleeding.

"What happened?" Sparkey shrieked.

Noah was panting heavily and couldn't speak. It was really

no mystery what had happened. The duplicate was supposed to discharge electricity into the ground every two hours. In the original duplicate, the discharge had been pre-programmed, so no one had ever gotten hurt. But with Sparkey in control, he had to remember to touch something metal every two hours. So far, he had managed, but it looked like his little nap had come at the wrong time. Noah proved the perfect energy conductor.

"What's going on in here?" The light came on, and Mrs. Fields rushed in. She took one look at Noah and gasped, "What happened here?" She took him by the arms and helped him stand up. He just shook his head and pointed at *Scotty*. Sparkey was at a loss for words. It wasn't like he could realistically explain how hundreds of volts of static electricity almost barbecued her son.

Mrs. Fields, however, did not interpret Noah's pointing correctly. After all, how could she possibly think her youngest son had nearly electrocuted her eldest? She instead thought Noah was pointing at the TV on the far wall, and Sparkey quickly said, "I think there is something wrong with the TV! Look what it did to Noah."

Noah was shaking his head incessantly, but Mrs. Fields ignored him. "Oh, never mind, where are your brother's clothes? I'm taking him to the hospital."

Sparkey picked up the teen's baggy jeans. Noah was becoming coherent enough that he painfully pulled them on, but he pushed away his shirt, unwilling to aggravate the burns on his chest, arms, and hands. Mrs. Fields nodded and draped the boy's blanket across his back. Then she turned back to *Scotty* and said, "Stay away from that TV!" Then she left with Noah.

Sparkey immediately turned back to the TV. He had gotten Scotty in enough trouble without his having to explain all this. He unplugged the TV and ripped at the cord with his teeth. That had little effect, of course, given Scotty's baby teeth. What he wouldn't give for his bear teeth right about now. He improvised and grabbed a pocketknife that was sitting on the dresser. He slashed at the cord, making the rubber coating jagged and exposing the wire. It would look like the dog chewed it up. He wasn't exactly sure a 19-inch TV could produce the kind of voltage that would cause the burns Noah got, but at least Mr. and Mrs. Fields could believe it could.

When he was done, he left the cord on the floor, turned off the lights, and slipped back into bed. It was then that he finally noticed the clock. It was programmed to turn off after one minute of incessant whining, which had come and gone in all the excitement. However, the message still flashed across the screen. It read *7649*. Since a human clock technically had no such time, Sparkey knew exactly what it meant. *7649* were the last four digits of Scotty's home phone number. The numbers had become Starananian code for *"Come home!"*

Sparkey smiled. It would still be several hours before he could go home, what with all the commotion in the Fields' house. But, at least, he could get back to where the real action was, and best yet, save his friend.

Noah and Mrs. Fields returned about an hour-and-a-half-later. Sparkey pretended to be asleep, but through half-opened eyes, he viewed his *brother*. The teen's hands were wrapped in bandages, and he was still shirtless, holding an ice pack to his chest. Most amazing to Sparkey was the fact that the young man was now bald, or nearly so. His hair had been shaved almost to the scalp. To use a human expression, Sparkey thought Noah looked *cool*. And he wasn't exactly sure Noah disagreed. He had a slight smirk on his face, and Sparkey saw the boy flexing his muscles in the mirror and admiring his scars. The cub laughed; humans were funny creatures.

Noah and the rest of the house had been asleep again for more than an hour when Sparkey turned his attention back to the clock. He stood from the bed and looked at Noah. He still had the ice pack over his chest, and his pillow was draped across his face. Even so, Sparkey wouldn't risk contacting home with Noah in the room. He didn't need the *Door* to get back, but he would need to contact his father to deactivate the mind link. He unplugged the clock and headed out to the living room.

Under the light of the Christmas tree, he plugged the clock back in and tapped snooze-time-radio-buzz-snooze, the code that would link him directly with the communication station in his father's workshop.

The alarm clock crackled, and after a moment, a worn voice replied, *"Sparkey, what took you so long? I contacted you hours ago!"*

"Sorry, Dad, we had a little excitement here. Anyway, can I come home yet?"

"Absolutely! We have another mission for you."

"*We* meaning you and mama?"

"*We* meaning General Shortstop and the rest of the Space Force."

Sparkey let his human mouth spread in a face-consuming grin. Spikey continued, "I'll deactivate the mind link, and be right upstairs to get you."

Chapter 24
Sparkey's Weapons

"They want me to do what?" Sparkey was sitting up on his cot in the gym of Cosmic Bubble Palace. Spikey was at the end of the bed.

"You are going to take command of the *fire glass* weapons on the *Zerubbabel*."

"But why me?"

"Well, in brief, because you share my DNA, and I felt it important to keep control of the *Zerubbabel's* essential components in the family. I can't be onboard her for the rescue, so you're the next best choice."

"But I've never manned weapons before, Dad. You've given me a few piloting lessons, and I'm not half bad with a sensor array, but weapons are another story."

Spikey smiled and said, "Think of them as a very large and powerful slingshot. Don't worry; General Shortstop will run you through the basics. As I understand it, these weapons are so powerful that just pointing them in the right direction would be devastating to the enemy, even if you are off target."

Sparkey bowed his head, and he rubbed the back of his neck, "You mean, I may have to kill people?" Three months earlier, it had been Scotty who had been opposed to killing, and Sparkey who had been gung-ho for it if it saved his dad. In the end, Scotty had found the courage to do what God wanted, but there was no denying the experience had changed the boy. He was no longer the simple dreamer Sparkey had found on the fourth-grade playground of Loan Oak Elementary School. In only three months' time, the human child had become the most extraordinary emperor in the history of Staranana. And if Scotty could find the courage to help Sparkey, Sparkey would find the courage to help Scotty.

Spikey shook his head, "That is unlikely. The *Zerubbabel's* objective is to keep the Cosmic Bubble away from the *Dragon's Blood*. General Shortstop would like you to fire a few warning shots, enough to distract the *Dragon's Blood*, and then set yourself between them and the Cosmic Bubble, which will be drifting in space. Once the *Dragon's Blood* has its sights set on you, the *Fire Cruiser* will commence its attack. If all goes according to plan, it should be a short battle."

"What about Scotty?"

"No one is to fire a shot until we have confirmed his safety. The *Fire Cruiser* will only use conventional weapons until we have rescued the *Dragon's Blood's* crew."

"Rescued the crew?"

"Yeah, your mother and this Stararockan doctor we met believe that we can use *Door* technology to cure *goonieness*. It's complicated, but at least we can get those bears back alive."

"That's great! When do we leave?"

"You'll leave with the General at 9:30 tonight. It's about 6:00 p.m. now."

Sparkey narrowed his eyes and smirked, "Good, that will give me enough time."

"Enough time for what?" his father asked.

Sparkey hesitated, "Uh, nothing, time to get a little nap, that's all."

Spikey nodded, "I'm headed back to bed myself. Want to head back to the apartment with me?"

Sparkey shook his head, "Thanks, Dad, but I'm already in a bed. I might as well take advantage of it. Besides, I have a few things I'd like to think over. Staying here will keep me from getting distracted."

Spikey eyed his son suspiciously. This was a fully equipped gym. There were few places in the Palace more distracting, other than perhaps the library. But he didn't press the issue. "All right," he said. "See you soon."

Spikey turned to leave the gym, followed by the attendants who had been keeping Sparkey from bumping into things. Sparkey lay back down and pulled the covers up to his neckline. The lights went off, and the outside door clicked shut. Sparkey waited another moment, then stood and left the room.

~

Spikey could smell his wife's cooking the instant he stepped into their apartment. If his nostrils weren't playing tricks on him, and they usually didn't, she was frying ice trout, steaming fresh green beans from the Palace garden, and, of course, baking a mouthwatering, honeysuckle apple pie. He also saw a basket of blueberries and a new fruit Scotty had introduced them to called the tomato.

"You up?" Spikey asked. "I thought you'd sleep for at least another two hours."

Gloria flipped a fish in her frying pan and then looked up at her husband. "I did too, but I'm too anxious. So, I figured I'd make us all a big dinner. After all, if we're going into battle, we're going to need all of our strength."

"Are you worried about your plan?"

Gloria shrugged, "I just hope it doesn't end up making things worse. I kind of feel like I don't have any faith. I mean, God healed hundreds of bears before. Shouldn't we give Him the chance to do it again?"

Spikey walked around the center island that held the stove into the kitchen and wrapped his arms around his wife. He kissed her gently on the back of the head and whispered to her, "Maybe He will." Then he turned her around to him and said, "But I think we have to do all we can too. Scotty once told me this story about a little boy who was diagnosed with a dangerous but treatable form of cancer."

"I've studied that disease," Gloria broke in.

Spikey continued, "Yes, well, so had many of the doctors near this little boy. However, his parents believed God would heal him. They prayed and prayed, but eventually, the little boy died."

"That's horrible!"

"Yes, it was. What is worse was the fact that the boy's parents probably didn't consider the fact that *every good and perfect gift comes from God.* God gives knowledge to man as He desires to do so. He gave the doctors in that situation the knowledge to fight the cancer, and He has given you the knowledge to fight *goonieness.* He may still heal them on His own, but in the meantime, you are being faithful by using the knowledge He has given you."

Gloria smiled, "I guess you're right." Then she looked through the kitchen into the living room, "Hey, I thought you were bringing Sparkey back up?"

"I brought him back to Staranana, *so to speak.* But he said he wanted to sleep down there until we launch."

"Interesting, he's probably up to something."

"Oh, probably."

"Any idea what?"

"I can't even imagine, and I've got a great imagination. I'm beginning to see we have raised a very unpredictable son."

"It's like I've said before, Sparkey follows his heart regardless of the consequences to himself or sometimes even those around him. I say we trust him."

Spikey surrendered, "Let's just pray God is guiding his heart."

"I don't believe any less from any of the past situations," Gloria replied.

"Okay, so let's eat!"

~

Sparkey nudged the door open slowly, and it squeaked from disuse. Scotty's empirical chambers were both lonely and dark. They were only half the size of Seth's former 100-foot by 100-foot suite just one floor below, but they were no less magnificent. Though Scotty very rarely slept here, he had taken the time to give the place the personal touch. There was a 92-inch plasma screen TV against the left wall closest to the door. It wasn't actually from Earth. Spikey had created it for Scotty to play video games on. Both Sparkey and Scotty had enjoyed several sleepovers and long video game tournaments.

On the opposite wall was a collection of swords from throughout Starananian and Earth history. There were broadswords, Katanas, rapiers, cutlasses, double-edged swords, and even some embedded with jewels. There was also a very small dagger in the center of the display locked inside a glass case that was screwed to the wall. All the other swords were hanging around it, and many were more impressive than the tiny orange blade; but Sparkey's eyes were drawn to it, nonetheless.

After a moment, he pulled his eyes away and examined the rest of the room. There were, of course, dressers and toy chests, and a closet filled with royal garments in Scotty's size. Unlike the bay window in Seth's chambers, Scotty's room only had three simple windows along the fifty-foot-long rear wall. His bed was up against the one in the middle, providing an idyllic view of the Ice Sea far below.

Sparkey walked over to Scotty's bed and fished under the mattress. He had never believed he would actually have to do this, but desperate times bred desperate measures. After only a moment, he found what Scotty had hidden there only a few months before. It was a tiny brass key.

Sparkey squeezed the key in his hands and ran back to the sword display. The orange blade glowed like a tiny star, and Sparkey slid the key into the lock of the glass case. It popped open, and he took the dagger in his hands. He had never held it before, and something about it made him feel strong and powerful and yet humble and God-fearing all at the same time. It only took another moment to find the holster in Scotty's dresser, and having slipped the dagger inside, he took it and left the room.

Chapter 25

Departure

"You okay?"

Sparkey took a deep breath and answered General Shortstop, "I hope so. The controls seem simple enough. I just put my hand here, and then I control the aim and the trigger with my other hand, right?"

Shortstop chuckled, "Well, yes, but that is not what I meant. I meant, are you personally okay?"

Sparkey could not help the fact that he was shaking slightly. Of course, he really didn't know why. In the battle to overthrow Seth, he hadn't been nervous at all. He had fought gators, recklor bats, and a dragon had frozen him. He had traveled to an alien planet, traversed the White Desert, and been present for the downfall of Seth. Yet when he thought of his feelings during that time, all he could remember was determination and hope. Now, however, he was actually nervous, even scared, and he didn't know why. Perhaps it was because if Scotty died, the survival of Staranana would be next to impossible. But the more likely reason was that he didn't know how Scotty would react to him once they saw each other again.

"I'll be all right," Sparkey replied.

"Good enough," Shortstop said. The General, at the helm, then turned to the Nakans, "All right, boys, keep those scanners of yours scanning far and wide. We need a nice sized asteroid with heavy mineral deposits. Hopefully, the alloys in our hull will blend in, and we won't be detected."

"Loud and clear, General!" Toby replied.

"Aye, sir," Cak piped.

Shortstop turned back to his controls. "Activating engines. Toby, clear our departure with Palace Command."

"Palace Command has cleared us. We are set for an ascent velocity of 1,000 kleps per minute," Toby responded.

"Sensors are online. I estimate twenty minutes to the rendezvous coordinates if we come in the back way through the asteroid field. There are several large asteroids in the vicinity of the vortex; we should be able to set down on one of those," Cak reported.

"Very good, Ensign. I'm taking us up." And with that Shortstop pulled back on the controls and the *Zerubbabel* rose into the sky.

~

"What do you have for me, Spikey?" asked Colonel Speedway, as the inventor stepped into the command center of the Palace.

"Good news, I hope, Colonel. I finished analyzing the virus cure. To put it simply, the anti-virus alters the programming of the virus so that instead of destroying a computer system, it destroys itself. It is actually fairly ingenious. We have been trying to wipe out the entire virus at once, but this anti-virus alters a single line of code. The virus may still infect our system, but the amount of computer memory lost will be less than 1000th of one percent."

"What about the sonic attack?"

"The anti-virus will eliminate it too. Still, I suggest we maintain our original defense system."

"The dual computer cores?"

"Precisely!"

Speedway nodded, "Very well. Did General Shortstop have all this data?"

"Yes, I briefed him and installed the program in the *Zerubbabel* before he left. How are things going with the

Bubble?"

Speedway shook his head and rolled his eyes, "You ever work with bolts a foot thick and covered in thousands of years of rust and ice?"

"Can't say I have."

"Well, we broke several industrial sized mechanical wrenches before they would finally give way. We also bent the crossbeam beyond repair. Not that it matters because it slipped from the crane and fell off the roof of the Palace."

"Fell off the roof! Was anyone hurt?"

"No, it fell off the back side of the Palace straight into the Ice Sea. By now, it is probably a few hundred feet underwater. It will have to be replaced, assuming this whole scheme works."

"Well, it had better work, because if Lizard Face gets the Bubble, it will be the end of Staranana."

"From what I saw of Cololot, any amount of *fire glass* in his hands would spell the same. No matter what happens, these *fire glass* weapons are going to have to become highly classified and restricted. It would also be a good idea to set a few guards on the Bubble once we have it back in place."

"I thought the glass could only be used by one person?"

"Well, we found a way around it for Sparkey. Who says someone else couldn't? I don't want to be grisly, but all it would take is a little blood or a severed limb placed on the access panel, and the enemy would be able to activate the array."

"I see your point."

"Knowing the power of this glass is going to vastly complicate our lives. We already know about three other alien species: humans, Takillians, and the *So*; but who is to say if there are others? Staranana and Stararocka could become galactic targets."

"You know, I've been thinking along those lines as well. Being on Stararocka again was amazing, but in many respects, they are centuries ahead of us technologically. In a way, they represent what we would have been like without Seth. They could help us out a lot. Maybe we should establish a formal alliance?"

"It's not exactly like we're enemies, and they helped us in the battle to take Staranana; plus, we have enjoyed great cooperation during this effort. Why do we need to get formal?" Speedway asked.

"Well, as it is now, Stararocka is basically self-governing. They do as they please when they please. Their society is thriving, but through their ancestry, they should be under the authority of the *Blood of the Land*."

"I can't say I disagree, and we could definitely use some of their technology. I also don't think they would object to being under the *Blood of the Land*. God was at work as much on Stararocka as he was on Staranana three months ago. But actually, I think we had better leave this discussion for another time."

Spikey nodded his head, "You're right. Here we are talking politics, and we're about to launch a major mission. How are we coming with that by the way?"

Speedway glanced at his watch, "The *Fire Cruiser* is going to begin its descent in about ten minutes. It will be delicate work, but Commander Honeytub will use the claw to nudge the Bubble off the roof and grip it firmly."

Spikey handed the Colonel a pad. "I've done some computations. With the added mass of the Bubble, the *Fire Cruiser* will only be able to make one-quarter of its top speed."

"That shouldn't be a problem. We still have plenty of time."

"I'm just worried that with the added mass of the claw and the Bubble, the *Fire Cruiser* will lack the maneuverability required for a battle."

"Well, we're releasing the Bubble into space. That will cut down some of the mass, won't it?"

"Some, yes, but the bulk of the mass comes from the claw itself. Captain Noble told me they used twice as much hydrogen to bring the claw back to Staranana as they usually would, and that was just using the primary thrusters. Trying to use the maneuvering thrusters will only increase the fuel problem as it will take four times as much thrust to rotate the ship."

"I'm sorry about that, but we can't abort the mission."

"Oh, I'm not suggesting that. I'm saying we should use this handicap to our advantage."

"What do you mean, Spikey?"

"Well, the *Dragon's Blood* is equally equipped, claw and all. They'll know about the fuel problem, and likely, they will have taken steps to counter it. They, on the other hand, are stuck with their claw until they get back to Evilanda."

"And we aren't?"

Spikey stepped down to the central control board on the lower level of the Command Deck. He tapped a few keys, and the image of the *Fire Cruiser,* claw included, appeared on the screen. He twisted a knob, and the image rotated until the ship was on its side, exposing the belly. Spikey punched a few more buttons, and five red lights began to flash at the base of each claw.

The inventor said, "In order to install the claw, we had to make significant modifications to five airlocks on the belly of the ship. Each finger of the claw slides into one of the airlocks where the base of it is then secured to the ship, and it is wired into the ship's computers. Captain Noble told me that the belly deck is completely inconsequential to the operations of the ship. Mainly, it is filled with storage bays."

"So?"

"So, I would like your permission to install explosive charges on each of the fingers."

"What?"

"If we install charges, we can blow the fingers off the ship and restore our maneuverability. The damage to the *Fire Cruiser* would not be significant enough to even stall us briefly. We can seal the deck above, and I can even adjust the wiring of the claw so that it won't send a surge back into the rest of the computers."

"It's a great plan, Spikey, but it's the Nobles' ship. Shouldn't you ask them before you start blowing it apart?"

"Oh, I already have. It's fine with both Will and Josh. I even offered my engineers to help repair the damage afterward. I just want to have every advantage over Lizard Face possible."

"I agree, but if you have the Nobles' permission, why

come to me?"

"For one thing, the plan wasn't finalized until about six minutes ago, so I couldn't ask General Shortstop. Second, after Scotty's government was established, you were given direct authority over the Palace armory, and I need the charges from there."

"Doesn't the *Fire Cruiser* have something that will work?"

"Nothing for a job this precise. All of their explosives are blunt and made for large-scale attacks. The charges the goons left behind are perfect for this kind of contained explosion."

"I see. Consider permission granted, Captain. How long will all this take to set up?"

"Gloria and Doctor Grizz shouldn't need me in the cargo bay with the *Door*. I taught them well. I'll still try and be there, but either way, it will take no more than twenty minutes to set up the charges. I can have it done before we arrive at the rendezvous coordinates."

"Good, well, it's about time to head up to the roof. Josh is going to bring a shuttle for us, and then we'll board the *Fire Cruiser*. After that, we'll get the Bubble in place. You ready to go?"

"Yeah, I'll meet you up there. I just want to go check on Gloria and Grizz one last time."

"Understood, see you up there."

~

"There, that is the last bit of data I can squeeze into this thing." Gloria Moonbeam stared down at the small electronic pad in her hands. For the last hour, she and Doctor Grizz had been giving themselves a crash course in goon anatomy. Added to what they already knew, the Palace's old doctors had surprisingly extensive records on the goons. There was nothing that even touched on a cure, for Seth had no intention of healing any of them, but there were significant records on goon DNA and brain development. The whole genetic mess screamed satanic prison, but their research was enough to convince Gloria and Grizz that their plan stood a fighting chance.

As payment for all his help, though he would have gladly done it for free, Gloria had given Grizz every record on Seth's anatomy she could find. He had been pouring over it for the last ten minutes while she finished downloading the goon data.

"You ready for this, Doctor?" Grizz asked.

"Please, *Lee,* after all of this, I think we can call each other by our first names."

"Very well, *Gloria,* are you ready for this?"

Gloria stared at her data, tapped her fingers on the back of the pad, and then looked Grizz full in the face and smiled, "You had better believe it!"

"How's it coming in here?" The new voice belonged to Spikey.

"We're ready," Gloria said.

"Great, you want to walk up together?" Spikey asked.

Gloria grinned, "How could I refuse such a gracious invitation?"

Spikey grinned too and extended his hand. They interlocked fingers, and Spikey drew her close. He was just about to kiss her when he noticed Dr. Grizz. It wasn't like he didn't already know Grizz was there. It was just that Spikey could easily tune out the rest of the world when it came to his wife. Grizz, of course, was as gracious as ever, though he was coming as close to a blush as was possible for a bear.

"Doctor! I'm sorry, I…" Spikey tried to apologize.

Grizz waved his apology away. "I have no intention of getting in the way of young love, Captain Moonbeam. You make me miss my wife."

"Yeah, I guess I'm just kind of excited about getting Scotty back."

"Well, what do you say we go get your friend back in time for his Christmas party?"

Spikey nodded and said, "If you'll follow us, Doctor."

"Lead the way."

~

"Captain on deck!" The officers of the *Fire Cruiser's* bridge crew snapped to attention when Captain and Commander Noble stepped onto the bridge, along with Colonel Speedway. Usually, Will did not require such formality out of his crew, but this was a special occasion. Except for the brief battle to take Cosmic Bubble Palace, this was the first major collaboration between cousin worlds that had been separated for more than 500 years. He needed his bears at their best, and he had no doubt they would be.

Josh stepped down to the helm, and Speedway took his place at the weapons board. Will would replace him when they started using the *fire glass*, but until then, he would man the conventional weapons. Captain Noble slipped into his command chair and flipped the switch that would open an intercom to the entire ship.

He said, "Attention, all hands, this is the Captain. In just a few short hours, we will wage one of the most important battles in the histories of either Staranana or Stararocka. I don't need to remind you that there are many lives at stake. Not the least of which is the promised *Blood of the Land*, our friend, Scotty Fields. We have no idea what he has gone through over the past three days, but could he have seen what you all have been up to, I know he would be proud. Starananians and Stararockans alike have given 200% of themselves. You've all sacrificed sleep and time with your families to bring all of our friends back home. And some of you have already paid the ultimate price, having had family or friends killed by our enemy. I know it may seem inadequate, but thank you all for your sacrifices. However, our job isn't done yet. I need to ask more of you than you have probably given already. I can't promise a positive outcome, but I promise I will give all I have to get our friends back. I hope you will do the same. Once again, thank you. You're the best crew in the galaxy and the best friends a bear could have. Now, let's get to it! All hands to battle stations - Red Alert!"

It was during inspiring moments like this that Noble's crew reminded him more of a well-oiled machine than the friends he had shared years of laughter with. Reports instantly started coming at him.

Josh reported, "Thrusters are at station keeping, holding us one hundred feet over the Cosmic Bubble. I have just transferred helm control temporarily to Commander

Honeytub in the claw control room."

Speedway added, "Captain Moonbeam reports that all the explosive charges are in place."

"Let's make sure those charges stay disarmed until we reach the coordinates. I don't want a slight jolt from the claw to set them off," Captain Noble ordered.

"That is confirmed, sir. Captain Moonbeam is now joining Commander Honeytub in claw control."

A voice chimed over the intercom, *"Bridge, this is Dr. Moonbeam. The Door is online and standing by. Cargo Bay One is now under quarantine."*

"Great job, Doctor," Noble replied.

Honeytub came over the intercom next, *"Bridge, this is Honeytub. I'm moving us into position."*

"Excellent, Commander," Noble said. Then he ordered, "Josh, place the image on the screen."

Commander Noble tapped his controls, and the image of the Bubble, as looked at from directly above, materialized on the screen. Ever so slightly, the fingers of the claw bent and descended upon the ancient glass sphere. There was a shudder throughout the entire ship as the claw made contact with the glass, and the fingers slipped into position around the Bubble. The ship moved slightly upward, as did the Bubble out of its housing. Honeytub maneuvered the claw one more time until the Bubble was in place, and the claw locked at its fingertips.

In another circumstance, the bridge would have been filled with cheers and applause, but the truth was, no one really wanted the Bubble removed from the Palace, especially under these circumstances. Honeytub reported, *"The Bubble is secure, Captain. I am transferring helm control back to the bridge."*

"Understood," Noble replied. "Josh, take us up."

"Aye, Captain."

"With the Captain's permission, I would like to put a full view of the Palace on the screen," Speedway requested.

"Permission granted."

Speedway tapped his controls, and a full view of the entire building was displayed. Its one hundred stories of ancient brick and finely carved statues, along with thousands of windows, were all very impressive. The towering walls and vast courtyard were breathtaking. However, the beauty of it all was diminished by the absence of the pink sphere that had rested on its roof for over one million Starananian years. Speedway prayed this was only a short hiatus for the Bubble.

A few moments later, when the *Fire Cruiser* achieved orbit, Captain Noble ordered, "Josh, set a course for the rendezvous, best possible speed."

"Aye, sir."

Chapter 26

The Final Trial

B y the time Scotty and Captain Gakic returned to the communications room, Scotty's entire right leg was covered in blood. He was convinced that TB had been destroyed, and the prospect of being rescued had all but vanished. Why had God seen him through the fire, healed his ribs, and protected him from Blackie, only to let him be killed now? It didn't make any sense.

Captain Gakic tapped several buttons on the communication terminal and remained focused on the screen for a few minutes. During that time, he all but ignored Scotty. It was very tempting to make a break for the unguarded doorway, but where could he possibly go? He was more than a klep underground, and by now, the *So* vessels were probably heavily guarded. His leg also didn't help matters. He decided to try a little conversation instead.

"So, are you and the other *Gakic* friends?"

For a moment, the captain was silent, but Scotty was surprised when he actually got a real answer, "I wouldn't exactly put it that way."

"What do you mean?"

"I mean, I never wanted him to exist in the first place. I protested, but Lord Lizard Face insisted. Several of his cloning attempts had proven less than successful. A lot of the other *real* goons had to walk around with imperfect reflections of themselves everywhere they went. A few even murdered their copies, only to kill themselves for fear of Lizard Face."

"Lizard Face told me he never hurt any of the *real* goons."

"Oh, he hasn't, but it is only a matter of time. The *Goon Omega* project is likely to make every other goon obsolete."

"Then why do you still serve him?" Scotty asked.

"Because Lord Lizard Face had faith in me first, and he has put me second-in-command of this empire. It is a position I wouldn't have dreamed of three months ago, and I have to believe I will keep my place here even with the *Goon Omega.*"

"It doesn't have to be this way you know. You could…"

"Shut up!"

"I didn't even say…"

"I know exactly what you were going to say, but let me let you in on a little secret about the goons. We are a proud and arrogant people. We lust for power and pleasure. We care nothing for the people we kill, and we will do anything to advance ourselves, even if it means betraying what you would call our friends. Your God is impotent and weak. You all bow before Him like fools ready for the slaughter. You are a weak and worthless people. And when Lizard Face has the Bubble, he will make an end of your Lord and Savior once and for all."

Scotty's blood was pumping with adrenaline, and he wanted to lash out with anger. He tried to think of the right words to refute Gakic, but the only words that came to mind were very strange indeed. *"But the Lord hardened the heart of Pharaoh; and he did not heed them, just as the Lord had spoken to Moses."*

It took a moment, but Scotty soon understood the purpose of the excerpt from *Exodus*. Even after enduring repeated plagues, the Pharaoh of Egypt refused to obey the Lord's command to release the people of Israel. Finally, God Himself hardened Pharaoh's heart, making it impossible for him to seek the will of the Lord. The same had happened to Captain Gakic. There would be no saving this goon.

Scotty fell silent and remained still. A moment later, Captain Gakic turned to him with a knife. Scotty's heart jumped into his throat. Both fire and fang had failed to kill him. Would a simple blade do the job?

Gakic stepped closer to him and said, "Give me the

computer."

"What?"

"The alien computer, give it to me!"

"I can't! Lieutenant Gakic destroyed him!"

The goon sneered beneath his mask, and then he grabbed the human boy by the arm and shoved him to the ground.

"Ah!" Scotty screamed, and Gakic was already on top of him with the knife. Scotty cringed, waiting for the jagged blade to pierce his already marred flesh. That never happened. There was a moment of pain as Gakic pulled the burned fabric on Scotty's hip away from his skin. Then Gakic slipped the knife inside the pocket and cut it off Scotty's pants. TB's remains clattered to the floor.

A tear welled in Scotty's eyes as he saw what was left of his friend. The emerald had melded and fused with the other components. The circuit chip was warped and charred. Scotty had no idea what would happen to TB after he *died*. He hoped he would go to Heaven, but that was a promise given only to humans. Scotty trusted in God's mercy, and perhaps TB could share in the promise given to the bears to join the *Blood of the Land* in Heaven as something altogether better than what they were. But whatever the outcome, he now felt completely alone.

Gakic picked up TB and said, "The memory unit and self-awareness chip survived."

Scotty wiped the tears from his eyes, "What?"

Gakic didn't reply. Instead, he stepped back to the communication terminal and opened a drawer beneath it. He pulled out a small device that Scotty guessed was some sort of scanner. Gakic pointed it at what was left of TB, and a clear tube running along the end of the device began to pulse with blue light. After only a minute, he put the device away and picked up TB. He walked back to Scotty and handed the boy the computer.

"What did you do?"

"I followed my orders. Now, let's go."

"Where?"

"Back to the lab."

Scotty sniffled, and Gakic pulled him to his feet. They left the room together.

Lt. Gakic had been arguing with the other clones for about half-an-hour. Lt. Clak recoiled at *Gakic's* words, "I can't believe you want us to betray Lord Lizard Face!"

"You are as good as lizard chow already as far as Lizard Face is concerned. But I don't believe that is true of Emperor Scotty and the bears."

"You aren't allowed to address him as Emperor anymore!" Clak refuted. "And besides, they slaughtered all the goons left behind on Staranana."

"And how many bears did the goons kill in the last 500 years? We were at war, and the bears won the planet legally, no matter what Lizard Face says. Besides that, I have seen this boy's God at work. I saw him thrown into the flames and tossed down to Blackie. I tried to shoot him in the head, and nothing happened."

"You hurt him just now," one of the others said.

"Yes, on a setting that should have vaporized him. His God has not forsaken him, and I am done resisting Him."

"So what is it you are saying?" Clak asked.

"I am saying that we abandon Lizard Face and Evilanda. We rescue Scotty, take one of the *So* ships, and head back to Starananian space."

"You actually think they will have us?" another asked.

"I don't know, but one thing is certain, I intend to become a servant of the Lord Jesus Christ and His servant, Emperor Scotty Fields. Now, who is with me?"

There was an intense, long silence, but then hand after hand raised into the air. Finally, Lt. Clak was the only one left. Lt. Gakic looked at him and said, "Well?"

There was another long moment, then Clak raised his hand and asked, "So, what do you want to do?"

~

Scotty had no idea why Captain Gakic wanted to take him back to the cloning lab. Perhaps they were going to try to clone him too or drowned him in one of the tubes. Regardless, he did all he could to stall the situation. That wasn't hard as his leg only allowed them to move at a snail's pace. With the lab being on the 60th floor, it might be hours before they got there.

~

"We're ready to get underway," reported Lt. Kyak.

Lizard Face jutted out his forked tongue in excitement and surveyed the bridge of the *Dragon's Blood*. There were a dozen goons at their stations ready for the greatest battle of their time. The ship, whose weapons were already impressive, had been outfitted with *So* weapons as well. Should the *Fire Cruiser* try anything unexpected, they would be blown out of space.

The plan was still to exchange the *Goon Omega,* disguised as Scotty, for the Bubble. Then, while the *Goon Omega* acclimated itself into Starananian society, Lizard Face would return to Evilanda and capture the secrets of the Bubble. The fake Scotty would slowly but surely make the bears hate him, but because of the *Blood of the Land* prophecies, they would never try to overthrow him. Within a few months, the bears would be back under slave masters' whips, and Lizard Face would return for his revenge.

The lizard master slid into the command chair in the middle of the bridge. *Scotty* was seated next to him. "How are your *sstudies* going?" Lizard Face asked.

The *Goon Omega* replied, "Excellent, Master! I have studied every intelligence report we have gained on the boy. I know the names of his human family, his school, and his hometown. I could repeat to you anything he has learned in school. I also know everything he has done on Staranana since he has been there. Should his friends engage me in a conversation about those events, I could recall detail for detail."

"Very good! I didn't realize our intelligence was *sso* accurate."

"The spider probe provided most of it, and Moonbeam's computer database was very helpful. Unfortunately, they discovered the probe, and that was the end of the data stream, but it is of little consequence."

"There were no gaps?"

"Nothing significant. Thanks to the boy's duplicate, most of his memory has been recorded into the Palace computers.

There was one problem, though. I was not able to obtain any information on the boy's religion. Every file dealing with it was heavily encrypted for some reason."

Lizard Face's large eyes grew wider, "Are you *ssaying* you know nothing of the boy's religion?"

"Only what you know and have told me."

Lizard Face bared his fangs in rage. If there was no knowledge of God, then all the other information about the boy was worthless. This was to be as much a battle against the Almighty as it was against the Starananians. If the *Goon Omega* could not at least give the appearance of being a Christian, he would be spotted for an impostor quickly. There had to be a way out of this.

Lizard Face said, "All right, we can figure this out. What I have told you *sshould* be enough to get you back to *Sstaranana.* Just be *ssure* to *ssay* things like *thank the Lord* or *God was with me*, or *praise Jesus.* Don't be too *sshowy* about it, but make *ssure* you mention how God helped you *ssurvive.* You can also mention the fact that three times we tried to kill you, and each time we failed."

"Impressive, Master."

"Now, when you return to *Sstaranana,* you must tell them you need *ssome* time, at least a few days, to yourself. Lock yourself in *Sscotty's* chambers and find his *Bible. Sstudy* it until you can adequately fake being one of those goodie goodies."

"A problem, Master. First, wouldn't the human boy return to Earth after such an ordeal? Will I be able to go to Earth?"

"I care little about what happens on that world. Let the boy's parents think him dead for all I care. Once Gakic is done with the boy, it will be true anyway. We know that *Sstarananians* can go to Earth. They just can't be *sseen* there. You will go through the *Door* when it is prudent to do *sso*, and the bears will never be the wiser. It will actually be a good intelligence gathering mission *sshould* I decide to conquer that world too."

"Second, according to the spider probe, we are nearing a day called Christmas. It is a huge human holiday, and Chef Berry is preparing a massive party at Scotty's request. I will not be able to not attend."

"Do what you must. But *sstudy* those *Sscriptures* quickly. We cannot allow this plan to fail."

Lt. Kyak returned, "The helm is standing by, and my security teams are ready. All claw systems are operational, and we have loaded the extra fuel you ordered, Master. I request permission to get underway, my Lord."

Lizard Face turned away from the *Goon Omega* and said, "Permission granted, Lieutenant. *Sset* a course for the vortex."

"Very good, Master," Kyak bowed. Then, as acting first officer, he turned to the helmsman, "Ensign Borak, ignite launch thrusters and lift us off the asteroid. Weapons officer, arm all laser cannons and torpedo tubes. All other hands, assume battle stations and take us to red alert."

The lights on the bridge dimmed to be replaced by the pulsing red status beacons. If all went well, in a few short hours, Lizard Face would be given the power of a god, and he would finally supplant the impotent Creator of the Universe.

~

Lt. Gakic stared at the tiny baby lizard clone floating in the glass tube, and he couldn't help but feel sorry for him. This baby, Leif, was an exact clone of Lizard Face and was intended to be the reptile's son. But what kind of life would that be? Growing up learning to mistreat and murder people was appalling. And of course, just having that thought was completely new to *Gakic*.

Only a day earlier, he never would have questioned Lizard Face, but what Being could protect a nine-year-old boy from three such deadly traps? The fire should have turned him to ash, Blackie should have gutted him, and at least one of the weapons' blasts should have vaporized him. None of that had happened, and now *Gakic* was convinced that resisting God was to invite death. He had been surprised, but grateful, that most of his clone friends had made the same decision as he. There were still hundreds to reach with the message of Christ, as little of it as he knew, but the Lizard Face loyalists had to be taken out of the way first.

He didn't exactly want to kill them, which was another alien feeling. But if they could not be persuaded, they would be deadly to the converts. The only way *Gakic* could think of to keep his people safe was to leave Evilanda, but he would not go until he had given each of the clones a chance to turn to God. The best way to make that happen was to seize control of Evilanda's computers. Hence his presence in the cloning lab.

Thanks to Lizard Face's obsession with creating the perfect soldier, the cloning lab had more computer access than anywhere else in the underground city. From there, a computer operator had direct access to every computer on the asteroid from personal units to the launch stations on the surface. And the best part was, there were very few security lockouts on the system.

There were two reasons for this. First, Lizard Face had programmed intense loyalty into his creations. That was why they were willing to walk into fire or let themselves be ripped apart by Blackie at the slightest order from their Master. It was against their genetic nature to betray him. Clearly, God had overridden that handicap in many of the clones.

Second, the lab literally gave most of the original goons the creeps. And that was saying a lot for a race whose faces were said to make people insane. As soon as feasible, Lizard Face had allowed the original goon team assigned to the lab to be replaced by clones. Very few *real* goons had stepped inside the lab since.

Lt. Gakic's first objective was to find out where Captain Gakic would be taking Scotty for yet another attempt to kill him. The other two times he had been thrown back in his cell. But as far as *Gakic* knew, nothing new had been planned. Besides, what worse torment could Lizard Face come up with? He had chosen two biblical forms of execution, and each had failed. It was odd Lizard Face had chosen methods that had been equally ineffective in the Scriptures.

Still, Lizard Face had planned the boy's death for months, and in his sinister imagination, he had to have had more than two options. He just had to figure out what the other plans were and fast, before the boy really did get killed.

He was working at the console next to Leif's tube, and his

feelings for the baby were overwhelming. He kept hearing the words over and over again in his head, *"And when she opened it, she saw the child, and behold, the baby wept. So she had compassion on him, and said, 'This is one of the Hebrews' children.'"*

Gakic had absolutely no idea what those words meant, but one thing was certain. Love, actual love, was building in him for this child. It was almost as if God was asking him to take the baby as his own son. He shook the feeling off. That was ridiculous. He focused on the console, sifting through the files.

He barely noticed that right next to him something was covered in a large white sheet. Whatever it was, was too small to be another cloning tube. It was propped against the rear wall of the room, and next to it were some very odd tools. There were a large hammer and a pile of huge, rusted, iron nails. He couldn't guess what they were meant for, and then he found the file.

The title read simply, *"God-killer."* He opened the file, and his eyes narrowed. *Was even Lizard Face capable of such blasphemy?*

~

Scotty's leg felt dead. He had no idea what time it was, but he guessed it was late. It had taken almost two hours to climb the stairs, and surprisingly, Captain Gakic had been very patient. Of course, he had also been sneering with pleasure, probably about what he was about to do to the boy. He hadn't said what that would be yet, but if the other two trials were any indication, it would not be good. Scotty clenched the charred remains of TB all the tighter as they arrived before the metallic doors of the cloning lab.

"Are you going to tell me what you are going to do yet?" Scotty asked.

"I think that will speak for itself. Let's just say, this is guaranteed to work. Even your God could not stop it!"

Scotty was beginning to wonder where these people got their propaganda from. If Seth had been spreading these kinds of lies about God, it was no wonder the bears had lost faith. After 5,000 years of the same lie, it might as well have been the truth. But Scotty knew better. There was nothing too difficult for God. Even now, in this dark time, all it would take would be a word from the Father, and this would all be over. He didn't know if he would be rescued, or if he would die, but one thing he did know was that God would win.

Captain Gakic pressed in the appropriate code to access the lab.

~

At the swish of the outside door, Lt. Gakic snapped his computer terminal off. He hadn't accomplished everything he had wanted, but he had done enough. First, all the converted clones had been sent to the same *So* vessel Scotty had been on. Second, he had downloaded all the data he had previously collected on Scotty's alien computer. Finally, he had planted a virus in the mainframe that, once activated, would give the converts permanent access to the most protected parts of the database, even from remote locations.

"Lieutenant, what are you doing?"

Gakic turned to see his counterpart, along with the human boy. Scotty looked pale and exhausted. He was barely standing, and even that was just a hunch. Captain Gakic pulled him into the room and shoved him to his knees.

"I'm sorry, Captain. I was assigned here this evening."

"By whom? I make the duty assignments, and as I recall, you're off right now."

Gakic had never been good at lying, but this was an especially bad time to be caught in a lie. He had completely forgotten Captain Gakic was the one who made the duty assignments. Then again, he could think of one legitimate reason for being there.

"Actually, sir, I am just doing what I can to obey Master Lizard Face's orders. I needed access to the equipment in here to continue my research on the alien computer."

"That will no longer be necessary. You destroyed it."

"I what?"

"It was in the boy's pocket when you shot him."

Lt. Gakic shook his head. This was not very good at all; perhaps God would not accept him because of this. He said, "I'm sorry, Captain, but I downloaded enough information to reproduce it in time. Besides, with respect, sir, if the fire had worked, the computer would have been destroyed anyway."

"Never mind. It is not that important now. I see you have a weapon. Come here and watch the boy."

The Lieutenant did as he was told, and he trained his rifle on Scotty's head, but he had no intention of firing. If need be, he would kill Captain Gakic before he would bring any further harm to Scotty.

Captain Gakic walked to the far side of the room, picked up the hammer and nails, and gestured that Scotty should be brought closer. Lt. Gakic pulled the boy back to his feet, and he limped to the end of the room.

Captain Gakic said, "So far, your God has delivered you from the fire and from the fangs of a giant lizard. He even saved you from our weapons, but our Master was smart enough to find the real weakness of your God. After all that He showed Himself capable of, all it took was a hammer and a few rusted nails to put Him in the grave. Now, you will share that fate!"

Captain Gakic took the sheet in his hands and pulled it away. Beneath it was a simple wooden cross.

Scotty's eyes flared, and he screamed, **"NOOOOOOOOOOOOOOOOOOO!"** But it was not out of fear. It was rage, pure, holy rage! This ended now! He shouted, **"YOU WILL NOT MAKE A MOCKERY OUT OF MY LORD'S CROSS!"**

And then there was light, pure, burning, holy light. But not that of an angel; no, this light surged from the human boy himself. It burned and exploded across the room. Scotty's eyes were now a shimmering sapphire blue, and his clothes had changed. He now wore a blindingly white robe, and his flesh healed.

Captain Gakic was not so fortunate. The light was ripping the room apart. Cloning tubes exploded, and the specimens within them vaporized upon contact with the holy illumination. Gakic stumbled backward into the light. Though he was not vaporized, Scotty saw him fall toward one of the shattered tubes, and then the light obscured him from sight.

Scotty couldn't even describe how he felt. Though, if he

had to guess, this must have been what it would be like when Christians finally received their glorified bodies. He felt powerful and humble all at the same time. God was ever before his thoughts, and he felt like he could fly back home of his own power. It was amazing! In that moment, he knew everything God intended him to be, and he *was* all those things.

Despite the fact that his enemies had been vanquished, (at least the ones in that room), the light persisted. Scotty glanced about him and immediately recognized someone else standing in the room. It was the angel Joshua, and he was cradling something in his arms.

Scotty had never admitted it, but in his few encounters with the angel, he had been very intimidated and even afraid of him. That was a very normal, healthy, and godly reaction to such a being. However, now, all that was gone. He felt as powerful and as privileged as the angelic host, so he boldly approached him.

Scotty said, "Joshua, servant of the Most High God, explain what has happened here, please." Scotty was surprised that even those words coming out of his mouth sounded like music. And he couldn't even be sure he was speaking in English anymore.

The angel declared, *"You have overcome the Devil, godly one. Be at peace."*

"Have I crossed over into Heaven?"

"Once before you thought the same. The answer is no. Because of your faithfulness to the Lord Jesus Christ, you have been granted a gift offered to only a few others, but for you, it will only be temporary. You will return to what you were, and you must leave here at once."

Had Scotty, in that moment, still thought as he had only minutes before, he would have been disappointed at the prospect of becoming mortal again. But everything was different now. The Lord's will was now his, and he would obey without reservation or complaint.

Joshua said, *"You must also take this."*

For the first time, Scotty noticed the baby reptile in the angel's arms. It was Leif as he recalled, Lizard Face's son.

Joshua placed the babe in the boy's arms, and then both he and the fiery light vanished. Scotty felt himself shrinking. Not physically, but spiritually as his body returned to what it had been before. Of course, his wounds were still healed.

He took a deep breath and turned toward the door. It was then that he noticed the two goons. Or rather, one goon and one corpse. Captain Gakic had fallen upon the jagged edges of one of the shattered cloning tubes. His body had been impaled, and blood was gushing from him. He was quite dead.

Lt. Gakic, on the other hand, was kneeling prostrate on the floor. His weapon was melted, and he was breathing heavily. Scotty approached him, fully aware of the danger he still represented.

When Scotty got close enough, the only living Gakic said, "Please don't hurt me, servant of the Most High God. I am for you!"

"You have a funny way of showing it. You have tried to kill me four times!"

"I'm sorry! Please, have mercy!"

"And you killed my friend!"

"Don't sweat it, Scotty. I'm just fine."

Scotty's mind leaped at the internal voice, and for a moment, he completely forgot about Lt. Gakic. The remains of TB had been in his palm throughout the entire ordeal. He pulled his hand out from underneath the baby. The voice had come from inside his head, but for a moment, he didn't want to open his palm for fear he had just imagined it. When he finally did, a smile spread across his face.

The emerald was no longer melded with the other components, the circuitry housing was once again intact, and TB's computer chip was in perfect shape.

"TB! You're alive!"

"Yes, it must have happened in the light. Though technically, I was never really dead. As long as my memory core is intact, I can be salvaged. And the Takillians made that extremely hard to destroy. Nothing short of a nuclear blast could do it."

"I'm just glad you're okay!"

"I'm glad you're okay too, but I suggest you turn your attention back to the task at hand."

Scotty nodded.

Lt. Gakic wailed, "I didn't mean to hurt him. Perhaps I can fix him? I have been studying his systems since you arrived."

"That won't be necessary anymore," Scotty said, though he didn't explain why. Good or bad, *Gakic* didn't need to know TB was all right. "What do you want from me?" the boy asked.

"I wish to pledge my allegiance to you and to serve you all the days of my life."

Scotty stiffened. *Was this a joke?* This creature had tried to kill him. They had fought each other in the *So* vessel, and he had been every bit as arrogant and cruel as the original Gakic. Scotty had no interest in slaves or false loyalty. All he wanted was to leave. If Lt. Gakic provided that, it would be enough. As it was, it would be wrong to hurt him in any way, much less kill him.

Scotty barked, "Swear your allegiance to Jesus Christ!"

"I already have, Your Majesty."

Scotty was taken back. *Was that even possible?* He prayed and got an immediate response, "***Forgive as you have been forgiven.***"

That sealed it. Scotty asked, "Are you sure you're related to Captain Gakic?"

The Lieutenant nodded shamefully and began to weep. Scotty placed TB in his remaining pocket and then knelt next to the goon. He whispered, "God wants you to know that your sins have been forgiven. He also wants peace to be multiplied unto you. Now, please stand. I need your help, my friend."

Gakic slowly rose and said, "I am at your service, Sire."

"We need to get back to Staranana."

"I have a crew and one of the *So* vessels waiting. And we must hurry; we have to get there before your friends give Lizard Face the Cosmic Bubble."

Scotty secured his grip on the baby and said, "Lead the way!" Then Scotty, his resurrected friend, the infant clone of one of his greatest enemies, and Lt. Gakic left the room together, ready to leave Evilanda behind forever.

Chapter 27
Trips

"One hundred-seventeen," Sparkey counted. That was the number of lazy asteroids that had drifted past the massive crater the *Zerubbabel* was hiding in. They were now positioned on a very jagged, very large asteroid, 5,000 kleps from the event horizon of the vortex. Normally, such a phenomenon would have dragged all the asteroids in the area into itself, but the gravitational forces from this vortex were surprisingly low. An added advantage of their asteroid was the fact that it had heavy deposits of minerals throughout it. The mix of iron, copper, gold, and even magnesium would effectively hide the metallic signature of the *Zerubbabel*.

General Shortstop had ordered the ship into black mode, and they had anchored into the rock. Their orders were to not lift off of the asteroid until signaled. And that would only happen once Scotty's safety was confirmed. Either way, their objective was to keep the Cosmic Bubble away from the *Dragon's Blood*.

Toby and Cak were playing a game called *Crazy Eights* that Scotty had taught them. The General was calibrating and recalibrating every system on the ship. Sparkey's DNA had long since been programmed through the filter that would make the glass think he was Spikey. Now, he was doing all he could to keep his mind off of his reunion with Scotty.

He would be glad to see his friend safe and sound, of course, but he couldn't escape the guilt of having left him behind. Though he hadn't told the Nakans or Shortstop, he had brought the *Dagger of Promise* with him. The transparent orange blade, made of brillium amber, was the bane of all evil. It had been the weapon Scotty had used to send Seth to the Black Lava Pits, and Sparkey hoped that if he got the blade to the boy again, he could do the same to Lizard Face.

That would mean that he would have to sneak off the ship, disobeying orders and leaving the *Zerubbabel* without *fire glass* weapons. But that was a chance he was willing to take if it helped Scotty to forgive him. He'd just have to watch for the right time to take his leave of the *Zerubbabel*. The *Fire Cruiser* still wouldn't be there for hours. He had plenty of time to figure it out.

"One-hundred fifty-eight."

12:30 a.m.

"We're making all of 1,000,000 kleps per hour, Captain, but we should make it to the rendezvous coordinates by 2:00 a.m.," reported Commander Josh Noble from the helm.

Gloria Moonbeam and Doctor Grizz were on the bridge with the Nobles, along with Colonel Speedway. Spikey and Commander Honeytub were still down in claw control. Will Noble, acknowledged his brother, "Steady as she goes, Josh. Let me know about any problems."

"Aye, sir."

Captain Noble turned to the two doctors, "Are you ready to proceed?"

"Confirmed, sir," Gloria reported. "The *Door* is ready, security is standing by, and I have the cargo bay filled with medical personnel. I have also set up a level ten quarantine of that deck. It has been completely isolated from the rest of the ventilation systems and even the computer systems. Any computer link will have to be done through remote access, and communication must be done over interstellar radio channels."

"We do have one concern," Dr. Grizz broke in.

"What is that?" Will asked.

"We are operating on the assumption that the bear-goons will still be on that ship, and that they will still be in the same location. It has been over four days since they were taken. They may have been moved."

Captain Noble took a deep breath. He had thought about that too. He just prayed it wouldn't be true. He said, "Let's hope for the best, but if they aren't there, I'm not giving up on them. I'll take the *Fire Cruiser* to Evilanda myself and rescue them if I have to."

"Understood, sir."

12:40 a.m.

"Take a look at this, Spikey," said Commander Sam Honeytub. He had been closely monitoring the integrity of the claw. By normal space travel standards, the *Fire Cruiser* was moving very slowly through space, but by any other standards, 1,000,000 kleps an hour was incredibly fast. As such, the claw had to be watched like a hawk to maintain its structural integrity.

His scans had also revealed some interesting things about the Bubble, including trace amounts of energy that had never before been noticed in the glass, as well as its highly complex crystalline structure. However, the most remarkable thing was what he was just about to show Spikey.

"What is it, Sam?"

Sam pointed to the screen of his console and an interior scan of the Bubble. He said, "There is oxygen in there, sir. A miniature atmosphere if you will."

"Well, that's not too surprising. There had to be oxygen around when the phoenixes created the Bubble."

"Yes, but that was more than a million years ago. If I remember my chemistry right, if oxygen is left under pressure for a long time, it will emit lethal levels of nitrogen. That would in turn cause nitrogen narcosis in anyone that tried to breathe it. But I am detecting nothing but a perfect atmospheric balance of oxygen and nitrogen in there. It might as well have been in there for less than a day. Anyone could breathe it."

"Maybe it leaked in?" Spikey suggested.

"From what the General and the Colonel said, this glass is indestructible. I don't see how anything could crack it enough to cause a leak. Besides, if it did have a leak, the air should be venting out into space by now, and we should be detecting a steady decrease in air pressure inside the Bubble. See for yourself, sir. The pressure levels are constant."

Spikey double-checked the Commander's work, then said, "Make a note of it, Sam. I don't know if it means anything, but it might."

"Aye, sir."

1:00 a.m.

"We are approaching the vortex, Master," Ensign Borak reported.

Lizard Face stiffened in his chair, "This is it, people. Let's *sshow* those bears who the true ruler of the galaxy *sshould* be. Helmsman, take us into the vortex."

"Aye, sir! With the added mass of our claw, it should take three hours to traverse the passage to the rendezvous. That will put us there at exactly 4:00a.m."

"Very good, Ensign. Maintain battle *sstation*s and red alert."

1:15 a.m.

Lt. Gakic reported, "We are approaching the vortex."

"How fast are we moving?" Scotty asked.

Lt. Gakic checked his display monitor and reported, ".99 of light speed, Your Majesty."

"We can go that fast?" Scotty was impressed. Riding in the *Zerubbabel* at one-half light speed was incredible, but this *So* vessel was almost twice as fast.

Gakic said, "The *So* left behind impressive technology. Still, the *Dragon's Blood* has a significant lead on us. Our speed won't be enough to catch them before they traverse the vortex. I estimate that it will take them about three hours. If you were dealing with a more capable pilot, I could probably get you across in one. Though, we would have to reduce speed significantly. However, with my limited skills, and I'm sorry, I'm the most trained pilot aboard this craft, it will take us three hours as well. Which, if I have done the math right, will give the *Dragon's Blood* a fifteen-minute lead on us."

"We'll just have to pray Lizard Face doesn't get his hands on the Bubble before we get there."

"Speaking of praying, Your Majesty, could you tell us more about your Lord?"

A few of the other goons came closer, and they all looked eager. They were thirsty for God, and why not? Living in such an environment as Evilanda was bound to leave one spiritually parched.

Scotty smiled and said, "Well, first you can call me Scotty. I'm not very formal when it comes to titles. But I would be happy to tell you about *our* God."

A few of the goons sat on the floor as if it were story time in kindergarten, and Scotty began his impromptu sermon, "The basics are this: God created humanity to be perfect and to enjoy perfect fellowship with Him. However, the Devil, or Licen in Starananian, opposed this relationship. He himself had already been cast out of Heaven for trying to supplant God. So Licen, in the form of a serpent, deceived the first woman, Eve, into disobeying God by eating of a tree God had forbidden them to eat from. She, in turn, gave the fruit to her husband, and from that point on, they were cursed and became spiritually and physically separated from God. Some might have thought Licen had achieved his objective of keeping men from God, and he probably thought so too. But God had a plan."

"What was it?" one of the goons asked. They were like eager children.

"God promised a Deliverer who would one day defeat Licen and pay the price for the sin of humanity. Thousands of years went by as humanity wallowed in their sin. During this time, the Lord destroyed the entire world with a flood, leaving only eight people to repopulate the Earth. He confused languages, scattered peoples, and finally established a nation for Himself. Through that nation, He gave the Law. Those *Ten Commandments* pointed out human sin, and try as they might, humans could not keep the Law, for sin was in their very nature. That put humanity in a very desperate situation, and so finally, two thousand years ago, God fulfilled His promise of a Deliverer.

"The *Bible* says in John 3:16, '*For God so loved the world that He gave His one and only Son, that whoever believes in him shall not perish but have eternal life.*' Because God is a holy God, He must have justice. He can't simply let sin go unpunished, but He also has no desire to send all of humanity to Hell. So He sent His Son Jesus Christ to Earth. This Christ taught in incredibly different ways, and He performed many miracles so that He amazed all and convicted the hearts of many. Of course, there were also those who hated what He represented, a threat to their power, and so He was put to death.

"Now, God could have annihilated the world for murdering His Son, but instead, He placed all the sin of all humanity throughout all time on His Son, so that He was very pleased to have His Son die. You see, in His death, Jesus washed us of all our guilt. He paid the price for our sins, and God's sense of justice was satisfied.

"Three days later, God raised Jesus up from the grave. And having conquered sin and death, He took His place as the name above every other name. Thanks to Him, any who now admit their sins, believe in their heart and confess with their mouth that Jesus Christ is Lord will be saved. And it doesn't matter how bad you have been. Anyone can be saved."

"Do the same rules apply for us?" a goon asked.

"We are still figuring that out on Staranana. There is an angel named Joshua, who basically serves as a spokesman for God to Staranana. He said that Jesus did not die for angels, and He did not die for bears, but for men alone. I think that the reason for that is that everything in this area of space extends forth from the human imagination; the human heart if you will. In other words, God created Staranana to honor the human imagination. According to the *Text of Iren,* when Christ comes again, all the bears will be transformed into something far better, and they will share the fate of the *Blood of the Land*."

"Who is the *Blood of the Land*?" another asked.

Scotty's face flushed, "Well, actually, I am."

Many of the goons sat up straighter. They had never been in the presence of a prophetic figure before.

Scotty countered, "You mustn't worship me! Or even come close to it. I am nothing holy. God sent me to Staranana to remind the bears to trust Him and to watch over them, but all glory and worship must go to God alone. Now, in answer to your question, I trust that if Christ called you away from a life of sin, He has a plan for your eternal souls. Continue to trust Him, and I am sure you will take part in the same glory as the bears."

The goons seemed even more excited as they returned to their stations. How very like God to send one of His servants into the realm of evil, only to bring out a people for Himself. If this persisted, Evilanda might just have to change its name.

2:00 a.m.

"All stop." Captain Noble rose from his command chair and approached the viewscreen. Along the edges, asteroid fragments drifted lazily in space, but in the center, the blackness of space rippled like a pond when pebbles break its surface.

"No sign of Lizard Face yet, sir," Colonel Speedway reported.

"That's all right. He still has two hours," the Captain replied. "Any sign of the *Zerubbabel?*"

"Yes, sir. They did a good job of hiding, but I've got their exact mineral signature on file. Plus, the fact that General Shortstop is hailing us doesn't hurt either."

"Put him on the screen."

"Aye, sir!"

Speedway tapped his panel, and an instant later Shortstop's furry face appeared on the screen. *"Status report, Captain?"* he requested.

"Everything is ready to go over here. I will order the garbage to be dumped as soon as we open the package. After that, I think our trash can will be worthless. We'll throw it away. Please don't come for the trash until we call you. We must be careful because shining the Christmas lights too quickly may hurt our presents. Stay in bed until it's Christmas morning."

Most of the bridge crew had no idea what Captain Noble was talking about, but the General heard him loud and clear. Before he had left in the *Zerubbabel*, he and Captain Noble had formed a code they could use to communicate for fear Lizard Face had any probes in the area. The garbage was the Bubble, the package was Scotty, the trash can was the claw, the Christmas lights were the weapons, and the presents were the bear-goons. Bed was Shortstop's asteroid, and Christmas morning meant to stay put until the bears and Scotty were safe.

Shortstop replied, *"Very good, Captain! Merry Christmas."*

2:07 a.m.

"All right, you heard the Captain. Everything is in place. Double check your systems and be ready to shove off this asteroid at a moment's notice. Toby and Cak, keep a sharp eye on your sensors. Sparkey, how are you feeling about those weapons?" Shortstop asked.

"Just fine, sir. And if it's okay, I would like to go back to the mid-compartment to fix a snack."

"Permission granted. I may join you myself in a few minutes."

"Us too," Toby replied rubbing his belly. "I just have to finish a few computations."

Sparkey nodded and headed to the back. The truth was, he hoped they would take a long time to come back there. He prayed this wouldn't be another one of those decisions that he would regret; though the truth was, he probably would. But he had things other than food on his mind.

His dad had taken the time to repair the *Zerubbabel's Door* after the last encounter with Lizard Face. He just hoped the inventor had added the modifications he had been planning on for weeks. Simply put, Spikey had designed a remote control for the *Door* that could function up to 1,000,000 kleps away from its base machine. So, if the remote was back there, Sparkey could open a *Door* from anywhere on the *Zerubbabel,* or anywhere in this area of space for that matter. As far as he knew, the prototype *Door* in his dad's workshop was the only one with a remote, but he could hope that his dad had gotten around to upgrading this system.

When he got into the mid-compartment, he found the lights low, as was standard in black mode. Though the cupboards were fully stocked with food, he had no intention of partaking of them. He approached the *Door*. There was no remote anywhere around. *Dang it!* He couldn't risk firing up the actual *Door* now, even if he could sneak back here later. The power surge would light them up like a Christmas tree. The remote, on the other hand, could fire the *Door* up in only a few seconds, and with the preprogrammed key, he could be gone a few more seconds later. Sparkey loved having an inventor for a dad! Unfortunately, it didn't look like he'd be getting off this ship, at least, not easily.

He was just heading back up front when he noticed the drawer marked *Spikey's tools.* It seemed odd that his dad would label a drawer with his name on a ship that he owned, but then again, in their apartment, something labeled in such a way meant to *stay away!* Spikey didn't go so far as to install locks on his various stashes of tools, but everyone knew how particular he was with his stuff. Sparkey opened the drawer and found the *Door* remote.

3:00 a.m.

"The *Fire Cruiser* has arrived at the vortex, Master. We detected a transmission coming from it," reported Lt. Kyak.

"Anything *ssignificant?*" Lizard Face asked.

"No, they must have been calling the Palace. It was about their Christmas party. I don't think it's anything we need to worry about."

"Very well, maintain course."

3:30 a.m.

"We're making better time than I thought, Your…Scotty, but we'll still be at least ten minutes behind them," Lt. Gakic reported.

"Get us there as quickly as possible, Lieutenant," Scotty said.

"With respect, sir, you can call me by my name too."

Scotty grimaced and squirmed, "I apologize for what I am about to say, and it is going to sound very childish, but your name sounds like something my dog threw up."

As true as it was, Scotty hated saying something like that in the midst of this new friendship. Thankfully, *Gakic* did not take it personally. He laughed and said, "You think so too? I never understood why Lizard Face made the clones keep the same names as their progenitors. Oh, well, you can call me Lieutenant."

"Or maybe I can call you *Gak* or *Gakie* or even *G*. What do you think?"

"Whatever you want, Scotty," *Gakic* laughed.

4:00 a.m.

"We're approaching the threshold, Master Lizard Face."

~

"The *Dragon's Blood* is approaching, General."

~

"Ten more minutes, Scotty."

~

"Captain Noble to all hands. The *Dragon's Blood* is entering the area. Maintain your stations. Stay on alert. Let's get this done!"

Chapter 28
The Exchange

For a moment, everything just hung in space. There was no movement, just two massive vessels staring down the barrels of each other's weapons cannons. Each seemed to be sizing the other up. The *Dragon's Blood* was conducting fierce scans for any traps. Thankfully, nothing was showing up, even with the *So* sensors. The *Fire Cruiser* was conducting its own scans, mostly for human life signs. Unfortunately, the *Dragon's Blood* was using some sort of alien dampening field to block their scans.

After another minute of stillness, Captain Noble decided to take the initiative, "Colonel, open a channel to the *Dragon's Blood*." And then, "This is Captain William Noble of the Stararockan vessel *Fire Cruiser* to the commander of the *Dragon's Blood*. Be advised, we will interpret any aggressive action toward this vessel as hostile, and we will respond with extreme force. We are prepared to release the Cosmic Bubble to you once you have released Emperor Scotty and his escape craft is successfully beyond your weapons' range. This condition is not open to negotiation. If you fail to comply, Scotty or no Scotty, you will be destroyed."

Will knew Scotty would agree with that. Even if he did get killed, the bears would be out of immediate danger. It was an ugly prospect, but Noble knew Scotty was willing to make the sacrifice. It also took some of the power out of Lizard Face's hands. Now they couldn't be manipulated.

Speedway's panel chirped, "They are responding, Captain."

"Put them on screen."

When the image of Lizard Face appeared in what had once been Captain Turrock's command chair, Captain Noble felt sick. Even the idea of someone like Lizard Face, a murderer several thousand times over, in command of one of the Starananian Liberation ships was appalling. Added to the fact that he had killed a close family friend of the Nobles, it was all Will could do to keep thoughts of vengeance from his mind.

"*Sstararockan vessel,*" came the hissing voice of Lizard Face, "*we agree to your terms of exchange. Please note your Emperor beside me. He has not been harmed, and he has been treated as a royal guest. He will be departing from this vessel in an escape pod, approximately two minutes after the end of our conversation. Three minutes after that he will be beyond our weapons' range. Therefore, we expect the Bubble to be released in five minutes.*"

"Acknowledged, please also be advised that we have developed a defense against your computer virus. Should you attempt to use it, that too will be considered an act of aggression and will result in your destruction."

"*We understand and will comply. Dragon's Blood out!*"

~

"That was very cordial, Master," the *Goon Omega* said.

"Yes, it was. Let the fools think they have the upper hand. It will *sserve* my purposes all the better in the future. Now, come, walk with me. We must get you to the escape pod."

~

"*Captain Noble, this is Doctor Moonbeam.*"

"Go ahead, Gloria."

"*Sir, the scanners in the Door were able to cut through the dampening field. We've confirmed 278 bear-goon life signs. It's less than we'd hoped, but at least we have those.*"

"Very good, Doctor. Remember the General's orders. We don't open our presents until Christmas morning."

"*Understood, sir.*"

~

Sparkey Moonbeam did his best to hide the *Door* remote under his console, but so far, everyone else was too focused on their sensor readouts. He had programmed the *Door* to take him to the deck just below the bridge of the *Dragon's Blood*. Unfortunately, he had run out of time to get there before Scotty would be released, and it was unlikely the boy would want to return just to use the dagger on Lizard Face. So Sparkey would do it himself!

The bears had it all worked out that they would destroy the *Dragon's Blood*. That would result in the death of Lizard Face, but in Sparkey's mind, justice demanded a direct ticket to the Black Lava Pits for the reptile through the *Dagger of Promise*. Actually, he saw it as a way to redeem himself in the eyes of Scotty. His parents would probably see it as an incredibly stupid thing to do. He would still do it, of course. He just had to wait for the right time.

~

"Can't this bucket of bolts go any faster?"

"We're at maximum, sir," Lt. Gakic assured.

"Scotty, calm down. We're on one of the fastest known ships in the galaxy," TB reminded.

"Not fast enough!"

~

"They've ejected the escape pod, Captain," Speedway reported. "Should we move in?"

"Wait for it, Colonel. Let Scotty come to us."

"Aye, two minutes forty-five seconds until we are to release the Bubble."

"Understood, inform Claw Control."

~

"You ready, Sam?" Spikey asked.

"Aye, sir. As soon as we get the word, I'll release the Bubble."

"Excellent, once Scotty and the bear-goons are safe, I'll blow the claw away from the ship."

"Confirmed, the lower deck has been completely evacuated, and the area is sealed off."

~

"I have a lock on the bear-goons," Gloria said. "This won't be pretty. Is everyone ready?" She looked around to the two dozen medical personnel and the fifteen security officers assigned to her and Doctor Grizz. Each one was wearing the white masks with the filter tubes over their mouths and noses. They nodded, and the security officers tightened their weapons across their chests, ready for anything.

"All right. I'm bringing the *Door* system online. As soon as we have the okay, I'll open the passage."

~

"It's time, Captain," Speedway said.

"Hail the *Dragon's Blood*," Noble ordered. Speedway complied, and when Lizard Face again appeared on the screen, Noble said, "Be advised, we are releasing the Bubble now, but you are not to approach this ship. Let it drift to you, and then we will part company peacefully."

"Understood. Dragon's Blood out!"

"Captain Noble to all hands, **MERRY CHRISTMAS**!" And it began!

~

"That's my cue," Sam said.

"It's all our cues," Spikey replied.

Honeytub twisted the compression valves on his claw controls, and then he pulled down the primary locking lever. There was a click and a shudder in the hull, and outside the ship, the Cosmic Bubble was dropped free into space.

Honeytub called the bridge, "The Bubble is free, Captain."

"Acknowledged, evacuate that section."

~

"That's our cue. Sparkey, get the weapons ready. Ensigns, sharp eyes. I'm taking us up," Shortstop said.

"Wouldn't it be better to wait for Scotty to get aboard the *Fire Cruiser* before attacking?" Toby asked.

"That's part of the trick," Shortstop began. "Scotty isn't going aboard the *Fire Cruiser*. We are going to use the *Door* to bring him over here with us."

"What!" Sparkey exclaimed.

Shortstop misinterpreted Sparkey's excitement. "You excited about seeing your friend again?"

"Yeah, sure," Sparkey whispered. The truth was his plans would be easier to carry out with Scotty on the *Fire Cruiser*. He'd just have to improvise. He asked, "Permission to man the *Door*, sir."

Shortstop shook his head, "You know we need you at the weapons board. Cak will man the controls." Then he addressed Cak, "Once we engage the enemy, get back to the controls. We'll only have a few seconds. I'm going to take us in for a close pass of Scotty's pod."

"Understood," Cak replied.

Toby reported, "General, they've spotted us."

~

"Master, there is another vessel emerging from the asteroid field. It's the *Zerubbabel*," Lt. Kyak reported.

"What! Those fools!"

"The *Zerubbabel* is targeting us. They are trying to put themselves between the pod, the Bubble, and us."

"If they want to be idiots let them! Target the escape pod!" Lizard Face commanded.

"Master? Why do you want to kill the *Goon Omega*? It's the only one we have."

"Well, it's not exactly the only one," Lizard Face said half under his breath. Then added more clearly, "We must keep up appearances. Take out the pod's engines. Then blast the *Zerubbabel* out of *sspace*!"

"Aye, sir!"

Another goon reported, "Master, I am detecting a *Door* field forming in the cargo bay where we're keeping the bear-goons."

"I expected *ssomething* like this." Lizard Face tapped his controls and asked, "Lizard Face to Dr. Amek, are you ready?"

Lizard Face could practically hear the grin across the intercom, *"Yes, sir!"*

Had it not served his plans, Lizard Face would have slaughtered every bear when he first took the *Dragon's Blood.* He had not allowed any impure goons to leave Staranana with him, and he had no desire to add any to his numbers now, especially with the *Goon Omega* project. But the remaining bears had served a purpose.

They had been kept in quarantine since the day that they had been captured, and little by little they had been exposed to a virus. The cure for this virus was *goonieness* itself. The bear-goons would only be carriers. However, should someone else be exposed to the virus in any way, it would instantly cause all the symptoms of *goonieness* to a factor of ten. Flesh would rot, and the infected individual's mind would contort. Only this time, the stress on the brain would be so intense that it would literally tear itself apart. Then the virus would consume the flesh of its victim in a very real, very painful way. Anyone who was infected would be dead within minutes. Lizard Face had implanted a dormant version of the virus in the *Goon Omega.* Given the creature's superior powers, it was a way to ensure its loyalty. All it would take was the introduction of one enzyme, and the *Goon Omega* would self-destruct. Now, however, it would be the bears that would suffer.

~

"That's our cue," Gloria said with the command from Captain Noble. She and Doctor Grizz manned the controls of the *Door.*

Grizz said, "We have to expect resistance from the other side. I am scanning for a *Door* repulser field, and I am vamping up our power levels to 120% of normal."

"That may be enough, but Spikey said we can take it as high as 250% if we need to before the system begins to burn out."

"There's nothing over there resisting us," Grizz reported.

"That's odd? They should have detected us by now. Keep an eye on it. It will take a few minutes for the field to form."

~

"They've opened fire on Scotty's escape pod!" Toby screeched.

Shortstop barked, "Cak, get back there! Get Scotty onboard. Sparkey, open fire!"

"Aye, sir," Sparkey complied. As he had rehearsed a hundred times, he gripped the weapons controls in his hands. It was not yet time to bring out the big guns, a.k.a. the *fire glass*, but this ship was more than capable of defending itself without them.

"I've got a target, sir. FIRING!"

Two purple beams of energy shot like lightning from the *Zerubbabel* and tore into the *Dragon's Blood*. The damage barely scratched the outer hull, but it was more than enough to tell them to back off.

"I'm putting us in between the pod and the *Dragon's Blood*, and I'm taking our shields to full. Toby, where is the Bubble?" Shortstop asked.

"About 4,000 kleps away, near a large asteroid, but it is still drifting toward the *Dragon's Blood.*"

"Can we keep it away from them?"

"Not as long as we're trying to defend the escape pod!" Toby screeched as the tiny ship was rocked with an explosive barrage.

"Cak! How's it coming back there?" Shortstop shouted.

"I'm having trouble establishing a *Door* field, sir!" Cak shouted back.

Shortstop maneuvered the *Zerubbabel* out of the way of another blast of fire and punched the intercom switch, "Why, Ensign?"

"*The targeting computer is already locked on another set of coordinates. I can't break the lock.*"

"Where is the target?"

"Deck two of the Dragon's Blood!"

"What! Why would…?" Shortstop began, but he was cut off. The cockpit of the *Zerubbabel* had begun to glow blue, and bolts of electricity were shooting through the room. Beyond Sparkey, dissolving the very bulkhead next to him, a *Door* field was forming.

"Sparkey, what are you doing?" Toby yelled.

The cub did not answer. He was already out of his safety restraint, and he was standing on his chair poised to jump through the *Door*. He dove headfirst into the swirling blue light. He had no idea what he would face beyond, and even as he flew, he wondered if he was doing the right thing. Scotty was as good as rescued, the *Dragon's Blood* would be destroyed by the *Fire Cruiser*, the bear-goons were going to be healed, the Bubble saved, and they would all be home in plenty of time for Christmas. He didn't have to do this, and yet he did. If only to prove himself, he did.

Sparkey was almost through the *Door* when he felt something wrap around his ankle, and suddenly, his head was slamming into the seat of his chair. Shortstop demanded, "I don't know how you're doing this, but it will stop right now! How could you be so selfish?"

Sparkey growled, and then with his foot still trapped in the General's hand, he kicked as hard as he could and slammed his foot into Shortstop's nose. The older bear immediately fell back, grasping his now bleeding snout. Sparkey was up again, and without even looking back at Toby's accusing glance, he jumped through the portal.

The vessel was again pelted with a round of fire. Shortstop gripped his controls in blood covered hands and ordered, "Toby, get up here. Take the weapons."

Toby unlatched his safety restraints and got up. He asked, "Are you okay, General?"

"I'll live," Shortstop said. "Cak, can you get Scotty now?"

"Yes, sir. I'm bringing him over."

Shortstop commanded, "Toby, contact the *Fire Cruiser*. Inform them of the situation. Once Scotty's aboard, I'm taking us out of here."

"What about the Bubble, sir?" Toby asked.

"We can't use the *fire glass* without Sparkey, and the *Dragon's Blood* has obviously been modified with alien technology. We can't put Scotty at further risk."

"Understood, General."

~

Cak Nakan had never been very good with Captain Moonbeam's inventions, but part of his basic military training had included full lessons in *Door* operation. Even so, the device wasn't easy. All sorts of things had to be factored in, including plasma and tachyon levels, distance computations, energy levels, and precise coordinates. All that was hard enough, and being in the middle of a space battle, with the ship jutting this way and that, wasn't exactly making it any easier. When he finally locked onto the escape pod, it was a miracle.

The blue passage coalesced, and when it had fully formed, Cak took a deep breath as *Emperor Scotty Fields* stepped back onto the tiny vessel.

Cak reported, "We've got him, General."

Chapter 29
Revelations

"**W**elcome back, Scotty," Cak said.

"Yes, thank you, Ensign. Praise God I'm back safely. It wasn't easy, though. You made the right choice giving up the Bubble."

"Well, no one is quite sure about that. We've got a plan to keep it."

"Oh, really?"

"Yes, sir, but I had best get back to my duty station. Do you have TB? We could use his help."

"Unfortunately, Lizard Face destroyed him."

Cak hung his head. TB was yet another to add to the long list of the dead.

Scotty said, "Let's go up front, and please, tell me more about this plan."

~

"SPARKEY IS WHERE?" Colonel Speedway shouted.

That had Captain Noble out of his seat. He said, "Put that transmission on the viewer, Colonel."

"Aye, sir," Speedway complied. An instant later, the face of Ensign Toby Nakan filled the screen.

Toby reported, *"Sparkey somehow opened a Door in the cockpit and jumped through it. It was targeted at the second deck of the Dragon's Blood."*

"Why would he do that?" Noble asked.

"I have no idea, sir."

The screen switched to the blood-stained face of General Shortstop. "What happened to you?" Captain Noble asked.

"It's not that important. Captain, the Zerubbabel is in no condition to continue in this fight. We're going to back off to a safe distance and keep Scotty out of harm's way. Can you rescue Sparkey and keep the Bubble from Lizard Face?"

"We'll do our best, but we'll need to figure out another way to get the Bubble back to Staranana. We're going to dump the claw to give us more maneuverability."

"Understood, keep me apprised."

"Yes, sir! Captain Noble out."

The image of the General was replaced by a field of stars, and Noble ordered, "Colonel, get me Spikey."

~

Honeytub noted the flashing green light on the control board of the claw. "There is a transmission coming in, Captain," he reported.

"I've got it," Spikey said.

He tapped the button next to the light, and Captain Noble's voice filled the room, *"Spikey, Sparkey is on the Dragon's Blood."*

"What!"

"From what I understand, he did this himself. The Zerubbabel has Scotty safe and sound, but he still went over. If we want to get him back, we need to dump the claw and get the other bears over now."

"Understood, we'll dump the claw in sixty seconds."

~

"Gloria to Captain Noble, the *Door* field is at full strength. We're bringing the bears over now."

"Understood," Noble said. He didn't mention a word about Sparkey. There was no need to worry her. After all, there were close to three hundred bears who would soon need her help. He just hoped her would-be cure would prove up to the challenge.

Gloria glanced about the room one last time, and everyone nodded that they were ready. She turned to Grizz, "Here goes nothing!" And she pulled the activation lever.

The lights in the cargo bay dimmed as power was sucked into the *Door*. Blue jolts of lightning danced between the gems along the doorframe, the air whistled at almost deafening levels, and finally, the blue passageway formed completely.

Gloria commanded, "Dr. Grizz, bring our modifications online."

Grizz grunted in assent and tapped a few more buttons on the control panel, and the mood of the room instantly changed. If Gloria had to describe the look of the original *Door* passage, she might have related it to gentle ripples on the surface of a pond. The initial lightning show, anytime the *Door* opened, could be a bit unnerving, but once the passage formed, it generally set people's minds at ease. Spikey said that the effect made people trust their lives and safety to the *Door's* ability to take them where they wanted to go.

Now, however, it was like looking right through the top of a tornado funnel, and a particularly violent one at that. Anything on the other side would be sucked into the passage and exposed to the tachyon and beta radiation. Gloria winced. She could almost hear the screams as the radiation further mutilated the infected ones' already marred flesh. Unfortunately, as a doctor, she knew that sometimes you have to make the pain worse before you can make it better.

~

On the *Dragon's Blood,* a gnarled hand scratched a patch of itchy fungus on a furry face. The room around him stank of vomit, urine, and other forms of waste, but no one seemed to care. It was like being in an insane asylum. There were random flickers of happy memories, but they were as elusive as the wind, brushing against you but never taking solid form. Madness had consumed them all. It was a miracle they had not killed each other. But the pain they now endured was nothing compared to what was coming next.

~

"I think I'll take the weapons, General," *Scotty* said.
"But, sir, I…"

"Are you questioning me, General?" *Scotty* asked, his tone both condescending and rude.

"No, sir, but I told Captain Noble we were backing off from this fight. We need to get you to safety. Plus, you couldn't control those weapons anyway. They're made of *fire glass*, and only Spikey, or Sparkey with a little technological manipulation, can use them."

The *Goon Omega* quickly scanned its memory. Sparkey was Scotty's best friend. In fact, Scotty was very close to the entire Moonbeam family. If anyone was going to notice that something was wrong with *Scotty,* it would be one of them. It might not be a bad idea to arrange a little accident for all of them as soon as possible. No need to have them snooping around wrecking the Master's plans.

Scotty asked, "Where did you get more *fire glass?*"

"From the phoenixes. We found, or rather, they brought us to their city. They allowed us to take two globes of *fire glass* from Emperor Iren's coffin."

"Emperor Iren?"

"Yes, it's a long story, sir."

"Well, regardless, the *fire glass* should make excellent weaponry. I can't wait to see the amount of power it can unleash."

"Yes, how did you...?" Shortstop began.

"Are Spikey or Sparkey aboard?" the *Goon Omega* interjected. He wasn't sure if he had slipped or not. Scotty probably didn't know anything about *fire glass*. Shortstop had as much as said it could be used as a weapon, but there was no way Scotty would have known its full capabilities. Thankfully, Shortstop didn't pursue the issue.

The General replied, "Sparkey was onboard, but, well, he abandoned ship. He opened a *Door* to the *Dragon's Blood* and transported over there. We think he wants to confront Lizard Face. We don't know why."

Scotty shook his head, "That stupid little bear!"

Shortstop was shocked at that. Sure his nose was bloodied, if not broken, but he didn't think of Sparkey as stupid. He had known the cub since he was born. Sparkey had always been filled with passion, often abandoning the rules if it served the greater good in his young eyes. Whatever his motives, the cub must have thought what he was doing was right. What was more disturbing was Scotty's attitude. It was possible the human boy held a grudge against Sparkey for leaving him on the *Dragon's Blood*. Plus, with the death of TB, who knew what Scotty was feeling? Still, his behavior wasn't very Scotty-like, and it definitely wasn't Christian.

"I'm sorry, Scotty?"

"Nothing, General. I've just had a rough few days. Um, Ensign Nakan was telling me about a plan to keep the Cosmic Bubble?"

Another red flag! Scotty was always respectful, and he typically addressed Shortstop and Speedway by their ranks. But usually, he called the Nakans and the Moonbeams by their first names. Something was out of place, but Shortstop let it slide. He was just glad to have Scotty back safe and sound.

He replied, "Both the *Zerubbabel* and the *Fire Cruiser* are now equipped with *fire glass* weapons. If it weren't for Sparkey, the *Dragon's Blood* would have probably been destroyed by now."

"Well, that's very interesting. Do you think we'll get Sparkey back okay?"

"I really don't know. This complicates things something awful. But if anyone can figure it out, it is the Nobles and the Moonbeams. In the meantime, we are getting you out of here," Shortstop said and turned back to his controls. "I'm setting a course back to Staranana. We'll let the *Fire Cruiser* clean up here."

"Very good, General. I think I'll head into the back and lie down."

"Good idea, sir. I'm sure you must be exhausted. We'll need to get you checked out by a doctor soon. But for now, take it easy."

The *Goon Omega* nodded and moved back toward the rear compartment. Of course, he had no intention of going anywhere near the bunk compartment. There was a transmission he needed to send.

~

"The mass levels in the passage are continuing to increase," Gloria reported. "It should be just another minute, and all the bear-goons will be inside."

"How long will it be before they exit onto the *Fire Cruiser*?" Dr. Grizz asked.

"Just a minute or two after they all enter the passage. We have to make sure they have all been fully exposed to…" Gloria paused and fixed her eyes on one of the *Door's* computer readouts.

"What is it?" Grizz asked.

Gloria pointed at a red bar on the computer screen. She said, "This is the *Door's* temperature gage. It's running hot for some reason."

"Well, we are pumping a lot of energy into it."

"Yes, but that should show up in the power coils, but they read as absolutely stable. This heat is coming from the motor. If the levels don't stabilize, I'm afraid the radiation generators will rupture."

"Maybe we should get Spikey down here."

~

Spikey Moonbeam watched the claw drift away through space. He and Commander Honeytub were back on the bridge. The Cosmic Bubble was still drifting, but with the claw now gone, Lizard Face could only assume treachery. Even so, the *Dragon's Blood* had remained motionless since the *Zerubbabel* escaped with *Scotty*. Its own claw was opening and closing as eagerly as a little boy waiting to catch a baseball.

Spikey asked, "So, how do we get Sparkey back?"

"We could use…" Captain Noble began, but a frantic voice broke out over the intercom.

"Gloria to Spikey! We need you down here now!"

"What's wrong?"

"The Door is overheating. We can't stabilize it, and all the bear-goons are already in the passage."

Spikey got up immediately, "I'm on my way. Drop the power levels to half of what you are using, and open the exhaust ports to full. That should buy you a few more minutes."

"*Understood! Gloria out.*"

~

"We're approaching the threshold of the vortex. We should be in communication range of your friends within one minute," Lt. Gakic reported.

The real Scotty sat up straighter in his chair. His finger itched over the top of the transmitter switch. By now, the *Dragon's Blood* had been on the other side of the vortex for almost ten minutes. God only knew how much damage Lizard Face could do in that length of time. Scotty only hoped Lizard Face hadn't used the *Goon Omega* yet.

~

"There is a transmission coming in," Lt. Kyak reported.

"What?" Lizard Face inquired.

"I can only assume it is coming from the *Goon Omega*. The signal is being routed from the *Zerubbabel*."

"Put it on the *sspeakers*."

Lizard Face waited a moment, and then the voice of *Scotty Fields* filled the bridge, "*Master, the bears are deceiving you! They have no intention of turning the Bubble over to you. You must destroy the Fire Cruiser immediately. Both of their vessels are equipped with fire glass weapons! And, sir, one of the bears has already boarded the Dragon's Blood.*"

Lizard Face cursed under his breath. So the fools had figured out the secret of the glass. And if that was the case, they would sooner sacrifice all their lives than surrender the Bubble. Well, that was perfectly all right with him!

He addressed the *Goon Omega*, "A change of plans. We'll engage the *Fire Cruiser*, but if we lose the Bubble, I *sstill* need you in place. Make *ssure* the *Zerubbabel* gets out of here. I'll take care of the *sstowaway* personally."

~

"Aye, Master," the *Goon Omega* replied and flipped the transmitter switch to off.

"Who were you talking to, Scotty?"

The *Goon Omega* turned with a start to see Ensign Cak Nakan. If the teen had heard even a portion of his conversation with Lizard Face, there was no alternative. He had to die.

~

"Quickly, Spikey, take a look," Gloria said as her husband approached the *Door*. The temperature gauge on the device was coming dangerously close to critical levels.

Spikey began to tap furiously at the controls, and he said, "I don't understand how this is possible. The motor is the last thing that should be overheating. Are you sure you followed all of my instructions?"

"To the letter! We haven't even taken the power levels as high as you said they could go," Gloria replied.

Spikey confirmed this and said, "Well, if I can't stabilize it, the radiation generators will be breached. That wouldn't have been a problem on a regular *Door,* but because of the modifications I made to this system, the leak will kill half the bears on this vessel. And the other half will have to abandon ship. Start getting these people out of here!"

"What about the bear-goons?" Grizz asked.

"I'm sorry, we can't help them anymore. Now move!"

Grizz began directing the medics and the security guards toward the exit. Then he followed them.

Gloria remained with Spikey, who was now on the floor pulling a panel from the base of the *Door*.

"Gloria, get out of here!" Spikey demanded.

"Not without you! Now, what are you doing?"

"Ugh! I'm trying to manually cut the motor. I'll have to sever the fuel line. But I have only…." Spikey paused and placed his hand against the now exposed radiator of the *Door's* motor.

"What's wrong?" Gloria asked.

Spikey shook his head and replied, "With temp levels like the computer is reading, the radiator should be boiling over by now, but it's completely cool." Spikey jumped up to the computer controls again, and his brow furrowed.

"Spikey, talk to me!"

"The *Door* isn't producing this heat. Something else is!"

"What is it?"

"I don't know. Come on, we have to go now!" Spikey grabbed his wife by the wrist and then punched the intercom switch on the *Door*, "Spikey to Captain Noble. We failed, Will. We can't save the bear-goons. You need to evacuate this part of the ship, and then jettison the entire *Door* system into space!"

Captain Noble didn't even ask for an explanation. He merely replied, *"Acknowledged! And, Spikey, we need you back up here right away!"*

"Why?"

"There is another ship coming through the vortex!"

"On my way!" Spikey began to pull Gloria toward the exit, and he thought he heard her start to sniffle. He couldn't really blame her. Three hundred friends were about to be crushed to death in a lonely realm outside what could truly be called reality. But there was nothing to be done. It was either those lives, or those plus eight hundred more.

Spikey and Gloria were just approaching the threshold of the cargo bay, when they felt the white-hot blast of light explode against their backs! Spikey pulled Gloria in front of him, trying to shield her with his body, as if that would do any good. It would probably only prolong her life for a billionth of a second, and then they, and most of the ship's crew, would be dead. Spikey clenched his eyes shut.

"Spikey, look!"

Spikey popped open a single eye. To his surprise, he was not dead, and Gloria was pointing back inside the cargo bay. He followed her finger back toward the *Door*, and there they saw the source of the light. It was a man in flowing white, and they both recognized him immediately. You just didn't forget people like this. He had his hands on the controls of the *Door*. He glanced briefly in their direction and shouted, ***"Be sober, be vigilant; because your adversary the devil walks about like a roaring lion, seeking whom he may devour!"***

"What does that mean?" Gloria asked, but she never got an answer. The cargo bay doors snapped shut, leaving she and Spikey alone in the corridor.

"Spikey, what was…?"

"We'll worry about it later. Obviously, God's got a plan. Now, you should get up to sickbay. I need to get to the bridge!"

~

"I can't identify the vessel, Captain," Josh Noble reported. "It's alien in origin, but I'm detecting much of the same technology that seems to have been incorporated into the *Dragon's Blood*."

"Great! Reinforcements for Lizard Face," Captain Noble cursed.

"I wouldn't bet on that, Captain," Speedway interjected.

"Colonel?"

"Sir, that ship is targeting its weapons on the *Dragon's Blood*, and they are hailing us."

Noble cocked his brow and ordered, "Put them on screen, Mr. Speedway."

Shock, confusion, hope, and a little bit of anger played their way across Captain Noble's face as the image of a human boy materialized on the screen. For some bizarre, unknown reason, Captain Noble was face to face with Emperor Scotty Fields.

Scotty wasted no time with pleasantries, *"Captain, listen to me! You can't trust Lizard Face. You have to keep the Bubble away from him. He has some new creature that can shape-shift. He created a double of me that he was going to use to try and trick you into giving him the Bubble."*

Noble eyed him suspiciously, "With all due respect, *Scotty*, you seem to be surrounded by goons at the moment. How do I know you're not this shape-shifter?"

Scotty saw Spikey step onto the *Fire Cruiser's* bridge and replied, *"Ugh! Captain, we don't have time for twenty questions. Look, the Moonbeams know me better than anyone. Have Spikey test me."*

Noble turned to Spikey, "Well, Spikey?"

Spikey was still trying to shake the shock of seeing Joshua again, and the added confusion of seeing Scotty in one place, when he knew for a fact that he was in another, had his mind spinning all the more. He focused and said, "All right. Um, do you remember three months ago when you, Sparkey, and I were crossing the White Desert?"

"Of course!"

"About the sixth night we were in a cave. Sparkey went to sleep, and you and I were talking. During that conversation, I compared Seth's throne to something. What was it?"

Scotty didn't even have to think before he replied, *"Actually, you compared it to two things, a baby's highchair and a toilet seat. And that was in relation to the throne of Jesus Christ."*

"He's right," Spikey said. "One last question though. Something I've neglected to enter into the security records for situations like this. Tell me, what is your favorite verse of the *Bible*?"

Again, Scotty snapped out an answer, *"My favorite verse is Joshua 1:9, and you know that because I quoted it in our would-be church service in the dungeon of the Palace when we were all captured three months ago. I can quote it if you like?"*

"Not necessary, Scotty," Spikey said. He turned to Captain Noble, "I'm convinced, Will."

Noble nodded and addressed Scotty, "Praise the Lord you're all right, Scotty, but we've got a few situations brewing. We could use your help, and maybe a little explanation about the goons."

"I'm all ears, Captain. And don't worry about these guys. I'll tell you the whole story later, but needless to say, they are new servants of God."

"Excellent! Well, first things first. Sparkey is onboard the *Dragon's Blood.*"

"What?"

"We don't know the whole story. We need to destroy the *Dragon's Blood,* but we can't as long as Sparkey is onboard. We…"

"Sir, sorry to interrupt," Speedway broke in. "I wasn't able to eject the *Door* system."

"And you're just telling us this now!" Captain Noble raged.

"Well, that's just it, sir. The system stabilized for some reason, and I tried to initiate a proper shutdown. Just blowing it out the airlock still powered up could have destroyed a quarter of the ship. Anyway, by the time I got ready to eject it, I lost all contact with that deck."

"How could that happen?" Will asked.

"I think I know," Spikey said. "The angel Joshua was down there."

"Hate to break this up, gentlemen, but have you noticed that the Dragon's Blood is closing on you, weapons powered?" Scotty was thrilled that God had chosen once again to intervene, but the time for discussion was over.

"Yes, sir," Noble replied. "Josh, evasive maneuvers. Colonel, hands on those weapons. Target only their nacelles for now. Let's wait a bit longer to bring out the big guns."

"Yes, sir, but you might want to know that our crew compliment has increased by about 278 bears."

"What?"

"That's what I was trying to tell you. If Joshua was down there, he must have brought the bears over. I am detecting absolutely no trace of *goonieness* among them. From what I can tell, they are in perfect health."

Captain Noble smiled and commanded, "Maintain quarantine of that section, but get Gloria and Grizz back down there right away."

"Yes, sir!" Speedway chimed.

Scotty asked, *"Can you use the Door to get me onboard the Dragon's Blood?"*

Spikey shook his head, "No, not before I check out and recalibrate the system. Besides, if anyone is going after Sparkey, it is going to be me."

"No, my friend, I need to do this. I suspect I am the reason Sparkey is over there in the first place."

Spikey knew better than to argue, "In that case, head toward the *Zerubbabel*. Their *Door* should be able to get you aboard."

"OH MY GOSH!" Captain Noble screamed.

"What!" Scotty exclaimed.

"If this is the real Scotty, then the shape-shifter is onboard the *Zerubbabel!*"

"I don't have time to play twenty questions with them too. Warn them, and tell them I'm coming. Scotty out!"

~

"With all due respect, sir, I asked you a question. Who were you talking to?" Cak again asked.

"Oh, Ensign, sorry. I was just checking in with the *Fire Cruiser*."

"No, I don't think so, *sir*. You called whomever you were talking to, *Master*. And unless the Lord Jesus Christ Himself has decided to make an appearance on the *Fire Cruiser*, you have no *Master* in Starananian space!"

Scotty sneered. Though lying was practically in his blood, there was a simpler way to deal with this problem.

Cak was waiting for an answer, and then his hands shot to his throat as his windpipe was suddenly being crushed and his throat being impaled by two clawed hands. Only, it wasn't his hands doing it. Somehow, *Scotty's* arms had extended a good three feet in length, and his hands had transformed into two green, scaly, reptilian claws. Cak had no idea what this thing was, but it definitely wasn't Scotty. Oh, well, it also wasn't the only person in the room with claws!

Cak grabbed onto the creature's arms and slashed, ripping away human flesh and lizard scales. The *Goon Omega* lurched away, and Cak prepared himself to fight. In ordinary circumstances, he would have shouted for help. But his throat was on fire, and it was all he could do to taunt the creature, "I don't know what you did to our friend, but you're going to pay!"

The *Goon Omega* jumped on Cak, and they crashed to the floor. Cak struggled against the beast's arms, which were obviously much stronger than a nine-year-old's, but they had yet to prove themselves against a bear's strength. Cak kicked and slammed the *Goon Omega* into the table. The more noise the better! It jumped up and went for Cak's jugular again, but he spun away and returned to his feet, just in time to see the thing transform again. Scotty's rather adorable face began to split, and crack, and bleed. His eyes swelled and became yellow, and a scaly green snout began to form from his mouth and nose. Within seconds, Cak was met with a very familiar face.

"Lizard Face?"

"No! Just a faithful *sservant!*" And the *Goon Omega* attacked again.

Cak grabbed it by the wrists and threw it into the far bulkhead, but the *Omega* was quick to recover. It jutted its tongue out across the entire room and wrapped it around Cak's neck. Yuck! It didn't get more disgusting than that! Cak dug his claws into the tongue and ripped it open. The *Omega* wailed and pulled back.

It jumped on the table and then right on top of Cak. Glass shattered, chairs went flying, and they continued to wrestle about the mid-compartment! *Where the blazes were Toby and the General?* The *Goon Omega* had its hands wrapped around Cak's wrists, and he felt the sting of acid make contact with his skin. Then he watched in horror as the thing began to change again.

Scales began to sprout hair, and lots of it! The snout became stubby and grew a black and wet looking nose. And the large, yellow eyes shrank to beady, black spheres. When the transformation was complete, Cak was face to face with himself.

Cak threw the thing off and jumped up again. "If you think I'll have a problem smashing my own face in, you're mistaken! I won't let you get away with hurting my friend!"

The *Omega* growled and lunged again at the young Starananian. Only to be stopped dead as a bolt of laser energy exploded between them.

"Hold it right there!"

Cak and *Cak* turned to see General Shortstop and Toby Nakan standing in the hatchway to the cockpit. Toby had an energy pistol pointed in their direction.

The *Goon Omega* shouted, "Quick, Toby, kill him! He's some sort of shape-shifter!"

"Don't listen to him, Toby! You know I'd never ask you to kill anyone. Besides, I'd hate to cheat Chef Berry out of the chance to hold a grudge against me!"

"Who are you going to believe? Me or this freak!" the *Omega* raged.

Toby rolled his eyes, aimed, and fired, and one of the *Caks* sizzled out of existence.

"Ensign, what the…?" Shortstop began.

"Don't worry, General. I think I know my own brother. We've got the whole twin thing going on."

"Yeah, thanks, bro. You had me scared there for a minute," Cak rasped. "But you didn't have to kill, whatever that was."

"It was called a *Goon Omega,*" Shortstop explained. "And if what Scotty told us about it was true, it was too dangerous to be kept alive."

"Scotty?"

"Yes, it seems he found some new friends, and he escaped from Evilanda without us. He's in an alien ship off the port bow. Are you fit for duty?"

Cak looked at the General's blood-smeared snout and tried to laugh. "Sir, if you can keep working with a broken nose, I think I can handle a sore throat."

"Excellent! Then get back to that *Door*. Scotty needs a bridge from his ship to the coordinates Sparkey went to on the *Dragon's Blood*."

"I'll have him over there within minutes. I just hope we get him back a little sooner than before."

Chapter 30
Bubble Battle

"Come out, come out, wherever you are!" Sparkey trembled at the sound of his enemy's voice. He had not expected to hear it this quickly. At the moment, he was hiding behind several crates of metallic paint and liquid metal in the deck two cargo bay of the *Dragon's Blood*. According to the schematics of the *Fire Cruiser*, which was identical to this ship, there was a crawlway that led directly from the cargo bay to an access port right under the command chair on the bridge. Assuming Lizard Face was sitting there, all it would take would be a slash to the legs, and the reptile would be leaving on a one-way trip to the Black Lava Pits. Then, hopefully, Sparkey could get back to either the *Zerubbabel* or the *Fire Cruiser* before the *Dragon's Blood* was blown to bits.

Either ship wasn't extremely appealing. He wasn't sure who he was more scared of facing, General Shortstop or his parents. The General would likely place him under arrest for the duration of the mission, and he had no clue what would happen after that. His parents, on the other hand, were sure to ground him for life, and that meant no trips to Earth, no more missions, and possibly even, no more fun at all. Scotty could overrule all that, but he rarely did. He respected Gloria and Spikey as parents, and though he was technically their superior, he was still a kid, so he usually did what they asked.

Sparkey still had the *Door* remote, which promised near instantaneous escape if he needed it, but he wasn't ready to give up. This was a big cargo bay, and if he could just sneak around and over crates long enough, he could make it to the access tube and get up to the bridge. He just hoped he could shake these goons.

~

"Return fire!" Captain Noble barked.

"Aye, sir!" Speedway complied, and another atomic charge shot from the *Fire Cruiser*. "Minimal damage to their thrusters. More incoming missiles!"

Noble braced himself as another round of enemy fire slammed into his ship. So far, even with the extra mass of their claw, the *Dragon's Blood* had proved a formidable enemy. Even so, she was being manned by a crew with less than a week of operating time aboard her. The *Fire Cruiser* was almost twenty years old, and most of her crew had been serving aboard for years. They wouldn't be easy to defeat.

Noble ordered, "Colonel, continue targeting their nacelles; fire at will!" Then he stepped up to Spikey who had taken over on the communications board. "Captain Moonbeam, what's the word from Scotty?"

"The *Zerubbabel* is prepared to send him over, but they need to move in closer."

"I thought the *Door* had an incredible range."

"It does, but the *Door* repulser field on the *Dragon's Blood* may become an issue again. If we could only…" Spikey began but was slammed to the floor as an atomic charge rocked the ship.

"Damage report!" Noble demanded.

Josh Noble reported, "Hull breach on deck ten, starboard side. No casualties. Weapons and engines are unaffected."

"You were saying, Spikey?"

"We need to distract the *Dragon's Blood*."

"We're already doing that!"

"No, we need all of their attention focused on us, which means we have to become more of a threat."

Will smiled and ordered, "Hail Scotty's ship."

Spikey tapped a few buttons, and Noble turned back to

the viewscreen. The image of a goon formed there. It spoke, *"I am Lieutenant Gakic. How may I help you, Captain?"*

"I was wondering if I might speak with Scotty?"

"He has already transported over to the Zerubbabel. He needed new clothes and weapons before he went after Sparkey. You can reach him there, sir."

Noble had to admit he was surprised at the goon's courtesy. He just hoped Scotty's trust in them was not misplaced. He would be counting on that trust. He said, "Actually, Lieutenant, you're the one I need to talk to."

"Of course, Captain!"

"I am assuming my ship and the *Zerubbabel* are going to be quite distracted over the next several minutes or more. We need you and your ship to keep an eye on the Cosmic Bubble. Don't let the enemy near it. Can I trust you with that?"

"Absolutely, sir!"

"And, Lieutenant, under no circumstances are you or your crew to come into physical contact with the Bubble."

"I understand, Captain. You can count on us."

Noble nodded, and the goon disappeared from the screen. Will addressed his brother, "Josh, initiate attack maneuver *Papa 1.*"

"Captain?"

"You heard me."

Josh gulped, and Speedway asked, "Our target?"

Will settled back into his command chair, faced the still firing image of the *Dragon's Blood* on the screen, and ordered, "Their claw!"

~

"What are they doing?" Toby bellowed.

"Maneuver *Papa 1*," Shortstop replied.

"Sir?"

"A very dangerous maneuver that pretty much guarantees that an enemy will have to devote all of their resources toward defending themselves. To my knowledge, no one has pulled it off successfully. The ship in question vamps its engines up to full speed and then sets its thrusters to spin the ship. It creates a nearly impossible target, especially if the ship has a high-velocity capability."

"But the *Fire Cruiser* can move at nearly half the speed of light."

"Exactly, and Lizard Face won't know how to counter it. But I imagine the crew of the *Fire Cruiser* will be quite dizzy by the time it's over."

"We're receiving a message, General. Captain Noble says we need to move in fast, get Scotty aboard the *Dragon's Blood*, and then fall back, but be prepared to join the battle."

"Acknowledged," Shortstop replied. Then he punched the intercom button, "Scotty, prepare to disembark."

~

"You're *ssure* he's in here?" Lizard Face asked. He had just entered the Deck 2 cargo bay.

Lt. Anic, who had taken Kyak's place as security chief, reported, "Yes, sir. Our scanners indicate a single Starananian presence in this room. But the lead compounds in the metallic paint and liquid metal are distorting the scans. We can't pinpoint its exact location."

"Keep *ssearching*!"

"Lt. Kyak to Master Lizard Face!"

"Go ahead."

"The Fire Cruiser is commencing a bizarre attack."

"Deal with it, Lieutenant!"

"Aye, sir, but they are targeting our claw."

Lizard Face spat and cursed and then ordered, "Close in on the Bubble. Forget their attack. They are trying to bait us. The *ssooner* we *ssecure* the Bubble, the *ssooner* I can destroy them!"

"Yes, sir!"

~

"Boy what I wouldn't give for the Dagger of Promise right about now," Scotty thought as he crept down one of the corridors of the *Dragon's Blood*.

"The dagger is a close-range weapon. If I had a body to hurt, I'd feel more comfortable with that energy pistol the General gave you," TB

commented.

"Yeah, easy for you to say. My mom and dad said I couldn't even touch a gun until I was at least twelve. I can't even point my toy guns at anything but this picture of an elk we have in our living room."

"You have toy guns?" TB giggled.

"Hey! It was pre-Staranana, all right?"

"Sure, buddy, sure!"

~

"Get away from me!" Sparkey screamed.

"Kill the little fool!" Lizard Face hissed.

There were only three goons in the room. And honestly, Sparkey hadn't expected to get out of this without a fight. It was time to put a bit of slingshot wrist action to use!

The first goon approached, arms wide, to grab him. This one was unarmed, but he nearly had Sparkey in his grasp. The cub kicked the thing in the face, vaulted up, and ascended a tower of crates. The goon recovered and was just climbing up after him as Sparkey pulled out the *Dagger of Promise.* With one solid flick of the wrist, the dagger went flying, and it sank squarely into the goon's chest. The goon staggered back and vanished in a whirlwind of shimmering heat before its body could even hit the ground. The dagger fell to the floor below.

"You don't have that thing to help you no more!" the second goon cursed.

But Sparkey wasn't out of the fight yet. He leaped from his crate mountain and landed right on top of the goon's head. Half of the creature's mask peeled away, but Sparkey snapped his eyes shut in time and held his breath. They both tumbled to the deck. When Sparkey was quite sure he would not open his eyes to insanity, he opened one halfway, exhaled, and spotted the dagger only inches away. He grabbed it and with a lightning-fast twist of the hips, he flung the dagger straight into the small of the goon's back. It fell to the ground and vanished.

Sparkey recovered the dagger and disappeared again into the jungle of crates. There was only one goon left, Lt. Anic. Unfortunately, he had an energy rifle.

"Not bad, little one," Lizard Face mocked. "*Ssay* haven't I *sseen* you before?"

Careful not to give his position away, Sparkey shouted back, "Yeah, I'm Sparkey Moonbeam! I escaped from you three months ago in the Palace."

"Ah, yes! I also recall that you fell on top of me and almost got me killed by *Sseth*."

"Yeah, sorry about that. I'm going to do a lot worse today!"

"Big words!" Lizard Face sneered.

"Not big enough!" Anic interjected, and Lizard Face heard the click of his rifle.

The reptile couldn't see either of them, but he heard a muffled scream, and a blast of weapon's fire, and then heavy footsteps heading back toward him. Anic had done it!

"Well, done, Lieutenant!" Lizard Face called over the crates.

There was no response, just more footfalls. Lizard Face stepped closer to the maze to see if he could meet up with Anic. And then, once again, he found his head being slammed into the deck.

"Did you honestly think your goons could stop the *Dagger of Promise*?" Sparkey had jumped from the top of the pile of crates, and now, he had his real enemy under the dagger's point.

"Maybe they couldn't, but I will, you little maggot!"

Sparkey was amused that Lizard Face, who was as good as dead, still had the confidence to talk trash. But a moment later, Sparkey realized his boast had not been in vain. Something slimy wrapped around his ankle, and the next thing he knew, he was flying through the air. The dagger went hurtling toward the exit. The *Door* remote landed next to Lizard Face, and Sparkey slammed into the far wall. He fell and heard his ankle snap on impact.

Lizard Face stood and flicked his tail, "Never underestimate *ssomeone* with a tail."

Sparkey did not respond. He was just panting on the deck. Lizard Face smirked and said, "Well, what do we have here?" He picked up the *Door* remote. "Is this what I think it is?"

Again no response.

Lizard Face stepped to the side wall and pressed the intercom switch, "Lt. Kyak, *sscan* the cargo bay. You'll find a new piece of technology I believe to be a *Door* remote. Link it to our *ssystem* and input the coordinates we discussed."

"Acknowledged, Master! And, sir, that So vessel that came out of the vortex seems to be collaborating with the bears."

"What?"

"It's true, sir. They have sent several encrypted transmissions. We haven't cracked much of the code, but apparently Lt. Gakic is in command."

"Traitor!"

"It gets worse, sir. According to the transmissions, the human boy is still alive!"

"Impossible!"

"Nothing is impossible!" The intercom panel exploded, and Lizard Face spun toward the exit of the cargo bay.

The surge of joy that shot through Sparkey was almost enough to completely block out the pain from his broken ankle. For there, standing in the doorway, was none other than his best friend, Emperor Scotty Fields.

Scotty had the *Dagger of Promise* and an energy pistol in his hands. He said, "Leave him alone, Lizard Face."

"How is this possible? The *God-killer sshould* have destroyed you!"

"You obviously didn't read the rest of that story. Three days after He was crucified, Jesus Christ rose to life again, and even His enemies fell down and worshiped Him. I am no Jesus, but He delivered me. And Captain Gakic and the clones in the incubation tubes were killed by God Himself."

"And Leif? What about Leif?" Lizard Face begged. It was very becoming for him to show even an ounce of parental concern.

"He survived, but I am afraid your *Goon Omega* is now nothing more than a stain on the *Zerubbabel's* carpet."

The reptile's eyes narrowed, and Scotty said, "Surrender, and I will…"

The deck bucked and sent them all flying. Lizard Face slammed into a crate, and it broke open scattering cans of paint all over the room. Some of them even popped open spilling their contents across the bay floor. Scotty landed next to his own pile of paint cans, and Sparkey, who had barely moved, had his hands wrapped around the handle of a bucket of liquid metal.

Lt. Kyak reported frantically over the intercom (there was another receiver near the exit), *"Master, your request is complete. But we can't shake the Fire Cruiser!"*

"Thank you, Lieutenant. It will be a nil issue *sshortly. Ssend* a full *ssecurity ssquad* to the cargo bay immediately. Tell them hoods and masks off!"

"Acknowledged!"

Scotty thought he saw Sparkey's pulse begin to race faster, but he wasn't worried. He was silent for a moment and then said, "Lizard Face, have you forgotten that I know a goon's face can't harm a human?"

"Maybe not, but your little friend has much to worry about. And they can *sstill* kill you."

Scotty shook his head, "So foolish you are. If a fire, a giant lizard, multiple laser blasts, and four days with you couldn't do me in, I doubt your goons could. Besides, they are never going to get near this cargo bay."

"What?"

"Yes, you see I have had TB link up with all their brains. By now, they will all be suffering excruciating headaches. They won't be of much use to you."

"And why haven't you done that to me?"

The ship rocked again, but they remained standing. Scotty replied, "Because I want to deal with you personally. If they happen to have *Bibles* in the Black Lava Pits, you might want to look up Psalm 94:1."

"Oh, don't worry. You won't get the chance to *ssend* me there!" Lizard Face mocked, and then he pressed his thumb against one of the buttons on the *Door* remote.

The room instantly went dark, and Scotty saw the power meter on his pistol begin to lower, and then it reached zero altogether. A chime sounded in the air, and a field of light began to grow from a single pinprick. There was only one possible place he could be going.

Scotty looked directly at Sparkey. And the cub didn't even need TB's mind link to know what the human boy wanted. He popped open the can of liquid metal, and Scotty did the same with his paint.

As the *Door* field finished forming, Lizard Face turned back to them and just laughed. He went to step through the *Door,* and Scotty shouted, "Now!" Both canisters of paint and liquid metal went jetting through the air, and their contents exploded over Lizard Face. Covered in red paint and thick globs of metal, he slipped on the floor and fell backward through the *Door.*

Scotty was heading over to go after him, and he threw several more cans of paint through the portal for good measure. Unfortunately, Sparkey beat him to the passage. He had hobbled over on his good foot and was now soaring through time and space after Lizard Face. Scotty had hoped to send him home, but it was too late now. With the dagger in hand and a drained pistol at his side, he stepped through the *Door* just before it vanished!

~

"The ship can't take much more of this!" A dizzy and exhausted Josh Noble reported, and he wasn't talking about enemy fire. The *Fire Cruiser* had literally been spinning like a top for almost ten minutes. So far, they had severed one finger from the *Dragon's Blood's* claw, destroyed its port nacelle, and produced several hull breaches on the lower decks. But *Papa 1* was beginning to pay more of a toll on the crew of the *Fire Cruiser.*

Spikey reported, "I don't think the *Dragon's Blood's Door* repulser will be an issue anymore. Guess where Scotty and Sparkey are now!"

~

"They're where?" Shortstop cursed.

"That's what the message says," Toby replied.

"All right, we're closer, but not quite close enough. I'm setting a course. Cak, open a channel to our goon friends on the alien ship."

Scotty had no idea how this was possible. Above him, all he saw was the velvet black of space, drifting asteroids, and stars. But he wasn't floating, and he wasn't suffocating. In fact, he was standing on very solid ground, though about an inch of mixed paint and liquid metal had formed beneath his feet. And the air was sweeter than even that on Staranana. A moment later, when the shimmering white sun moved from behind an asteroid and sent a rainbow down through a pane of pink glass, Scotty confirmed where they were. They were inside the Cosmic Bubble!

Sparkey was on his knees in the paint, crawling toward Lizard Face, who was digging through the liquid, trying to expose the glass enough to touch it. Each time he seemed to be almost there, though, the paint would rush in and cover it again.

"Blast!" the reptile raged, and then the paint next to him exploded.

"Stand up, Lizard Face, and toss that *Door* remote over here." Scotty's pistol had recharged.

The lizard slowly rose and faced his enemy. Scotty shot at his feet and said, "I see what those claws are doing. Don't even think about digging toward that glass! Just stay right where you are."

Lizard Face held his hands up, and Scotty said, "Sparkey, get over here." The cub began to hobble over, and the remote landed in the muck at Scotty's feet. He picked it up and said, "Sparkey, you need to get out of here."

"I can't. That thing is linked to the *Dragon's Blood's Door*."

"I don't mean that you should use this. I can contact the *Zerubbabel*, but you need to go!"

"But, Scotty, I…"

Scotty smiled, "It's okay. In my eyes, you did nothing wrong. You just helped out a friend, and God used what happened to His glory in a big way."

"Really?"

Scotty nodded and said, "I'll tell you all about it soon, but you need to go."

Sparkey surrendered, and with his eyes and pistol still locked on Lizard Face, Scotty tapped the transmitter button on his new belt. "Scotty to General Shortstop."

"Shortstop here! Are you all right?"

"For the moment. I need you to open up a *Door* inside the Cosmic Bubble. Sparkey is coming over. He'll need medical attention."

"What about you?"

"Standby for now, but get all of our ships over here right away."

"But, Scotty…"

"Get on it, General," Scotty snapped, and then he clicked the transmitter off.

A *Door* field formed within seconds, and with a smile, Sparkey hobbled through and was gone.

"*Sso* what have you got planned for me?" Lizard Face sneered.

"Don't make this hard on yourself. You're going to the Black Lava Pits one way or another. You get to choose how painfully. Seth chose the most painful way."

"*Sseth* was a fool!"

"Exactly my point. So, you just let me prick your finger, and you can be on your merry way."

Lizard Face chuckled, "*Sseth* was a fool because he let a child defeat him. But you *ssee*, you're not the only one with friends in the area."

Scotty was going to ask him what he meant by that, but never got the chance. A blast of rainbow light exploded above him, and the Bubble began to spin. He fell, and his pistol got caught up in the centrifugal force and flew away. When the Bubble stilled, Lizard Face was running toward the far side and away from the paint.

"No!" Scotty screamed and took off after him. Outside, the image of the *Dragon's Blood's* underbelly had come into full view, its now four-fingered claw aching to squeeze around the Bubble.

Lizard Face was nearly past the paint, but then he was tasting it as he fell into the slimy mess again. Scotty's hand was around his ankle. "You are not going to touch that glass!" the boy screamed.

Lizard Face thrust his tail hard into Scotty's stomach and bellowed, "And you think you will?"

Scotty recovered quickly and jumped back onto the lizard. He jabbed punch after punch into the beast's gecko-like snout. Lizard Face countered, sinking his razor-sharp teeth into Scotty's arm. Scotty screamed, but he did not relent. He wrapped his legs around Lizard Face's waist and twisted hard. Though he couldn't be sure, he thought he heard a few of Lizard Face's ribs snap. The reptile continued to struggle, and Scotty pulled out the *Dagger of Promise.*

Lizard Face stilled as Scotty brought the blade toward his neck. Scotty felt the shudder and heard the grind of the claw taking hold of the Bubble, but he ignored it. As long as he touched the glass first, it wouldn't matter what the *Dragon's Blood* did. He held the dagger just above Lizard Face's paint-covered throat, and said, "There is only one God, lizard lips! And Bubble or no Bubble, you would never come close to being Him. Goodbye! Tell Seth I said hello."

Scotty was moving in for the kill, and then he went flying again. And the Bubble was spinning away from its would-be captors. When the sphere settled, Scotty saw Lt. Gakic's *So* vessel hovering next to the Bubble. There was significant damage to the forward hull. They had rammed the Bubble to keep it away from the *Dragon's Blood.* It was very thoughtful but unnecessary, and it had allowed Lizard Face to escape again. He was heading back toward the clean glass. Enough was enough!

Scotty pressed the recall button on the *Door* remote, and a passage crackled into life. The wind it generated began to churn the paint, and before Lizard Face could reach any clean glass that too had been covered, and Scotty was on top of him again. The blade of the dagger was now covered in paint, but Scotty assumed it would still work. He clutched Lizard Face by the throat and slammed his head into the paint.

Lizard Face's eyes were wide, and Scotty was bewildered at his newfound strength. For some odd reason, Lizard Face couldn't move, despite the meager nine-year-old muscles that were restraining him. Scotty met his gaze and shouted, **"God to whom vengeance belongs – SHINE FORTH!"** Then he twisted the dagger in his hands and plunged it right into Lizard Face's stomach.

The creature choked, and his stomach poured blood, but he wasn't entirely dead yet. Scotty couldn't be sure what was taking so long for him to vanish. Though, as he recalled, it had taken Seth a couple of minutes to vanish when he had been stabbed. Regardless, Scotty didn't want to risk Lizard Face's blood making contact with the Bubble.

He pulled the blade from his enemy, wiped it on his pants, and then threw it down next to them. Lizard Face was still gasping for breath, but his hand made contact with a metal hilt. Scotty, still with a strength that defied reason, took Lizard Face by the left arm and left leg, picked him up, spun, and flung him into the *Door*. There was an additional flash of light, and Scotty could only assume Lizard Face was now the newest resident of the Black Lava Pits.

The passage vanished, and Scotty stood and pressed the transmitter button again, "This is Emperor Scotty to all ships. Let's get this done!"

Captain Noble's voice came over the transmission, *"This is Captain Noble, time to open the big presents!"*

Scotty hurried over to the now extended perimeter of the paint. He wiped his hands and then knelt. Outside the Bubble, directly in front of him, was the *Dragon's Blood*. The ship was cowering, surrounded by three heavily armed vessels and the Cosmic Bubble. Scotty nodded, as if the other ships could see him, and then he touched the glass!

He hadn't known what to expect when he did finally touch the glass, but it was amazing. Pink circles of energy began to ripple over his body, and they were building in intensity. Light formed next, and it filled the interior of the Cosmic Bubble until the thing looked like a tiny star in space. And then it exploded!

A shock wave of heavily concentrated, violent pink energy shot from the entire Bubble and enveloped the *Dragon's Blood*. The same energy (though admittedly a reduced amount) was surging from the *Fire Cruiser* and the *Zerubbabel*. The *So* vessel was maintaining a safe distance, but it was still firing its own laser cannons at the *Dragon's Blood*.

The *Dragon's Blood* was making a meager attempt to escape, but it was futile. The claw had already been incinerated. Airlocks were exploding. Windows were shattering, and bulkheads were twisting. Though it was impossible, Scotty could have sworn he heard the screaming of hundreds of goons who were now being burned in phoenix fire. After less than thirty seconds of fire, there was nothing left of the *Dragon's Blood* except ash and a few twisted compartments drifting lazily away into the asteroid belt.

Scotty pressed his transmitter again, "Scotty to General Shortstop. Prepare to bring me onboard. Let's go home!"

"Acknowledge, sir. Standby."

Scotty sighed and looked around. *Where was the Dagger of Promise?*

Chapter 31

Christmas

"**O**uch!"

"Just hold still, Scotty."

"Yeah, easy for you to say," the boy complained. He was now in the *Fire Cruiser's* sickbay, sitting on a medical bed. Slightly cold and slightly embarrassed to be in the large, busy room with only a pair of blue boxer shorts on, he had medical monitors hooked up all over his chest and torso, and Gloria and Grizz were poking and prodding him in various places. Gloria had treated and bandaged the lizard bite on his arm. And Grizz was feeling all over his ribs just to make sure they were healed like Scotty believed.

Scotty tried to make conversation to take his mind off of what they were doing, "So, how are the bear-goons?"

Gloria replied, "Well, they aren't exactly goons anymore. They have all been fully checked out. Aside from the emotional trauma they will still have to endure, they should be fine. Captain Noble put them all on a transport shuttle and sent them back to Stararocka."

"Did you ever figure out what happened with Joshua?"

"Spikey looked back over the modifications we made to the *Door*. They should have worked. Joshua likely caused the overheating. The bears have only distorted memories of their experience, but one of them seemed to remember someone on the *Dragon's Blood* saying their *goonieness* had been impregnated with a deadly virus. If Joshua hadn't intervened, everyone on the *Fire Cruiser* would probably be dead."

"I think it's safe to say God knew what He was doing in this entire situation."

"I read your report. Did you really transform into your glorified body while you were on Evilanda?"

"Yeah, well, I assume so. And it was only for a few minutes right at the end."

"What was it like to change back again?"

"I feel small, but excited, because when Jesus comes back, I'll be like that forever."

Gloria smiled, and the sickbay doors swished open. Spikey and Sparkey stepped into the room.

Scotty tried to jump up, but Grizz pushed him back down, so he just said, "Hey, guys!"

Spikey asked, "Scotty, really, are you all right?"

"Better than all right!"

"That is yet to be determined," Grizz quipped.

Scotty ignored him and said, "Well, it wasn't an easy few days. Heck, I could use a word to describe them that I am not allowed to say. But God was alive, and He did save some people who might have otherwise never heard His message. Speaking of which, where are Lieutenant Gakic and the others?"

"Still on board the *So* vessel. It may take a while for everyone to adjust to them, but they did promise to come to the party."

"Well, I'm not sure how long they will be around. The Lieutenant will probably want to go back to Evilanda and continue sharing the message of Christ."

"What do you want to do about Evilanda?" Spikey asked.

"If we leave it alone long enough for *Gakic* to do some good, it might make a great vacation spot."

"Scotty!"

"I'm serious. You should see the place. It's amazing. But you know, what I think would be more amazing is us offering to use your goon cure on *Gakic* and the others."

Gloria shook her head, "I'd love to, Scotty. But the system is calibrated for bears that were only goons for a short time. I have no idea how it would affect goons who have been goons for their entire lives."

Scotty nodded, but said, "Well, God hasn't chosen to heal them yet. Maybe because He still needs them to reach the other goons, but keep working toward a cure. With Lizard Face dead, there is no reason to maintain hostilities with the goons."

"Speaking of our dear departed reptile, we've scanned and re-scanned the Bubble. We still have to clean up all that paint mess, but there is no sign of the *Dagger of Promise*," Spikey said.

"Lizard Face must have grabbed it somehow," Scotty said.

"If he did, then the dagger was either destroyed with the *Dragon's Blood*, or it is sinking toward the bottom of the Black Lava Pits right now."

"Let's just hope God decides to give us a little reprieve from evil, for a while at least."

Spikey nodded, and then Scotty asked, "So, when do we get to go down to the party?"

Grizz interjected, "Hold it right there, kiddo! The party isn't until tomorrow night, and you need to stay in sickbay at least that long for further tests and observations."

"Ah, come on, I feel fine, and I want to see how Chef Berry has decorated the Palace."

"Feeling fine and being fine are two completely different things. And besides, I think the surprise is worth the wait."

"You've been down there?"

"Briefly, when we got back to Staranana a few hours ago. All the *Fire Cruiser's* crew were assigned quarters in the Palace for the duration of the celebration."

"Yeah, but I have to stay up here in space, while the rest of you get to have fun down there."

"It's only for a day and a half."

Scotty consented, and then he asked, "Could the rest of you excuse Sparkey and me?"

Gloria, Spikey, and Grizz nodded and stepped away, leaving the two friends alone.

Scotty asked, "So, how's your ankle?"

"Great! Dr. Grizz used this bone regenerator thing on it. I had broken it in about three places, but it is as good as new now."

"That's good. That's good," Scotty said. Then he looked awkwardly down at his bare toes. He began, "Sparkey…"

"Yes," Sparkey said, now finding his own toes extremely fascinating. Scotty had more or less forgiven him in the Cosmic Bubble, but he had a pretty good guess as to what this conversation was going to be about.

"Thank you!"

Sparkey was stunned. He hadn't expected that. "What?"

"Thanks…Thanks for being the friend I always wanted."

"I left you on the *Dragon's Blood!*"

"True, but you saved Toby's life. And the General tells me Toby and Cak found the spy at the Palace. And your mom told me that you took my place on Earth. Sparkey, I have to say, that is amazing!"

"Yeah, well, you and Noah might have a few issues when you get back."

"Still, it was pretty cool of you, and though it wasn't really necessary, your willingness to confront Lizard Face alone meant a lot."

"Scotty, I…"

"Sparkey, don't say anything. As far as I'm concerned, you did what you had to do. You followed your heart, and I believe you followed God. For that, I have no hesitation in saying you're the best friend I have ever had."

Sparkey had no words. He expected a lecture, a dressing down, or an all-out reprimand. But Scotty offered nothing but love, friendship, and unconditional forgiveness. God obviously made an excellent choice in his *Blood of the Land*. What the boy did next topped it all.

Scotty stood, half pulling the medical monitors off his body. He approached Sparkey and wrapped his arms around him. Then he said, "I love you, buddy. Thanks for being my friend."

Sparkey continued to be stunned for a moment, but slowly, he embraced his friend as well. And they stayed like that for what felt like one perfect, eternal moment.

"Scotty! Get those monitors back on!" Gloria shouted from around the corner.

Scotty pulled away and called back, "Sorry, Gloria." He stuck the monitors back on his chest and belly, and then he slipped back onto the bed. Then he asked, "So, Sparkey, exactly how much trouble are you in with everyone else?"

Sparkey chuckled, "Well, General Shortstop, was a little more forgiving when my mom told him his nose wasn't broken. Though it does have significant bruising. As a punishment, I have to help clean up all the paint from inside the Bubble, and I have to do a few extra chores around the Palace. The General also told me to expect a little bit rougher treatment when I begin my basic military training in a few years."

"And your parents?"

"Well, let's just say, I'm grounded until further notice. I don't expect I'll get to go to Earth again anytime soon."

"That's rough, man."

"Um, Sparkey, we need to head down to the surface," a new voice said. It was Spikey. He had just come back around the corner.

"All right, Dad," he replied, and then he turned back to Scotty, "See you tomorrow?"

"Count on it!"

~

"I don't see why we couldn't take the *Door* down to the surface?" Scotty complained. "Why do we have to land the ship?" At the moment, he was on the bridge of the *Fire Cruiser*, along with Captain and Commander Noble, Dr. Grizz, Commander Honeytub, and Lt. Gakic. The ship was being lowered to a rest in the plain just beyond the former slave camps outside the Palace.

Will replied, "We won't have any crew aboard during the party. The ship will be safer on the ground. Besides, this helps build the suspense."

Scotty laughed, "I think you guys are just nervous. After all, you haven't had a Christmas expert like me helping you get ready for this party. But Christmas is more about the heart of a person toward Christ than fancy decorations."

Will input, "Well, we're all hoping you'll find an ample

supply of both."

Scotty looked at the viewscreen. The Palace looked absolutely naked without the Cosmic Bubble. He asked, "So, what are we going to do about the Bubble?"

"Lt. Gakic has that all taken care of," Noble replied.

"Really?" Scotty asked, turning to his new goon friend. "How?"

Gakic replied, "It seems *surprise* is the word of the day, so I think it will have more of an impact if I wait to tell you."

Scotty rolled his eyes, "This is worse than waiting for Christmas morning!"

"Begging your pardon, Captain," Josh interrupted. "We've touched down."

Will nodded and flipped the intercom switch on his chair, "Captain to all hands, secure your stations, and you are dismissed. Enjoy the party, people."

~

The courtyard gates creaked open as Scotty, and his Stararockan entourage approached the Palace. Lt. Gakic had taken the *Door* back up to his ship still in orbit. He had promised he and his crew would be at the party later that night. No one had mentioned what had become of the Bubble, and Scotty had been so busy being poked and prodded that he had just assumed they had gotten it back to Staranana. How was another question. The *Fire Cruiser's* claw was still drifting somewhere in the asteroid belt. Oh, well, Scotty decided he wouldn't worry about it, especially, not tonight.

They began moving across the courtyard, and Scotty asked, "Captain, do you think you'll build another *Dragon's Blood?*"

"We still have a lot of grieving to do. So for the moment, no, but one day, I'm hoping both Staranana and Stararocka will have a fleet of ships we can use to explore the galaxy."

"That would be awesome!" Scotty beamed. "But this time, let's stay away from any insane lizards."

Will chuckled and then he stopped short, right by the outer door of the Palace. "You ready for this?"

"I've been ready for days!"

"All right, here we go!" Noble rapped on the large metallic doors, and they slowly began to pull open.

Scotty was all teeth after that. The instant the doors were open, he was overwhelmed. There were literally thousands of bears. The entire entry chamber was filled with them, save the center of the room. There were also bears leaning against every balcony on every story clear up to the hundredth story of the Palace. He imagined every bear on Staranana had come, and at least a thousand Stararockans.

Directly in front of him was a table piled high with food. There were whole turkeys and chickens, which had been brought from Earth. There was also oboca steak, tubs and tubs of mashed potatoes, hundreds of varieties of pasta, thousands of fruits and vegetables, and, of course, no shortage of every type of food made with honeysuckle apples. Though Scotty wouldn't be frequenting this particular dish, there was also an abundant supply of ice trout.

Right next to the doors into the banquet room, which also seemed to be crowded with bears, was a band playing Christmas music. Remarkably, since they had never had Christmas here before, the music was beautiful. Grizz had also mentioned something about Gloria singing later. That was sure to be amazing. Scotty had heard her a few times in the Moonbeam apartment.

Almost everyone he knew was there. Garlan and his assistant Sam were present, as were Toby and Cak and their parents. Colonel Speedway and General Shortstop were there and in civilian clothes. There were also two elderly bears, whom Scotty did not recognize at first, but he later learned they were Spikey's Stararockan grandparents. And Scotty recognized many more faces. About the only one who wasn't present was Hydro, but Scotty knew the dragon would still be mourning in the mountains for quite some time. Scotty was looking around for the Moonbeams when his eyes landed on his pride and joy, the Christmas tree.

It was fifty feet high and deep, forest green. There were dozens of strings of colored lights circling the tree all the way to the top, and Scotty's heart skipped a beat at the beauty of those lights reflecting off an endless rainbow of glass bulbs. As the old song went, there was no shortage of silver and gold decorations on this tree, and Scotty spotted a toddler chewing on the end of a string of popcorn. Also, though he couldn't see them yet, each guest had added his or her own unique ornament to the tree. It was truly breathtaking, and the whole thing was topped off with a simple, brass cross.

Scotty finally saw the Moonbeams. They were standing directly in front of the tree, and their arms were filled with presents. And theirs weren't the only ones. The fountain had been turned off so that it and the rest of the area surrounding the tree could be filled with presents.

Scotty started toward the Moonbeams and stopped dead as the room exploded with applause. *Oh, no, here they go again!* Scotty looked at his feet and started kicking at the marble floor. Spikey and the rest of the Moonbeam family came up to him. The elder Moonbeam pushed his present into the boy's hands and then wrapped his arm around Scotty's shoulders and addressed the crowd, "My friends, here before you is a boy unlike any other boy!"

More applause!

"A boy whom the enemy could not defeat!"

And more applause!

"A boy who has been our friend and stands in the full light of God, and on that note, I think it is only appropriate that we thank our Heavenly Father for bringing him back to us."

With that, everyone fell silent, and Spikey prayed, "Lord, we are so grateful to You. We know none of this was by our strength. Our friend has testified to Your power and Your saving grace. You delivered him from the fire, and the pit, and turned even some of his enemies toward You. Oh, Lord, we confess that we are still grieving the loss of many friends, but You have proven their loss not to be in vain. Thank You that You are always true to Your Word. Please give us joy this first Christmas on Staranana. And Lord Jesus, *Happy Birthday!*"

A resounding *amen* filled the Palace, and Sparkey said to Scotty, "Welcome home, my friend, and merry Christmas!"

~

The next few hours were spent opening presents and eating. The Moonbeams gave Scotty a new bike, several books, and his own *Door* remote. Spikey also promised TB that he was working on a new device called an *audio* that would make him even more portable, and allow him to travel to Earth. Gloria sang a breathtaking rendition of *O Holy Night* that had everyone in tears. And, of course, Chef Berry was fussing all over the Palace, trying to make sure everything was just perfect. Scotty would have to tell him later how well he had done with the party. In fact, Scotty doubted that any Christmas party in history (save perhaps the first one) could have topped this celebration.

There was still no sign of *Gakic* and the other clones, but according to Shortstop, it had been decided that *Gakic* would adopt the baby Leif and take him back to Evilanda for the time being. Scotty hoped there wouldn't be any begrudged clones who would want to take revenge on the son of Lizard Face. However, the two lizards did have one distinct difference.

While living, Lizard Face had had a strip of black scales down his back. Leif had a strip of white scales down his. According to *Gakic*, they hadn't been white until the angel Joshua held him. Scotty hoped that was a good omen that Leif would not turn out like his father.

Of course, there were tons of games at the party. Scotty and Sparkey became quite fond of bowling in the throne room. Scotty rarely used the throne room, and he still thought of the throne as Seth's. And, in fact, the bowling pins were carved to look like Seth, Lizard Face, and the goons. The boys had a blast for hours. And the best part was that, at least for that evening, the burden of responsibility and expectation was off their shoulders. They could just be kids and have lots and lots of fun.

When the Palace clocks began to gong twelve midnight, General Shortstop approached Scotty and the Moonbeams who had once again convened at the base of the Christmas tree. "It's time. We had best get to the roof," he said.

"What for?" Scotty asked.

"You'll see," Spikey said, and he began to lead Scotty and his family toward the lift tubes. The crowd parted for them, but they were obviously not the only ones headed to the roof. Every lift tube was filled, and hordes were heading toward the stairs. Whatever was going on must be something really big.

~

Scotty shuddered as he stepped out into the frigid night wind of the roof. He was only wearing his regular clothes, so he hoped whatever was going to happen, happened quickly. Spikey led them right up to the edge of the large crater in the center of the roof where the Bubble once sat. Another ten minutes passed, and the entire roof was filled with bears. And there were still many more watching on monitors inside the Palace. Scotty wished he could be one of those. This cold was ridiculous. It was times like this that he wished he were emperor of a warmer planet.

Scotty was going to ask yet again what was going on, but then he found himself squinting as a bright light formed over his head. He looked up and felt the rush of wind as an unidentified craft lowered toward the roof. Scotty couldn't figure out what it was, but from the center of the descending craft, a multi-colored beam was rotating. The blackness of the night still concealed most of the vessel's features, but every so often as the beam rotated, Scotty made out the silhouette of a sphere.

General Shortstop commanded, "Activate beacons!" And from the four corners of the roof, four highly illuminated spotlights were directed at the vessel above. It was then that Scotty recognized Lt. Gakic's *So* ship. The spinning rainbow beam was some sort of magnetic energy tether, and secured firmly in its grasp was the Cosmic Bubble.

Everyone watched in awe as the ship and Bubble continued to descend. The whole crowd stepped back, and those near the edge of the roof found themselves praising God for the guardrail. It was the only thing keeping them from falling to certain death as throngs of bears pressed against them.

The Bubble bumped against the edge of the crater and then slid back into place. The *So* vessel released the magnet beam and moved to hover just beyond the eastern edge of the Palace. On the other side of the roof from Scotty and the Moonbeams, Colonel Speedway operated a crane and swung a curved beam over the top of the crowd. Several people had to duck, but in no time at all, the beam was being lowered into place. Once it was in position over the Bubble, several of Spikey's engineers moved in to bolt it back to the roof. When they finished, they stepped back, and the night erupted with deafening shouts and applause. After all, they had been through in the last week, it was finally over, and Cosmic Bubble Palace was whole once more.

Scotty wrapped his arms around the Moonbeams and said, "Merry Christmas, guys! And God bless us all!"

"Amen!" they all chimed.

"And, guys, can I ask one more favor?" Scotty asked.

"Of course!" Spikey replied.

"Can we go back inside now?"

The Moonbeams all laughed, and Spikey led them back inside. The party was far from over, and without a doubt, it would be a very merry Christmas indeed!

After

'*R*enounce God or die!*" Slimy scales slipped between razor-sharp rocks, unperturbed by the vacuum of space. Fire, rock, twisted metal, and death were constants. There was no one to hear the demonic chant, but it continued still.

Was that a structure up ahead? Perhaps? Onward it slithered, its cold, black form invisible in the night. Something was crushed there. But what? It crawled over broken bones and through floating blood. The taste of it was sweet, but it wasn't here to feast.

"Renounce God or die!" it continued. But then, *"Renounce God and live!"*

Finally, it came upon its target, five broken and bloody fingers loosely holding a metal hilt. It cringed at the sight of the orange blade and moved no closer. It remained still and watched. There was nothing for the longest time. And then, yes, there it was, a twitch. And then another. Yes, this was the right place. This was the right one. The fingers attached were moving. The fingers attached were alive!

Author's Note

The cosmos are filled with countless wonders. Some scientists estimate that there are more than 200 billion trillion stars in the Universe. However, would it surprise you to know that God knows every one of those stars by name? Not only that, He created them all. God says of Himself in Jeremiah 23:24, "Do I not fill heaven and earth?" With a God that big, it is hard to imagine that He cares about people as small as you and me, but He does. In fact, He cares more about *you* than all those stars combined. However, there is a problem. As Scotty explained to Lieutenant Gakic, humanity is separated from God because of its sin, meaning the bad things we do. God cannot allow sin to go unpunished, and that punishment is eternal separation from Him in Hell. Many humans face that punishment even now, but there is still hope. God doesn't want to send anyone to Hell, so He provided a solution. He sent His Son, Jesus Christ, to Earth. As described in the *Bible*, Jesus lived a life without sin, and then, because many hated Him, He was put to death on a cross. Three days later, God brought Him back to life, and He accepted Christ's death as payment for humanity's sins. Now, any who admit their sins to God, believe in what Jesus did on the cross and that He rose again, and commit their lives to Him will be saved. That means you will live with God and Christ for eternity! If you have not yet asked Christ into your life, I invite you to do so. A sincere heart is all He requires. Take care. You will be in my prayers.

About the Author

David Scott Fields II is an author, teacher, publisher, and Christian journalist currently residing in Jupiter, Florida. At the time of this publication, his works include the novels *Staranana*, *Lizard Face*, *Old Covenant*, *New Covenant*, and *The Noble Dragons* in the *Chronicles of the Imagination* series. Additionally, he has published the novellas *The Betrayal of Kelcott*, also from the *Chronicles of the Imagination* series, and *The Prism's Echo*, *Salvage*, and *Allegiance* from the *Parallel Encounters* series. His educational writing includes the children's writing workbook *Green Elephant*, and curriculum supplements for several classic pieces of literature. Each of these titles is published through *Thrive Christian Press*, and they are available through various retailers. In addition to his writing career, Mr. Fields has served for almost 20 years as an English teacher in various Christian schools. Both as a teacher and writer, Mr. Fields seeks to remind the young people in his life that God is alive. His goal, above all else, is that his life will be a testament for Jesus Christ and that his writings will help bring many people into a saving relationship with their Creator.

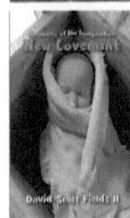

Also available...

Parallel Encounters
The Prism's Echo

To the naked eye, The Prism's Echo is just a dusty old book, but to a reader with the right question, it opens the door to infinite possible realities.

Visit www.amazon.com to order.
ISBN: 978-0692329962

Parallel Encounters
Salvage

Captain Brooks hopes to salvage an alien vessel and incorporate its resources into those of the rebellion. But there's a problem - the Nazis have spotted the alien ship too!

Visit www.amazon.com to order.
ISBN: 978-0-692-35235-9

Parallel Encounters
Allegiance

Things are on the up for the rebellion, but the tides of the war become turbulent again with the return of a former ally who has now become the bitterest of enemies.

Visit www.amazon.com to order.
ISBN: 978-0692375457